Albert Emil Brachvogel, Therese J. Radford

Beaumarchais

An historical novel

Albert Emil Brachvogel, Therese J. Radford

Beaumarchais
An historical novel

ISBN/EAN: 9783337393793

Printed in Europe, USA, Canada, Australia, Japan

Cover: Foto ©Andreas Hilbeck / pixelio.de

More available books at **www.hansebooks.com**

BEAUMARCHAIS.

AN HISTORICAL NOVEL.

BY

A. E. BRACHVOGEL,

AUTHOR OF "NARCISSUS," "BENONI," "A NEW FALSTAFF," "A STORY OF THE MIDDLE AGES," ETC., ETC.

"*Ma vie est un combat.*"—*Beaumarchais*

TRANSLATED FROM THE GERMAN, BY

THÉRÈSE J. RADFORD.

COMPLETE IN ONE VOLUME.

Illustrated by Gaston Fay.

NEW YORK:
D. APPLETON & COMPANY,
90, 92 & 94 GRAND STREET.
1868.

CONTENTS.

BEAUMARCHAIS.

BOOK I.

CHAPTER I.

GAUCHAT THE BOOKSELLER.

THE dwellers in Paris from 1828 to 1830, who revisited it in 1861, after an absence of thirty years, say that it was almost impossible to recognize the city as the same. This change has not reference to mere outward appearance, for the Hôtel de Ville, the Louvre, and such structures, are still there, and will remain ages after we have passed away ; but the ancient spirit and manners, and the charm of historic reminiscences, have in some way grown less and less distinct, until they almost cease to be. And it is not an uncommon experience that we are less saddened by the actual absence of a loved object, than by its presence so altered—so brought under different and unexpected circumstances —that its existence seems a mockery of the past.

Louis XIV. built the "New Paris"— the "world-ruling Paris." He endeavored to accommodate to his times the more recent mediæval taste—the Gothicism of his ancestors with a more antique and classic purity, and this again with that ostentatious style of decoration known as the "renaissance." Paris was a second Rome. The conflicts which entered so largely into the national history, from the days of the Maid of Orleans to the abolition of feudal rights, and the brilliant recollections reaching back to the death of Jacob Molay, gave a variegated and poetic character to the edifices, streets, and squares, and moulded the peculiarities of the men and manners of the age.

The "New Paris" built after the revolution is an insipid imitation of the former glory of the city ! I say insipid, simply because it is so, notwithstanding all the eulogies of enthusiasts, who are overwhelmed with admiration on beholding the Rue Rivoli !—Two hundred years hence, we shall have, in all parts of the world, boulevards, straight streets, elegant façades, charming ladies in fashionable dresses—but all these will not of themselves inspire us with enthusiasm. The truly educated find nothing interesting which has no historic memories, for they have the same effect as the hallowed ruins of some mystic temple, which no one but a barbarian would remove from a landscape of contrasted freshness and beauty.

What the former kings, from Henry

IV. to Louis XIV., created—that characteristic tone which made Paris unique among the cities, has been destroyed by the temper of the present, and especially by the empire. "Chauvinism" is now the new uniform of that city; it has been deprived of all distinctive qualities, in order to insure its tranquillity. To judge the French capital by what it formerly was, would be as absurd as likening the populace on the boulevards to the columns once led by Dumouriez and Custine, or to the hereditary guests at the Palais-Royal, the race-course, the "Cercle l'Espinasse," the Hôtels Bourbon, Penthièvre, and Ventadour.

Let us rebuild "Old Paris," for it was the place of our story, beginning with what remains of the former city: Notre Dame, the Palace of Justice, the Palais-Royal, the Luxembourg, the Temple, the Hôtels de Ville, de Dieu, Sorbonne, the Louvre, the Tuileries, several venerable convents, and private mansions in St. Germain. Fancy the Rue Rivoli extended, the Tuileries and Louvre closely surrounded by gabled house-tops, the Café Régence, and the renowned Chestnut Avenue as a public promenade, in the midst the "Arbre de Cracovée," the Exchange of intriguers and politicians. Notice the edifices with roofs in all styles, lighted only by glimmering lamps, in streets about half as wide as they are now, with all kinds of outbuildings, projections, wooden benches, steps, and various appendages! Take away two-thirds of the stores; and imagine those left with narrow windows, very dark and deep. Listen to the grating of the rusty weather-vanes, the swinging of the tin sign-boards and the rattle of the shutters. Now look up to the smoky atmosphere covering this chaos of stone, brick, tile, and wood, and we have a slight conception at least of the locality.

The Luxembourg looks distrustful, like a fortress. The whole region around the Temple is gloomy, haunted by misery, crime, and the fearful thoughts conjured by the innocent blood of the templars that was shed there. Dark secrets slumber in its recesses, shunning the light, and no unarmed man by night passes that way. Iron gates shut off the thoroughfares in this neighborhood, and, if we go through the crooked Rue St. Antoine, in an easterly direction toward its outlet, on our right we see the Convent of St. Mary's Daughters; on our left, the two broken walls (all that remain) of the Castle Tournelle, Hôtel Sully, and the Place Royal. Here we stand before that vast prison and terror of Paris, the Bastile, with its drawbridges, portcullises, and ditches. Above its inaccessible walls arise its eight towers, like colossal organ-pipes, as if prepared to indicate the unending *miserere* of those languishing within. A *lettre de cachet* from a nobleman against a citizen, a husband against a wife, a father against a son, the powerful against the weak, drawn and sealed in blank by some complaisant minister—and the drawbridge falls, the portcullis rises, a carriage escorted by policemen enters, and the victim is entombed. His accuser in an hour of remorse may remember and restore him, or he may sigh from year to year until death brings his release.

The Seine has but nine bridges instead of eighteen. The boulevards near the northern town, the avenues St. Anne, Montmartre, Richelieu, Caillou, and Honoré, are just commenced, as well as the Champs Elysées. Beyond is open country—not a sign of the faubourgs of the present day, except St. Antoine. South of the Seine, in the districts of St. Jacques, Université, and St. Germain, no boulevards are to be seen. The lines of the walls surrounding the Quartiers St. André and Bénoit, uniting them, by fortifications, with the city, are hardly traced. We look in vain for the Champ de Mars; and the numerous gardens and parks are the sites of the palaces of ancient families—Brissac, Leonville, Crecy, Noailles, Chevreuse, Grammont, Soissons, Polignac, Penthièvre, Guise, D'Estrée, Aumont, etc. The last scions of these houses were emigrants, whose bones crumble in the soil of foreign lands.— Here is the shell, now let us look at the kernel—the people.

Yonder, that gigantic captain of the Royal Swiss, in his blue velvet coat and white cockade, thrusts the small grocer contemptuously out of the way; he despises the chattering Parisians, and thinks proudly of his native mountains and the lilies on his breast. That noble guardsman, in a red uniform, with his cavalry boots, and gilt basket-hilted sword, with his hat on one side, is half a courtier. He is pinching the cheek of the pretty flower-girl in her cap with its lappets and narrow neckerchief. He is about to go either to an hour's exercise at arms, or to the Royal to dine—maybe to game at cards or dice, or who knows but he has a rendezvous with some one in the neighboring alley?

That is the notorious Picpusser monk, with a broad, smiling face, who is talking so solemnly to a slender abbé, carrying his cloak over his arm and wearing a steel sword. Two members of Parliament are driving past in their red robes and high mortiers. Farther on, several nuns from Port-Royal are carried in sedan - chairs, closely muffled, so as not to betray their age; and on the other sidewalk a company of ladies and gentlemen, vividly gesticulating, and talking loud and merrily. The latter are philosophers, lawyers, and learned men; all dressed extravagantly in embroidered clothes; and the former are *des esprits* from the circle of Mlle. l'Espinasse. If you look closely at the faces of the gentlemen, you will recognize Diderot, Marmontel, Mably, or Raynal.

What approaching noise is that? The Duke d'Orleans, or the Prince de Conti, the Duchess de Grammont, or perhaps Monseigneur the Dauphin, is driving by, accompanied by running footmen; outriders, some of them Moors, and a dozen lifeguards, bring up the rear, gazed at by Jansenists and Molinists, surly Brittany peasants, and fish-women from the Halle, musicians in braided jackets, and fantastic charlatans in flowing cloaks! They all smile, as if life were a perpetual round of pleasure. Each form of folly or of wisdom has its own mask and costume, demeanor and gesture, color and cut. One supposes the other peculiar because he thinks of himself; each is amused at the expense of all, loves himself most, and thinks Paris is the universe. The distinction of rank, the arbitrariness of the laws, the grim Bastile, as well as the stern halls of justice, do not trouble the people individually. Every one believes that certainly prisons do not concern him. All were merry in the former Paris, because it was a privilege to talk of their discontent; now all are sad, because of their tedious contentment.

About the year 1758, at the corner of the Rue de la Chaussetrerie, near the Rue Tirchape (one of those small but very lively alleys leading from the Rue St. Honoré to the Rues de Lombards and St. Antoine), in the centre of the old town, was a bookstore, kept by a man named Gauchat, who at that time was wealthy, and had the best right to be proud and self-important. He always wore mouse-colored serge and a white necktie, notwithstanding his fondness for snuff. His bobwig was so essential an element of his dignity, that he often went to sleep without taking it off. Wearing only one office-sleeve, and with a pen behind his ear, he thought he made a very impressive appearance; and this, with his sharp and unsocial manner, terrified many whom he wished precisely to inspire iu that way. His establishment, which we would now consider rather mean, seemed to be stuffed with the worthless literature of the day, and old moth - eaten works that no one even looked at. He had no show-windows, for they were only used by milliners and hair-dressers.

In this damp hole there lived, besides the proprietor, a deaf and dumb clerk named Quinet, an inestimable friend to the man of books, a shopman, and a good - for - nothing apprentice, who attended to the retail trade, supplying with impudent importance the intellectual wants of seamstresses, tradesmen, citizens—in fact, all the so-termed lower classes. If, however, a man of distinction entered, such as a philosopher, a high official, a collector of the revenues, or a courtier, the treasures of Gauchat were displayed according to the degree of his patron's consequence, who was invited to ascend to the upper apartments.

There, arranged on oak shelves, were all the poets, from Racine and Molière to Nivelle de la Chaussé, the great law and historical works, maps, plans, valuable old copperplates, as well as all that was new in literature. Gauchat himself printed and published quite extensively. He was on the best terms with the Board of Censure—the inquisition of those times — aud did just what he pleased, taking care to follow the prescribed formality. When any thing was forbidden in Paris, he had it printed in Liège, Amsterdam, or London. • If a man of rank, well known to Gauchat, wished to purchase a prohibited work, the bookseller did not have it, and he assured the gentleman that nothing but licensed books were sold at his store; but as soon as double the price (wrapped in the paper on which the name of the required volume was written) found its way to the desk of the deaf and dumb Quinet, the customer was sure to discover what he was seeking, under his hat, when he took it up on leaving. It was none of Gauchat's business to know how these goods were obtained—he was not the censor of distinguished people.

M. Gauchat had several poor authors in his pay, who had been rendered tractable by hunger. These men received his orders as soon as any one was interested to have a rival denounced. He himself was silent—gave not the least indication of concern in such a matter—he delivered only what would make a noise in reference to others. Since the time of Jansenism, Voltaire, and the Encyclopædia, the goose-quill, type, and printer's ink, had become a mighty power, setting at defiance censure, the Bastile, and the galleys. Gauchat knew this very well, and his greatest pleasure was to be, by virtue of his business, a kind of general, or at least command a regiment of writers, all under his control, who would be led into the field for pay, or a patron in high position.

This was the real era of pamphlets, libels, anecdotes, and poetic libelling, and the bookseller enjoyed it. His pleasure was greatly heightened by the secrecy and danger attending such undertakings. It is scarcely necessary to say that he despised the poor writers he employed, keeping them in proper discipline and dependence; he had so little idea of the dignity of authorship, as to suppose that no word could touch the masses which he had not printed. He knew rich people only, who wrote for pleasure, and who therefore had the right to be celebrated and independent. Toward Messrs. Voltaire, Holbach, and

Marmontel, he was a devoted servant—toward poetasters, protected by cliques in high places, with whom he did not wish to be at variance, he was polite; but people that lived by their pen he considered as a sportsman would his dogs, ready to run after any game, coming and going without any such audacity as to exercise a will of their own.

Worthy M. Gauchat was at the high desk near a window of his store, looking over printers' bills and various letters, now and then communicating with Quinet by signs, when a man approached from the direction of St. Innocence. He was walking leisurely and dreamily, and it was difficult to say to what rank he belonged; but one thing was certain—he was young, poor, and interesting. His tall, straight, and slender figure had the elasticity of youth, for he was about twenty-six years old, and his graceful movement gave some evidence of a person probably of good family and superior education. At all events, he must have associated much with people of refinement, and mother Nature had given him facility in acquiring the style of polished life. His face was one of those that even in youth have something striking, and which does not much change by age, remaining young for many years, particularly when they reflect so much mind. He was of fair complexion; his light hair curled beyond his small hat, and completed the "Titus head," so called by some who began to wear their hair by powdering it and tying it in a bag at the back, the black ribbon crossing on the breast. He supported himself by a strong cane, holding it in his left hand, while in his right he carried a small scroll, wrapped in an old number of the *Mercure Française*.

The young man was naturally sportive, but he did not seem very merry as he walked along; misanthropy was plainly settling on his brow and lips; when one equipage passed on after another, his eye flashed darkly, as with secret hatred, and he betrayed the restlessness of a man striving to conceal his emotions when hunger struggles with an independent and proud behavior. As he walked faster when he came within sight of Gauchat's establishment, any one seeing him in his dress of dark-green but very faded satin, with ripped seams and imperfect embroidery, his large shoes with copper buckles, very clean but much darned ruffles, would have pronounced him a poor *littérateur* going to a publisher with his manuscript—his last hope! As a curious contrast, this man wore a watch, probably a costly one, to judge from the heavy gold chain, with trinkets and agate seals, hanging from his vest pocket; on his right hand sparkled a ring set with large rubies.

The literary man entered the bookseller's store. "Good-morning, Gauchat; how are you? Again at your accounts? It must be elevating to write bills for payment, and receive money for the labor of other men's brains, friend. You agents are a lucky set! You take a completed manuscript with your left hand, paste your name upon it, expend a few hundred francs, give it away with your right hand, and put a few thousand francs into your pocket—a short way to become rich!" Saying this, the new-comer threw himself upon an old chair, and played with his watch-seals.

Gauchat raised his head slightly, held his pen a moment in the air, and looked coldly into the face of the speaker. "M. Beaumarchais, I did not know I was your friend. I am commonly called M. Gauchat, especially by people dependent on me. You have a way of talking so that one never knows whether to take it as a compliment or an insult. I do not care for either. Probably you have another manuscript which you expect me to be fool enough to purchase!" He resumed his labor at the desk with his accounts.

"If you are not my friend, common M. Gauchat, I am very sorry for you; I should have supposed that an old practitioner like you had more sense! How can you say openly to any one that you are not his friend, since no one knows to what honors he may attain, and whether he may not hereafter be useful to you?"

"I can tell what will become of you, after paying you thirty francs in cash for an *École pour la Harpe*, and wasting paper and printing, when no one has the remotest idea of buying it!" He pointed spitefully to a long row of books on a top shelf and a packing-case in a corner. "One copy was sold to a lady! Truly, a prosperous trade! I your friend! Ridiculous! I have been cheated—robbed of my money! The book is the merest scribbling in the world — waste-paper, nothing else! You become something!" He laughed sardonically and shrugged his shoulders.

"I am only not appreciated, Gauchat. People generally fail until they make their fortune by some work; all great men have passed through that experience! One is lucky earlier, another later. Can you know beforehand whether the public will patronize a book or not? To do that you ought not only to be better educated, but possess something that cannot be acquired, and which will remain an eternal mystery in spiritual things—the perception of results! Among five books that you print, three at their very birth return to original rags; one scarcely pays its cost, and another makes you handsome returns! Still, you continue to publish; for you know that one good sale pays for many bad ones, and by degrees you even dispose of the books remaining on your hands

to those good provincial souls who consider it an honor to throw away their money in Paris. At twenty-six, it is true, I am nothing; but in five years I may be a millionnaire and the idol of France! In this small parcel the whole metamorphosis may lie! Will you look at it?"

Gauchat's countenance was distorted by a malicious smile, as he said, "To look at this metamorphosis would really be a droll business!"

"I should think so, particularly if you have a share in the profits!" Saying this, the author rose and placed the scroll upon the bookseller's desk.

Gauchat opened the manuscript. *Eugénie, a Drama in five Acts!* "Ha! ha!" He carelessly wrapped it up again. "No one will read a theatrical piece written by you—no one will act it either; for that, you must be a Voltaire, a Diderot, or, at least a Marivaux. Pray, become a millionnaire and an idol without me, I thank you!"

"You repulse me! Without knowing the contents, you refuse to accept this?"

"Yes!"

"Gauchat, or common M. Gauchat," said Beaumarchais, his countenance flushed, his eyes sparkling, and his voice trembling with excitement, "joking aside, take the manuscript—I want money! It would be both a noble and judicious action—something that seldom happens to you!"

"No, sir! If you want money, that is your affair; I desire none of your writings! I take nothing more, even if you give it me for nothing! Do you understand?"

"Certainly," and the author put his manuscript in his pocket. "Now, I shall be just as plain!" He drew out his watch, holding it before the bookseller's eyes; it was set with brilliants, a real morceau for a cabinet of curiosities. "It is now a quarter after ten;

I give you time to consider until half-past ten! If you have really read the *École pour la Harpe*, and if you have the slightest idea of what intellect is, you comprehend that I know how to wield a pen! I am in need, and that sharpens people's inventive faculties. I might hit upon something that would be very disagreeable to you, therefore—reconsider your answer!" He put away his watch, sat down again, took out a soiled memorandum-book, tore off a leaf, and began to write.

Gauchat was astonished. "Do you threaten me? Ho! ho! And with your pen? But who are you, that I should be afraid?"

"You have a quarter of an hour for all these arguments!"

"And—and who will force me to take all your scribbling? Why do you not offer your—drama, or whatever else you may call the thing—to Lorrant or Le Jay, and defraud them for once?"

"Because I have better offers to make to Lorrant! He is a man of honor, but you are a swindler, and to run a risk does not hurt you; you always make others pay the damage. Decide to take this work, or—be my enemy! You have still eight minutes!"

M. Gauchat felt rather strangely, especially as Quinet was making signs to him. The publisher had a strong desire to have this knight of the quill kicked out; on the other hand, it occurred to him that the man might be insane and dangerous—this was confirmed by the motions of the deaf and dumb clerk. Could there be a real foundation for this bold audacity, so that he should be on his guard, having precarious speculations enough on hand already? "M. Beaumarchais," he began, forcing himself to assume a calmness he did not feel, "why do you not sell that magnificent watch, which must be worth at least a thousand francs, or that ring with the large pearls and rubies!"

"Because I intend never to part with either, even if hunger stares me in the face! All my hopes, the strength of my soul, the confidence in my good star, are associated with them—as long as I possess them, I can never quite sink! I would rather sell you a manuscript than rob myself of these my last resources!"

"And I will not buy it!" cried Gauchat, losing all self-control; "I do not wish to have any thing to do with you. Yonder is the door!"

"I will make use of it as soon as it is time." The author looked at the watch. "Aha! the respite is past!" He rose negligently, and went slowly toward the counter. "In spite of my trouble I have a more humane heart than you, I leave you my address that you may repent!" He laid the memorandum-leaf on the table. "I shall wait until this evening! But if you are not at my house at that time with twenty louis d'ors, and I am to starve, with my wife, then, good friend, I begin a libel, entitled *Monsieur Gauchat and the French Board of Censure, two Historical Antitheses of Civilization*. To-morrow, it will be written; the day following, printed, and read by every one; and you may use the money you saved on *Eugénie* to obtain a few comforts in the Bastile. I acknowledge that it is very severe to act thus, but I would be a fool to treat a rogue in a different manner; I adapt my treatment to every species of animal according to its habits! Now I shall take advantage of your door. Adieu!"

Gauchat had furiously crumpled and thrown on the floor the address of Beaumarchais, when the latter began to speak, but, as he continued, the bookseller became alarmed, and did not notice that Quinet picked up the paper, smoothed and placed it in his desk.

When the author left the store, whistling, the proprietor stood as if paralyzed. A pause ensued. Quinet regarded his master with a shake of his head, and little Jacques Parol, the apprentice, crept into a corner to smother his laughter.

"That—that—that monster has become acquainted with all my trade! He — he has proofs against me! He knows my connections! The other booksellers hate me, and will rejoice at any slanderous reports raised at my expense, particularly now, when all are distrustful and excited, on account of the attempt of the assassin Damien on the king—when all are ready to believe the most incredible stories! And the fellow has such an impudent tongue that I have no doubt he writes well! Perhaps he has been hired by some one to libel me, and if I had had any sense I would have bought him off?—M. Caron!" He ran like a lunatic toward the door, hoping to recall the man he had turned away. But this good intention was frustrated by the appearance of a splendid equipage, with a ducal coronet upon the panel, which stopped in front of the store. The ornamented lackeys sprang from the footboard, and, while one opened the carriage-door and let down the velvet-covered steps, the other hastened toward Gauchat, asking: "Are you the proprietor of this place?"

"Yes, certainly! Benoit Gauchat, bookseller!"

"The Duke de Fronsac and Chevalier de Piron honor you with a visit! I hope you appreciate it properly!"

"Oh dear, yes! M. Valet-de-chambre, and—" The words died on the publisher's lips, for the gentlemen themselves approached.

The one who first descended from the coach was Chevalier de Piron, about forty years of age, and the most graceful man of the society of his day.

He wore a coat of rose-colored satin, with raised white embroidery, straw-colored vest, and grayish pants, a large diamond-pin sparkled in his lace shirt-ruffle, a steel sword in a silver sheath dangled from his side, and a wig with large curls surrounded his jovial and handsome countenance. His charming and unaffected manner confirmed the supposition that he knew how to make himself acceptable at court.

The Duke de Fronsac was about the same age, but taller and thinner, stiff as a mummy, cold and measured, as if he were beyond all the vanities of this world. Those, however, who knew him better were aware that this air was merely the result of boundless contempt for those beneath him, and, in a very great degree, of intellectual poverty. He seemed to be in ill-humor, and followed hesitatingly, while displaying his gold eye-glass (a new invention), and looking at the sign of the bookseller. Piron walked first, and, on approaching the door, said, "Are you Gauchat himself, good man!"

"At your service!"

"Duke, we have arrived, will you be pleased to enter?" Fronsac unceremoniously took the lead, passing into the store.

"*Fi donc*, how dark! what a hole this is!" Fronsac ejaculated. "And this mouldy smell! It cannot be worse in the Temple or the Bastile." He took a pinch of snuff, with every sign of disgust at the place.

"If your grace will take a view of my warehouse on the next floor," replied Gauchat, submissively, "you will perhaps be pleased. This department is only for common people, and contains common things; but in my rooms above—"

"Oh, that is not the question," smiled Piron, "we do not desire to remain longer than necessary. Have a better chair brought for his grace, and send away your people; we wish to talk to you in private."

"Make haste!" cried Fronsac.

"This man," and Gauchat pointed with a trembling hand toward Quinet, "is only a poor deaf mute!"

"That will not prevent him from leaving the room, I hope!" laughed Piron. "I had one of them in my service, who was the greatest scamp under the sun, and I dismissed him because he stole more than the value of ten tongues and twenty ears." The apprentice and shopman brought two oak seats, and then disappeared, followed by Quinet.

Fronsac leaned back negligently, holding in his hand a gold snuffbox, and looking sternly into Gauchat's face. "Listen, and answer truly, as if you were at confession, and never dare to mention anywhere or to any one the object of our visit, if you are not willing to make the acquaintance of La Force or Châtelet! Send us a few of the newest literary works, that we may have an apparent reason for entering this den!"

"Very well, your grace!"

"Have you not published a book, entitled *École pour la Harpe*, written by a certain Caron Beaumarchais?"

"Yes — yes, your grace, it is so," said Gauchat, pale as death. "I hope, gracious duke, that — that no expression appears in the work, that—that is displeasing? I have as yet sold only one copy, and, if you desire, the whole edition shall be—"

"Sent to my house?" interrupted Fronsac, horrified. "By Heaven, you are an insolent fellow! If you send us two hundred copies, they would—" turning to the chevalier — "be sufficient, I will have no more. But, aside from such a trifle, since you do business with this Beaumarchais, you must be acquainted with him. You will tell us then, honestly, what kind of individ-

ual he is; how situated; whether he has any *savoir vivre*, rendering him capable of entering good society, that is, as far as you yourself have any idea on these subjects. In short, say what is praiseworthy or blameworthy in the author of the *École pour la Harpe*. Consider well, that any false statement will result in severe punishment, as individuals would thereby be deceived of so high a rank that their names cannot be mentioned in this hole!"

Gauchat trembled in all his limbs; he was literally breaking down under the weight of surprise, uncertainty, remorse, and fear. Two gentlemen from the court, a duke and a chevalier, make inquiries about Beaumarchais, and buy two hundred copies of a work, at which no one had previously looked! And he had, moreover, as good as kicked the author out of doors! The publisher breathed hard, and his words were broken.

Piron could scarcely suppress his laughter at this scene, and, as he had reasons to wish for a successful issue, he assisted Gauchat out of his embarrassment. "Although I am not concerned in this matter, and am in a certain sense the innocent cause of it, I take the liberty, duke, to draw your attention to the fact, that a plain man like M. Gauchat rarely receives so noble a visitor, and that your dignity and determination quite oppress him, as you may perceive. Will you permit me to question him?"

"Hem, yes!" and Fronsac's countenance relaxed a little, "I see he is in consternation! Not accustomed to people of rank, dazzled, frightened! Good, very good; he seems a loyal man —no foul-tongued scandal-monger! Have the kindness to speak to him, chevalier!"

"Now M. Gauchat," said Piron, smiling, "as soon as you have recovered yourself, tell us what kind of man is M.

Beaumarchais. It may be depending on your testimony, that unthought-of happiness is in store for him!"

"Provided he is worthy of it!" interrupted Fronsac.

"As you are in the presence of—very distinguished personages, do you understand?" and Piron placed a peculiar stress on his words, "and may be made responsible for your statements, you will not fail to place in a true light a man who has excited attention in such high circles of society!"

Gauchat was certainly so astounded by the sudden change preparing for the destiny of Beaumarchais, that he half fancied all this a dream; but he was well enough acquainted with the upper classes, and had penetration enough to comprehend the intimations of Piron, that the duke was one of those old coxcombs who are the plague of all around them, high and low. "Ah! now I understand the sense of your grace's words, I see what you wish! Oh, what a question! Do I know M. Beaumarchais?—my dearest, most honored friend—a most cultivated man, and an accomplished musician—a genius of wit, intrigue, grace, and irony, having gifts to become in five years a millionnaire and the idol of Paris! I know him as I know myself, and—" Piron raised his finger stealthily but threateningly. Gauchat ceased speaking.

"Nonsense, what babble that is!" exclaimed Fronsac, disdainfully. "Such qualities are not found among lowborn citizens! Whence is a man to obtain grace, wit, elegance, and *bon ton*, who never breathed a respectable atmosphere, and gains his daily bread as a musician and a book-maker! I will wager that the man would sell his soul for a hundred francs to do any mean action for which you might bargain with him; then, he is a plebeian!"

"Oh, I beg your grace's pardon!

This man has a great soul and a distinguished style of thought—he possesses something like a natural nobility. I acknowledge that his circumstances at present are none of the best; his position is such as we *bourgeois* call—a calamity. But will you believe, duke, that he was here a quarter of an hour ago; and, though in great want, would not sell me a splendid drama, called *Eugénie*, which he has written, because I was so inconsiderate as to offer him five hundred francs instead of seven hundred? He showed me scornfully his watch, set with diamonds, that must at least cost a thousand francs, saying: ' M. Gauchat, I will not sell you my manuscript at all, even if I break one stone after another from this piece of jewelry, in order to live!' Before I could make any compromise or apology, he vanished."

"Why, duke," said Piron, "that shows an exalted character, noble pride, and the consciousness of great mental qualities, such as are unusual in persons of his class. I almost think he will answer certain expectations!"

"It really seems so! It is quite an uncommon thing," said Fronsac in surprise; "if this musician is as loyal and tractable as he seems disinterested and amiable (but this I doubt), the affair would be void of danger. We must see him. Give us his address."

"His address?" repeated Gauchat, anxiously. "Ah, yes!" And he searched everywhere. "I know it, he gave it me just—no—a long time ago. I,—oh permit me to call my book-keeper. Quinet knows every thing. Jacques! Jacques Parol! Where are you? Call Quinet! Ask him whether he has the paper left by Beaumarchais!" The boy rushed out into the coach-house, but soon reappeared, gesticulating with Quinet, who nodded, unlocked his desk, and smilingly handed the previously despised address to his master. "Thank Heaven!" exclaimed the bookseller, "business papers are never lost in my house! Here is his residence: 'M. Pierre Augustin Caron Beaumarchais, No. 30, Rue Bertau, fourth floor in the Pigeonnier, cross-street of the Rue Beaubourg.' That is the street running parallel with and between the Rue St. Martin and the Temple, your grace. Let me copy it, so that it may be plainer."

"If I recollect correctly, that is a shocking neighborhood, an ominous district; and in the fourth story!" sighed Fronsac. "It is dreadful to think that any one can live in such a place, who is destined to be so highly honored —" the duke hesitated, and shrugged his shoulders. "Of course, the fantasies of the elevated in rank must not be discussed; let us end the affair, chevalier."

"With pleasure, and as I am the cause of this hunt for M. Beaumarchais, duke, I will assist you as much as possible in the difficult enterprise." Piron took the address. "M. Gauchat, do not fail to send the books to the Hôtel de Fronsac; you will remember that we came merely to make this purchase, and you must forget all the rest if you wish yourself well!" The chevalier opened the door; Fronsac walked stiffly toward the carriage, while Piron gave the address to one of the lackeys, and the equipage rolled down the Chaussetrerie, through the Feronerie, toward St. Martin.

When Gauchat rebounded from the humble posture he had assumed while the two cavaliers took their departure, he looked stupidly at Quinet, and then slapped his hands together, saying: "He said so! In five years he will be the idol of Paris! Oh, what a fool I am! But he must not let any one else publish for him; I shall visit him to-night, Quinet." And he accompanied his words by signs, to make himself understood. "Write a laudatory advertisement of the *Ecole pour la Harpe*, and have it inserted in the *Mercure Français!* Say it is a book for the court, and that we sold two thousand copies in one day. We may put it in that form—the extra cipher will, of course, be credited to the compositor! Instead of one franc, the price must now be five! Jacques, call the shopman! Pack two hundred copies, and have the rest carried above. One hundred must be bound in morocco, with gilt edges, gilt letters, and lilies! Trade is prosperous. The book sells! In a week this edition will be exhausted!"

CHAPTER II.

THE PIGEONNIER.

WHILE Beaumarchais, driven from Gauchat's threshold, was walking along the streets like one in a dream, whistling the then popular song, "*Je vais revoir ma charmante maitresse,*" he sought in vain to ameliorate his sense of hopelessness, and, what was worse, degradation. That man suffers doubly who has enjoyed a careless and happy youth, but who, in his manhood, is poor and unemployed, with some dear one dependent on him, and who moreover has wealthy relatives—a father, perhaps, whose heart has long been hardened against him.

Under such circumstances even the best have sometimes evil thoughts, and the soul darkly hovers over the abyss of crime or suicide. Perhaps even this strong man would have bowed beneath the weight of his misery, and in despair have done that which would have brought him to the morgue or the galleys, but he very truly remarked that the costly watch and ring kept him from folly. So long as he felt in possession of something valuable, he did not altogether lose courage, though he knew there is much deception in all final resources. A day might come when the last louis d'or realized from them would be expended, and he none the better off in his hopes than when he had something to fall back upon. The bold confidence which he had shown at Gauchat's was only a sad manœuvre to gain subsistence; for to let the knavish publisher notice anxiety and extreme poverty was only to expose himself. In mental pain at his rebuff, and wandering about without object, Beaumarchais finally recovered his calmness, and resolved to go home. Perhaps his young wife Susanna had been more successful! As if driven by some presentiment, he hastened his steps.

While the author was on this expedition to the publisher's, and an accident (or whatever else you choose to call it) was about to change his lot in life, by the appearance of the two cavaliers at the store, a very curious occurrence was taking place at Beaumarchais's dwelling—an important event in his career, and more than all else influenced his whole future, becoming the origin of many struggles, but also of a renown that resounded through all France, uniting his name with that of the great of the land.

The Rue Beaubourg, commencing at the small cross-streets Maubue and Simon le Franc, which unite at the south end the principal thoroughfares of St. Martin and the Temple, runs parallel with the latter, and ends toward the north at the Church of St. Nicolas de Champ. It was a narrow, dirty lane, in bad repute, like the rest of that *quartier*, inhabited by those who could not afford to live in dearer neighborhoods, and also by many who preferred cheapness to more convenient and respectable dwellings. Many small streets traversed the Beaubourg, various *culs de sac* entered it, where the houses were gloomy and unsightly. It was celebrated for its filth, and the irregularity of the buildings was no small puzzle to the tax-gatherer, in discovering their occupants.

An alley such as we have described entered the Beaubourg, about the middle on the west side, called the Rue Bertau. The houses on the right as you entered leaned against the old convent and church of St. Lazare, with its bell-towers, stone water-spouts, and smoke-blackened walls. The background, that formed the *sac* was a square edifice, larger than usual in this neighborhood, the front of which was hidden by the church. On the left was a small space between this building and the adjacent row, locked by a narrow wooden gate, protected by iron prongs, over which you had a view of a dirty courtyard.

This structure had long been known as the Pigeonnier, not only on account of its windows, (for, on the side visible from the Rue Bertau, there were thirty-six,) but for its roominess and numerous outlets, so that by day and night many could pass in and out, without the knowledge of the uninitiated. The lower floors were of Gothic origin. The principal gate, apparently on one side, but really in the front, with its arched windows and vaults, as well as the cloistered lines of the interior, indicated that this locality must formerly have been used for sacred purposes, and was probably an extension of St. Lazare. The upper floors, as well as the roofing, were in the style of the "renaissance." The Pigeonnier was at this time rented to very many lodgers. In the basement was the store of a harness-maker; by its side a large smithy, from which resounded the anvil-hammer. Passing through the gateway you entered the interior courtyard, which was once a convent garden.

Besides the gate already described, this building had a small outlet to the left, and another opposite the principal one, leading to another alley. Fancy this large edifice, inhabited by five or six hundred persons of all ages, some of them mysterious characters, who came and went as they pleased, as long as they paid the rent for the day—ten cents, for which they received receipts, and which were ingress and egress tickets, to be shown to the different porters. Certain persons of quality, who paid for a length of time in advance, had free admission everywhere about the premises.

In the left wing looking toward the Rue Bertau, and occupying the whole lower floor, dwelt Mademoiselle Coralie Raucourt, an actress of the grand opera, who at that time was in the bloom of her beauty, and was the *enfant chérie* of the celebrated Duni, and of Piccini, as well as of others. In the story above her, a Jew pawnbroker was flourishing, for, as there were many in need of money in the neighborhood, his stairway was seldom without visitors, who had to show their tickets as they passed out, to confirm the fact that they came on legitimate business. In the third story dwelt a tailor, a shoemaker, a turner, and a briefless lawyer, all equally poor, and therefore intimate. On the fourth floor, in the garrets, lived a curiously-mixed company. On the first door there was no sign; on the second, was one bearing the inscription: " Batyl, Music-Teacher, Artist at the Opera." Beyond the staircase was a third: " Louise Duchapt, Fashionable Milliner."

On opening the door without a name, you entered a large garret. There were four small box-like windows looking upon the inner courtyard. It was light enough, but badly furnished, cold, and dreary. To the right a door of communication led to

Batyl's room; to the left, at one of the windows, stood a small table covered with writing-materials and many closely-written pages; at another, a kind of work-table, with blonde, tulle, ribbons, and other articles of finery. To the right of the door was an old closet, corresponding with a bureau on the other side. Upon the latter lay an old piece of oil-cloth, a few books, cups and saucers, and some keepsakes. Above it a mirror was fastened; on one side hung a violin, and on the other a guitar by a blue ribbon, and between the strings was an artificial rose, from some lady's head-dress. It was a melancholy little place, and yet it could tell of sweet hours that had passed away like the sounds of pleasant music.

Farther on, the room was divided by a patched cotton-curtain, behind which stood two clean beds and a trunk; and a few steps more brought you to the corner window, which looked down upon the Rue Bertau. It was a separate chamber, cut off by an improvised wooden partition, with a door in the middle. At the window stood a worm-eaten desk with a stool; on the left, a miserable bed; on the right a closet, and on a comparatively large table lay classic works, writings, and, strewed about in confusion, the usual apparatus of learned men. Three parties had a right to this apartment. An old schoolmaster named Morelly, who had claims to the little corner; Batyl, who used the foreground as an eating-room; and Beaumarchais and his wife, whose sleeping-chamber was behind the curtain, in front of which they had their workroom.

Nothing could have added more to this poverty-stricken scene than the young woman, sitting at her work, her feet upon a narrow bench, holding a milliner's head on her lap, upon which was fitted a fanciful cap, with which she was busily engaged. She might not have been so much as, certainly not more than, twenty years of age. Her complexion and small, graceful figure, her neck, shoulders, and bosom (that the old red silk handkerchief did not altogether hide), had lost none of their youthful freshness. Her charming countenance still had all the naïveté and loveliness which for a long time preserve with some women an expression of childlike innocence, especially if accompanied by dimples in chin and cheeks. But her eyelids were inflamed from weeping, her breath came irregularly and heavily, she often started, looking shyly at the door; then she sewed more rapidly, as if urged by some fear. Her whole being expressed something wearied and spasmodic, and a deep flush was passing over her brow, to be succeeded by a deathly pallor. It was evident that she was suffering.

Madame Beaumarchais was annoyed by the noise from the street and corridor, as well as by the melancholy variations of Batyl's harp practising in a minor key. She could no longer control herself, but, letting fall her work, wept; then she sat thinking—thinking. "To work!" she murmured, suddenly starting in her reverie. "By dinner-time I must have this cap finished, so that I may receive money from Louise Duchapt, or we must starve! What a merry life Mlle. Raucourt leads! she rented the lower floor two months ago, and has damask curtains and gilt furniture! Of course! she has sold herself to the dissipated courtiers, why should she not be gay? One might almost doubt the existence of a just Providence!" Hastily she seized her needle, when she uttered an exclamation of pain, and blood flowed from the forefinger of her left hand, staining the white tulle. Quickly she put aside the cap. "It is ruined!" she cried, and tears stood in her eyes. "Instead

of receiving any thing for it, I have lost a whole night, wasted oil and labor, and now I must repay the damage done! Lie there, stupid thing!" She angrily cast the milliner's head upon the floor, and walked up and down in despair.

"A crowd of knaves, who are far inferior to Caron, dress in silk, enjoy reputation, office, and money, proudly pass us with gold-headed canes, perhaps smile pityingly; and you, poor Beaumarchais, do what you will, nothing prospers in your hands! You are a man of talent, but alas! a mere *bourgeois*, and these two facts do not well agree! Why was he not born a blockhead? we should then be well enough provided for! When he was a watchmaker, and lived peaceably with his father, he was happy; oh, if he had only remained obedient, like other sons who have fathers to bequeath them wealth. Ah, I was his misfortune! When he saw me at Passy three years ago, and we fell in love with each other, he led me to his parents' house; I shall never forget that day—a day when the father cursed the son for marrying a poor girl, of whom he knew nothing, and she herself was ignorant of her parentage! I am his bane!" She stood wringing her hands. "And if he does not succeed in selling his *Eugénie*, what shall we do? The grocer will trust us no longer, Batyl is becoming impatient, and Morelly is as poor as we are! We shall have to part with our last treasure, the watch—ah, the ring—the only clew that might possibly lead to the discovery of my miserable birth!"

Perhaps the poor woman might have fallen into more unhappy thought, when Batyl, the musician, stopped his harp, and gently opened the door.

Some people continually remind us, that, aside from the nobler attributes of the mind and the gift of language, we have many qualities in common with the brute. Batyl was an excellent musician, but he was vain; and, as neither his art nor his restless self-love procured him a position in the royal chapel, he became wicked, uniting in his character absurdity with villany, and impertinence with a rare delight in the misfortunes of others. Entering softly, and seeing the grieved woman before him, he whispered to himself: "She is ready for anything!" The wife of Beaumarchais seemed instinctively to feel the approach of danger, and turned toward him in a startled manner.

"Why, Madame Susie, are you again so sad?"

"He is going to dun me!" thought Susanna, but she replied: "Ah, Batyl, sadness is the companion of poverty."

"Well, well, Caron is out, eh?" Batyl looked around, and, placing his hands behind him, walked toward that part of the room curtained off, to assure himself that no one was there or in Morelly's division.

"But he will return unsuccessful! We have become accustomed to misfortune. What a pity that we were ever born!"

"Your parents ought to have been proud, Susie, of such a pretty creature as you are."

"How proud my parents were of me," exclaimed the young woman angrily, "they very plainly showed by rejecting me, and to this hour keeping from me, exposing their child to temptation and sorrow. The only proof I have of their identity is a ring that will probably find its way to the goldsmith rather than discover my family! I am very miserable!"

"Miserable! fie, you sin in speaking thus. Are you not young and pretty! These evil days may soon pass—"

"And worse may follow," she interrupted. "There is no use in trying to console one who has no prospect of a dinner."

Batyl looked at her craftily, sighed, and smiled: "Ah, in an hour all could be changed!"

Susanna cast an inquiring glance on him. "Batyl, I think you ought to be sent to Bicêtre."

The musician drew from his pocket a package. "Can you guess what I have here?"

Susanna smiled. "Something to eat for Caron and myself?"

"Not exactly, but something which could provide plenty to eat!"

"You are jesting!" exclaimed Susanna, irritated. "A package of banknotes? Is that it? And from you who are continually dunning us for the hundred francs!" She shrugged her fair shoulders disdainfully.

Batyl came nearer, his voice sank to a whisper. "A person of distinction, who wishes you well, sends this."

"A person of rank wishes my Caron well? Who is it?"

"Will you keep it a secret?"

"Yes; but give me the present!"

"Hold, Susie! it is not sufficient that you are silent, you must also agree to certain conditions.

"Conditions?" She became cool and guarded. "And what are they, M. Batyl?"

The musician smiled in embarrassment, while opening the parcel. "Let us first look at the gift, then we can talk." The wrapping fell, and he held a costly casket in his hand, turning it around. "Well, is it not beautiful?"

Susanna looked at it with as much distrust as surprise. "Truly wonderful! And real velvet!"

"The ornaments and clasp are gold!"

"Gold!"

"And the lining also!" Batyl opened it. "It contains three thousand franc bills, and a note for you."

The poor woman, so recently disturbed by thoughts of her condition, with its immediate want, rejoiced at the sight, forgetting all else. "For me? What beneficent lady has discovered our wretched circumstances?"

The musician still smilingly retained the present. "This lady, I beg your pardon, is a gentleman—an Apollo in amiability—a Pluto in riches; it depends only on yourself to see him at your feet, and to live henceforth in splendor! send him a favorable reply, and—" He presented the casket to her with a bow.

Susanna soon awoke from her dream of beneficence; instead of gratitude she felt profound indignation. "You and your Apollo are scoundrels!" she said.

Batyl stepped back. His flattering politeness assumed a natural malice. "Indeed! But I lent you a hundred francs from mere sympathy! And as to the count, no man is a scoundrel who has an income of eighty thousand francs, and is the heir of a millionnaire."

"When, you infamous scraper," asked Susanna, pressing her hands together, "did you learn to despise me in this manner—to imagine, for one instant that I could possibly sell myself? Men like you should be beaten to death!"

"To death?" grinned the musician. "In a civilized state! Fie! I am only attempting that of which the highest men of rank are not ashamed. Only look at Mademoiselle Raucourt. She lives like a princess just for the trouble of civilly receiving certain noblemen. Now, jesting aside—"

"Take the present away!" cried Susanna, angrily. "If my husband were here, you should have all your notes discounted on your back!"

"That is the reason I waited until he was away," replied Batyl, coolly. "Your husband cannot support you, Madame

Beaumarchais, much less repay me my money. In a few months, you will reach the lowest depths of poverty."

"I would rather beg than be guilty of dishonor. However unhappy our circumstances may be, there is comfort in Caron's love and a good conscience! Who can be so inhuman as to filch them from me?"

Batyl put both casket and letter into his pocket. "I will go, as reasoning has no effect. The day before yesterday I demanded my money of your husband for the third time, in presence of Morelly, as enjoined by law. He has not paid me. You must therefore accept the present and proposition, or Beaumarchais is sent to the debtor's prison—that is the result of your prudery!"

"My husband in prison! Are you a man?" The unfortunate woman wrung her hands despairingly.

Batyl put on his hat and took his cane. "Certainly, as soon as I leave here! The count has taken measures to have the execution levied as soon as possible, and your husband incarcerated, at the expense of Apollo, until you have earned a hundred francs, or have abandoned your scruples."

"Be merciful, Batyl!" weepingly entreated Susanna.

"Good - morning, madame!" He went quickly toward the door.

"One word, Batyl!" She turned pale and trembled violently.

"Yes or no?"

A deep blush crimsoned her countenance; she looked around as if for help, then, suddenly coming to a determination, she whispered: "Yes!"

"Ah, that is good!" laughed the harpist, turning back, and drawing the casket and note again from his pocket. "I will inform Count de la Blache—"

"La Blache!" cried Susanna, horrified. "Falcoz de la Blache?" she murmured. "I shall die with disgust and shame! Why, sir, this count has a wife?"

"That is one more reason why he has discovered your beauty. I see you are acquainted with him?"

"Oh yes," she said, shuddering, "I know the oppressor of my youth! And now—"

"It is your fate, my dear; however, you can bear it with an income of six thousand francs, and a splendid dwelling, as this letter will inform you. Read it." He handed her the casket and billet with a malicious pleasure.

Susanna took them, and walked as one stupefied toward the work-table, laid both upon it, and sank into a chair, pressing her hands before her face, and whispering, "What will Caron say?"

"He will be at first raving mad, but afterward he will become reconciled to the arrangement. You must read the count's letter, and answer it at once."

"Not this moment, Batyl!" she replied, weariedly. "My head aches. I can find no words now. Say to La Blache that he must have patience."

Batyl looked at her with a piercing eye. "You intend to prepare Beaumarchais! I have to give a lesson at the bookseller's in the Rue Beaubourg; that will give you sufficient time. When I return I will put on my state-dress, and carry a note from you to the count, announcing to him the first rendezvous. Such trifles can be written in two seconds. Farewell, Susanna!" He nodded and opened the door, when, hearing several well-known voices on the corridor below, he again turned. "Listen! Morelly is coming with Lamoignon and Turgot, but, be careful, unless you wish to see Caron in a dungeon!"

The beautiful but wretched woman was in agony. Leaning her head on her trembling hands, she wept bitterly, because the last and precious sources of her earthly happiness were assailed.

She did not sit long alone. The door opened, and three men entered in lively conversation, without noticing Susanna, who was crouching in the window-niche; they passed on to the division of Morelly.

The oldest of the new-comers was a teacher engaged in instructing the pupils of St. Lazare in the secular sciences, especially the classes in elementary branches; he was half despised and half pitied by his clerical superiors. His dress was so poor that it required all Susanna's ingenuity in mending to keep it at least decent. His figure was small and delicate; his head well formed and thoughtful, with a vast forehead towering above bushy eyebrows, and a few white locks about his temples. His was the countenance of a thinker—melancholy in meditation; but at other times it had something gentle, bright, and happy. A smile played winningly about his lips, expressing contentment, which, with a ruddy hue of health and strength, reminded one of the presence of some philosopher of antiquity. This poor teacher, Morelly, now sixty-two years old, and almost in rags, was the Diogenes of France—one of the first, and decidedly the most profound of the men before the French Revolution, whose successor was Jean Jacques Rousseau, with his *Contrat Social*, *Emile*, and *Sur l'Inégalité*; on which Mably, Holbach, Raynal, and all the reformers of that school, based their theories. Morelly beheld clearly the heights to which the revolution might rise, but which it never reached, because a bloody partyism blinded its conceptions of the sublime and happy in social life.

Morelly was the anonymous author of the *Basiliade*, a poem on the human sovereignty of the world, published in 1753, long before the appearance of Montesquieu's *Esprit des Lois*, and before the philosophers even thought of forming a system of their doctrines of denial, by gathering them in the *Encyclopédie*. He also wrote the *Lois de la Nature*, which for a long time was ascribed to Diderot. The literary men of the drawing-rooms, and the profounder students, admired by all the world, cut their garments from the remnants left by this man—perhaps the greatest idealist since Plato. Jean Jacques Rousseau's son (Babœuf) turned Morelly's misunderstood *Basiliade* into a farce for the theatre, but paid for it with his head. The ideas of Louis Blanc, Fourier, and Cabet, are mere plagiarisms from this man's works, or, at best, half-social, half-political variations. He was neither vain nor passionate, and considered himself happier than a prince, if he only had a piece of bread when he needed it, a glass of water, a bed, paper, pens, and ink, and a true friend. He refused every effort to draw him from his poverty and solitude, by saying, "*Je suis assez heureux!*"

The youngest of the three, about thirty-one years old, was Anne Robert Jacques Turgot, a son of the president, and secretary of the intendant of commerce, De Gournay; he was a follower of the economists of Quesney's school. His faculty of analysis, and a certain habit of calculating, gave dryness to his speech, and to his bearing and physiognomy a Cato-like sternness, somewhat moderated in society by the forms of intercourse, as well as by his mental polish and morality. He was elegantly attired, preferring, however, dark colors, and no other material than cloth, avoiding the dandyism with which the young men of those days variegated themselves.

The third was no less than the son of the Chancellor of France, Lamoignon de Malesherbes, first president of the *Cour des Aides*—a man of about thirty-six. His figure was full and well proportioned, without being athletic; he had not the stiffness and apparent unsociability of his friend and colleague, but yet the quiet dignity of a patrician, conscious of his rank, without troubling himself with any special intimation of it. His mild eye, and the delicate smile on his lip, were in keeping both with his intellect and a nature that had long disencumbered itself of the constraining formalities and ceremonious privileges of his class, without precisely despising them. He wore a dark-blue coat and pantaloons of silk; a kind of gray-cloth lawyer's cloak, and a dress sword (the sign of a nobleman), completed his costume.

However obstinately the aristocracy still clung to the old forms and distinctions of rank, exaggerating every trifling act, as if conscious of the approach of a time when they would cease altogether, the influence of new ideas was already so great that many superior men, like Lamoignon, anticipated this social change, choosing secret companions, remarkable for intellect, from among the people, though poor, and in positions that inexorably excluded them from contact with the nobility.

"Rest assured, my dear friend," said Malesherbes, ardently, "the facts will overwhelm us sooner than we expect; and that which was with one a mere deduction, and with others—as you, for instance, my Diogenes — a sunny dream, will become a reality—a reality wrought out by the nations! America is already in a ferment! After the British government rejected the project of a constitutional union, neglecting Chatham's warning voice, Franklin has gone to London (as we hear from Mlle. l'Espinasse) to make a last effort at reconciliation. He bears peace or war in the folds of his mantle! And that terrible attempt at murder by Robert Damien, who was publicly executed on the Place Grève by an equally barbaric justice, is it not a "mene tekel" for monarchs? The secrecy in which the process was conducted, the reports among the excited populace, the anxiety with which all was suppressed that might lead to a discovery of the motive for the deed,—all point to a terrible commotion. Do you not think that if the great struggle between slavery and liberty begins in America, all oppressed hearts among us will awaken, and abolish forced service, *lettres de cachet*, the *jus primæ noctis*, corrupt farming of the revenues, arbitrary taxation, and the prerogatives of the clergy and feudal lords?"

"No!" Morelly hung his hat on a nail, and exchanged his coat for an old gown of lambskin. "No, I hardly believe it, my friends! The movement of the people beyond the ocean sprang from a sense of intolerable oppression, and the necessity of independence to a youthful nation, conscious of its strength. A new people arising from the mixed blood of European emigrants, is a very natural result, just as the Romans sprang from the Etruscans, Pelasgians, and Latins. We, however, are old and indifferent—a condition similar to that of a man who, approaching the verge of life, and, having lost all vigor, compensates himself by logical abstractions. We shall not probably imitate America! It is true, the world is ever young, humanity is in continual development, and we are already a part of the future, at least in its introductory features, but not as a national body—not as the France which is to be, but only as atoms tending to some settled and fixed form. We are rather destined to be like the Greek colonists, who entered into new combinations with the youthful Italians, and I believe that would be the best."

"Never!" exclaimed Turgot, sharply. "This proud France will remain the first people upon earth—the think-ing, guiding head of the human race! It is the only Romanic nation that has preserved hitherto the manners of the ancients in their purity, that ruled during the Middle Ages, and is now burying old institutions by the mere power of thought. Its natural law is to remain isolated and to govern. The North American movement is strong and deep, but slow. We shall therefore have time and opportunity to make the hitherto uneducated masses conscious of what we have already gained, of the conquests of philosophy, physiology, natural sciences, and, above all, agriculture. By involving the old delusions in doubt, and especially while the transatlantic nations are obtaining liberty by a gradual movement, we shall long have been prepared, and in a moment our burden will be cast off."

"Cast off!" echoed Morelly, nodding thoughtfully. "I tell you, do not be precipitate! You might serve Satan, fancying you were doing God service. If what you say could really happen, I pity France and all her sons and daughters, for we live for the promotion of evil. Divine Providence, however, sees farther than we. No, Turgot, in spite of your natural consequences, you are as pleasant a dreamer as Plato and the ridiculed Morelly. I merely imagine what in future a more enlightened race of men might become; but you both wish to make your dreams realities. Let your Diogenes, aided by a practical lantern, look at the state of France.

"History proves that it has always had a hot and rebellious temperament, and is accustomed to domestic strife. The arm of Richelieu, the revolution of the Fronde, the power of Louis XIV., invaded the independence of the aristocracy, and turned their influence in favor of a strong monarchy. Sully and Colbert were the first to think of the freedom of the people. So far all went well; but the social power of the nobles remained—that very power by which they could not oppress those beneath them. They now devour three-fourths of the state income, they receive the taxes, tithes, lands, offices, patents, and sinecures, without obligation to make any return, or to respond to any complaint. Do you not yourselves illustrate what I say? Would your Jansenist fathers not consider it greatly beneath the dignity of their coat-of-arms, if they found you in the Pigeonnier with shabby Morelly?

"Here is the state of the case: The lower classes labor, groan, and pay; poverty is universal, and the revenues of the state are smaller. Luxury increases extravagance and national debt, for a continual pumping will at last exhaust the well. Another John Law is at hand. This state of affairs may last a long time, for the people are blinded, their souls are in possession of the priest, and their bodies of the landed proprietor. Suddenly you interfere, Messrs. Philosophers!"

"Fortunately, my dear Diogenes," said Turgot, banteringly, "you well describe the development of our plan! We philosophers say to the masses: 'The hierarchy is a worn-out affair, and the teachings of the priests stupefying; but a free mind is independent of tradition—is a law to itself. What can you say? Did not Holy Mother Church, with her Augustine—did not the Jansenists point out the way?'"

"But you, followers of Quesney," said Lamoignon to Turgot, "only make things worse. You say to the nobles: 'Matter is the only enduring thing; it must be in motion to exist; it is eternally in motion; and therefore is itself eternal! It moves according to an inner law, to a force inseparable from it; consequently matter always in motion is alone spirit, and nothing exists besides!'"

"The only sensible idea in all this," interrupted Morelly, hastily, "is the endeavor of the economists to turn their doctrines to practical utility; they say, 'Man and the state are just such moving matter.' Upon this doctrine of philosophy they curiously found moral qualities, and then social and intellectual ones, and then the division of land, and the laws of consumption and production; they demand from the government a balance-sheet of income and expenses, that where a tax is paid, an 'equivalent may be received; that where there is a prerogative, there may be a duty, and this they call 'national husbandry.' But you have overturned your own doctrines of equality and reciprocity. To whom do you preach? To the rich and aristocratic; no one else in France knows much about you. What are the results? You have put additional means of oppression into the hands of those in authority—that is, craftiness, to defend themselves. Messrs. Voltaire and Holbach wish to be understood at court and by the nobles, but not by their shoemakers, tailors, and lackeys; intellect is not for the people any more than money, honor, and freedom! When Christ taught, every one understood Him, and the poor the best of all. Your friends act in a contrary manner. The world is indeed moving; America will become free without your learned drawing-rooms, where what is affirmed is nothing more than that all power lies in the pocket! Suppose our poor oppressed people are seized by a desire to imitate those beyond the ocean, then the weight of matter in motion will be such that we shall be horrified! Oh, if ever the masses comprehend your principles, they will kill aristocrats, philosophers, and priests, with a full knowledge of what they do. They will not, however, reach that point during our life.

"In my *Basiliade* I essayed to ennoble the inherent divine humanity. From the fogs of the Middle Ages I tried to define and bring out the simple and sublime religion of the Saviour of mankind; but the philosophers do nothing but destroy! That fact separates us forever. That is why I will not go to their reunions to countenance their babble. Let us three remain together, as we have hitherto done, and though we may differ in opinion, we have one object—the elevation of the human race. Avoid the materialists; but, as far as lies in your power, ease the oppression weighing down the people, that they may be better, freer, more humane, when the time comes for Liberty to enter the world as a second Pallas. Your memorials on administration and commerce, that you so often read to Caron and myself of an evening, will give you enduring fame as public benefactors. Leave the tearing down to those who consider a denial of everything a sign of superior intellect!— Listen! what was that? It seemed like a sob!"

The old man went to the other part of the room, followed by his companions. Turgot was about to make a morose reply, when Morelly pointed to Madame Beaumarchais, still in the corner.

"What is the matter? Again grieving! Is there no prospect for Caron?" Lamoignon placed his hand on her shoulder.

Susanna sprang up and stared at them. "Prospect? Yes, such as that of the condemned upon the scaffold! To die quickly would be a blessing, but, to pine away by inches from shame and repentance — who, as you know every thing, has discovered such a torture? Tell me his name that I may curse him!" She seized Morelly's arm, and looked at him with a wild glare.

"But, dear me," cried Turgot, "can you do more than starve?"

Morelly patted her hand, saying: "Calm yourself, Susie; tell us what is the matter."

"If you will not betray me."

"Have you ever been deceived by old Morelly?"

A pause ensued. Susanna could speak only at intervals. She related with a blushing face all that had occurred between her and Batyl, and showed the casket and the letter from La Blache. She threw herself sobbing into the old man's arms.

Turgot paced the floor furiously— all his moral feelings were outraged. "Now, you gray dreamer, will you still say it is not necessary to purify the sacred hearth of our native land? Can this state of corruption continue one day longer? The excess of wickedness cries for vengeance! When will the Nemesis appear?—La Blache is the name of this brute?"

"Do you know him?" Morelly inquired of Susanna.

"Too well! You are aware that my parents have always disowned me. I was brought up at the house of Antoine Garnier, the intendant of Passy, which belongs to the rich Duverney, the royal banker, whose nephew and only heir this La Blache is. He saw me there, and persecuted me with his propositions. Caron released me, for I ran away and became his wife. My obscurity has hitherto protected me, and now he makes use of our poverty to conquer my aversion and honor."

Turgot searched in all his pockets. "And I have only twenty-five francs left!" He attempted to press the money into her hand.

"That is of no use, Turgot, if we cannot pay Batyl. We must sell Caron's watch, our last hope, or perhaps even the ring—the only thing that can possibly assist me to find my parents."

Malesherbes seemed to awake from deep thought. "Some one is coming;

it must be Beaumarchais. Be calm, I hasten to my father the chancellor; and Caron shall be protected."

"Oh pray, tell him nothing of this!" entreated Susanna.

"No, you must tell the truth to your husband; no evil is remedied by secrecy," said Morelly.

The door opened. Beaumarchais entered, looking fatigued and discouraged. His countenance bore an expression of utter despair. He cast a glance at his friends; then, turning to his wife, said: "Did you receive any money for the cap?"

"I have nothing!" she replied in a sad tone.

"Nor have I! I have been at least to ten booksellers, but not one would purchase. Gauchat, the rascal, showed me the door. He has sold only one copy of my work, and has not yet ceased repenting the thirty francs he gave me for it. How many scoundrels have good tables, and positions of influence! Honest or dishonest, I alone, it seems, am the only one who does not prosper. But it is all right, I suppose; I have discovered that I have no talent. Your husband, Susanna, is as incompetent as any man to be found between the poles!" He threw the manuscript on the bureau.

"You no talent!" she exclaimed. "He is losing his self-esteem!"

"Do you know what it is to be a genius? It is the high art of knowing how to wear your mask, and make an attitude."

"What are you talking about?" and Morelly shook his venerable head. "Is only the contemptible falsifier a man of genius?"

"Well, suppose you are as gifted as Apollo," continued Caron; "if you do not look like him, you are a fool. To paint a good picture, or compose a piece of poetry, is nothing; but to astonish people by some bungling work,

to be called wise at small expense, to dress up men's passions, to choose your mask, your dancing-master attitude, and thus to pass through life, is the sign of intellect, and brings money and honor! O holy Providence, see this poverty—this pale woman in tears, and teach me my true position! Blind old Chance, put in my way a few blockheads, that I may try my hand on them, and become the factotum of the world."

Morelly witnessed this wild irony with sorrow. "Tell him, I beg you; it is better!" he whispered to Susanna.

"Not now!" she replied, trembling.

"Would to Heaven," exclaimed Turgot, who was pacing up and down, but now stood before Beaumarchais, "that poverty were the worst that is threatening you!"

"What else is there?" asked Caron, turning pale. "Wife, Morelly, what is the matter?"

"I cannot tell you," groaned Susanna.

"And yet it must be told," exclaimed Malesherbes. "Be a man, Beaumarchais!" He handed the casket and the letter of the count to Caron. "Batyl has sued you for the debt you owe him, and, unless you accept M. de la Blache's proposition, you will be sent to prison to-day."

Caron stared at the case, the note, and those around. "Batyl!—I in prison?—Let me see what it all means." He opened the box. "Three thousand francs in bills—a gold-and-velvet casket!" Placing the money on the table, he opened the perfumed note, and scanned it. "La Blache offers a yearly income of six thousand francs for—for Susanna's love!" He trembled violently. A legion of passions seemed to toss him as a tempest the ocean. He clinched his teeth, and bit his lip until the blood came, that a word might not escape him—a large tear or two rolled down his cheeks.

"Caron! Caron!" wailed Susanna. "Oh sacrifice your watch—every thing —only—"

"Leave me," he answered; "I will soon be calm."

Morelly was about to address Beaumarchais, but a repelling gesture silenced him. Turgot regarded the man with folded arms, and Malesherbes was endeavoring to think of some means to help the unfortunate couple, while Caron paced the room. It was a sad sight, the struggle of a strong man with himself.

"This is shocking, and will end in insanity!" whispered Morelly.

"Recover your self-possession, my friend," said Turgot, gloomily.

"I beseech you, only speak, Caron!" begged Susanna.

"He is beside himself," said Malesherbes, anxiously seizing the young wife's hand.

Beaumarchais was near the curtain, with his back to his friends, when suddenly he turned. His anguish seemed to have ceased, for he assumed a very merry mood. "Ha! ha! triumph!" He kissed his wife passionately. "Dance, my love, be gay! Morelly, Lamoignon, Turgot, congratulate me! The great Caron has found his mask." He pressed the count's letter to his lips, as if it were a keepsake from a loved friend.

"Oh I understand him," said Turgot. "With the anger of injured virtue, he will appear publicly and say: 'This is what is offered to the children of France! Permit your wives and daughters to be dishonored, or rise for human rights and dying liberty!'"

"Of course," laughed Beaumarchais. "You philosophers have made such cries your profession. Do you think my grief may be used as a weapon by you? Poverty drives neither my wife to dishonor, nor me to become a hound of your factions."

"Well!" replied Turgot, half disdainfully. "What will you do? I believe you should be sent to Bicêtre."

"Really?" rejoined Beaumarchais, "Now, pay attention! One of these thousand-franc bills" (and he gave it to his wife with comic emphasis) "must immediately be changed at the Jew's, below. Either you or I will pay Batyl before witnesses. And that this rascal La Blache may know what it is to feel disgraced through his wife, I shall copy his letter to you, sign my name to it, and send it with the casket to his countess. Good reputation does not protect us from the wiles of the wicked; but if we can obtain a certain notoriety for immorality, let us take advantage of it. We are then feared, and every wretch becomes grinningly friendly, lest we might do him harm. I have my mask, if fortune will only give me the right position!" Laughing, he went to his table to write the note to the countess.

Susanna breathed freely; she felt relieved at the thought that Caron had found some way of escape. "My dear husband, if you only regain your courage, I am quite happy. But, we must eat—"

"Certainly, and we must dine well to-day," replied Caron. "Go, therefore, and change the bill. Then, fry a chop for us, and get a few bottles of wine, will you not?"

"And you do not feel degraded in making use of this money?" asked Turgot, harshly.

"Degraded!" and Beaumarchais shrugged his shoulders. "If I force La Blache to buy me off, instead of making him the lord of my honor, why should I feel degraded? Cato, you have lost your reason in abstractions. Cunning against cunning—that is the game, and the most stupid must pay. You three will be our guests. Morelly says that the true idea of nature is community of property, and I shall endeavor to reëstablish this order.

Morelly shook his head. Lamoignon laughed heartily. Turgot said coldly: "I am much obliged to you for your invitation. Let us go to your closet with Malesherbes, Morelly. I have something more to say to you." He took the old man's arm and drew him away, followed by Lamoignon.

"You refuse?" laughed Caron. "Well, Roman virtue should never interfere with the good things of life! Be merry, Susie; run away to the grocer; it is high time to strengthen our poor bodies with a little food."

"I will lock up the rest of the money," said Susanna, concealing her treasures in the bureau drawer. "Here is the key, that from this pigeonnier these strange birds may not fly away. Thank Heaven, we need not part with either your watch or my ring!" While, enlivened by new hope, she pressed a kiss upon Caron's lips, put the bill into a purse, hid it in her bosom, and looked around for her old hooded cloak, to prepare herself for purchasing the materials of a good meal, such as they had not enjoyed for a long time. Beaumarchais finished his billet-doux to the countess.

At the same time, this most curious of *hôtels garnis* was honored by a visit from the Duke de Fronsac and Chevalier de Piron. They had driven in their equipage as far as the Rue Maubue, and there, by the advice of Piron, sent it back to the duke's mansion, and engaged a hired coach, that brought them to their destination. This only increased Fronsac's disgust at the mission with which he was intrusted; but he was completely exhausted by the exertions he had made, as well as by his indignation, when, after having found No. 30, the porter put certain inquisitive questions to them, ending in a contribution, without showing any special

reverence for such distinguished personages. They at length discovered where Beaumarchais lived, and, after losing themselves several times in the labyrinth of passages, and, being set right in a surly and suspicious manner, climbed to the fourth story.

Piron concealed, as well as his politeness permitted, his amusement at the misery of the old courtier, and having assisted him up the stairs to the nameless door, he said: "Here we are; here, the middle door! The Argonauts already see the golden fleece! Approach, my dear duke!" Opening the door, he continued: "Do not stumble over the high threshold! These are certainly not the marble stairs of Versailles and Trianon."

Beaumarchais had finished his note, and, on seeing the strangers, sprang up. Susanna, who was about to leave the room, retreated, and let her cloak fall. "These are gentlemen from the court!" she said, in a subdued voice.

"We have arrived, I think," smiled Piron to Fronsac, casting a glance on the couple and around the desolate apartment.

Fronsac groaned. "By our Lady, I have never before ascended such stairs!"

"They are those which lead you, duke, to an unknown country—Poverty!" said Piron.

Beaumarchais bowed politely, and was going to address the new-comers, but Fronsac gave him no time. Turning his eye-glass full upon Caron, he said, dryly, "Who are you?"

Turgot, Malesherbes, and Morelly, stepped out from the recess; on seeing the extraordinary visitors, however, they remained behind the curtain at the other end of the garret.

Caron's face reddened. "Yes, who are *you?*" he returned.

"I ask, *who* are you?" replied Fronsac, in irritation.

"I am a man."

"That means nothing."

"So I see!" and Caron turned toward Piron, and bowed. "May I ask what is the object of your visit?"

"I, my good fellow, visit only men," said Piron, laughing. "I present to you his grace the Duke de Fronsac, one of our most intellectual men at court, who is seeking a certain M. Caron de Beaumarchais, having just received his address from the bookseller Gauchat."

"Why, that is our name!" and Susanna clasped her hands in astonishment.

"Our name, my pretty child!" said Piron, patting the young woman's blushing cheek. "Is our name Beaumarchais?"

"I am Caron Beaumarchais, sir," interrupted the author, coldly, "and that is my wife."

"Are you he, himself!" exclaimed Piron. "Excellent!—I beg your pardon, madame, courtiers are sometimes very nonchalant."

"So, you are Beaumarchais?" Fronsac fastened his piercing eye upon the young man, apparently measuring all his qualities.

"Yes, your grace," said Susanna, quickly. "He is the one whose *École pour la Harpe* M. Gauchat printed, and my husband." Caron made her a gesture of disapproval.

"He is the man we are seeking; therefore, duke, execute your mission at once."

"You will immediately make your toilet," Fronsac commanded, "and follow us to their royal highnesses the daughters of his majesty, the princesses Adelaide, Sophie, and Victorie, to be honored with a private audience. The carriage is waiting.—Woman, give me an arm-chair."

Piron glanced around, mischievously. "Yes, an arm-chair!" He placed one of the old chairs for Fronsac, and seated himself on a stool.

"Their royal highnesses demand my presence!" exclaimed Beaumarchais, almost beside himself. "But that is impossible!"

Even Fronsac smiled. "Oh yes, in your lowliness you are overwhelmed!—Chevalier, have pity on the poor plebeian, and confirm the order, which, I must confess, is incomprehensible to me."

"You, man, called Beaumarchais," cried Piron, in a jovial manner, "I verify the order that you are to appear immediately before the princesses. But quickly, my friend! say not another word, and make your toilet."

"Oh dear!" sighed Susanna, "what shall we do!"

"Toilet!" exclaimed Beaumarchais, uneasily. "Just Heaven, I have none! I cannot go as I am. Excuse me until to-morrow, your grace, while I endeavor to get another coat."

Fronsac stared. "To-morrow? Not instantly obey the command of the royal princesses? Wait until to-morrow? You must go now!"

"Must!" and Caron's brow glowed. "You may speak in that manner to your lackey, duke; I am not at present your servant! I will obey, but not in a style that makes me blush, and which would be an insult to their royal highnesses."

"Indeed, your grace!" interrupted Piron. "You see that he is right. He cannot appear at the audience in such a dress; but I will have him at your mansion in five minutes, if you will leave me here alone."

"Very well!" and the duke rose. "I rely on you. Make haste!" He turned to the door.

"Oh, your grace," said Susanna, "let me lead the way, or you may stumble on those wretched stairs!"

"Condescend to lean on the arm of

this charming little woman," laughed Piron; "she will have care of your gracious person. Take firm hold of the duke; you are not the first of your rank who has supported. an ancient house."

"Chevalier!" said Fronsac, coloring with indignation. "I must very—"

"You must lose no time, my dear duke, or you will exhaust the patience of the princesses. It is best to howl when we are among wolves."

Susanna offered her arm to the peer of France, which the latter took with an embarrassment that would have done honor to a schoolboy. Both left the room and slowly descended the staircase. Piron could scarcely suppress his laughter while he closed the door.

"I must be either bewitched or insane!" murmured Beaumarchais.

"Now, quick!" said Piron; "what are you going to do?"

"Alas, I do not know! Where am I to get a better coat?"

"That is bad!" Piron looked around. "How very poor you are! but I wish you to make a sensation. Your future and that of others may depend upon it.—I have it!" he took off his coat. "Let us exchange — the princesses no doubt will smile; however, that does not matter. It is better than to neglect the moment that may lead to fortune." He held his embroidered coat toward Caron.

"No, chevalier!" and Beaumarchais stepped back. "Poverty is less ridiculous than borrowed plumes. I will not wear a coat belonging to a gentleman from court, and whose name I do not even know."

Piron offered him his hand in a hearty manner. "Well, I am a colleague, Aimé de Piron, who begs you to have the goodness and put on this variegated article."

Susanna returned, and remained standing in the doorway when she saw the gentleman in his shirt-sleeves.

"Piron! The charming poet, the witty chevalier, with an artist's soul!" exclaimed Beaumarchais. "*Your* coat I can wear!" He was about to take off his own.

"No!" and Susanna hastened toward him, "the garment of a courtier? I shall not permit it! He must not appear in any thing unsuitable to him!" She laughingly added: "I have a resource!" Running into Batyl's room, she soon brought a brown coat with silver braiding. "It is Batyl's state dress; he must lend it to you. Ha, ha! Caron, he cannot go to Count de la Blache to-day."

"That is true!" exclaimed Beaumarchais, quickly changing his costume. "Take back your coat, my generous chevalier."

Susanna assisted Piron in dressing. "Well, little tyrant!" he said, smiling. "On a signal from you, the god Vishnu is transformed to his original appearance. But, upon my word, your husband would have looked very well in my clothes!"

"M. de Piron," said Beaumarchais, conquering his emotion, "whatever may be the consequences of this hour, it shall be as unforgotten as your amiable behavior. Permit me to offer you a small token of my gratitude." He took his manuscript from the bureau and gave it to the chevalier. "It is my first drama, *Eugénie*, composed in the midst of starvation and torment. No one will look at it—no one will publish it. Perhaps you may not find it too contemptible to keep it as a memorial of poor Beaumarchais in his garret."

"Why, that is charming!" cried Piron, pressing the author's hand. "I accept the present, but only on condition that I may take care of its public recognition. Another thing: act boldly in presence of the princesses, and toward all behave as you did to Fronsac."

Caron embraced Susanna, crying in a glad voice, "I have found my position!"

"Take it as if all around you were opponents," remarked Piron, "you will find enough of them; Fronsac is one already."

"He is haughty, proud—"

"Stupid—you may say; however, that is not his fault; Minister Silhouet is his cousin, so you see it is a family failing. You are handsome, ready, talented, and—a commoner; no Fronsac can pardon that. He who has no foes can never be a victor."

"You remind me of an enemy!" Beaumarchais seized the note he had written, took the casket, placed the letter in it, covered all with an envelope, and put it in his pocket.

"*You* have an enemy?" said Piron. "Are there any people in existence having no weapon of defence?"

"Oh yes, and my opponent has great power, and the will to use it dishonorably. However, I will be at his service. Permit me to pass the Hôtel St. Albin on the way—I must leave a parcel there."

"Is La Blache your foe?"

"He is!" breathed Susanna, softly.

"You had better be careful," replied Piron, gravely. "Count de la Blache is to be presented to the princesses to-morrow, by his father-in-law, the Duke de St. Albin, in order to receive the patent as commander of the body-guards of their royal highnesses."

"What!" cried Caron. "Is there any possibility that I may be present at this formality?"

"It may be; that is, if you please the princesses! All depends on to-day's audience."

"But, chevalier, what are the intentions of their royal highnesses toward me?"

"They alone have a right to tell you. At all events, this is not the place to converse on such a subject. I only caution you, that you must bring forward all your resources of wit, knowing that your fortune is at stake; therefore—"

"Enough, chevalier! Come, I feel within me the strength to wrestle with all France!" Again embracing Susanna, he said: "Do not forget our dinner!"

"And do not let it burn," exclaimed Piron, seizing her hand and pressing it to his lips. Both gentlemen left the room. Susanna, Malesherbes, Turgot, and Morelly looked after them, then at each other, and felt as if awaking from a strange dream, which they did not comprehend.

CHAPTER III.

THE KING'S DAUGHTERS.

No man, however great his self-control, can resist the emotions arising from a sudden and unexpected change in his circumstances. It is hard to endure a fall from happiness to misery, until tyrannous necessity at last gives us patience to suffer; but to rise without any preparation—as by a magician's wand—from humiliation to honor, or what the world calls "fortune," is much more difficult, and the first step in this joyous path is often also that which leads toward shame and ruin.

From the moment when Beaumarchais returned to the Pigeonnier after his fruitless efforts at Gauchat's and elsewhere, until he found himself seated in the coach beside Piron, he had not recovered himself. This change in his destiny—from wretchedness and utter despair to opulence and fame—was too unexpected not to impress him deeply. He was therefore silent the first part of the way, and the chevalier possessed sufficient delicacy and knowledge of the world to appreciate Caron's feelings and give him time to recollect himself. If Beaumarchais did not express himself overjoyed, but rather gave evidence of fear and anxiety, it was owing not so much to the presence of the courtly poet, as to a certain distrust in the ascendency of his lucky star. He knew well that all depended on his own behavior, and that presence of mind was especially necessary. The surprise and enthusiasm that glowed in his features at first soon gave way to doubt, and a consideration of what was really to come. He was still profoundly occupied with his thoughts when the carriage stopped before the Hôtel St. Albin, in the Rue de Francs-bourgeois, Quartier Grève.

"This is the residence of Count de la Blache's father-in-law; the count inhabits the right wing. Pray, do not stay longer than is absolutely necessary."

Beaumarchais rose quickly. "Not a moment longer, chevalier, than to deliver this parcel to the porter." He glided from the vehicle, and, hastening to the gate, handed the package to the Swiss guard.

"To Madame le Comtesse herself—and secretly?" asked the man, with a suspicious air.

"As you please, my good man. You may give it to the countess, or her father, either openly or privately; but on no account must it be handed to M. de la Blache while he is alone; for it has reference to a family affair. Do not forget that."

"May I ask who sends it?"

"From M. Caron Beaumarchais." He turned haughtily, walked toward the carriage and reëntered.

"You have executed your mission, and, as I see from your smile, successfully!" said Piron.

"Executed it? Yes, chevalier! But to-morrow will show whether it is well ended, or only well begun. Permit me to say a few words before explanation becomes impossible. You have seen my dwelling, and have an idea, therefore, of my poverty. I bore this change of my former circumstances bravely, for the sake of my wife. You can judge from her appearance whether she is not probably worthy of any sacrifice. If you could fathom my sorrow, to which is added the secret malice of a man of rank, you would comprehend that the prospect of the favor of the royal princesses inspires me with hope, it is true, but also with anxiety. I am a man of the *bourgeois* class, the first who makes his fortune at this court. I am certain that I am not to be raised to prominence merely by a whim—conditions will be made—I am poor, unprotected, and open-hearted; my degradation can afford you neither renown nor advantage of any kind—what is the object of my call to court?"

"I have long expected that question. Sir, I cannot answer it frankly until their royal highnesses have seen you; but, indirectly, I will draw your attention to a fact which your shrewdness will probably teach you how to make use of. If you cannot do that, premature revelations will help neither you nor us; they would only be dangerous to all parties. Any one having the *entrée* at court must assist in managing intrigues, invent or suffer from them; and, in case you please the princesses, you will not be spared—you understand—"

"That I must become an intriguer! Very well; plotting is a kind of passion with me, as dice and cards are with others. Now the question is, for what am I to plot? I never coquette with morality, and am only skilful when my heart enters into the scheme."

"Good! I leave you to come to a conclusion. Consider the place to which I am taking you, observe the persons, and all the rest follows as a natural consequence. The Marchioness de Pompadour is all-powerful—aided by Choiseul and Maupeau. She has the king entirely under her control, at Versailles. On the other hand, her majesty the queen lives in almost cloistered solitude at the Tuileries. The noble dauphin and his wife are hated by the marchioness, and are dependent on her humor; every action of theirs is watched, since the attempt of Damien. The dauphin is persecuted by slander, and his intercourse with his royal mother rendered very difficult. However, the prince is a man of heart and genius, and no Jesuit, as his enemies are trying to persuade the nation. He despises the chains that oppress both him and the people. Madame de Pompadour fears him. No one, besides, has any influence over the king except his daughters. Their residence, the Hôtel Bourbon, is therefore the gathering-place of ambitious spirits—there are the hopes of parties and the emotions of a whole people. The Orleans family are merely tolerated, because they are relatives, but we know from sad experience how injurious they have been to the house of Bourbon. Again, the Jesuits are endeavoring to prevent the ruin threatening them since the crime of Damien, and ardently desire to make a compromise with the government. At their head are the Abbé Terray, the Rohans, Aiquillow, the Ventadours, and St. Albin, and they wish to give the princesses a mentor in Count de la Blache, as Fronsac has been forced upon them by the marchioness, and their royal highnesses have no cause to refuse the appointment. Reflect well on all this! If you are the man we want, you understand me; and no foe, whoever he may be, can do you harm."

"Before you express yourself plainly you wish to fathom me. I comprehend

very well that a commoner, a man standing alone, is more suitable to perform certain offices than a man of birth and family; and—"

"We are entering the Bourbon gate —more words are useless. Be inoffensive to every one; observe all, but be frank with their royal highnesses."

"Mask, position!" these words resounded in Caron's ears.

The carriage stopped and the door opened. Looking around, Beaumarchais found himself in a vaulted corridor, and presently followed Piron up the flight of steps leading to the antechambers of the princesses. Two lackeys in light-blue velvet, with white cords and satin bows on their shoulders, opened the door to an apartment which both gentlemen passed through, entering an audience-hall decorated with gilt ornaments, looking upon the Quai des Theatines, the Seine, with the Pont Royal, and, beyond, the magnificent façade of the gallery of the Louvre.

"Announce me and my companion to their royal highnesses, my dear Lafleure," said Piron to a valet de chambre covered with silver trappings, who disappeared immediately by a door on the right. "Be quite unembarrassed, Beaumarchais; courage is the bride of fortune!"

"And I am about to form the union under your protection. In this instance, more is at stake for me than you imagine; and where gain and loss are so near, a bold throw is always the victor!" His countenance expressed decision as well as a winning politeness. Glancing rapidly at the large metal mirror, he seemed satisfied with himself. Piron smiled.

Some moments passed. The right door opened, and M. de Fronsac walked in, solemnly. "Their royal highnesses the princesses!" He remained standing in the doorway, and made a low bow, which the others imitated. There was a rustle of silk, and then appeared the Princess Adelaide, a tall, elegant woman of about thirty, a brunette, somewhat pale and thin. She wore a violet moire dress, and in her powdered hair deep-red roses; in her right hand she held a book bound in morocco. Nex came the second sister, Sophie, also a brunette of about twenty-seven, nearly as tall, but much stouter than her sister, and having a quite delicate complexion; her shoulders and arms were very beautiful, set off by a robe of silver-gray brocatel, ornamented by a pattern of gold flowers and green leaves; her hair was adorned with a diadem of white plumes and pearls. The youngest princess, Victorie, who was always quarrelling with Fronsac about etiquette, was twenty-two years old, fair and rosy; much shorter than and not so well developed as the Princess Sophie. She wore a dress of white-ribbed silk, looped with bunches of forget-me-nots, thus displaying her skirt of cherry-colored satin. A wreath of the same kind of flowers covered her head, that never seemed intended to be seriously occupied.

As soon as their royal highnesses entered, Fronsac and two ladies of the court, who followed, hastened to place chairs for them. Adelaide inclined her head and sat down slowly. Sophie took a seat noisily by her side, measuring Beaumarchais with piercing eyes; and Victorie, leaning on her eldest sister's chair, nodded to Piron.

"Is this the author of the *École pour la Harpe*, chevalier? Beaumarchais, I believe?" asked Princess Adelaide, opening the conversation.

"At your service, your royal highness; and I hope he will justify the opinion you have formed of him from his work."

Adelaide smiled, making a motion with her hand, and Piron stepped back. "It is true, M. Beaumarchais, your book has greatly pleased my sisters and myself. Any one who can write so elegantly and gracefully about a mere musical instrument, must be a master of it, and be able to express himself equally well on other subjects."

"Your royal highness, if I have written well on the harp, does it follow that I play it well? Is it necessary to be able to do every thing on which we pass judgment? Ah, if you are pleased to be so strict, who in all France can pass the ordeal? Our priests talk of virtue, our judges of justice, our ministers of human happiness, our poets and philosophers of liberty, and I—of the harp! If we all really understood that of which we so easily write, there would be quite a new order of things."

The ladies smiled in some surprise. "Ah, sir," said Adelaide, with a more winning expression, "you prove conclusively that you must be the author of this work, and it is much more pleasant to hear such ideas spoken than merely to read them. In the one case, they are like a bouquet of living flowers; in the other, an artificial one—both brilliancy and perfume are wanting."

"Nothing but the sun can render a flower fragrant. It is only because my words are uttered in your presence, that I think they breathe real life. If I were a cavalier of rank, that would be flattery, but the heart of a sorrowful man is warmed by a simple glance from the elevated and pure; he would feel that I am right in saying that the privilege of sovereignty is that of making others happy!"

"Truly, sir," said Princess Sophie, breathing quickly, "you speak well! I seldom meet with men so sincere, and never so gallant. I think under your instruction we shall soon become mistresses of the harp."

"Mistresses of the harp? Your

highness, through my instruction?" Caron turned pale.

"Of course, M. Beaumarchais," replied Madame Adelaide. "Surely you do not intend to make us doubt your skill through false shame? You must be our teacher. If we had had time to procure an instrument, you should give us a specimen of your ability now. I am willing to believe that a man of talent can write intelligently on any thing—can even defend the bad with as much apparent reason as the good, but only the virtuous can describe the beautiful and true in their own greatness; and I maintain that no one can write about the character—I had almost said soul—of an instrument as you do in your work, if you had not yourself the power to draw from it all the charming sounds of which it is capable. So the matter is settled.—M. de Fronsac, M. Beaumarchais is appointed professor and music-teacher of the royal princesses for an indefinite period. Have the goodness to write the contract and lay it before us to sign, as we wish to begin our lessons to-morrow. The next time we go to Versailles we shall have the confirmation of it from his majesty."

"Your royal highnesse.!" and Fronsac bowed. "Your word is law, and I hasten to fulfil your wishes. I take the liberty, however, to remind you of that which I considered it my duty to inform you. This step is so extraordinary, mesdames, that—"

"What, sir?—that what? I thought that our having once refuted your scruples would be enough! I beg—"

Beaumarchais stepped forward, and bent his knee before the Princess Adelaide.

"Are you also going to make objections?"

"I never object to what a lady says, least of all to any thing from such noble and kind patronesses; but I ask permission to hear what the duke has to oppose against my person in reference to your royal highnesses' commands. It is not only necessary for me in my future position here to know what prejudices I shall have to encounter, but how I have fallen in the estimation of M. de Fronsac, who had taken the trouble to ascend so high to find me—to the fourth story in the Pigeonnier, No. 30 Rue Bertau."

The princesses smiled. "Well, mention your scruples, duke; a chevalier should always be frank.".

"Although I do not know why I should explain myself in presence of this M.—Beaumarchais, I do so in obedience to the command of your royal highnesses; and I repeat, that I beg you to consider what an affront it will be to see a commoner at court. Such a thing has never happened before, and is contrary to all the rules of etiquette, in which rests the charm of royal prerogatives. This Monsieur Beaumarchais dwells in one of the worst districts of the city—in a house in which the lowest people in Paris seek shelter. It is doubtful whether such a person can act as professor to the princesses in the Palais Bourbon. Besides, he is a literary man, of whose talent nothing is known, obscure, without any professional character at all; while there are such masters as Rameau, Duni, and Lulli, at your command. M. Beaumarchais may possibly write and talk well; but your highnesses may have already perceived, from his short conversation here, that he is a man of the same loose principles as those published by Diderot, Holbach, Marmontel, and Rousseau. Such characters are very dangerous. It was my duty to obey, and, with the aid of Chevalier de Piron, seek and gain information about the man, and present him to your royal highnesses. If, however, you really mean to tolerate him about your illustrious persons, I am sure you will permit me to relieve myself of all responsibility, and personally acquaint his majesty with the affair."

"You see how frank the duke is, M. Beaumarchais!" said Sophie, smiling.

"Oh dear!" cried the youngest, "if our dear Fronsac gives us an account of all that took place, and did not take place, from the time of Louis XIV.— a chronology of the bows and a list of the liveries—in order to prove that he is correct about a matter of etiquette, we might as well resign ourselves to that inexorable victor—*ennui*."

"At all events it is but just, that, since we have heard what can be said *against* M. Beaumarchais, he may have an opportunity to speak *for* himself. What do you think of the duke's arguments?" and Adelaide looked uneasily at Caron.

"They are worthy of his magnanimous mind! As to my being a commoner, I acknowledge that it is so, but it is the fault of my parents. It is a mistake, however, to say that no one of my class ever before appeared at court. Louis XIV., the haughtiest of monarchs, with whom originated the ceremonies practised at every court in Europe, sat at table with Molière, an actor, without troubling himself about etiquette. If you are so very strict, why are royal courts so often controlled by women of low birth? Why do noblemen destroy the honor of the commoners? Is it not better for your royal highnesses to accept talent, wherever you find it respected and cultivated, as a heavenly gift? The Rue Bertat is certainly in a disreputable part of the city, and the house called 'Pigeonnier' is not inhabited altogether by persons like myself—poor and unsuccessful, or rather, as the noble Duke de Fronsac says, the lowest of the people of Paris — but more, the vilest reprobates visit there —that is, they call on Mlle. Raucourt,

the well-known opera-singer. In a short time I will hand a list of these persons to your royal highnesses. But, I am a literary man, and that probably makes the duke dislike me! Are authors and thinkers, then, dangerous, because they have to do with intellect? Oh, my most gracious duke, only very small minds fear us, and you will permit me to suppose that the word *fear* is unknown to a Fronsac!" He bowed almost to the ground with comic gravity.

The duke turned pale, stammered, and left the audience-hall, on a sign from Adelaide, who wished to save him from further confusion. A glance sent Piron also into the antechamber.

"You have given us proofs," said the princess, "that you are a man of mind as well as of heart. Are you also honest and faithful? I do not mean the honesty to which all lay claim, and that fidelity of which just sufficient is guarded to save one's reputation. I mean, are you a man such as would sacrifice his existence for his patrons? Tell us, M. Beaumarchais, are you capable of such disinterestedness?"

"If I am not, your royal highness, it is useless to ask me, for the inducements to utter a falsehood are very great. In this instance, doubly so, for behind me is misery; before me, happiness. You wish to know whether this dexterity in defending myself, does or does not arise from a species of immorality. You desire to patronize a man of the world, but not a Machiavelli. I will drop my mask for one moment; look behind it, your highness; smile and pardon me. You say I have talent. Alas, for what purpose? Whether I really possess any, I do not know; I am but twenty-six years old. Permit me to tell you the story of my life—the best intimation of what a man may be, is what he has been.

"I am the only son of a wealthy

watchmaker, who is still living at his store in the Rue Dechargeur in St. Jacques de la Boucherie. I have five sisters. My father is a prudent but austere man, and ruled me with a rod of iron. I learned his trade, I became an artist in my line, read much, made verses; in short, educated myself as only a young and ambitious man can. Music was as natural to me as speech. I made a discovery in our branch of business, that of watch escapement. My father intended to get a patent for it, but the idea was stolen from me by a colleague with whom I was too frank. That was the first lesson my ingenuousness and imprudence taught me. I will not trouble you with an account of the old gentleman's anger; the lawsuits did him no good.

"My father had always more mind than heart. He forced me to marry a woman, Mlle. Leonora Ségurier, who was of respectable parentage, had a large fortune, and was dying of consumption. She loved me as much as I detested her, and I was obliged to marry her without complaint, as if I had been a—prince. Luckily, heaven had mercy on me, and she was soon in her grave. Of course, as we had no children, her property reverted to her family, and I was forced once more to take a wife, who was still more abominable to me—Leonora's sister Frances. My father would not give up the prospect of Segurier's fortune. She also died; so that at twenty-three, I was the happy widower of two wives! I breathed freely. The money paid to our firm reconciled my father.

"One day I was walking to a pretty country-seat in the neighborhood of Paris, where I saw a lovely, but very poor girl, who was so unfortunate as to have been abandoned by her parents from her birth. When, notwithstanding hard work, her beauty became remarkable, the poor child was perse-cuted by the propositions of a nobleman of the court. My love saved her, and I presented Susanna to my father, as the woman of my choice. The result was, that he cursed us both, and dismissed us from his house. He was too virtuous to suffer an illegitimate daughter in his family. From that day—three years ago—Susanna and I have lived miserably in the Pigeonnier.

"Laboring to gain our daily bread, disinherited by my father, sometimes not knowing whence we were to get food for the morrow, again persecuted by the same man of rank, who wishes to avenge himself, because a poor maiden had more honor and sense of shame than he, the hand of God raises me out of the dust, and I stand in the Hôtel Bourbon, in presence of your royal highnesses! Such is the brief outline of my life. It required all the love Susanna and I have for each other to bear it. And you ask am I honest? Can a man confide in the world, be frank with it, when even at such an early age it has used him so shamefully? I confess, I cannot; and therefore wear a mask to protect my heart and happiness. I am faithful only to myself and the poor woman who has innocently caused me so much suffering.

"I might assure you that gratitude would attach me to the service of your illustrious persons. I could take many oaths as to my fidelity, honesty, and disinterestedness; but must these not first be proved? I do not wish to experience the disgrace that your royal highnesses were deceived in me. They trust us too much who, thinking that our advantage is associated with theirs, rely on gratitude only, a mistake which makes many hypocrites. Your highnesses cannot have strong confidence, as you ought not to have, in him who appears before you for the first time. I have however one petition," and he threw himself at Adelaide's feet, took her hand in his left, and Sophie's in his right, pressing both to his lips.

"What petition?" said the sisters, greatly moved.

"That your royal highnesses will never judge me unheard, that I may have the right to repel such attacks as may soon be made against me, because I am a commoner, dangerous to certain persons, a poor man of talent, and your obedient servant."

"You have our word for that," cried Adelaide.

"No one shall drive you from us but you yourself, M. Beaumarchais," said Sophie.

"And any one that would rob us of him, my dear sisters, must first defend himself against me to the utmost," laughed little Victorie.

"Then I have only to ask, your royal highnesses,"· and Caron rose smiling, "whether the lesson may not begin to-morrow about the hour of audience? It is important, as I should like to give you a proof of my services at that opportunity. The first lesson will of course be only preparatory."

"At the audience?" said Adelaide, "that is somewhat unusual."

"My presence may perhaps be necessary. Permit me now to be silent on the subject. It is sufficient for me to be prepared for evil reports."

"I do not see why M. Beaumarchais should not be there," said Sophie, "for it is no levee. Besides, it is well if he show himself to the people, that his engagement may not be regarded in a bad light, as it is sure that remarks will be made."

"And what harm is there, dearest," said Victoria, "if we take a lesson until it is interrupted by the audience, and continue it afterward? Is Fronsac the judge and controller of our will?"

"You are right, my sisters," replied Adelaide. "You will be present, sir. —Ah, the duke!" She rang the bell.

Lafleure introduced Piron by one door, as the duke entered by another.

"Have you written the contract?"

"At your service, your royal highness. Here it is." One servant held the silver inkstand, while another placed a small table in front of the princess. She signed her name, handing the pen to her sisters, who did the same.

"The personal report you intend to make to his majesty will be unnecessary, duke, as we intend to go to Versailles to-morrow after dinner. If you should still think it desirable you may accompany us.—Here is your appointment, M. Beaumarchais; your salary is four thousand five hundred francs, and as you are probably not ready to appear becomingly, you will receive three thousand francs for wardrobe expenses. The duke will present you to our intendant and give him the check. You will come to-morrow morning at ten o'clock for our first lesson." The princesses rose.

"Chevalier de Piron!" The chevalier approached Adelaide. "I am very well satisfied with the service you have rendered us. We shall all endeavor to find means of expressing our gratitude." She smilingly gave him her hand to kiss, and, after he had paid the same homage to the other ladies, they retired, followed by their two attendants and Lafleure.

"I will take you to the intendant, sir," said Fronsac, somewhat rudely.

"Will you permit me to accompany M. Beaumarchais?" asked Piron. "You know I must conduct him back to his residence."

Fronsac had an impertinent answer on his lips, but he repressed it and nodded coldly. They went to the intendant's office. Beaumarchais was presented, exhibited his appointment, received three thousand three hundred and seventy-five francs, put his money and the contract into his pocket, and, slightly bowing to Fronsac, left the Hôtel Bourbon with Piron.

When both were in the carriage the chevalier could not restrain his delight, pressing Caron's hand. "My friend (for so you must permit me to call you), I have never before witnessed such eloquence, grace, and intellect! You cannot fail! It would be an injustice if such endowments were suffered to decay in poverty. The first thing you must do is to leave that wretched Pigeonnier, and live suitably to your present position. I will make you a proposition. Take possession of the left wing of my house in the Rue des Ormes; the windows look out upon the garden. It is a refuge for love and poetry when one is tired of court intrigues. We can then sit and talk in the open air, rejoicing that we are free, and—well, you are silent, what is the matter?"

"Chevalier, I feel like a man just recovered from intoxication! The bold step has been made; the burden is on my shoulders, and I must bear it. But let us abandon these thoughts. Your offer is very enticing, and I shall soon take the liberty of reminding you of it. My present dwelling is too valuable for many reasons, so that I ought not to leave it immediately. I must retain some connection with this place of my misery as long as I live, not only from gratitude, but for useful purposes that you will hereafter appreciate."

"Very well, make your own arrangements. For a few days it will not much matter; but you will soon find yourself such an object of curiosity, that an exclusive apartment will be the only protection against intrusion."

"That is true, chevalier," said Beaumarchais, thoughtfully. "Be kind enough to have the garden rooms of your residence put in order. I see the Rue Maubue, and I will not let you take me any nearer home. I will wait on you to-morrow with my wife, after the first lesson."

"*Au revoir!* Keep up your courage to-morrow; you will stand face to face with your enemy, Count de la Blache. I am very anxious to know how you will manage him. Be prudent."

"Certainly, chevalier. I recommend myself to your continued favor." He pressed Piron's hand, drew the cord, and descended, bowed once more, and then walked quickly away. Piron leaned back smiling. "An excellent man, amiable and intellectual; we could not have desired a better. He will enter difficult conflicts, but he is the right man for them. He will obtain everything, not I; he is young. I am beginning to like a little ease, and am not made to find my way out of labyrinthine paths. The commoner will make a sensation; but, because he appears powerless, all will be regarded as a musical whim of the princesses—the effort of young ladies to amuse themselves. There is Pont de Bois, I am curious to know what monseigneur will say." He had the carriage stopped on the other side of the bridge, and walked down the Quai Orléans to the Hôtel St. Louis, the palace of the dauphin, where he disappeared at a side-door.

CHAPTER IV.

THE LETTRE DE CACHET.

It was very natural that those who remained in the garret should feel great astonishment at the sudden call of Beaumarchais to the princesses, and the appearance of the two courtiers in the Pigeonnier. Madame Susanna's newly-risen hopes were too bright, and her conviction of her husband's abilities too firm, that she should long remain in mute surprise at the unexpected change that had taken place in their circumstances. Her misery had been too deep to restrain her from expressing her happiness. So the flower beaten down by the storm, raises its head to the first ray of the sun, unfolding its leaves and blossoms. With cheerful activity, the little woman ran hither and thither, laid the table, placed glasses and chairs, that, as she said, laughingly, "the gentlemen's appetite might be awakened by her preparations, and do honor to her cookery." Then she put on her cloak, and hurried away to purchase what was necessary for the repast so long desired.

Morelly, Turgot, and Malesherbes, the witnesses of this strange event in Beaumarchais' life, were competent to appreciate Caron's transition from extreme poverty to probable honor and position, and they were vastly surprised.

"Truly," said Turgot, "it is most extraordinary! It resembles a miracle, and if Marmontel had been here he would immediately have founded a story on it!"

"I should really like to see the moral he would draw from it," replied Malesherbes, shaking his head.* "There are things in the world, like the caprice of fortune, coming uncalled and leaving unasked, loading one with benefits and neglecting another, just and unjust at the same time, and apparently acting without reference to wisdom or morality. All of us will be glad at Caron's luck (for we know that he is highly gifted), if it be permanent and real; but this audience with the princesses seems to be a result without obvious cause, and I am more alarmed than pleased. What do people know of Beaumarchais? If he is talented, no one is aware of it. His genius only fits him for the sterner duties of life, not for the

court. His first step to public favor is his work on the harp! Suppose it good (I understand nothing of music, but I know it must be written well), is it comprehensible that this book should be of sufficient importance to attract the author to such high society—the court of France—where unite arrogant frivolity and haughty grandeur, assisted by intrigue, and infected by envy and self-conceit? I may be wrong, but this production of Caron is a mere pretext, and he is destined to some danger."

"The same idea has passed involuntarily through my mind," said Turgot, "and first ideas are generally correct. I know Piron; he is a courtier, who has taken the trouble to learn something, and has taste enough to write verses that please his illustrious patronesses. He honors authors, is something of a philosopher, and really a noble person, but too good-natured, jovial, and rich, to burden himself with serious matters, much less with troublesome court intrigues. He likes to push others forward when action is needed, and always protects himself by prudent reservations."

"I will swear to it that he intends to make use of Beaumarchais in some such way, and that the question is not merely the harp and a drawing-room entertainment. We must warn Caron," said Malesherbes, anxiously.

"If there is still time, my good friends," exclaimed Morelly. "I know that Turgot, the follower of Quesney, will smile, but I believe that neither chance, the blind caprice of fortune, nor mechanical force, is the ruling power of human life; but rather the omnipresent God, who created the soul, and gave it that all-involving faculty of freedom of choice, for its own weal or woe, and permits every one, however hard and long he may have to struggle, to reach that measure and kind of happiness, best suited for him, provided he does

---

* Marmontel, "Contes Moreaux."

right and adheres to his choice. Let the princesses and Piron have their secret objects, I know Beaumarchais, and am certain he will raise himself in his own way, and be useful, as you are in yours. The spirit of the *Basiliade* is on his brow, and distinguishes his thought, just as yours with the doctrine of human sovereignty—yes, you may smile, Turgot! Each one of us, however he may fancy he is living for himself, must fulfil his destiny, and we ought to serve mankind, and prepare for more enlightened times and nobler minds, the problem which Christianity has furnished, and which the Middle Ages could not solve."

"Well for him and all of us, my good Diogenes," answered Malesherbes, mildly, "if it is as you say; I would gladly believe it. You are happy in spite of your proud poverty, and on approaching you one feels refreshed and strengthened."

"That is true, Lamoignon!" smiled Turgot. "Even if we do not altogether believe our old friend—if our stern analysis contradicts his dreams—our feelings always urge us to agree with him."

"Your heart," said Morelly, "is the best thing about you, although Turgot says that it is only a machine to supply the body with life."

"Now, that is mockery!" said Turgot, "Before you acknowledge Quesney's tenets, the world would go to pieces. The prophets of two different systems cannot be just to each other. As to the rest, Malesherbes; suppose we contribute to the garret banquet by some confectionery for Susie. Come!"

"Indeed, that will pleasantly surprise the little lady, and reconcile her to our refusal. Though it was not in our power, like the deities, to change her condition, we may play the part of the friendly spirits that embellish life, and crown the cup of joy. Let us go, then, before madame returns." Male-sherbes put on his hat and drew Turgot with him.

Morelly looked thoughtfully after them. "In the mind of this young generation slumbers the question of universal liberty, though false prophets bring to market their ruinous opinions. Let them go their way." He nodded, smiled, and went to his division of the garret, among his books and writing materials. In a few moments he was absorbed in his studies.

It was extraordinary, that men of Turgot's and Lamoignon's rank and position, although they acknowledged Caron's genius, and wished both him and Susanna well, could do so little for them, as to protect them from the temptations from which they had but just escaped. Stranger still and appearing almost suspicious, was the fact that the gentlemen at first refused to accept the invitation to dinner, to which they now seemed to invite themselves; and that though they formerly thought but little of Beaumarchais' importance, he was suddenly of great consequence in their eyes.

We must first take into consideration the prejudices of the age—prejudices that such men, notwithstanding their enlightenment, could not banish, and by which many excellent characters are governed even in days of higher knowledge. Turgot and Malesherbes descended from ancient and wealthy families, belonging to the official world, the aristocracy, and the higher magistracy, who, like the parliamentary members, formed a strictly separate caste, and who believed the domain of public justice to be their exclusive right— families whose favorite doctrine was Jansenist predestination, to which their position in most respects gave actual expression. From father to son they belonged to the learned world of the Sorbonne, with its boastful traditions. It is almost unnecessary to say that such men did not particularly esteem Beaumarchais, the son of a watchmaker, who had run away from both his father and his trade, and was floundering in all kinds of literary labor; nor did they greatly respect talents that they permitted only to men of quality and leisure. They never thought therefore of introducing him into the spheres of life in which they themselves moved, and tacitly refused him any prospect of public service.

Morelly was as poor as Caron; but Morelly was a philosopher whose destiny seemed an injustice of nature ,and science; and yet to whom the drawing-rooms would have opened of their own accord, if the old man had not rejected every such facility of elevating himself, from a strange peculiarity of temper, arising from a disagreement with the spirit of the Jansenists, the school of Quesncy and Locke, and the Encyclopædists. Like Rousseau, he was independent in thought, and singular in his habits of life. Turgot and Malesherbes for various reasons hesitated to offer Caron either recommendations or money. He was proud, too much opposed to their views and learned exclusiveness; he often vexed them by his sarcasms, and would receive no alms from those who he felt were separated from him by his father's trade and his own aimless existence.

Paternal control, and the dependence of families on their head, were at that time so common, that Secretary Turgot and President Malesherbes were still as much under authority as if they were children. Both were obliged to act according to family dictation in reference to their dignity, their companions, the persons they should assist, as well as those they should not, all their enjoyments, and general conduct. Morelly could therefore banter them about their associating with him, and Caron belonged decidedly to those

they could not patronize, and whose acquaintance was calculated to expose them to reproach. A son who had violently withdrawn himself from the authority of his father, as Beaumarchais had done, was a monster; and one who could do so in order to marry a woman ignorant of her own parentage, was something not recognized in the respectable society of those days. The more dissipated the court—the more scandalous the life of the king—the more the middle classes insisted on an austere morality; and this was transmitted from father to son, how much soever a more charitable and generous intellect might endeavor to define the boundaries of real immorality. The influence of the old customs, and to some extent of false ethics, made slaves of them.

We can in some degree understand the astonishment of Turgot and Lamoignon when Beaumarchais was sent for, to have an audience with the princesses. If a frivolous nobleman, such as Choiseul, the minister of the war department, or even the Marchioness de Pompadour, had received him, it would not have been half so significant. All knew that such persons were not very particular in a choice responding to a purpose of their own, because they themselves had made their way in a somewhat questionable manner — but the *princesses!*

The daughters of Louis XV. exercised an influence greatly respected or feared. Without any concern whatever the monarch had neglected his consort Maria Leszinska, and condemned her to solitude; subjected the disobedient dauphin with his family to the same fate, and the espionage of the marchioness, because at the first and only royal levee she attended, the prince, while embracing her according to instructions, made a grimace, thus rendering her an object of the ridicule of the court, and indicating that he regarded her with indignation. But the king had not sunk quite so far as to be insensible of shame in the presence of his daughters. He ordered Madame de Pompadour to behave respectfully, and absent herself whenever the princesses appeared at Versailles. He allowed them secretly to have great influence on him, and endeavored to compensate them for the disgrace he had brought on his family, at least so far as the marchioness and her clique permitted him to have a will of his own.

The princesses thus maintained a universally-honored position—a kind of mediating power between the different members of the royal family, so inimical toward each other. All eyes were fixed on them; their drawing-rooms were the most brilliant, and the rendezvous of courtiers coming from Versailles to Paris. These ladies sent for Beaumarchais! There was no question but something more important than the *École pour la Harpe* was at stake; a chain of peculiar and mysterious events was somehow connected with it. Caron involuntarily became an object of respect to both Turgot and Malesherbes. They felt that he must possess qualities with which they were unacquainted; and, moreover, induced by the pleasure of seeing the young couple saved from their wretched poverty, the two men wished to share in the garret dinner, awaiting with impatience the result of an interview they would have considered as a special fortune for themselves.

Morelly had not been long engaged with his studies when Batyl returned in a very good humor. "Well, philosopher, again at your dreams for the happiness of mankind? When will your ideal republic, à la Rome and Athens, be ready?"

"As soon as the last dishonorable man in France is buried."

"H'm—then you will have to wait a long while."

"It cannot exist during your lifetime."

Batyl stared. "Indeed!" turning and putting down his hat. "Is madame not at home?"

"She is out making purchases."

"Purchases?" The musician glanced at the table laid for dinner, smiled, and walked to his room.

Soon Susie returned, with a heavy basket on her arm, and looking as if she already enjoyed the happiness in store for her. "How tired I am!" She threw off her cloak. "In my whole life, Papa Morelly, I never carried such a load! Come and help me unpack."

Morelly rose, but pointed to the musician's door—"Batyl has returned."

"Returned? Then he intends to go to La Blache. Be quick and write a receipt for his money; I have the change."

While Morelly was writing, Caron's wife unpacked her basket. "Well, we shall have some quarrelling, but my husband cannot remain away forever."

"Ah, Madame Susanna!" said Batyl, entering, "back from market? I am going to him immediately!" The last words he whispered, and went to the clothes-press near the door.

"You need not be in a hurry, M. Batyl."

The musician stepped back in surprise. "My coat? Where is my coat? It is not in my room, nor here, either."

"The coat? What coat?" Susanna raised her face and looked at him with a very natural expression of ignorance.

"I say, my coat!" cried Batyl, violently. "My state‑dress, the one I wear when I visit people of rank. I cannot go without it."

"Your—ah, your state dress? Yes, I believe—it is gone!" Morelly was obliged to suppress his laughter.

"Gone!" cried Batyl, standing motionless.

"Yes, I think so! On some one's person,—probably it went by that door." Morelly rose with the receipt in his hand.

Batyl acted like a madman. "You —you wish to prevent me from going to Fal—to—! But I will go, I must go. Where is my coat?" He ran searching in every corner of the garret, while Morelly and Susie laughed heartily. This changed the musician's anger into fear. He turned to Susie. "I desire to have the letter, casket, and money, that I gave you."

Susanna was greatly astonished. "Casket? letter? money?—Did you see that I had money, Morelly, or those things that Batyl is talking about? Did you see any one give me any thing? I believe, my good man, you are dreaming. However, as we are speaking of money, here are your hundred francs; sign this paper in the presence of Morelly."

During this scene Turgot and Malesherbes reappeared, carrying various parcels, and remained waiting in expectation at the entrance.

"A hundred francs?" Batyl slapped his forehead convulsively.

"With interest for six months," said Morelly dryly, taking the money from Susanna. "Be kind enough to sign the receipt!" and he began to count out the money on the table.

"Oh what a fool I have been," gasped Batyl, "to be outwitted by an artful woman! I am deceived, robbed!"

"Sign!" and Morelly held the pen toward him.

"Well, if he will not sign," interrupted Turgot, "you need only take both money and receipt to the mayor, and force him to depose under oath why he will not receive payment. That will be a suit of refusal to do justice, with an intent to injure others!"

"And we shall hang him with pleasure, according to law!" laughed Maleherbes.

"The mischief! you are a woman! They have conspired to ruin me!"

"I never heard that a man was ruined because he received his own money!" said Susanna.

"There!" Batyl wrote his name, trembling, and put the hundred francs into his pocket. Drawing Susanna toward the curtain he whispered. "Return the letter, casket, and money, Susie. Surely you do not wish to bring me into trouble!"

"You have your own, and I cannot recollect any thing else—Ah, there is my husband!"

Batyl started, and stood without reply; for Beaumarchais entered, with a countenance pale and disturbed.

"He is wearing my coat!—I thought so!" said Batyl to himself.

"But Caron, my husband, is it thus you return from court?" and Susanna hastened toward him.

"Were you not successful at the audience?" asked Morelly.

"'Not successful?'" replied Caron. "Oh if it only were so, I would feel less miserable! As it is, I am ruined! Is it not a mockery—to succumb to my incompetency just as I am about to ascend the path of honor? In future, when Parisians speak of a braggadocio, a fanfaron, they will say: 'He is a real Beaumarchais!' Do you feel what it is? Worse than hunger—it is public contempt—to be a pariah of such ridicule!"

"Husband, what do you mean?"

"But if your audience terminated well," said Turgot, smiling ironically.

"Did your illustrious patronesses manifest a kindly disposition toward you?" Lamoignon interrupted.

"On that very account I am disturbed!" sighed Caron, blushing. "I have pleased them. The princesses are angels of condescension; I received an appointment immediately. Piron is delighted, Frousac confounded. My fortune is made, and yet—I am to give them lessons on the harp!—Morelly, Susanna, can I play that instrument? They might as well command me to overthrow the Chinese wall with my teeth, or dance a Spanish *pas* on a cobweb! And to-morrow I must go to my execution! To-morrow Fortune will close her domain against me, and to my shame and dishonor!"

This afflicting confession of Beaumarchais was listened to by Susanna with perplexity. But the scene was so comical, that Turgot, Lamoignon, and even Morelly, could not refrain from smiling. Morelly was about to obtain further information by a few questions, when Batyl, who heard what was going on, and understanding the painful position of Caron, burst into exclamations of malicious joy, and approached the musician: "So you intended by one bound to enter court, while such as I must consider it an honor to be knocked about by lackeys in the antechambers. Oh, yes, you literary men think you understand every thing. You write about a harp, but cannot play it. Well, scribble away! but when the question is to do any thing, you are out of your element. Oh, the royal princesses, who are too proud to admit true artists, will be highly edified with their lesson to-morrow!"

"So they shall be!" cried Caron, with a cheerful face. "You have just come at the right time, for you are a harpist. Susie! Batyl is our deliverer! I shall take a lesson from him every day, and give what I learn to the princesses. As I play the guitar well, the other accomplishment is soon learned." All burst into laughter.

"I give you lessons, that you may shine with what does not belong to you!" exclaimed Batyl. "I shall do no such thing." The merriment ceased, for Batyl's object was well understood.

"You will not?" asked Beaumarchais, dryly.

"Never! I shall have the pleasure of seeing you disgrace yourself."

"Has he given his receipt, Susanna?"

"Here it is. Signed in my presence," said Morelly, handing Caron the paper.

"Now, Susie, bring Batyl's harp from his room. While you attend to the dinner, I can study the elementary parts with him."

"Sir, what liberties are you taking?"

Caron seized the musician by the collar. "Now, you wretch, either you must give me a daily lesson for a fair remuneration, or I shall denounce you to the princesses as a corrupter of morals, and you will be driven from the opera—If I do this, both you and your Count de la Blache will be dishonored before all Paris! Now it is my turn to laugh. Will you do as I say?"

Batyl stood as if petrified; he was entirely in the power of Beaumarchais, and his fear made him cowardly. "Yes Caron, I—I will do it, on condition that you return the letter, casket, and money."

"And then I shall have no lessons? You will run to La Blache, return his package, and all the rascally conduct remains concealed! No, no, my good fellow! I shall certainly return you the three thousand francs, and take a receipt for them. If you are honest enough, you will give them to the charming La Blache; but the note is too valuable a treasure—on it depend your fate and his. As soon as you miss a lesson, or he dares to move in any manner against me, you had both better be on your guard. The casket and a love-letter from myself, I have already sent to the countess, who is said to be almost as pretty as my wife. If you go to the Hôtel St. Albin you know what kind of welcome to expect. I advise you, in presence of these excellent friends, to be wise, leave this Count Falcoz to his evil conscience, and the contempt of his family, and comply with my requests. When I have learned all I wish from you, I will not prove ungrateful, you shall have your desire—a situation in the royal chapel, and you may tell every one that I am your pupil. Consider well what you do."

"You will do me no harm on account of this miserable affair ? "

"No, on my word ! I promise it before these witnesses."

Batyl breathed heavily. "Well, I am at your service ! "

"Ah, that is right, Batyl ! — Come, friends, let us eat; and then I must attend to my lesson. What have you for dinner, Susie ? "

"Only cold dishes; it was too late to cook any thing," she replied, placing the food and wine upon the table.

"Well, then, give me your arm, *Madame la Directrice des Concerts*—to their royal highnesses ! Take your places, my friends, and pardon me for not receiving you at •this time more suitably. I beg, however, to have the honor of your company in my new dwelling, which is already taken, and where I hope to do better at another time. Permit brave M. Batyl also to share our repast; anger must have given him an appetite, and a little wine will wash down his envy."

The company were very merry, and helped themselves freely. Morelly's features expressed pleasure at the good fortune of Beaumarchais. Turgot, and especially Malesherbes, were animated by the same feeling, while they seemed to struggle with their astonishment at the dexterity and boldness of a young man whose birth they knew was far inferior to their own, but who was nevertheless the favorite of the blind goddess. Batyl alone was reserved, coolly polite, and silent. He could not quite disguise his heart. He was attentive to discover all about the circumstances that raised Beaumarchais from poverty to such a height as to be the musician's master and punisher. He knew that no opponent was so invulnerable as never to discover some weak point; and that, if he had lost La Blache's favor, the count would need him for some future scheme of revenge.

"Now, tell me, dear Beaumarchais," asked Turgot, in the course of conversation, "how did you manage to please the illustrious ladies ? Relate all that took place at the audience. I confess, that I am moved not only by sympathy and natural curiosity, but by anxiety, to know how you will manage to escape the envy and countless intrigues that must be expected in such a position ? Good fortune often dazzles the wisest, especially when the change is so remarkable and unexpected."

"My dear Turgot," smiled Caron, sipping his wine, "this question involves much that affects you all as well as myself, and which I gladly answer; but there is something that does not concern you, and which for the present requires silence. It is the failing of fools to tell all they know; to reveal what is necessary, and no more, injures no one. As to ourselves (the friends of the garret), you know, Turgot, how often we have had opposite opinions—how often you have given me to understand that I am an ignoramus, and, in return, I have laughed at your learning; we did not quite love one another, for I was pleased when I had you at a disadvantage—but, at any rate, we did not hate each other."

"But I do not see," said Lamoignon,

"what that has to do with what occurred in the Hôtel Bourbon?"

"Very good, Malesherbes! In this way I shall be able to answer in a manner that must satisfy all, explain what relates to this business, and give a few hints without betraying myself. Lamoignon and myself come nearer to each other, because he is not one of the extreme philosophers whom I despise. He has more liberality and good-nature in the management of a subject. As to my dear old friend Morelly, he is my brother, father—aye, the sun that warmed me during my affliction. I will always love you three, for I have learned and expect to learn much from you. Turgot is my intellect, Malesherbes my heart, and Morelly my reason, the sublimest faculty, the guide of my life. You are necessary to me, or I —fall; do you understand?"

Turgot and Malesherbes looked at each other in surprise. "Oh, let him alone," said Morelly, smiling, "he is giving us very plain intimations, and will probably inform us how much we need him." Malesherbes looked surprised, and Turgot could not refrain from a pitying gesture.

"That is my intention, though you smile contemptuously. I am necessary to you, however extraordinary it seems, gentlemen, that the former watchmaker, the unlearned author, the vagabond wit, the fellow that scribbles about an instrument without knowing how to play it, should maintain that he might be useful to you, men in the service of the state. Until this morning I knew how insignificant and useless I was, and how my name was recognised with a shrug—at best, with a sympathy that preferred to retire from any practical good."

"You are becoming bitter, dear Caron," said Malesherbes, embarrassed.

"No, my friends! But my heart trembles at the thought that you understood me so little as not even to perceive that I possessed talent and soul enough to appreciate your best qualities, profit by them, and acknowledge your good intentions for the future well-being of our country. And I think I understand why it has pleased a wise Providence to bring me out of obscurity and appoint me a place in the Hôtel Bourbon. Are further explanations necessary? Do you not think the career opening to me is a happy one?"

Turgot and Malesherbes offered their hands with profound emotion; Morelly embraced him, saying: "That is what I expected from Caron!"

"But tell me only one thing," said Lamoignon. "Did not the princesses inquire about your birth and past life?"

"Certainly; and I answered, mentioning some names, but not that of a certain count," and he cast a glance at Batyl, "and the place where I made Susanna's acquaintance."

"And the royal ladies found no objections?" cried Turgot.

"On the contrary, they signed my appointment."

"Who was present at the audience?" asked Malesherbes.

"Besides their royal highnesses, two ladies of honor, two lackeys, and Piron and Fronsac."

"You did not speak to the princesses alone? Did no one come or go during the interview?" and Turgot looked at Caron with a curious smile.

"I acknowledge, my dear friend, that I was so occupied with the conversation between my patronesses and myself that I paid no attention as to who came or went."

"You see," said Morelly, laughing, "the beggar has become a diplomatist in one morning. How quickly the soul may blossom from germs that lie invisible and unsuspected."

"Whatever the future may have in

store, I hope I have proved to you that we are very necessary to each other; that the friendship of the garret must become more intimate in the drawing-rooms, and that no pride or good fortune can for an instant make me forget my present residence, and the watch-maker's son."

"I drink this glass to our old friendship and the Pigeonnier!" said Morelly. The friends touched their glasses and pressed each other's hands, while Susie shed tears of joy.

The conversation became general. Caron spoke of his new residence; Turgot and Lamoignon mentioned personages at court, gave information about different characters, and replied to some of their friends' questions. The little feast became a happy celebration of the good fortune of Beaumarchais, and all were at ease and familiar, except Batyl, who sat as if upon burning coals, irritated at hearing so much with so little satisfaction. Caron still wore the musician's best coat. The audacity of Beaumarchais, however, was apparently soon to be punished, and the day made more remarkable by another event. While the merriment was at its height, and Batyl fancying the family scene at the Hôtel St. Albin, caused by the casket sent to the countess, rough voices and numerous steps were heard on the old staircase outside, so that the company became silent.

"What is that?" said Turgot; "some persons are at the door." It was opened, and a commissioner of the police entered, his officials occupying threshold and passage.

Beaumarchais grew pale. "Who gave you permission to enter here, sir?" he said, angrily setting down his glass.

"My uniform will inform you," replied the man. "I am also not quite unknown in this region. Besides, I am in the habit of asking not answering questions. Who of those here present is Caron Beaumarchais?"

Batyl sprang up. "That one!" he said, pointing to Caron with a triumphant smile.

"What do you want with him?" asked Susanna.

"If you are Beaumarchais," and the lieutenant placed his hand heavily on Caron's shoulder, "I take you prisoner in the name of his majesty."

"Wherefore, sir?" said Turgot, rising.

"The warrant is usually shown!" said Lamoignon. "I have the honor of being myself a royal official."

"Certainly!" said the commissioner, drawing forth a stamped paper. "Here is the royal *lettre de cachet*, for Caron Beaumarchais, No. 30 Rue Bertau, in the Pigeonnier, fourth floor, garret, second door to the right, issued on complaint of his grace the Duke de St. Albin, for insulting his daughter, Countess Rosa de la Blache, consort of Count Falcoz, by said Beaumarchais, and attempting the degradation of her honor and rank. You are the man; therefore, forward, my dear fellow, let us take a walk to the Bastile!" Susanna clung sobbing to her husband, while Batyl laughed aloud.

"Sir!" said Caron, maintaining his firm self-possession, "I shall certainly not resist a command of his majesty, and you may rely on my obedience as soon as you have proved that I am the person meant in this warrant; and I doubt that you can do this."

"How is that!" said the lieutenant, roughly, "you are Caron Beaumarchais, and found in the place designated."

"That is my name, but I reside no longer here; I am professor of music to their royal highnesses the princesses! May I ask your name?"

"And do you think," exclaimed the man, "that I will allow myself to be fooled by such nonsense?" De Sartines, commissioner of his majesty's police, knows how far to go; and he is well aware that persons in the employ of their royal highnesses are not found in the Pigeonnier. If you think you are right you may remonstrate from the prison; but, first, you must come willingly with me, or I shall have you bundled up like a bag of dirty linen and driven off in a cart!"

"On the contrary, M. de Sartines, you will retire quietly and politely, or you will be cashiered to-morrow. According to this royal autograph patent of their highnesses, I am their professor and concert director. The illustrious ladies might well be surprised that a De Sartines could ignore their orders, to execute a *lettre de cachet*, dated last year, of which the Duke de St. Albin has probably a few dozen blanks. If the duke thinks he has any complaint against a royal official, he knows where to apply; I am not subject to *your* jurisdiction." Caron handed his patent disdainfully to the alarmed lieutenant.

M. de Sartines looked into the paper. "It is so, music professor to their royal highnesses!"

"You now see that at the audience to-morrow, I might complain of your inconsiderate conduct. You need only make inquiries at the Hôtel Bourbon, to confirm the truth to your own disadvantage. If you should ever have another commission for me like this, you will find me at my residence in the mansion of Chevalier de Piron, secretary to their highnesses, Rue des Ormes!"

"M. Beaumarchais," and the officer returned the letter with a bow, "I beg your pardon for having disturbed you. Of course the duke must carry his complaint to a higher tribunal. No serious reproach can be laid to my charge, for it is certain you are the person intended, though you escape this warrant by a fortunate event. I do not think you
4

will make me suffer for an attempt to perform simply my duty in arresting you—the blunder was committed by the duke. I have the honor!" He raised his hat, and departed.

Caron's laughter broke the painful silence. "Now, Susanna, I really believe that I shall become a great man! Fill your glasses, friends, and then, farewell for to-day. This great rascal Batyl must not cheat me of my lesson! Let us pour out a libation to the goddess Audacity!"

CHAPTER V.

LESSONS ON THE HARP.

THE eventful day ended in quiet happiness, mingled with that gratitude with which the ingenuous and honest receive benefits and enjoy them. After Beaumarchais had escaped from the *lettre de cachet*, by his self-possession, and forced his friends to acknowledge that he was born to be a diplomatist, it was arranged that Turgot, Malesherbes, and Morelly, should visit the young couple on the following evening at the Hôtel Piron. Turgot, who had business to attend to in the neighborhood of the arsenal, undertook the delivery of a note to the chevalier, in which the warrant was mentioned, and the request made to have apartments ready for Beaumarchais and his wife early in the morning. The friends separated, not without many curious thoughts on the favors of fortune.

Beaumarchais returned the three thousand francs of the count to Batyl, taking a receipt for them, and gave him also one hundred and fifty francs for the coat, saying: "A dress in which I appeared before their royal highnesses shall be worn by no other person."

Batyl, finding his hope defeated of seeing Caron in the Bastile, and having put himself more than ever in the author's power, could do no better than gain his good will by obedience. The first lesson was given, and with astonishing success. Beaumarchais was naturally of a musical turn; he sang with taste, and played the guitar very well. He had written his *École pour la Harpe* relying on this talent; and, urged by the necessity of the case, he was an exceedingly attentive pupil. The value of his work was perhaps not very important, but he had enriched it with so much taste, so many philosophic thoughts, and beautiful fancies, that it greatly interested the princesses. Batyl was requested to attend the following afternoon at the Hôtel Piron.

Caron received one more visit, that of M. Gauchat. It is unnecessary to describe the author's polite coolness, and the numerous apologies and assurances of friendship of the bookseller. Gauchat insisted on publishing *Eugénie*, but Caron refused, saying, that the manuscript was already in the hands of the princesses. Gauchat begged him to write something else—anything he pleased, to be published by the firm, entreating him to accept five thousand francs on account, that it might at least be known that he had the honor of some connection with M. Beaumarchais. The latter smiled and took the money, writing a note to the effect that all he composed, amounting to that sum, should be published at M. Gauchat's. Caron was prudent, for he comprehended that such a man as the bookseller would be useful to an author at court.

At last the three—who had hitherto lived in the garret like parent and children—Morelly, Caron, and Susanna—were alone. They talked of the future, and gave themselves up to their happiness, made many arrangements, and reminded each other of possible dangers. Beaumarchais and Susanna ob-

tained a promise from the old man that he would share, in some degree at least, their good fortune. "What is the use of your community of goods, papa, if you never try to realize your dreams?" said Susanna. Morelly was obliged to yield, and accepted their offers with the emotion of a father. As, however, he would not leave the Pigeonnier, and as it was well to retain this place as a refuge, and to watch Batyl as well as Mlle. Raucourt and her followers, it was agreed that direct and frequent communication must be maintained between the Quai des Ormes and the Rue Bertau. Unlike others, the young couple felt that they ought to remember the place where they had suffered so much. There was a feeling of fidelity and modesty in this, and from it was to arise much that was connected with what appeared a brilliant life, but in reality a continual conflict.

On the morrow, quite early, M. and Madame Beaumarchais left the garret, taking friendly leave of Morelly. They had nine thousand francs in their pocket, and did not forget to take the old guitar with the blue ribbon and the artificial rose, and appeared at the Hôtel Piron, where they were received by the chevalier and his consort.

Piron was exactly such a person as described by Turgot and Malesherbes. Noble, elegant, humane, rich, and indolent, but cautious. Besides, he was too frank to play the intriguer for the illustrious ladies; he merely entertained them and attended to their official correspondence. But with all his ingenuousness he was cunning in a certain way. No man was better acquainted with the court, its characters, and the influences at work, and if he did not trouble himself with them, he could give good advice, adopt the proper means to defined aims, the right persons to accomplish certain purposes, and yet he always assumed the appearance of pure disinterestedness. No one knew so well as he to pretend ignorance and surprise. It was he who had discovered Beaumarchais. He saw in his work on the harp not so much the musician as the superior intellect, the witty and ready *littérateur* — a man unknown, no philosopher, and therefore not exciting suspicion, and attached to no exclusive circle.

The reception of Beaumarchais at the audience informed the chevalier that Caron was a real acquisition, and by the manner in which the princesses appointed the musician it was seen he surpassed their expectations, and that Piron could make no mistake in assisting him in his passage from the garret to the court, attaching Caron to himself as well as their royal highnesses, by all means at his command. He therefore had the left wing of his mansion put in order immediately after the interview, receiving Beaumarchais and his wife very warmly on their arrival.

He who has ever felt the change from sorrow, want, the narrowness and rudeness of low life, to happy circumstances, high social intercourse, and honorable activity, can alone have any conception of the profound but silent gratitude Caron felt — of the naïve pleasure and surprise of Susie, who only on the preceding day went out with a basket on her arm to buy food, but who now entered lofty and richly-decorated apartments, with their Venetian mirrors and downy sofas, and regarded as her own the many elegant and costly things which at Passy she had only been permitted to see from a distance in the villa of M. Duverney. Poor Susie, making caps for Louise Duchapt, had become Madame Beaumarchais, wife of the professor to the royal princesses—a lady who could wear just such head-dresses herself as she formerly made for the wealthy. Of course, she knew how charming she

was, and that she conquered the heart of Chevalier de Piron and his wife by her simple and sportive manners.

When people of rank overcome their prejudices, and can appreciate their fellow-creatures, they are generally very amiable in their condescension. Such was Madame de Piron. As soon as Susanna recovered a little from her astonishment, and the gentlemen began to talk of serious subjects, she was conducted to a boudoir by her attentive hostess.

"Quick, my dear, you must surprise M. Caron with a better toilet. You must make up your mind to borrow one of my dresses and shawls. While our husbands are at the audience we shall drive to the milliner's and silk mercer's, and buy what is necessary for you."

"But, most gracious lady, who—who is to pay for all that? How do we know whether we shall always be in such prosperous circumstances? The court is said to be a very bad place; and how shall I, a poor simple woman, look in such rich garments? Like a doll bought at a country fair."

"No such thing, what are you thinking of, my dear child! you will look very well. In a few days you will become accustomed to these brilliant scenes. Believe me, many of the ladies looking so grand have very common minds, and have risen by somewhat equivocal means; but the higher circles of society learn to tolerate them, for they that have pure hearts can endure every thing. Your charming figure would make any costume appropriate. As to the expense, do not trouble yourself about that, we know what we have to do to please the princesses. Now throw over you this wrapper and powder-mantle, my maid shall arrange your hair. When you are ready, ring that bell, while I go and see what my wardrobe can provide for you; for, as the wife of a member of the royal court, you must be careful of appearances.—Not another word, I love you, and you must obey."

It was not extraordinary that Susanna and Caron should be so pleased with their new dwelling; for every thing was in perfect taste—noble without pretension, uniting comfort with beauty, and avoiding excessive ornament. The Hôtel Piron consisted of but two stories, built in the elegant style of the times. It fronted the Rue des Ormes, the Quai des Theatines, and the Rue St. Paul. On its right was the Hôtel Grammont; on its left, the Pont Marie and the Fauconniers. The front windows looked upon the northern branch of the Seine, and the Isle de St. Louis. In the vicinity were the mansions of the Aumonts and Fourcys, and the church Ave-Maria. It was altogether an aristocratic neighborhood.

The residence of Piron might have been almost termed a villa, the centre being built somewhat back, so that the wings projected, and in front was a cheerful little garden, separated from the street by an iron railing. The upper story on the right was occupied by the chevalier, and that on the left by Beaumarchais. The ground floor contained the kitchens, servants' rooms, gardener's and huntsman's dwellings. The manner in which Piron had chosen and arranged the apartments for his friends showed delicacy as well as prudence. On passing through the garden, you came to a corridor, leading to a staircase to the upper story. A door immediately opposite opened into the sitting-room, of sky-blue and white stucco, its windows looking upon the Rue Fauconniers. To the left of this was a square sleeping-chamber, with its huge bed and heavy green canopy. By a tapestry door was the entry into Caron's study, ornamented in gilt—one window looking on the Seine, and two

toward the garden. Adjoining this was a small cabinet, intended as a dressing-room.

On returning to the sitting-room and opening a door to the right, you entered a large drawing-room richly decorated. On the ceiling was represented the triumph of Pallas, and from the centre hung a chandelier. Glass doors led to the broad garden terrace, set with orange-trees. The reception-room connected with the staircase, and through its great windows your eye rested upon the soft green of the foliage, where finches and nightingales mingled their songs with the murmur of the fountain.

This abode was not altogether an Elysium for Caron and Susanna, though they were for a long time happy there, for it was the witness of many sorrows, such as they had not suffered even during the time of their greatest want in the Pigeonnier. Still, as Beaumarchais acknowledged, he never felt so much joy as at the Hôtel Piron, and he left upon its threshold his youth as well as his sensibility to pain. Nothing afterward could make him either happy or miserable.

Caron found his residence pleasing chiefly because it was so to Susanna. He regarded his condition with an eye of wordly wisdom and distrust, considering himself but as a transient guest. He understood how much he was under Piron's observation, which was oppressive to a man of energy and independence. He therefore resolved to take advantage of the safest occasion to free himself. He was willing to be serviceable, but according to his own notions; and a favorable fortune rendered such a temper only more troubled.

While a collation was brought into the drawing-room, Madame de Piron and Susanna entered, the latter dressed in a robe of brown and gold silk, trimmed with white lace, a hat of black velvet with a white rosette, a small satin cloak over her gloved arm, and carrying in her hand a bag containing her handkerchief and smelling-bottle, à la Pompadour.

"M. Beaumarchais, what do you say to your wife?" asked Madame de Piron, smiling.

Caron kissed the hand of Susie, who was half ashamed. "Oh, gracious lady, a good husband is in duty bound to confess his wife pretty under all circumstances, and I am certain my little Susie knows well enough that I do so. But, in truth, I would rather see her in the simple costume in which she won my heart."

"But I pray you," said Piron, "this is a toilet à la Duchesse de Grammont, introduced by the sister of the Duke de Choiseul, and the latest fashion of our ladies."

"My dear sir, you cannot, as a member of the court, permit your wife to appear publicly in a style of dress that, however choice the materials may be, is not suitable to the station you now occupy."

"I do not mistake your intention, gracious lady, any more than the praise the chevalier bestowed on the costume à la Grammont. Of course, my wife must have a promenade dress as well as one for the drawing-room, that she may not expose herself to ridicule, or bring contempt upon my illustrious patronesses. The occasions for Susanna to be publicly seen, can only be when she accompanies you, gracious lady, on a shopping expedition, or if it should be found absolutely necessary to have her presented, which, by the way, I am not particularly anxious about. Here is her world, and one in which she may be very happy in the midst of true friends. And I beg you to have her dressed as I love to see her, à la Susanna. I assure you, such costume is natural and pretty, and harmonizes with her diminutive size. It may be that you yourself, madame, will one day admire this ordinary toilet of Susie! I have another reason," and Caron became more serious, "you may call it superstition or prudence; but, in short, I wish to be continually reminded of my past, and remain the same in all this luxury. I consider this a means to reconcile myself to all circumstances, and, should misfortune come, be enabled to bear it. I distrust neither my royal pupils nor you, but myself."

"That is what I told madame!" exclaimed Susanna, almost as if complaining. "And if you will permit me to dress as I am accustomed, only perhaps a little more tastefully, you will see that it will be less expensive, and you will like me a great deal better."

"These views, my friends, are too honorable to you that I should seek to contradict them," replied Piron.

"I ought to be displeased because you do not admire your wife in my dresses, but I comprehend your caution. We shall make our purchases accordingly, my dear, and I am curious to know what you will choose."

"The hour for the audience approaches, no doubt you have preparations to make; in half an hour the carriage will be at the door, and I beg you to meet us in our reception-room." The chevalier offered his hand to Caron. "Apropos, where is the harp for the lesson?"

"The harp? Yes, chevalier, it is true, I cannot use the old one. It needs repairing, and another, a better one, must be bought for the use of their royal highnesses. However, that makes no difference, as the first instruction is always given on the guitar. Will you have the kindness, gracious lady, to send me a new blue ribbon for my guitar?"

"With pleasure. In half an hour we meet again, Madame Susie." Piron and his wife withdrew.

Susanna put her arms round Caron's neck, and looked at him long and anxiously. "Do I not really please you in this toilet, or do you fear, as I do, that this is all a dream?"

"Susie, I really prefer to see you as you appeared a maiden at Passy. Buy finer material—that I leave to your own good taste and your needle, but fear the stability of our good fortune—only fools, and those who despise life, fear nothing. You know our enemy well enough, and I am to meet him in the presence of the princesses to-day. Do you feel that it is either my ruin or his? I must conquer him, and before the royal ladies! Will his hatred not increase? Certainly! The terror, therefore, with which I inspire him must be greater than the feeling of his humiliation. He must dread me, so that he may not interfere; our destiny is an unceasing warfare. We must be prepared for every thing; be economical wherever we possibly can, in order to possess; for there are but three things that can make us independent: birth, knowledge, riches; and if we are deficient in the first, we must make it up in the last."

"Alas, if we could only discover my parents!"

"You remind me of my duty to put on the ring. I hear M. Duverney will be at the audience; I will see whether he recognizes it."

"And do not forget your watch."

"And the billet-doux of the count, addressed to you!" He put them all in his pocket. "One thing more, my love. We entered this house with nine thousand francs; I have placed them in the secret drawer of this secretary, as well as my appointment papers. I give you the key; use as much money as you may consider necessary for our expenses; but remember that for every hundred francs we spend, two hundred must come in, or these apart-ments and this dress will certainly turn out a mere illusion. Now, be of good courage; be merry, and do not forget that we expect our friends to-night." He kissed her forehead, took his hat, put on the sword and gloves brought by Piron's servant, and soon all four were rolling along the quai over the Place Grève, through St. Germain - l'Auxerrois, across the Pont Neuf, along the eastern bank of the Seine, to the Hôtel Bourbon. Arrived at the palace, Piron and Beaumarchais descended and took leave of the ladies, who returned to the northern portion of the city to engage in shopping.

There never existed a court society, great or small, that did not, so to say, live on slanderous stories, whose most important business was not to pry into the life and conduct of others, and whose greatest pleasure did not consist in making use of the weaknesses, follies, and vices of its members. They who surround a monarch are therefore of two classes—the feared and the ridiculed. The former obtain power, the latter descend to ruin; and never did this courtier life flourish so successfully as under the Bourbons.

It would have been extraordinary, if the appointment of Beaumarchais, and all connected with it, had not already been known in the court circles. Frousac, the ladies of the princesses, and the lackeys, had taken care of that. All were aware that Caron was a commoner, the son of a watchmaker, a poor creature living in the Pigeonnier; that he had been so unfortunate as to insult the Duke de St. Albin; had but just escaped a *lettre de cachet*, and become known to the royal ladies by means of a pamphlet. Incredible! Was not this enough to cause the greatest commotion? Was not this array of facts sufficient to turn every one's hand against the unhappy new-comer?

An hour before the official reception the antechambers were filled with persons who, either for others or themselves, wished to obtain information about this latest court phenomenon, or whose rank or duty permitted them to be present at the audience. Questions were asked; whisperings heard; smiles, shrugging of shoulders seen—all listened to Fronsac's sibylline intimations, and were not ashamed to draw aside Lafleure, the head valet de chambre; for, of course, he knew every thing. Among those present were the three chamberlains of the princesses, the Chevaliers de Bouvé, d'Epernon, and de Lesdiguier, as well as Messrs. d'Aumont, de Noailles, and de Comartin, the three lieutenants of the body-guards of their royal highnesses. It was natural that they wished to be present at the presentation of their chief. M. d'Aumont was gloomy and silent; he was the senior officer, and not very well pleased at the nomination of Count de la Blache; Noailles seemed to share these feelings, but he gave vent to his vexation in petty sarcasms and ironical remarks; while Comartin, by his careless conversation, manifested more enjoyment than ambition. The group were discussing the topic of the day when the door opened and Piron and Beaumarchais entered, the latter carrying a music-book and a guitar.

"There he is, gentlemen!" and Fronsac cast a glance at the party.

"What an abominable affair!" exclaimed Noailles, in a whisper. "How self-satisfied the beggar looks, as if the Hôtel Bourbon were an ordinary mansion!"

"Can we not embarrass him a little. He is nothing but a comedian with a rather passable exterior."

"I advise you, gentlemen, to let the man alone," said Aumont, calmly. "His head shows intelligence, and he conducts himself well; as to the rest, he has nothing to do with us. I never have cared to avenge myself for my own degradation by despising the elevation of others. The man is an excellent harpist, which cannot be said of any of us."

"According to your idea, we should be hand and glove with all kinds of people, my comrade," said Noailles, pointedly. "If that Beaumarchais is to belong to our sphere, let him understand how he is to pass muster with us. I will try him."

While this half-whispered conversation was indulged in, purposely in such a manner that Piron and Caron might notice it, the chevalier asked Fronsac whether their royal highnesses had finished their breakfast.

"It is not my duty to know that, chevalier. You must apply to the head valet de chambre.—Lafleure, M. de Piron desires to speak to you."

"You see the storm is brewing! The atmosphere will be warmer than yesterday!" whispered Piron to Beaumarchais.

"So I think, from the words of those behind me."

The chevalier spoke to the valet in a low voice, desiring him to announce their arrival. As he was about to answer, M. de Noailles left his friends and touched Caron's shoulder. The latter turned: "What are your commands?"

"I believe your name is Beaumarchais?"

"At your service."

Noailles drew out his costly watch, handing it to Caron. "I wish you would look at this, it does not go well. What is the matter with it? *You* ought to know." Piron, Lafleure, and the rest, were motionless.

"Will you permit me?" said Beaumarchais, politely. Just as Noailles was handing the watch, Caron dropped it, and it broke into pieces.

"Sir!" cried Noailles, frightened.

"You see that you addressed yourself to the wrong person. My father always said his trade did not suit me. I generally destroy what does not interest me." A giggling was heard at the expense of Noailles, and, while he returned to his companions with a burning countenance, Lafleure hastened into the audience hall.

"I am glad, gentlemen," said Aumont, gravely, "that a citizen possesses enough mind and courage to defend his dignity."

Beaumarchais turned and bowed. "Monsieur, I thank you in the name of all citizens." Lafleure reappeared, making a signal to Piron and Caron to enter.

The audience chamber was vacant. "I beg you, chevalier," whispered the valet, "to step into the presence of their royal highnesses in the green drawing-room; they wish to give you some commissions. The Marchioness d'Irmac waits to introduce you." Piron left the hall, and Beaumarchais remained with Lafleure. The latter, pacing the floor pompously, cast many a glance upon the new-comer not quite free from self-complacency, however good-natured the old lackey otherwise seemed.

"I see you have a guitar, sir," Lafleure began after a while, "but I thought you were to give lessons on the harp?"

"Certainly, as soon as a suitable instrument can be found for their royal highnesses."

"I am very fond of music," rejoined the valet, more politely. "You are said to excel in it. My daughter sings, and plays on the guitar. I am only sorry she has no teacher."

"Your daughter doubtlessly requires no instruction; a few suggestions will be sufficient; perhaps she has no suitable pieces. If your office does not prevent you, I would be highly honored by a visit from yourself and daughter to-morrow evening; probably I can find something for her."

"You are very good, sir;" said Lafleure, greatly flattered. "I gladly accept your kindness, if you will permit me to assist you by my advice."

"You really overwhelm me, M. Upper-chamberlain. You have seen how enviously a poor commoner is looked upon here, as if people of rank were not obliged to make use of those who have learned something, like you and me."

"Truly, and it is laughable how very necessary we are to them! But, patience. I will teach you how to treat these gentlemen. They harassed me enough before I understood the ground. But do not call me upper-chamberlain; I have an important position, it is true, but I might be accused of vanity. Head valet de chambre, if you please! We shall talk of such matters to-morrow evening. I can tell you in the mean time that the princesses are enchanted, and —" A bell rang. "*Au revoir;* the principal lady of the household calls; their royal highnesses will soon be here!"

Beaumarchais bowed to the valet, and could not restrain a laugh. "My dear Caron, if you wish to succeed, you must by all means make friends with the lackeys, cooks, and grooms; they are a sort of Chinese wall around the higher circles." He walked up and down, smilingly tuned his guitar, and then, attuning the strings, hummed softly the song, "*Schönster Junker, Hans von Lyra.*" He was presently silenced, for Lafleure opened the door and the princesses with their attendants entered.

"I see you are ready, M. Beaumarchais," said Adelaide, kindly. "I have been informed that one of our cavaliers had the delicacy to give you his watch to repair. I am glad you repaired it so thoroughly."

"But you have a guitar!" said Sophie.

"Yes, your royal highness. The harp tires the fingers, for it requires strength. It is better to learn the elements on this instrument."

"And you have already taken up your residence in the Hôtel Piron?" asked Victorie, a little ironically.

"Certainly, your royal highness, especially as it pleased the Duke de St. Albin to honor me with a prison-warrant on my return yesterday from the audience; I escaped by showing the commissioner of police my appointment."

"St. Albin!" exclaimed Adelaide. "What induced him to do that?"

"He fancies that I insulted 'his daughter, the Countess de la Blache. and he meant thus summarily to avenge himself. I told the official to inform the duke that any complaint against me must be brought before your royal highnesses. Whether he was aware of my engagement and wished to render it void by degrading me personally, I do not know, but as I expected some attack of the kind, I yesterday requested my gracious patronesses to permit me to be present at the audience."

The princesses looked at each other in astonishment. "I cannot comprehend how M. Beaumarchais could have so irritated the duke!" said Victorie, interrupting the silence.

"I can easily explain it," rejoined Sophie. "I fear certain persons are more cunning than we imagine."

"Do you think so, my sister? Is it possible that something deeper lies at the bottom of Fronsac's resistance, La Blache's presentation, and the *lettre de cachet*, that—" Adelaide ceased, looking in consternation at her ladies of honor.

"Will your royal highnesses permit me to tranquillize you?" said Caron, smiling. "It is true that plans are forming soon to be realized by certain persons, but, on such occasions, it often happens that insignificant circumstances produce a coincidence leading us to ascribe greater depth of intention to the originators than they deserve. I absolve the duke from all such ideas. His party think they have gained an important point, if Count Falcoz de la Blache become attached to your personal service. M. de St. Albin's affair with me is quite a separate thing; he really feels greatly insulted. He does not imagine, however, that by bringing his accusation before you, he renders the very worst service to his family and cause."

"Explain yourself a little more," said Sophie, quickly.

"That would look, your royal highnesses," and he glanced at the attendants present, "as if I wished to give you an evil opinion of persons on the point of being highly favored by you. Besides, I like to see people caught in a net by their own movement, and would not deprive you, illustrious ladies, of such a pleasure."

"I am afraid you are capable of malice!" said Adelaide, thoughtfully.

"Very much so; and, to my shame, I own that malice affords me enjoyment when I can entertain it towards those with whom I have old accounts to settle."

The door of the antechamber opened, and Fronsac entered. "Will it please your highnesses to grant the audience? It is the usual hour. His grace the Duke de St. Albin, Count de la Blache, M. Duverney, as well as the cavaliers and officers of your suite, are waiting, and the Marchioness de Ventadour may be expected from Versailles at any moment."

Adelaide turned to Lafleure. "Be kind enough to request the Chevalier de Piron to bring the commission. M. Beaumarchais, you can continue your instruction afterward." She seated herself on au arm-chair between her sisters, ordered Caron to step behind her among the ladies of honor, took the patent of La Blache's appointment from Piron, and was glancing over it, when a noise was heard in the ante-rooms; the door opened, and a tall, stately man entered; the princesses immediately rose, and the rest bowed profoundly.

François Louis de Bourbon, Prince de Conti, Grand Prior and Knight of Malta, was a man of about thirty-three years, of a handsome, but, for his age, very grave, and indeed melancholy countenance, which greatly enhanced the dignity of his presence. He was dressed in black velvet without any embroidery. On the left breast sparkled the eight-pointed cross of St. John. A portion of his vest was seen, of red cloth with a gold border, and at his side glittered the steel handle of his sword. He held in his hand a hat adorned with short ostrich plumes; around his neck hung a triple gold chain, made of long clasp-like links united by small rings, from which hung a large gold cross. Without any further ceremony he approached the princesses and kissed their hands.

"You must pardon me, dearest cousins, that I so unexpectedly add to your company; but as I was informed that it had pleased his majesty to supply a vacancy in your household, and the person being already selected, my hearty interest in you led me hither to witness a ceremony of so great importance. May I ask a private word with you, previous to the presentation, dear Adelaide?" At this hint the others withdrew. He led the princess to a corner window. "Can you not elude this La Blache, my cousin? Your royal mother sends me in order to warn you. It is certain that Madame de Pompadour and the ministers have formed an alliance with the party of Terray and the Marchioness de Ventadour, of which this choice is the result, threatening to crush your independence completely. The king was persuaded to assent, as he usually is concerning any thing!"

"We have been duped in this matter, my dear Conti. After long and vainly desiring to appoint a captain of our guards, to which post we wished to raise Aumont, and introduce the Prince de la Tremouille, the scion of a faithful family, into the third lieutenancy, his majesty at our recent visit, unasked granted our request, but proposed La Blache immediately. Choiseul stood near. How we are to escape I do not see, and we have been caught in our own plans. I have but one hope, that a favorable accident may occur to prevent what we so much dislike. The Duke de St. Albin has a complaint against one of our servants, our new teacher on the harp, but the latter seems sure of his justification. Perhaps this may be a support."

"A very weak one! I heard about this Beaumarchais yesterday; with all his talent however he will have enough to do to maintain his position here, if he is to be useful to you. Piron spoke highly of him to the dauphin. How he, in this affair—"

"Excuse me, I will obtain some certainty on the subject — Chevalier de Piron!" The chevalier approached the window. "Will you be kind enough to ask Beaumarchais whether he is sure of being able to frustrate the appointment of the count, and invalidate the accusation in reference to the Countess de la Blache, when I return to my seat. He need but say yes or no. Make room for his royal highness near me." Piron hastened to Lafleure, who placed a chair for monseigneur; then the chevalier spoke a few moments with Caron in a low voice. As

Adelaide and Conti advanced, both looked at the author.

"Certainly, your royal highness," said Beaumarchais, "discord will disappear and harmony succeed!"

"I thank you. The prince disputed that passage in your book, sir.—Well, duke, order the gentlemen to be admitted." The folding-doors opened.

The Duke de St. Albin, a haughty old man, entered, accompanied by his son-in-law, Count Falcoz de la Blache, about twenty-eight, good-looking, but pale, and having an air of dissipation. Notwithstanding the humble manner he had assumed for the occasion, it was evident that his restraint was irksome, while he endeavored to conceal his nonchalance and levity. He was one of those handsome men that make no favorable impression. They were followed by Paris Duverney, the maternal uncle of the count, the richest citizen in the capital, and the court banker. He was of ordinary stature, rather inclined to corpulency, but having an intelligent and subtle mind, appreciating his own worth and never making a mistake in business matters. The chamberlains stationed themselves at the left, and the officers at the right of the princesses.

"His majesty," began Adelaide, "has been so gracious as to consent that the appointment of commander of our guards should be made, and it has pleased him to nominate your son-in-law Count Falcoz de la Blache. The wishes of the king are a law to us, and we feel happy in being able to show our favor to the illustrious house of St. Albin as well as to M. Duverney. We do not hesitate to present the commission at once, but, to our sorrow, we are informed, duke, that something disagreeable has occurred between you and one of our officials that may have evil consequences. We understand that you wish to hand in a complaint against this person on account of great injury done to a member of your noble family. Will you have the kindness to express yourself on this subject now?"

"Your highnesses," replied St. Albin, "it is impossible to express my gratitude for the honor you are conferring on my son-in-law; and I am yet happier that you yourselves wish to dispel the dark cloud which at the last moment seemed to threaten his presence near you. As to the accusation, I shall express no opinion of the individual in question. He has the extraordinary fortune to be in your service—a fact which protected him against his imprisonment in the Bastile. A warrant was issued against a certain Caron Beaumarchais, who yesterday dared send this casket and note to my house, addressed to my daughter the Countess de la Blache, attempting an infamy against the honor of a lady of rank, which is probably unparalleled in the crimes of citizens! I have nothing to request, your highness, but that you should read for yourself." In silence St. Albin handed the case and letter to Adelaide.

All eyes turned toward Beaumarchais, whose fall seemed certain. Adelaide took the paper in great perplexity, turning pale as she read.—"Beaumarchais, step hither!" He obeyed, casting a fixed glance upon La Blache.

"Is it possible—is it credible—that you could have written this note, sir?"

"And why not, your royal highnesses?" He drew forth La Blache's note to Susanna. "When the Count de la Blache set me such a good example, I considered it no infamy to imitate him in that copy! If it be no crime in the count, surely it is not in me. Or is it your opinion, gracious princesses, that the wife of a commoner is honored by that which disgraces a countess? I affronted the Countess de la Blache, a lady with whom I am not acquainted, and who has power, wealth, a hundred swords, a *lettre de cachet*, and the Bastile, at her command—it required some courage to send her that note! But to insult a woman of the people, because she is poor, has no protection, and no possibility of retaliation, except the anger of her husband, who is powerless, unless the king's daughters interfere—to do that, count, needs nothing but cowardice and a detestable immorality! Such a man is proposed to his majesty to be the guardian of his royal children!"

Words like these had probably never before been heard in the Hôtel Bourbon. The Duke de St. Albin shrank back involuntarily, uttering a cry of amazement, and staring at his son-in-law, who was gazing at Beaumarchais with a pale and frightened look. Conti arose hastily and seized his sword, the officers of the guard approached, murmuring, and struck their falchions against the marble floor. Duverney pressed his trembling hand upon his forehead.

Madame Adelaide was silent, but the red color on her cheek indicated her emotion. "Duke de St. Albin and M. Duverney, approach and look at this paper. On your word of honor, who wrote it?" Both advanced, and Adelaide held the writing toward them.

"That — for heaven's sake!" exclaimed Duverney. "Falcoz wrote it!"

"It is his hand-writing!" groaned the duke. Regaining his self-possession, he said, "I take my accusation back, your highnesses! The disgrace falls upon the dishonorable man whom I unfortunately call the husband of my daughter!"

"Accept our sympathy, duke. It is unnecessary to say that it is now impossible to execute the wish of his majesty. My dear Lieutenant d'Aumont, we confer the captaincy on you; Messrs.

de Noailles and Comartin will be advanced, and the young Prince de la Tremouille appointed third lieutenant. Order him to appear at the audience to-morrow; M. de Piron will draw up the commissions. You, M. Beaumarchais, remain to continue your lesson on the harp. Let all men know that talent and honor are esteemed, even in a lowly garb, at the Hôtel Bourbon!— Your arm, cousin." Adelaide bowed and withdrew, conducted by Conti; her sisters followed, the ladies of honor, as well as Piron and Fronsac.

La Blache now awoke from his apparent indifference, and roamed around like a madman, uttering words of hatred and vengeance. "Oh, terrible!" he groaned. "A nobleman so disgraced, annihilated in the face of all the world! You malicious *canaille*—you serpent in my way, shall pay for all—" He drew his sword to strike Caron. Count d'Aumont turned the blow, and the other officers stepped before Beaumarchais to protect him. Duke de St. Albin seized the furious man, and forced him back, saying: "Do you intend to degrade yourself beyond redemption, and be cited before the Parliament?— Be charitable, gentlemen, let it never be known that such a scene occurred in a royal mansion. Let the wretched man do penance in the obscurity of exile!"

"I wish I could forget that my sister was your mother," exclaimed the court banker, "and that Duverney is nothing for you but a money-chest and a reference! I renounce you! I wish to hear nothing more of a fellow too stupid to make his own fortune, and too unschooled to conceal his gallantries."

"Oho!" laughed Falcoz, ironically, "he renounces me! Very well! I can do without your society, but I should like to know whether you can deny our relationship in view of the law of heritage. And you—" as he gnashed his teeth, "I hate you more than I love my own pleasures, and I will at last prove it to you." He turned away.

"Oh," replied Caron, "as with your pleasures, so with your hatred, you shall pay dear!" The chevaliers and officers laughed aloud. The duke took La Blathe's arm and left the Hôtel with him, while Duverney paced the hall, only now recovering from his confusion, humiliation, and fear, and beginning to consider the consequences of what had just occurred.

After La Blache and his father-in-law had left the apartment, Count d'Aumont approached Caron and took his hand. "Should I thank you in our name, it would appear egotistical, M. Beaumarchais; but we wish to express our admiration for your shrewdness, your courage, and the charm of manner by which you have gained the favor of the noblest persons. Nature has given you a nobility that makes us forget your birth, and so long as the Aumonts, Noailles, and Comartins live, La Blache cannot harm you."

"Include us also," said the chief chamberlain, Le Bouve, advancing with his colleagues, "we can even better appreciate the blow M. Beaumarchais has struck to-day, thus happily delivering their highnesses from an offensive personage."

"Gentlemen," smiled Caron, "do not think better of me than I deserve. Nothing is so disadvantageous as too high an opinion in the estimation of our patrons. I have simply defended my conjugal honor and happiness; and that requires but little courage; it was a necessity. Where a man cannot use his sword, he must not spare his tongue. If I have at the same time rendered a service to their royal highnesses, you must not forget, gentlemen, that it is my business to remove discord, and perfect those harmonies without which no one can play the harp. You will

oblige me if you bestow your friendship and assistance as a free gift of the heart, of which the noblest are most capable." The conversation was interrupted by the entrance of Fronsac, who came to call the chamberlains and officers to the princesses.

Duverney and Caron remained alone. The latter took his guitar, and seated himself, looking ironically first at the banker and then out of the window. His fingers ran over the chords of the instrument, and his ruby ring sparkled in the sun.

"Ruined, dishonored before the princesses, who were always so kind to me, and to whom I owe so much!" growled Duverney in an undertone. "Must they not think that I am in agreement with this priestly coterie, while I only yielded to the claims of relationship to introduce that pitiful fellow! By what mysterious accident did all this occur? What connection is there in these opposite events? What demon has discovered the threads that—You are the one, sir!" he exclaimed, approaching Caron with tears in his eyes. "All this is your work!"

"True, your honor," and Beaumarchais continued to play, "I return every malicious action twice, and love him most who excites my hatred, for from boyhood I have a propensity for ruining characters. I never execute a scheme of spite and cunning by giving way to mere savage passion—that is not the way; but I employ the highest art, and therefore you will comprehend that I shall soon send the uncle after the nephew. Judge for yourself! Madame de Pompadour wishes to separate the royal family. Choiseul, Maupeau, Terray, as well as St. Albin and La Blache, are her allies, and, to finish the work, this atheistic mistress and her companions unite themselves with Jesuits. But a poor citizen, called Beaumarchais, appears one day and kindles a fire under the witches' caldron. Ah, you are surprised that I tell you this so honestly? Well, I am sometimes governed by milder impulses. I see you are an excellent man, a financier, to whom merchandise is every thing, and who have been duped because you had a sister unfortunately given to the La Blaches to prop up that falling family. What will you say if I promulgate with my tongue and my pen, seriously and wittily, that M. Paris Duverney has become a Jesuit propagandist, has introduced a pious spy, a relative of his, to their highnesses, and who is at the same time a friend of Mlle. Raucourt?"

"M. Beaumarchais," cried Duverney, "I—I beg you, spare an innocent man! You have great information on some subjects. I give you my word of honor that I will renounce the Albins and La Blaches!" He seized Caron's hand. "Do not act against me! You are poor; wealth makes people independent. Let us make a compromise, I am rich—"

"But I am not your nephew, longing for your louis d'ors."

"—I can, however, offer you advantages you—" He suddenly drew Caron's hand nearer to his eyes, and, looking at the ring, became very pale. "That ring! —just Heaven, how did you get it?"

"I have been moving it in the sun some time to attract your attention, and remind you of the way out of all your difficulties. The ring? Would you like to know? It is a legacy."

"From whom?"

"From my dear parents."

"Your parents? Never! The child was a girl!"

"Indeed? I suppose it was she who was brought up as a peasant's daughter, at Passy, in the house of Antoine Garnier, the steward of M. Duverney, and who, almost in her childhood, was persecuted by the nephew of the banker, who probably considered her his as part of his inheritance! You see your

sins increase, and, as I can produce the proofs, nothing remains but for you to make a thorough confession."

The court banker was in an agony; the perspiration stood in drops upon his forehead, and he trembled in such a manner that he was forced to hold himself upright by grasping a chair. "You are merciless; you know not what you ask! As the price of your silence and friendship you demand a secret the discovery of which would ruin me. Of what interest can it be to you to know it? Can you profit by the misery of others?"

"Perhaps! But, in short, the poor, disowned girl, so oppressed until now, is *my wife!* Do you now understand that I must either know her parentage or ruin the millionnaire Duverney?"

"Your wife? Little Susanna?"

"Yes, that is her name. I fancy I am not far wrong if I salute you as a near relative. How delighted their royal highnesses will be at this history!"

"No, on my word, you are mistaken! Had I ever had a child—a daughter, do not doubt that my paternal love, and the hope of leaving no money to that wretched La Blache, would have induced me to give her the best education, and introduce her into society with just pride. Susanna is the offspring of others—persons of rank—the child of sin! I took her out of the convent of the Ursulines, because I was obliged to, and brought her and the papers attesting her birth to Passy. I made my fortune by means of those documents, the Abbé Terray became friendly to me, and gave me a chance for financial operations; it is only right to remunerate Susanna for this."

"Ah," laughed Caron, putting down the guitar, "that is an easy way of becoming a millionnaire at the expense of the state!" He arose, and looked piercingly and tauntingly at Duverney. "Then the Abbé Terray is the fa—"

"Take care! I never said that! When did I say so? I—"

"We shall soon see. I will take care that their highnesses ask the abbé himself, to-morrow. What a pretty parliamentary process against one of the members! and, besides, some ecclesiastical punishment will follow, such as lifelong penitence on the Isle of St. If I am somewhat acquainted with methods of inquiry."

"Do you mean to ruin me?"

"Heaven forbid! As soon as I am put in possession of the papers attesting the birth of my wife, and the name of her mother, we are the best of friends, and you need fear nothing either from me or others."

Duverney wiped his brow. "Very well, you shall have the documents to-day; but not before you have signed a contract, which makes you a partner in my bank as long as it may please you, and whereby you promise to make no use of the documents while you remain in connection with me. It is the fact that I have those papers, and know the secret of Susanna's parentage, that facilitates my business operations with the government, and protects me from the hatred of certain persons."

"That sounds better! I am then to be the partner of a millionnaire; I am to expect you to-day after dinner, with the papers and contract, at my dwelling, Rue des Ormes, Hôtel Piron. But now, the mother? You acknowledge that she must be a very interesting person." The answer was prevented by a loud dialogue in the antechamber, in which the determined voice of a woman was especially remarkable.

"The Marchioness de Ventadour has arrived from Versailles! After what has happened I dare not meet her.

You do not know that woman! Let me escape by some door; detain her, show her the ring, and remind her of the — Ursulines! This afternoon I bring the contract!"

"Excellent," laughed Caron. "Go in there. If any one see you, only say that I wished it!" He pushed the financier through the left door, among the female attendants of the princesses. Just as Caron turned, the marchioness entered from the anteroom.

Diana de Ventadour was a tall woman, of about forty. Her resemblance to Susanna could not be mistaken, only that her hair and eyes were of the deepest black, and her complexion of that yellowish white common among Italians, with an *embonpoint* often noticed among the more heartless ladies of rank, who are given up to selfish enjoyment. She wore a long robe of black satin, very low in the neck, and trimmed with an extravagant quantity of black lace. On her bosom was a gold crucifix, suspended by a string of pearls, and in her hand a rosary. Her head was covered with the hood of her wide mantilla, fastened to her velvet cap by a pearl clasp. This was the costume of a lady who had renounced the pleasures of the world, and was animated by pious sentiments only. Her face still retained much of its beauty, though a certain harshness betrayed her haughtiness and presumption, and her low, heavy eyebrows, and subtle glance, made an unfavorable impression.

Caron grew very red, and his heart was full of bitterness. He saw at once that this woman would be his most dangerous enemy, but his determination was strengthened, and he bowed.

"But I tell you, Lafleure," she exclaimed violently, to the valet de chambre, who was anxiously following her, "the princesses are always at home for me, even if the audience is over! It will be considered incredible at Versailles, that the son-in-law of the Duke de St. Albin — the nephew of Duverney, a La Blache, a man of the oldest nobility, nominated for this position by the ministers and his majesty himself—not only lost it, and in the presence of their highnesses, but was insulted and disgraced by a beggar, a worthless fellow who calls himself Beaumarchais."

"Quite right, marchioness," and Caron advanced toward her, "his name is Beaumarchais, and he stands before you. If you wish to take the news of this terrible crime to Versailles as soon as possible, you need not trouble the princesses or yourself any further; you can obtain all the information you desire from me, the most reliable authority."

The marchioness stood as if changed into marble. Her large eyes, flaming in anger, were directed at Caron, and her features wore an expression of the most profound contempt. "So that is the individual himself? Indeed! Tell me, what extraordinary talent you possess that you, yesterday sleeping in a garret and dying of starvation, have to-day become the confidant of the king's daughters, your first act being the dishonoring of two noble names, and disturbing the peace in all the court circles?"

"Ah, gracious madame," said Caron, smiling and shrugging his shoulders, "I possess so many and varied talents that I am too modest to mention them in presence of so noble a lady. They do not all consist of the pious arts acquired among the Ursulines, but simply in the use of *this ring*, and some other trifles." He held the ruby toward her.

"Heaven help me!" and the fan fell from her hand. "That is — O annihilation!" She fainted. Beaumarchais received her in his arms. Lafleure was about to call for assistance.

"No, not yet. I know this kind of disease; people do not die of it. Only have the kindness to push a chair toward us, for it would not be desirable to be discovered with such a full-leaved rose on my bosom." He placed her in the arm-chair. "Now, step back a little, and you shall see how miraculously I can cure her." Lafleure bit his lip, and took his station at the door of the royal private apartments. "She is really quite faint," continued Caron, ironically. "I could not have believed her strong mind capable of this. I must use means for her recovery." He whispered: "Are you any better, *mother-in-law?*"

The judgment-trumpet will not awaken the dead more quickly than this question aroused Diana de Ventadour. She started up in a twinkling; her confused eyes glanced toward Beaumarchais. "Oh, my heaven, it—it is only too certain—he is her husband!" she murmured.

"Certainly," replied Caron, in an undertone, "and you can comprehend my great delight, at last to make the acquaintance of my mother-in—"

"Hold your tongue, sir! you are a wretch!"

"Because my relationship is inconvenient to such a pious lady? But that is just what amuses me; I have long been looking for you."

"Sir, you—unfortunate man, I—oh, listen to me! People of your description care only for money. I will give you to-day a million francs if you will go to England with—with her — this very night, never to return."

"A million? Not so ungenerous!" he replied, softly. "That is a large sum; my father-in-law, the Abbé Terray, will have to use the treasury. But, mamma, a man like myself has some conscience; the poor country is taxed enough already. And then, dear mamma, Paris, the service of the princesses, society (where slanderous anecdotes are retailed), and the booksellers, for whom we can write scandal, are all too pleasant here! We cannot move away. And consider also the pain of parting from such a sweet, long-looked-for, beautiful mother! We would rather remain here, and be content with five hundred thousand francs." Lafleure, who was watching them, disappeared in the inner chambers.

"He is a demon—my ruin!" groaned Diana.

"No, indeed, mamma. If I receive from you a check for five hundred thousand francs, payable at sight by M. Paris Duverney this evening—if you never trouble yourself about me and my wife—silence the St. Albins and La Blaches, and, wherever you recognize my presence, refrain from meddling with my affairs, I will keep your secret, and never make use of the papers in my possession. If, however, you disregard these conditions by a hair's breadth, madame—if you or any of your clique only make a wry face at me, I will tear from you the mask of hypocrisy, and expose you before all Paris; I will forsake you, as you forsook your unfortunate child!"

"And I am not to hate you as a poisonous reptile in my way?" She gnashed her teeth, and rose pale and exasperated. "How can you hurt me? What can you betray? We know how safe the papers are, and that you possess nothing but vain rumors, miserable falsifier!"

"Can so intelligent and influential a lady believe that I would attempt all this if I had not the proofs in my pocket? I really have. Paris Duverney is in my power, and if you rouse my anger I will persecute you from one end of France to the other. I will hold you up to the ridicule of all mankind. Ah, Madame de Pompadour will be delighted to see you ruined, without

herself suffering from your fate. You know, besides, how your position is threatened, since the murderous attempt of Damien! And you see what a good match your daughter has made."

The marchioness was alarmed and humiliated. She looked helplessly around and began to totter, but leaned on her enemy and bowed her head. "It is in vain," she whispered; "this is the curse of my life! Be merciful! You married Susanna as a poor girl; you must have some feeling. Do not kill the mother of your wife! I agree to every thing. Become as rich as you desire! Become as powerful as you may, I will avoid you; your path shall never be obstructed by me! Only—be silent for the sake of your dying hour, and the honor of a woman! Be silent forever!"

"I will if my demands are complied with. I will even refrain from informing Susanna, for I love her too well to reveal such a mother to her." The door leading to the royal apartments opened softly, and the princesses and Conti curiously regarded Caron and the marchioness.

Diana de Ventadour raised her head, and her glance fell on the ladies. She uttered a shriek, and almost fell; but, regaining her strength, looked with profound hate on Beaumarchais. Murmuring an oath she pressed the crucifix to her breast, and bowed to Adelaide and her sisters. "Excuse me, your highnesses, a—sudden illness prevents me from—paying my respects to you!" She disappeared, and a pause of astonishment succeeded.

The princesses and Conti entered. "Let the suite remain where they are; we wish to be alone." Lafleure locked the door on the inside. "We are almost accustomed to your miracles, dear Beaumarchais; but this new scene is so strange, that I think you owe us an explanation."

"Your royal highnesses, I understand that very well, but my meeting with the Marchioness de Ventadour was so painful—there was in it so much that disturbed my own serenity—that I beg you to leave the matter within my breast until compelled to reveal it. You asked me yesterday if I could be faithful. I did not reply. Just now Madame de Ventadour offered me a million francs if I would leave the country. I remain, and I declare that this woman and her followers will never again trouble the king's daughters. To accomplish this I have given her a—lesson on the harp, or rather a lesson on dissimulation."

"Ah," exclaimed Conti, "if you could do that, you are a valuable man! I beg you to visit me to-morrow. The dauphin and her majesty the queen also desire to take lessons on the harp!" Beaumarchais bowed low and concealed his emotion while kissing the hands of Adelaide and the prince.

CHAPTER VI

"THE DESIRED."

ALTHOUGH the vicissitudes of contempt and authority, neglect and power, characterized so capriciously the court circles of Louis XV., where all anticipated a daily surprise originating in the whims of Madame de Pompadour, or some exposed intrigues, yet the appearance of Beaumarchais, his good fortune and talent, were as strange as they were indispensable. Success in gaining the royal favor was the standard of merit, and every one ran after Caron.

In those days ideas of conduct consisted in the most rigorous formality—a sort of Spanish ceremonial gravity; language was robbed of its directness and power, confused by metaphor and silly notions of euphony, and always expected to convey some sentiment of love, attempting what is simple and natural in manner, but in reality affected and absurd. All this, however, prevented none from finding pleasure in questionable plottings, gambling, and revelry. Even the Marchioness de Pompadour, who had built the "Parc aux Cerfs" for her royal lover, was exceedingly careful of outward behavior and etiquette, and could render an orgy apparently respectable, reminding one of pagan times.

None conducted himself with so much truthfulness and grace, or with so much self-possession, as Beaumarchais, while he had at the same time ample opportunity for the enjoyment of his irony. Because all others could only move in certain forms of etiquette, they were the more surprised at the freedom of his speech and actions, while he never exposed himself to attack, by needlessly hurting any one's feelings, and never failed in any respect from ignorance. To complete his triumph, Duverney called on the afternoon of the audience-day, handing to Caron the documents, a check from Terray for five hundred thousand francs on the treasury, as well as a contract of partnership. It was also known that the Duke de St. Albin had banished La Blache from Paris for an indefinite time, and that the latter had been seen to leave in a travelling-carriage, accompanied by a pious Jesuit father. The Marchioness de Ventadour now seldom showed herself in public at Versailles, and Maupeau and Terray took every opportunity to prove their devotion to the princesses. Certain secret influences ceased, and the astonished courtiers began to perceive that the citizen Beaumarchais could not be put down easily or with impunity. They considered him very different from the rest of his rank, called him

M. Caron de Beaumarchais, and were desirous of demonstrating that he was the descendant of an ancient family forgotten in the obscurity of the Middle Ages. It was not considered proper to acknowledge so brilliant a representative of plebeians.

It followed, as a matter of course, that, in the eyes of Piron, Turgot, and Malesherbes, Caron gained in importance, and that Batyl, who had lost the patronage of La Blache, endeavored to banish every suspicion of Beaumarchais, and exerted himself to be successful in his instruction on the harp. Caron was so industrious that he was soon considered a master, and could really give lessons on that instrument to his illustrious pupils. He also devoted himself with zeal and remarkable good fortune to financial matters, in which he was the apt scholar of Duverney. He was one of those geniuses who refine every thing they touch, who always know how to improve the right opportunity, and, as if by intuition, avoid that which has become dangerous, or at least useless. He entered into extensive speculations; and as no one, except those interested, knew that he was half a millionnaire by means of an unknown mother-in-law, his bold investments and success caused the greatest astonishment. He became famous as a business man, and made many secret enemies among the nobility, the officials and moneyed men of the Rue Quincampoix. He was, in the mean time, the confessed favorite of the princesses and of Conti, and it was well known that he was also received by the dauphin and the queen.

Paris Duverney was a man of honor; he abandoned his aristocratic relatives, felt heartily attached to Caron, and devoted his time partly to charitable purposes in the construction of buildings, and partly to the charming little circle in the left wing of the Hôtel Piron, where Madame Susie, in her peculiar costume, ruled and gained all hearts.

Those hours were never to be forgotten which were spent in the bright apartments, upon the fragrant terraces, and in the vine-arbors of Beaumarchais. —Here were united cheerfulness and freedom, simplicity and high intelligence, where assembled Piron and his wife, Turgot, Duverney, Aumont, Morelly, Malesherbes, Marmontel, Caron, Susanna, and even old Beaumarchais.

Caron, when he found himself in good circumstances, could no longer live estranged from his father, who at last felt the loss of his son grievously, the more so since the latter had become a person of wealth and consequence. He had five daughters, of whom the eldest, Florine, had married Gilbert, a French merchant living in Madrid, and taken one of her sisters, Marie, to live with her; but both had been so long in Spain that they hardly knew their brother. The three younger, however, loved him dearly; and the less indulgence was shown toward Caron the more troubled were his sisters, and the more unhappy the relation between father and daughters, so that many sad scenes darkened the old watchmaker's days. Slowly but deeply came this regret, and his longing for his son rendered him more morose and whimsical. He struggled to resist the idea of having committed any wrong concerning Caron. His pride, his notions of paternal dignity that he could never err in reference to his child, prevented him from taking the first step toward a reconciliation, especially now that his "son had become a great man at court, and did not care for his father."

One day, to the no small surprise of the old gentleman, as well as of his daughters, an equipage stopped at the door. Caron and Susanna entered the store, kissed their father's hand, and asked him if he was still angry. As with most rough and obstinate characters, this unexpected visit operated so wonderfully that the old paternal feeling long suppressed broke through all restraint, and his desire for the love of his son became irresistible. Papa Beaumarchais now never passed an evening in which he did not go to the Hôtel Piron, either alone or with his daughters Margot, Claire, and Jeanne, to sun himself in Caron's happiness, listen to the conversation of intellectual men, or entertain Susanna, whom he seemed especially to have taken to his heart. It was amusing to witness his attempts to excuse his former cruelty and supposed paternal right. He would say, whenever there was any occasion: " Yes, indeed, children, you always considered me cruel—a very barbarian; but would Caron and Susie have become what they are, if, as a wise father, I had not sent them to a school of sorrow? There you learned to love each other, and to work for your living; there you became prudent! Oh, yes, I knew what I was about; I was aware that an experience of suffering makes the man!" Though those interested did not perhaps feel the truth of this, so far as his conduct was concerned, they jestingly assented, as well as their friends, and permitted the good man to enjoy an illusion necessary to his self-esteem and happiness.

Beaumarchais had not such success in the secret political mission in which the princesses employed him. Part of it he managed with surprising celerity, for he destroyed the alliance of the Jesuits with the ruling mistress (Madame de Pompadour) and her party, whose object was to abolish the influence and position of the king's daughters, to estrange altogether the already-separated royal family, and to cover up in forgetfulness Damien's attempt. Caron, as a professor of music, had the entrée, notwithstanding the court spies of Ver-

sailles, at the residences of the queen, the dauphin, Conti, the most powerful parliamentary members, the families of Richelieu, Machault, Noailles, and Luynes, and knew how to make use of all means in instituting a closer alliance among the different members of the royal house. But the power of Beaumarchais seemed to end there, and every step beyond, which the princesses expected from him (particularly as to the fall of Madame de Pompadour), by degrees made him certain that all such interference would only increase the common misery, at the expense of his own sacrifice. The signs of the new times, though still apparently unimportant, increased, and the hopes of Caron, Morelly, and their friends, were turned to higher subjects than cabinet intrigues.

It was toward the end of 1760 that Beaumarchais finally and irrevocably came to that conclusion. The long and wearisome attempt to withdraw Choiseul, the minister of war, from the interests of the Marchioness de Pompadour, was completely frustrated about this time, and the mode of operation had to be changed, if the princesses and their party did not wish to leave themselves in some respects exposed. The younger members of the royal family, therefore, desired a secret meeting. Every thing was arranged in such a manner by Piron and Caron that no suspicion was excited at Versailles of this family council.

The autumn was already tingeing the foliage of the vine, when the Chevalier de Piron, with the princesses, accompanied only by two confidential ladies-in-waiting and Count d'Aumont, drove from Versailles, their winter residence, to St. Cyr, pretending that they wished to devote a few days to the inspection of this celebrated establishment. Beaumarchais, who was freed from official service for the present, left Susanna under the protection of his family and Madame de Piron, and persuaded Turgot, Malesherbes, and even Morelly, to an excursion to Saint-Cloud, Vaucresson, and Roquencourt. They passed the Barrière Vaugirard in a hired carriage. They did not stay long in Saint-Cloud; for Morelly disliked the palaces, and the artificial forms of the trees, and longed to go farther into a freer nature, where he could find simpler people, and pastoral peace. They soon reached Roquencourt, but the vicinity of Versailles, the high-road leading in a southerly direction from Marly to Maulle, thence to Evreux and Conches, deprived the village of all prospect of a retired and quiet sojourn.

As it was still early, Caron proposed that they go a little farther, to Bailly, and, leaving the public road, remain over night at Rennemoulin, a solitary hamlet on the declivity of the mountains reaching from Marly. They could return on the following day through the valley and Versailles, or by way of the lovely Arcis. Arrived at the inn, they were rather tired, and soon slept, except Turgot, who remained up an hour contemplating the heavens. The materialist became a poet in the presence of infinite space, with its innumerable suns.

It is conceded that no other capital possesses such charming landscapes in its environs as Paris—with their parks, chateaux, hills, forests, and waters. The Vale of Arcis is beautiful because it has been preserved from unnatural cultivation, the glaring buildings of the wealthy, and public intercourse. On the north it has the heights of Marly; on the east the Park of Versailles; the summits of the Arcis Mountains tower toward the south, and gently slope to the plains of the west. Louis XIV., a sovereign of taste, had preserved this neighborhood from the ravages of art. When Le Notre had displayed his genius at Versailles, he left the vale untouched, so that it remained as Nature made it, with its wooded heights and flowery plains. The king enclosed it within the circle of his possessions, but would not suffer any thing there that could remind the beholder of the refinements of cultivation. The contrast of the architecture of Versailles with this natural landscape made a very pleasant impression on every mind.

The friends sat for some time after breakfast, the following morning, in silent delight, at the beauty and prodigality of Nature, never wearied of conferring benefits on mankind. "If I were a hermit," finally began Morelly, "a real professional one, I would build my hut here, that I might die in view of this landscape."

"And why not live here, peacefully, like a philosopher, a free man among free men?" asked Malesherbes.

"Among free men? That will scarcely be in our day?" said Turgot.

"And the happiness of the philosopher is also not certain! To be wise is to feel that all that is earthly is transient, and to experience misfortune is to become wise. The progress of human well-being is slow. Even a divine idea needs centuries to bear all its fruits among men. Can a philosopher, therefore, be happy? Never, or he must have no heart, and, in his own enjoyment, hear not the groaning world around him. This landscape is indeed beautiful; and perhaps yonder, in that little cluster of cottages, there may be a paradise, where all hopes are realized, and where great and sacred principles may be venerated, such as might practically rule and bless all mankind.

"And how different is the impression of Nature from that of the pompous fashions of man!" said Malesherbes, in a melancholy voice. "Nay, how different from that of the condition of the people that call themselves children of the soil! Those charming hamlets conceal ignorance and misery; and the blooming fields, on which twice as many persons could live, are robbed by the covetousness of officials, by devouring tax-gatherers, paralyzing both energy and contentment. The people are dying beneath the yoke of slavery, and are little better than the brutes; in some respects worse, for they are conscious of their shame."

"To reconcile them to it," said Morelly—"to prevent them from murmuring against this earthly slavery, by promising them heaven—is the business of priests calling themselves servants of Christ!"

"But when the consolation ceases to have its effect, and long-suffering is at an end," exclaimed Turgot, sarcastically—"when the deluded understanding of the century begins to think and demands its right—when the day-laborers, beggars, and serfs, remember that there, to the left of us, at Versailles, lies the origin of all their sufferings, where unchaste women squander what is obtained by the sweat of honest brows—that yonder, in Marly, the nobles in their hunts destroy whole fields, and that before the eyes of the oppressed stand the columns of a proud palace whose master has absolute power,—when they come to think of these things, there will be a prospect of dangerous discontent and a new order of affairs!"

"Let us not think of them now," said Beaumarchais, "let us not attempt to anticipate! It is the duty of all real friends of their country to prevent social agitation. The chains of an oppressed people should be broken only when they are worthy of freedom—when they can bear it without licentiousness. Is not that the better idea, Father Morelly?"

"If it were only true! Yonder paradise seems suitable for one to make a trial. I should like to know to whom it belongs."

"That is what I am endeavoring to recollect. In this vicinity ought to be Trianon, the villa of the dauphin. I see no other edifice which better corresponds to my idea of it!"

"Just like us!" and Turgot laughed. "We are natives of Paris, and know so little of its environs! The side toward Versailles, however, is not the one the heart of a patriot would care to explore."

"To decide the question, particularly as the villa is so near," said Caron, smilingly, "let us visit the proprietor, and ask him whether he would not like to give his subjects a good education, and see for himself if it would be of service to them."

"That would be realizing Utopia in a very naïve manner!" laughed Morelly, "Caron certainly does not lack courage. How confidently he turns to the field-path where that horseman is, as if he supposed we should receive an invitation!"

"I rather think we would be enlightened in our reforms by means of foresters and bull-dogs," replied Turgot.

"If that is Trianon, we need not fear such treatment," said Malesherbes, "for the dauphin is civil; but that he would shrug his shoulders and laugh at us, is certain."

"But suppose I insist on my plan, and show you how you are mistaken?—That is Trianon. On the heights, the pavilion with the cupola is Little Trianon, and the dauphin—expects us!"

"The dauphin!" exclaimed Malesherbes.

"Expects us?" asked Morelly.

"Beaumarchais, do not indulge in a bad jest!" exclaimed Turgot.

"I can only repeat that the prince is waiting for us," replied Caron; "he ordered me to bring you to Trianon, and without making any stir about it.

That is the object of our excursion. You will find the princesses and Piron, and I believe yonder rider is M. d'Aumont, in citizen's clothes, probably intending to meet us. Versailles is near; therefore, prudence!—you understand!"

"Caron, I pray you," said Turgot, "what made the dauphin think of us?"

"For myself," said Morelly in excitement, "I am a plain old fellow; he cannot desire to see me!"

"My dear friends, do you remember, at our farewell banquet in the Pigeonnier, that I remarked you would have need of me? I am no philosopher, no economist; I cannot control great influences to restore the state; but I can open the door to the highest places for physicians, men of honor and truth. Do you now comprehend? The dauphin is pious, simple, of strict morality and beneficent heart; the people know this, and call him the 'Desired.' Some say he is Jesuit; but Piron, myself, and a few other intimates, know that he has a magnanimous mind, secretly glowing with hopes for a renewed and better condition of the people. Since the attempt at the king's assassination, priestly prejudice has no more power over him. For us he is really the 'Desired,' to whom we wish nothing but long life!"

The friends of Beaumarchais were much moved: "And what does he know about us?" asked Malesherbes.

"I gave him your memorials and a copy of the *Basiliade*, and he said to me: 'If these men are really such as their writings indicate, I must make their personal acquaintance.' But, truly, there is D'Aumont—I was not deceived. Let us meet him."

"I never could have expected this!" exclaimed Turgot.

"It would be surprising if all the storms threatening our political hori-

zon were suddenly dissipated. How much the nation would owe you!" Malesherbes seized the hand of Beaumarchais.

"He is the son of my heart, who will never disgrace me," whispered Morelly. "Well, then, let us go. The future monarch must take us as he finds us." They descended the declivity, at the foot of which they met the jovial D'Aumont. After a short greeting, Caron and the captain spoke a few works in a low voice, when the latter rode quickly away, the others following slowly on foot.

"Will not our coachman wonder we remain so long?" said Malesherbes.

"I told him to wait for us. We are financial directors, inspecting this region."

"You have exercised great prudence, even toward us!" said Turgot, smiling.

"Certainly; it is necessary that we should be cautious. I have now no more reason for secrecy, and you may estimate the value of an incognito. The princesses succeeded in escaping to Trianon only by pretending that they wished to visit St. Cyr. If in Versailles it were known that they are here, you would soon see the roads swarming with embroidered spies."

"Very possible!" replied Malesherbes. "We must therefore be very careful in making our appearance."

"We shall avoid the palace, and go up by the village. Piron will await us at the back of the park, and take us to Little Trianon, where we shall find their royal highnesses."

The party hastened their steps, in order to reach the cool banks of the Mauldré. The sun was oppressive, and they passed on in silence, each occupied with his own serious thoughts. When they stepped on the bridge, Caron said: "To elude suspicion, Morelly and myself will go in advance, but not so far that you lose sight of us. Besides, you cannot miss the road."

The friends separated as they walked in the shadows of the stately poplars, through which could be seen the palace with its shining colonnade, and high above all the kiosk. They felt grave, though an indefinable pleasure possessed their minds in view of hours that rarely return, and which the pride and sometimes the sadness of old age brings to the brooding memory.

Trianon! What a mournful yet sweet sound—a minor chord—in the drama of France! Trianon! the cradle and the grave of a century's hope—of a new epoch in history!

Little Trianon, built in the form of a Moorish temple, was nothing but a rotunda with three entrances. The kiosk was united with it by a short passage, the lower floor of which, lighted by four windows, formed a small drawing-room, from which a winding staircase led to the cupola, where was a perfect panorama for miles around. The rotunda itself contained four apartments, each having a different prospect, all opening on a court-yard surrounded by pillars, or rather a green-house, receiving light and warmth from above. In the centre of this temple, couches and chairs invited to rest and solitude.

In the flowery court, several persons of high rank were talking familiarly. They were the princesses Adelaide, Sophie, and Victorie, and the dauphiness, Maria Josepha, the daughter of Frederick Augustus III., King of Poland, a fair and charming woman of about twenty-four, of transparent complexion, and remarkable gentleness of manner, as if the result of sorrow. But she was not unhappy, for she loved her husband, and was undisturbed by the jealousies and cares incident to her rank. Her temperament was naturally melancholy, increased by her educa-

tion at the court of Dresden. While yet very young, she had experienced the consequences of the rule of Madame de Pompadour, in her grandfather's case, and had seen her family humiliated by the war of the Austrian succession and the complicated quarrels with Frederick II. She witnessed the same unhallowed authority in the demoralization of France, still more glaring and shameless. It was a great trial for her that her consort should be censured before the king and the nation, and that the abyss between father and son widened day by day. Her piety and honest German feeling made her a quiet housewife, realizing her happiness in her own family, and, in nervous sensitiveness, withdrawing from intimacy with the outer world. Holding her white hand in his, sat her husband, four years her senior, whose grave yet winning appearance impressed every one.

Monseigneur the dauphin was tall, and his movements graceful. A sallow complexion and deep-sunken eyes indicated some desease, that, notwithstanding the skill of physicians, did not appear to be relieved. The people loved him, and called him "*Le Désiré*," to whose throne they would carry their complaints, and by whose wise and beneficent reign they hoped to become prosperous and happy.

On this occasion no courtier, no troublesome lackey, no marshal, with his ceremonious constraint, was present. Two little boys were amusing themselves in plucking off the leaves and buds of the flowers to plant a miniature garden of their own; they were the eldest sons of the dauphin, the Duke de Bourbon, and his younger brother Berri, who afterward, as Louis XVI., was the last, before the revolution, to wear the crown of the Capets.

"From all appearance, my dear brother," said Adelaide, in reply to some remark, “our object has miscarried. Our royal mother can hope nothing from Choiseul, however friendly he may appear; it is either cunning or embarrassment that makes him delay a decision.”

“He will persist,” said the dauphin, “even against the marchioness, until the German war is over. He will not be in earnest with our royal mother until Madame de Pompadour is about to disappoint his hopes, arising from the unfortunate alliance between Austria and France—nay, perhaps not until he is near his fall. You must never believe a slanderer.”

“And how can a discredited minister assist us against a woman who has undisputed sway over the king?” sighed the dauphiness.

“It is said that Choiseul has become more popular with the nation and the Parliament since his disagreement with the marchioness,” said Sophie.

“He has gained but little,” replied monseigneur, “if Frederick II. obtain such another important victory over us. A minister of war is always needing money, and the Parliament detests that; besides, as I infer from our cousin Conti’s observations, Choiseul relies on a very different support to keep him in his position—the secret assistance of our old foe, our cousin of Orleans. He holds the peerage in his hand, coquets with the dogmas of the philosophers, and empty Jansenism, and will devote himself to any party that will serve the ambition of his house.”

“And this unhappy, inimical family,” exclaimed Maria Josepha, “are associated with the Bourbons to their detriment; our children will have to combat their pernicious influences, as we are doing, and as our ancestors did.”

“If our children have the energy of Louis XIV., and the sense of their father, to foresee the convulsions of the times, they will not have much to do,” replied the dauphin. “We must, in the mean time, bear the misery of these days, until the decree of Nature puts an end to it—I see that well enough. However, Henry and Louis, Xavier and Charles, shall see better times, if God give me strength, as I hope He will. Every family causes its own ruin; passion and its weaknesses are universal enemies. Perhaps Providence permitted us to live through so much shame and affliction, that we may root up from among us those worst foes of monarchs!” He looked at the innocent boys with profound emotion; all eyes turned in the same direction. He felt as a father who lives but for the future of his children; and the princesses, as members of a family relying on a younger generation —on two children playing with the flowers, that withered as soon as planted.

“May Heaven graciously grant it! What parents can do, if they live long enough, that—” the lady looked fervently at her husband. Something like terror lay in her glance. A slight noise aroused them from their musings. Count de Mouy opened the side-door, and the dauphin beckoned to him.

“Well, my dear count?”

“Beaumarchais has arrived from Paris. The three gentlemen monseigneur wished to see are with him.”

“I hope all has been done quietly!”

“Certainly, monseigneur. Caron merely asked his companions to make a little excursion into the country with him. He did not acquaint them with his object until they left Rennemoulin on foot. If your enemies know any thing about it at Versailles, they must deal in secrecy.”

“Will it not be necessary first to see the professor alone, my brother?” whispered Adelaide.

“Call Beaumarchais, count, and let

the others take a collation in the Swiss house; the morning is warm. Let Prandin wait on them, he is reliable." Mouy hastened away; and Caron, who was waiting in the anteroom, appeared.

"Well, my brave fellow," smiled the dauphin, "do you bring us bad news and a welcome visitor?"

"I fear the former, but to find the other true, would make me very happy, monseigneur. Will you please hear what I wish to say?"

"Speak without ceremony."

"Choiseul's advances were mere feints, and her majesty the queen must not allow herself to be deceived any longer. His royal highness the Prince de Conti has probably already explained that Orleans and Choiseul have formed an alliance. Of course, it is a union of two persons, where each will endeavor to dupe the other."

"Very possible!" jeered the dauphin. "But in what manner does Choiseul intend to delude Orleans?"

"Exactly as he acted with her majesty. His object is to become prime minister, and govern France. Even should the marchioness fall from her position or die, he will find means to retain his place. He has a very handsome sister!" A cry of indignation followed.

"The Duchess Beatrice de Grammont?" asked Maria Josepha, in surprise.

"How did you obtain that information?"

"Your royal highnesses are aware of the intimate relations sustained by Madame de Pompadour with Terray, Silhouet, and Maupeau. My partner Paris Duverney has great influence on Terray, and as the abbé would like to deprive M. de Silhouet of any share in the financial department, and Maupeau makes pretensions to the premiership, all were not a little terrified when one day Choiseul managed to present his sister to the king. Madame de Grammont made a deep impression, and the Marchioness de Pompadour became very anxious about herself. This was the real cause of her disagreement with Choiseul, who is always frightening her with his sister. But the marchioness knew how to regain her empire, and the game will end in the displacement of one or the other, or, perhaps, with a reconciliation. What can her majesty expect?"

"And is there no hope that the king will finally become disgusted with his own conduct?" The dauphin rose: "Your opinion is, that one mistress removed will only make way for another; that neither age nor satiety will cure the king—"

"Nothing but death can do that!" interrupted Beaumarchais. "It is a severe decision, monseigneur, but I vouch for its truth. And more, I aver that Madame de Pompadour, though she is cursed by the whole nation, is not the worst; that her successors will surpass her in wastefulness and immorality, without possessing her shrewdness and refinement. Vice becomes grosser with age. It is sad that I must say so—that I must give expression to what you have long felt, but it must be said, that the situation may become clear. Orleans is speculating on this growing prodigality."

"How do you know that?"

"The duke is intimate with Mlle. Raucourt, the singer, whose husband Debrelon is in my power."

"And do you deny the possibility of any change for the better?" asked Adelaide, excitedly.

"Not exactly, your royal highness, for who can calculate the power of destiny or accident? We can only judge the future according to the past. The illustrious royal family must accustom themselves to expect no improvement during the king's life. All attempts to reason with him will only end in proving the folly of hope; there are too many foes of virtue, and his majesty stands at their head, even if only on account of his weakness."

"In the interim, time passes, the discontented become more clamorous, the condition of affairs more complicated. It is quite certain that North America will rebel against the mother country, and such examples are contagious! I should think we had enough of inflamable material as well as persons to make use of it."

"That is all true, monseigneur; we may believe we see great coming events very plainly, even if at a distance, and perhaps better than the next generation, though nearer to them. We should not forget that a calm precedes the tempest."

"But what do you mean by all this, Beaumarchais, what do you wish us to understand?"

"I mean to point out the only thing to which the nation yet may look forward—your government, you yourself, monseigneur! You are doubly the 'Desired,' you will be a father to the people, and educate your own son so as to make him wiser. Then all these troubles will not hurt us; Orleans will be powerless, and so will the example of a rebellious foreign land. You will prepare and grant those benefits of your own accord that other nations must obtain by bloody conflict." A pause ensued.

"And so you have again arrived at the *Basiliade*, my friend, have you?"

"I have not come to that, monseigneur, but to the certainty that you are not insensible to the spirit of Morelly, Turgot, and Malesherbes, because they are concerned with the future—men who are not solely occupied with ideas of destruction, and who would build up as well as destroy."　.

"You are right, and I thank you. Conduct the gentlemen into the blue-room." Beaumarchais withdrew.

"You see, my dears, how correctly I judged. Hope nothing from our father. It is disgraceful enough for a son to be obliged to confess that the death of his parent would be the greatest benefit of Providence! Wretched mother! It is a hard blow, let us hope it is the last! Courage, dearest Josepha! Let us place all faith in ourselves and our children, and in the Great Father above, who never deceives." He pressed young Bourbon to his heart, raised little Berri in his arms and kissed him. "For you, for you!" he murmured, leading them back to their amusements. "Let us shake off the old world, before we are buried in its ruins. I will try the new one those men are attempting to construct." He left the rotunda.

In the mean while Caron, Mouy, and Aumont conducted the three visitors into the blue-room, and all awaited in excitement an audience as unusual as it was dangerous. The door of the adjoining study opened, and the dauphin entered with a friendly greeting. "As this first meeting must naturally be unceremonious, let us dispense with formal presentation. If I am not greatly mistaken, this venerable gentleman is the author of the *Basiliade*, our modern Plato, but who has the advantage of founding his state upon the truths of Christianity. Am I right?"

"Yes, monseigneur," replied Morelly, "I wrote the work to which you refer, and the Book of Laws."

"Are you an abbé?"

"No, monseigneur. I have taken orders, but have not, however, received any other position than that of teacher at St Lazare."

"Your superiors did wrong. A man of your talent would have suited better the pulpit, the academy, or the lecture-room of the Sorbonne."

"I do not think so, your royal highness. I have all I deserve. 'Suffer little children to come unto me, for of such is the kingdom of heaven!' And I have entered, I trust, this heavenly kingdom."

"I should think your work must have procured for you many admirers and patrons. But I am afraid, while you were thinking how to render the human race happy, you yourself have gained nothing."

"Oh no, monseigneur! Others in my place would probably consider themselves poor, for I possess none of what are called the luxuries or even conveniences of life. But I have a garment to clothe me, though it may not be new, and a dwelling, though a very humble one. I have always had enough to eat, and never wanted books or paper. Your royal highness asks after my patrons? I published both my works anonymously."

"Are you not known there in Paris? Are not your colleagues, the philosophers, aware of your ability?"

"They are acquainted with my books," smiled Morelly, "but not my person. The reason is, that I do not wish to belong to their circle. What am I to do there? Those people expatiate upon what ought not to be, or what must necessarily decay. Or they arm themselves offensively, and use their energies only in attack. Shall I increase their number? And that for the sake of my own profit? Their dogmas are not mine, and yet I am as little inclined to assail any new truth really discovered by them, as to give up, so near the grave, the happy dreams in which I have grown old."

"Do you consider yourself a dreamer?" said the dauphin, jestingly. "That is at least a frank confession!"

"Indeed, monseigneur, I hope you do not consider me in any other light. Can a man in our day have become old without considering my work a dream?"

"I am glad you judge of yourself in that way, as it will be easier for us to come to an understanding on many things. But suppose your ideas contain errors?"

"Then the fault lies in my weak perception, your royal highness. I may yet have too many prejudices, and be too narrow-minded; I may belong too much to the old times, to have a clear insight as to what is practicable in these days. I will sacrifice all my errors to you, but not my dreams."

"You are an extraordinary man!" exclaimed the dauphin. "But if you are aware that the *Basiliade* is a mere poem of a paradise on earth, and you admit that it may contain errors, why do you believe in it with an almost religious fervor? Suppose I ask you how you would at present realize your fancies?"

"I answer, your royal highness, that I could not realize them. Why do I believe in them? Because they are founded on the enduring precepts of Christ, on true conceptions of humanity, on the simplest laws of fraternity and equality, on the consciousness of our common descent, and that redemption for which He died. I believe that, by and by, a purified and developed human race will establish that which now I only imagine. Some errors may be personally mine, but the truths I anticipate will stand. I consider what I have published as involving the best and final destiny of our race, from which the Middle Ages deviated. Ah, a deep longing is felt in the generation of the present day to return to those old paths! From this feeling originate indeed the bold and too often bitter thoughts of our philosophers; but we must not therefore quite despise them. From a yearning for the good came my poem, and yet the same feeling may also produce passions demoralizing and destroying all. Oh that some monarch with a great heart arose, who would guide the world gently back to the almost forgotten period of Christian faith and love—one who would imperceptibly loosen the chains, and take France painlessly over the hazards of the age! I stand before you, monseigneur; shall I say you alone can do this?"

The dauphin laid his hand on the old man's shoulder. "I would do all this, Morelly. *You* may think, but *I*, even when a king, can only act within the limits of the possible. What is the possible?"

"You must not ask me that, your royal highness; my only worth is in the truth and perspicuity of my ideas. My friends Turgot and Malesherbes can answer you much better than I. But one thing I can say. As we were coming hither, and beheld with glad eyes the smiling village of Trianon, an Eden in itself, my poem occurred to me. No man can render the universe happy; he would find it difficult even to become the benefactor of a nation, but to bless a village is a task not so difficult."

"You think we might make a trial with Trianon?" The dauphin mused a few moments, and then said, "this is not our last meeting, Morelly! Well, let realities take the place of fancies." He approached Turgot and Malesherbes. I have seen your memorials, gentlemen. I am greatly pleased with them; you may dedicate them to me when you publish them. What do you propose, in order to make a beginning in the improvement of the people? Speak in plain terms."

"That unequal taxation may cease," replied Turgot, "and the corruption associated with it of farming the taxes—that the pressure of serfdom and feudal ascendency be first diminished and then wholly abolished, and that work be provided for the people by manufacturing and agricultural industry,—these reforms will become sources of wealth and contentment. Men deteriorate when they are idle, and still more so when they are egotistic; but if their attention is turned to the noblest ambition, that of education and a freer enjoyment of life, then much evil will be destroyed by the root. We must begin where Colbert left off."

"But to render this mental culture possible," continued Malesherbes, "the Board of Censure must be abolished, your royal highness. No evil is prevented by that inquisition; for the most immoral writings creep anonymously into the hands of readers, and much that is good is suppressed. Even when errors arise in literature, they are refuted by means of the same liberty that gave them utterance; and for a public criminal, let a public court be established. Schools and churches should be a serious consideration of the state, and the rich livings dispensed with in favor of the lower clergy. We must reawaken the Estates-General, that they may take part in the national regeneration and hear the wishes of the people. The nobility must be gained over by honorable positions; the citizens, by rewards and various advantages. Believe me, monseigneur, a renewed life and prosperity will bless the country, and the troubles that have accumulated since the days of Madame de Maintenon will disappear."

"Do you honestly think all this practicable?"

"Under your firm government, yes, monseigneur!" exclaimed Malesherbes.

"Gentlemen, be assured, that if I—ever become king," and the prince's frame trembled, "all this shall be done. May God grant that it be not too late!"

"It is never too late to do good,

your royal highness!" said Turgot, enthusiastically.

"Let that be our consolation, gentlemen. I wish you in the mean time to gather experience and make preparation. I will procure you opportunities to gain a deeper insight into abuses, and to make recruits for our future purposes. The people call me by a happy name. My heart bleeds that they have occasion thus to designate me, but Heaven is my witness that they shall not be deceived in me. I do not say farewell!" He saluted them in great emotion and withdrew, followed by Count de Mouy.

Morelly, Turgot, and Malesherbes, pressed each other's hands in delight. "Well," smiled Beaumarchais, "I do not think we need longer be ashamed of the garret in the Pigeonnier."

"If we ever felt so, Caron, it is time to repent of it."

"The day on which this prince ascends the throne will be a day of jubilee," whispered Lamoignon.

Count D'Aumont entered. He had received orders to show them Trianon, and attend to their convenience and amusement. The dauphin intended to present them to his family in the evening.

The sun was setting. A day had passed whose results were expected with anxiety. The friends, guided by D'Aumont, had wandered upon the hills, through the gardens and forests, and the little village. Everywhere they observed signs of industry, good feeling, and appreciation of refinement. Great Trianon, however, was avoided, to escape the curious eyes of the courtiers, who had followed the dauphin in that direction—a retinue that always had a double object. The visitors were descending from the mountain ruin to the garden of Little Trianon, where the roses and the lilies bloomed side by side. On the right was a Swiss hut, concealed by maples and oaks, and on the left, a grotto, surrounded by elms and chestnut-trees, near which was a marble fountain with its shells and Nereids. In this place, to enjoy a rural repast, were assembled the family of the dauphin, as well as his sisters, attended only by Piron, Mouy, D'Aumont, and Saubret, the old forest-keeper of the prince. When Caron and his companions appeared, monseigneur slowly went to meet them.

"Well, how have you amused yourselves, gentlemen? I hope the count treated you with all politeness."

"Yes, your royal highness," replied Lamoignon, "we have passed the day in continual enjoyment."

"I am sorry I could not share it. But our circumstances require caution, and I wished leisure to consider our conversation of this morning. Did not some of your paradisiacal illusions, encouraged perhaps by the distant heights at Marly, vanish on a nearer approach, Father Morelly? One of our new philosophers, I think Voltaire, says, that heaven appears beautiful only because it is so remote; and that if we chance to get there we shall find it to be an infinite nothing—its charm is its unattainableness."

"That is a very skeptical remark," said the old man. "I will credit it when Voltaire sends me a confirmation from beyond the grave. But I am always willing to believe that whatever heaven we have here is nothing, if I am only clearly informed of the other. In most cases it happens that the prevailing philosophy knows little of either; religion satisfies me best. Men are of the earth, and very apt to bring their modes of measurement to judge of spiritual things. Our outward organs cannot apprehend what does not belong to their sphere. It is not half so absurd for a ploughboy to pass sentence about a ship, or a blockhead about a work of art. We should presume to give positive verdicts only on matters with which we are familiar, and even then with caution and modesty; for we have not reached the limit of even this sort of worldly knowledge, and, by further discovery, what we now believe true may be false.—But this is really an Eden; I find it more beautiful than I had imagined. You have rendered our parting very sad, monseigneur."

"But, according to your philosophy, you do not consider it completed."

"Heaven itself is not completed. We shall still progress. God alone is perfect! His own creation is but a shadowy reflex, and, where art intervenes, it should be in reference to what we really know of Him, thus guiding our aspirations after the absolutely good and true."

"Just as Trianon develops the ideas of the *Basiliade?*"

"That would be too bold, your royal highness; it is not due to me or my poem."

"Advance, gentlemen. I wish to present you to my family." The dauphin led them to the front of the grotto, where the ladies were. "Here is Madame Josepha, my wife, the dauphiness; there are my amiable sisters, their highnesses, Adelaide, Sophie, and Victorie. I introduce to you, my dears, the poet and philosopher, Father Morelly, who will convince you that he is not poor. This is the secretary of the Chamber of Commerce, M. de Turgot; and this, Lamoignon de Malesherbes, president of the Chamber of Taxation. Come here, Bourbon and Berri." The little princes came running and took the dauphin's hand. "These are my hopes; I live only for them and France. Look at these men, my children; they are your father's friends. Remember their names. This gentleman is Turgot."

"Turgot," repeated young Bourbon. "Malesherbes and Morelly."

"Malesherbes and Morelly," exclaimed Bourbon. "Oh, I remember in my heart all whom you love, my father."

"Do you also, Berri? Never forget these names; you will need them, when I—am no more." He kissed his sons. Bourbon, a boy of precocious mind, approached and offered his hand to the visitors:

"I shall think of your names when I am a man, and then I will always ask you how it will be best for me to do what I desire."

Little Berri looked timidly at the strangers, and hastened to his mother. "Turgot, Malesherbes, Morelly. Do I know these names now?" He hid his face in her bosom.

This was a great moment. Tears were in the eyes of all present, and sad thoughts came with the rustling of the elms in the evening wind.

"Take part in our Platonic repast," said monseigneur. "A lucky leisure exempts us from etiquette to-day."

"Father Morelly," said Maria Josepha, "you must sit at my side. Our royal sisters will have Messrs. de Malesherbes and de Turgot near them."

The dauphiness entered into conversation with Morelly on the manner in which he thought the inhabitants of Trianon could be elevated to a condition of the greatest possible earthly happiness. The princesses received from Turgot and Malesherbes an analysis of the financial and productive affairs of the country. The dauphin listened first to one, then to the other, introduced remarks and questions, and thus began a general and eager interchange of sentiments on the highest objects of life.

"But our privileged classes, our barons and bishops," laughed monseigneur, "what will they say to the paradise of Trianon and the endangering of their interests?"

"Of course, they will make resistance," replied Turgot; "but the example of a king, the awakening of a noble ambition, the results of enterprise and emulation, will do much. Many prerogatives can be abolished; others, like those of rich convents, can be rendered harmless by enjoining on them new duties in the cause of education; of beneficence, in its numerous and varied practical forms; and of science, in its unexplored and boundless departments."

"And then, sire," exclaimed Malesherbes, "the gratitude of the nation—the ardent blessing of millions! Will not these carry before them the paltry minority in favor of exclusiveness, and force egotism from its limited circle, that, for the benefit of all, it may even do good to itself? Who, monseigneur, will long be able to bear the curse of being a tyrant among free men, and the only one that remains lingering in the rotten ruins of a nation? That a freer development originates from the head of the people—from its educated and best men—makes the change peaceable, and gives less occasion for passion. Suppose that some must suffer, there would still be a vast diminution in the number of those that are now oppressed. Can France ever be politically ennobled, if her social and civil life is not reorganized?"

"Should your reformation at first be regarded distrustfully, monseigneur," added Morelly, "the most difficult trial will be accomplished before any one is aware of it. This little Trianon will become a model. The dauphin of France is the lord and proprietor of it. Bondage is the condition to which the people are born, and in which they work in common according to their strength. When separate possessions, and the pride which a selfish independence awakens so easily, have become the fashion—in short, when the community are fifty years older, and have violently broken their chains, my ideas will not be realized. Other centuries must reduce them to practice, new suffering must buy the experience that a common virtuous fraternity alone satisfies the desire for happiness—a doctrine, I contend, that nature as well as religion implants within us and urges us to observe."

"I feel that you are right," exclaimed the dauphin, warmly. "If this task succeed, the most desirable that ever fell to the lot of monarchs, my sons and myself would be the happiest sovereigns on earth!—Messrs. Turgot and de Malesherbes, I confide to you these two letters for his royal highness the Prince de Conti, member of the Chamber of Peers. He is my confidential friend; present yourselves to him, and you will soon be installed in higher offices. Do not forget this day! I shall know how to have intercourse with you when I desire it."

. "And do not by any means fail to visit the Hôtel Bourbon," said Adelaide, bowing.

"But you must not forget our dear Trianon," said Josepha, with a smile. —"Father Morelly, monseigneur appoints you pastor of this parish, to succeed him who has recently died. I believe that is your proper place, where you may best speak to the hearts of those you wish to educate. I shall often be present with my children at your religious services."

"That is my secret wish!" said the old man, pressing his lips on the lady's hand.

Beaumarchais had carried a harp from the grotto, and, under an elm, was gently touching the strings. The dauphin motioned to him, and he sang the *Profond Amour*, a song he had lately composed for the dauphiness:

“ Im Herzen ruhen stumm und still
  Allmächtig grosse Triebe,
Wer sie in sich erwecken will,
  Braucht nichts als—tiefste Liebe!

“ Sie ist der hohe Gottesgeist,
  Der uns in's Herz geschrieben,
Was Alles rings um Leben heisst,
  Es ist ein tiefstes—Lieben.

“ O weisses, holdes Lilienbild,
  Der Opfer-Liebe Zeichen,
Auf meines Vaterlandes Schild,
  Sollst nur im Tod mir weichen!

“ In Deinem weissen Gotteskleid
  Magst ring sum Du erblüh en
Als siegreich duftig Diadem
  Des Fürsten Stirn umziehen.

“ Die Liebe ist ein Königsrecht!
  Die Lilie auf den Fahnen,
Soll einst ein besseres Geschlecht
  Den Weg zum Heil sich bahnen!

“ Im Herzen ruhen stumm und still
  Allmächtig grosse Triebe,
Wer sie in sich erwecken will
  Braucht nichts als—tiefste Liebe! ” *

Profond Amour! how often the emigrants sang it at a later period, on the Rhine, as an anti-Marseillaise! The trembling notes had not yet died away, when the princesses rose softly, took leave of their brother and his consort, and disappeared in the groves, accompanied by Piron and Aumont. They returned to St. Cyr, where the evening bells were ringing.

“ Farewell, gentlemen; may our next meeting be as fortunate!—Father Morelly, I expect to hear you next Sunday in my church; Beaumarchais will inform you of my arrangements. Farewell!” The prince gave his hand to all; then offered his arm to the dauphiness, who smilingly bowed. Count de Mouy took Bourbon by the hand, and the old forester carried the tired Berri in his arms.

Beaumarchais and his friends walked in the bright moonlight through the village down the hill to the vale, and up the heights of Marly. They were happy, for their minds were filled with ideas of the future reign of the “ Desired.”

---

* Deep in the heart's untroubled rest
    Great impulses may be;
  And he who would their might attest
    Needs but love's energy.

  That is the highest grace divine
    Breathed on us from above;
  What we call life is but a sign
    Of the profoundest love.

  O lily on my country's shield!
    Love's emblem there I see:
  To death alone shall memory yield
    My tender thoughts of thee.

  Sweet flower of the fountain, thou,
    Of Nature's crown the gem!
  What fairer symbol for the brow
    That wears a diadem?

  A race of better days our fear
    Shall turn to happiness;
  Love's bannered lily may he bear
    Whose right it is to bless!

  Deep in the heart's untroubled rest
    Great impulses may be;
  And he who would their might attest
    Needs but love's energy.

BOOK II

CHAPTER VII.

THE MARCHIONESS DE POMPADOUR.

THE beneficent effects of the day when a truly enlightened heir to a throne had formed an alliance with the quiet workers for a better period, were soon apparent. To the astonishment of his superiors, Morelly quitted the school of St. Lazare, as well as the garret in the Pigeonnier, in which no one but Batyl remained. The latter, probably from avarice, did not wish to change his residence, though Beaumarchais, true to his word, had procured him a place in the royal chapel. Whether it was that Morelly shared the views of Caron as to the instability of earthly prosperity, or that he could not surrender at once all regard for his old domicile, it is certain that he arranged with the porter that the garret must be still at his disposal, "so that," as he jestingly said, "he may have a lodging in Paris, as all great people had." Trianon, however, became his real residence, where in a short time he felt most at home.

Morelly's mild nature, like that of St. John, together with his practical effort to obtain first the earthly happiness of his congregation, well fitted him to be the pastor of the poor. He soon enjoyed, therefore, the love of all his parishioners. During the summer no Sunday passed that the pious dauphiness, with her two eldest sons, Bourbon and Berri (accompanied by some of her more confidential ladies, and sometimes even by monseigneur), did not attend the ministry of the venerable poet and philosopher. Not a week passed in which the dauphin did not admit Morelly to an audience at Little Trianon, or called on him. The seed sowed by the preacher bore good fruit. Always remembering the first disciples of Christ and presenting them as the noblest models of pure religion, he awakened his parishioners to a sense of dignity and fraternity; and as the land as well as the people belonged to monseigneur, who agreed with the pastor's opinions, and the laborers as yet knew nothing of either liberty or selfishness, it was easy to inculcate an equal distribution of labor and a common enjoyment of life, responding in some measure to the ideal of a community of goods, as described both in Morelly's *Basiliade* and Plato's *Republic*.

The dauphin and his consort were themselves surprised at the growth, the industry, the increased wealth of the little village, the flourishing schools, and the numerous manufactures. It was during this period that Henry de Bourbon, the eldest of the young princes, in his intercourse with

Morelly, whom he dearly loved, manifested his talents; and Louis de Berri, the second son, a quiet, docile child, laid the foundation of his preference for mechanics and the *bourgeois* arts of peace.

Turgot and Malesherbes, through the recommendations of the dauphin, became acquainted with the Prince de Conti, who influenced the Chamber of Peers and a large majority of the Parliament in opposition to his secret opponent Orleans. Malesherbes was appointed Parliamentary Councillor and Attorney of the Chamber of Peers; and Turgot, a year after, became Intendant of Limoges, a position, in which he succeeded, by his wonderful genius, in raising the poorest province of France to an unexpected prosperity. He became the idol of the Limogians, and produced a sensation among agriculturists and the world of officials; while Malesherbes gained new converts in the Parliament to his ideas of liberty, and prepared the way for reform in the management of the revenues of the country.

The family of the dauphin, his royal mother and sisters, were at this time, rejoicing in the birth of the Princess Elizabeth, monseigneur's youngest child. The old and failing house of Bourbon seemed to be strengthened by a new generation of nobler sentiment and more hopeful promise. Yet how short and futile was this anticipation! The dauphin's eldest son, the Duke de Bourbon, Morelly's beloved pupil, whose genius and temper justified the highest expectations, died of disease within three days.

"In this precocious boy," exclaimed the bereaved father, " we have lost the emulator of Henry IV.! Our hopes now rest on Berri, a good child, but destined to be an inactive and solitary dreamer. Which has lost the more, France or I?"

Since 1740 the public spirit had made giant strides. The suppressed Jansenism, raising its head since the conflict of the Parliaments with the clergy, especially the Jesuits, whose influence was diminishing, was greeted with sympathy by the people; and the *Encyclopédie*, to which the great reformers contributed, had taken such deep root in the heart of the nation that Pallissot's comedy, " The Philosophers," in which Diderot, D'Alembert, and Helvetius were ridiculed, raised a perfect storm of contempt. On one side was a last struggle between the Jansenists and Loyolaists, Parliament and clergy; on the other, slowly moved the nation, restless and excited. At Trianon industry and a strong hope in the future reigned among the people. At Versailles was the accustomed dissipation—the same old desire, by extravagance, sensuality, and intrigue, to maintain high position, and continue the usual corrupt style of living. The tempests of foreign war also assailed the foundering state. Notwithstanding the alliance between France and Austria, Frederick II. remained a victor. In America the indignation at the tyranny of Great Britain was becoming more intense, and a spirit of defiance prevailing against the power of George III., the slave of his mother, who was the mistress of the despicable Lord Bute. France began gradually to awake to the consciousness of its rights and the necessity of a free and equal government.

The relation between Beaumarchais and Paris Duverney, though entered into by the latter through fear and constraint, soon became hearty, and a confidence existed between them as sincere as between a father and his son. This resulted as much from Duverney's peculiar position as from his character.

Every one has heard of the five celebrated brothers of Paris, the wealthiest financiers of the time of our history, the favorites of the Marchioness de St. Prie and of the Duke de Bourbon, under the regency. These brothers merited the gratitude of their country for accomplishing the ruin of John Law, as well as its curses for their dangerous strategy in concealing the state bankruptcy and providing for the extravagance of Madame de St. Prie. Paris, surnamed Duverney, was the youngest of the five. He had some heart and conscience, and entered the business so young that he was not involved in the immorality of the higher financial gambling. During this part of their career, the Paris family were ennobled, and their only sister was married to the impoverished representative of the ancient house of La Blache, which, of course, cost them a vast amount of money. With the fall of Bourbon and the Marchioness de St. Prie, the brothers also lost influence and position. It was fortunate that they were so immensely wealthy. But they could not bear their deprivation of power: two of them died, the two eldest were exiled by Cardinal de Fleury, and Duverney alone was left in peace, because he was politically of little account. He became richer by inheriting from his brothers, but their misfortune made him more cautious. He had ambition, but it was different from that of his relatives. The government required money; stock-jobbing had become, since the time of the Scotch banker, a fashionable amusement of the nobles; Duverney could not dispense with them, nor they with him. He became associated with Maupeau and the Abbé Terray, the financial councillor, who was head of the Sorbonne and the ecclesiastical portion of the Parliament. Duverney was connected with the La Blaches through his sister; and later, with the St. Albins and Ventadours, by means of his nephew Falcoz—these

houses led the Molinist aristocratic party, and were intimate with the monks of St. Nicole, St. Sulpice, and the powerful Ursulines.

The elder Marchioness de Ventadour had been the first governess of Louis XV. during the regency, and at first obtained some influence over the dauphin and the princesses. She endeavored to bequeath her court favor to her daughter-in-law Diana, especially when the latter became a widow, still young and beautiful. But Madame de Pompadour, who had already enslaved the king, permitted no rival, and the Ventadours lost their authority, particularly as the dauphin entertained a hatred toward them from the time of the attempt at the king's life. The elder marchioness, it was said, died from vexation; Diana was supported by the Jesuits, and allied herself with Maupeau, and especially with Terray. The result of the latter connection was, that Duverney one day brought little Susanna, then a few weeks old, from the convent of the Ursulines to Passy, and henceforth had the whole coterie under his control.

Duverney was a good-natured man, but shrewd and attentive to his own interests; he was honest, complaisant, incapable of any baseness, and wise enough to keep aloof from all party disputes. His appearance was mild and melancholy, from the effects of a childless marriage, and the death of a beloved consort. The St. Albins and La Blaches had always treated his wife badly, and reminded him of his low origin. He detested Jesuitical cunning, and lived with his relatives on a footing not very agreeable, merely maintaining an appearance of friendship. The feeling he entertained toward them was not ameliorated by the thought that the dissipated Falcoz was his rich uncle's heir; but, as such was the case, Paris exerted himself to his utmost for La Blache, on account of the relationship existing between them. He did this with the reluctance of a man who is condemned to make a show of courtesy against his will.

The affair of Beaumarchais at the first audience of the princesses — the discovery of Susanna and her birth— was the turning-point in the banker's life. He shook off the yoke of his relatives, and even thanked Caron for having given him his liberty. Caron's talents, magnanimity, wonderfully good fortune, and Susanna's amiability, as well as the feeling that accidentally he knew of and assisted in the concealment of her unfortunate birth, united Duverney with almost paternal love to both. He was pleased with the mental freedom of their friends; and the ambition to stand well with the princesses, the dauphin, and Prince de Conti, made him a member of a party in opposition to that of the La Blaches and St. Albins. He paid homage to the rising sun.

Three years had passed since the partnership of Beaumarchais and Duverney, and they had great success in all their business operations. Caron owed the banker gratitude for many favors, and endeavored to repay them by obtaining for the latter the higher confidence of the royal ladies, and the goodwill of monseigneur. He did more. Duverney, in many respects a solitary man, receiving no company, and responsible to none for his actions, was, however, zealous in the welfare of several benevolent institutions of Paris, and the erection of the new buildings on the boulevards. This perhaps was to satisfy a noble desire, or to gain popularity, or he may have caught the reformatory spirit of his friends. The military school at the Champ de Mars, was especially the result of his beneficence and sagacity. The dauphin, Conti, and his friends, as well as Marshal de

Richelieu, appointed chief of the future institute, thought that such patriotism should be duly honored. But they could not influence the indolent king— not even Richelieu, the friend of his youth; for he was now no longer welcomed at Versailles, since the Duchess de Chateauroux had been forced to give way to the *bourgeoise* Madame d'Etioles (Pompadour). Beaumarchais at length induced the princesses, a few days before the dedication of the edifice, to apply to their royal father personally, and influence him to be present, taking that occasion to thank Duverney publicly. The king gave an embarrassed and undecided answer, and when they urged him more seriously, he begged them to wait until he had consulted with Maupeau. He retired for a few minutes to his cabinet, and then gave them his promise to comply with their wishes. "A favor, however," he added, smiling, "demands a return. I hear that for some time you have had in your service a professor of the harp whose talents are highly spoken of; is he not a partner of M. Paris?"

"Yes, your majesty, it is M. Beaumarchais; you were pleased to permit his appointment."

"Very well, we wish to hear him perform at Versailles — send him here immediately after the dedication; we are curious to see him."

"Your majesty's command shall be obeyed!" stammered Adelaide, and the princesses withdrew in great perplexity.

Evidently the king had not spoken with any of his ministers, but with Madame de Pompadour. The latter was prejudiced against Duverney, and consented only on condition of seeing Beaumarchais. This seemed very suspicious to their royal highnesses and their party. However great their confidence in Caron, they feared that he might lose his presence of mind while in the camp of the enemy, and injure some of their plans. But there was no escape, and Caron gave them the most tranquillizing assurances. They agreed that no one should know any thing about it until after the expedition to Versailles, when informed of what the marchioness desired of Beaumarchais; of course, Durverney heard nothing whatever of the affair.

The day for the opening of the military academy arrived. Richelieu, Duverney, the princesses, the dauphin and his consort, the ministers, Choiseul, the generals and officials, awaited the king. His majesty appeared surrounded \ by a dozen courtiers; he greeted the dauphin slightly, the rest in a more friendly mannner, and offered his hand to his daughters. The ceremony commenced. Richelieu presented the banker; and Louis XV., who could be very amiable when he chose, eulogized the founder in an extravagant manner. His majesty permitted Duverney to conduct him about the building and explain its plan, conversing familiarly with him. Before leaving the institute, at the end of the solemnity, the king remarked: "I forgot to request you to remind your partner, M. Beaumarchais, of our wishes. He is expected to-day at Versailles."

The uninitiated were astonished at this additional distinction of Caron; in an hour it was the topic of conversation in all the higher circles of Paris. The others, such as the dauphin and Conti, were alarmed, and the princesses saw, in this repetition of the king's desire, that something serious was intended in reference to their professor. At the same time, the report prevailed that the marchioness and Choiseul were reconciled, and the latter had been proposed for the premiership. Duverney, as much surprised as he was

before delighted, hastened to the Hôtel Piron to speak to his friend.

"You are to go to Versailles to Madame de Pompadour! The king reminded me in public of this request. What can they want of you? Your patrons are indeed greatly concerned."

"You see I am already in state costume; the harp is in my carriage, and in two minutes I shall be on my way. Monseigneur, the Prince de Conti, and their royal highnesses, need not be troubled; my honor and character vouch for my fidelity. You ask what they want of me? If they desire to learn any of our secrets, they will find me too cautious to reveal them; if they wish to gain me over, it will not take them long to discover that I am too independent, and devoted to my friends. I fear no other danger."

"But do you not know that Choiseul has become reconciled to the marchioness, and is already prime minister —the same man whom you so ardently endeavored to win for the queen's party?"

"That is truly very unfortunate, but I shall make my way out of this complication. We have no time now to talk. If you have more evil tidings, drive with me, and we can take counsel in the carriage."

"I have much to tell you; for, as usual, troubles do not come singly. Clouds are gathering at the same moment from every quarter."

"Then I will use you as my lightning-rod with Terray; therefore, accompany me. After the audience, let us dine together. I will only say good-by to Susanna." He left the apartment, returning speedily, and was soon on his way to Versailles. —"Well, what else, Papa Paris?"

"You are aware that Choiseul has made an alliance with Orleans, in order to gain a safe party in the Chamber of Peers—the party in opposition to Conti.

Orleans will be admitted to the marchioness, who will identify herself with his intrigues. If this combination is not threatening enough to your friends, it will yet be strengthened by other enemies."

"By whom ?"

"Your old foes, my dear relatives, are moving themselves against you. Diana de Ventadour is an intimate of the Orleans; the Sulpicians and Jesuits are regaining courage. Falcoz has returned and is reunited with his father-in-law, St. Albin, and his wife; the Duke de Penthièvre, an early friend of the king, has also made advances to Orleans, and there is some talk of a marriage between Mlle. Adelaide de Penthièvre and the Prince de Chartres, the son of Orleans. Is he not making preparations for a grand conflict ? "

"If they should succeed, our interests would be certainly endangered. However, I know his strategy, and can disappoint him and his party. Let me think a little." The carriage passed on over the high-road, and the royal palace drew nearer.—"Orleans is the leader, and will profit by every thing, if we do not boldly attack him ! "

"Very possible! But how will you do it ? He has the advantage of being the most unconscientious man living.— I hear a carriage behind us, Caron, rapidly overtaking us. It is Orleans himself ! "

"Really ! Let him pass us, and draw down the blinds." Scarcely was this done, when a state carriage, drawn by six dapple-gray horses, rolled by. On the panel was the crest with the oblique chevron.

"I am thoroughly alarmed, Caron; I would rather have dispensed with the presence of the king than—"

"We cannot help it now, my friend. You can do one thing, however. Go immediately to Terray and say to him: ' Some one desires that the Duke d'Or-leans should not be admitted to Versailles a second time, and that certain old conditions must be respected, or else—the publication of a history among the Ursulines.' You owe that to the princesses and the dauphin."

"Very well; where shall I meet you ?"

"At the 'Red Horse,' Madame Paulmier's, with whom his majesty himself formerly had a well-known adventure; she keeps a good table, they say.—Here we are! Adieu, papa !"

"Farewell, Caron ! I never prayed more heartily for your success than I do to-day."

"First go to Terray, and then continue your prayers; heaven will not run away." He sprang from the carriage, took his harp, and entered the gate.

In the rear of the palace of Versailles, the rotunda called *Œil de Bœuf*, shutting off the perspective of the castle, and projecting into the park, were the apartments of the Marchioness de Pompadour. She held in her chains the monarch, the court, and the kingdom; and, though a woman of low origin, obtained that in which Mesdames de Mailly and de Chateauroux, ladies of the highest nobility, failed — an obeisance and outward respect from every one. Even Madame de Maintenon, who had been in fact married to Louis XIV., scarcely expected to be so distinguished.

The marchioness had at her command a graduated retinue of ladies, courtiers, lackeys, Swiss, and other guards, reaching from the chambers to the court-yards, making her as inaccessible as a reigning queen. It was permitted to dukes and princes only, to enter by the large portal to the royal audience-hall adjoining the apartments of the favorite. Simple noblemen and officials were obliged to be content with introductions by the side-doors in the wings. Commoners or citizens were conducted secretly through numerous passages and winding-stairs (as if the inhabitants of the palace were ashamed of them), and posted in some small cabinet, until called, like servants, by the tinkle of a bell.

When Beaumarchais announced himself to the officer on duty, he was disposed of as a commoner. The harp was carried by a footman, and Caron found himself in a closet-like room, opening into the toilet-chamber of Madame de Pompadour, and separated from this by heavy velvet portières. The boudoir was on the left of the marchioness's fairy-like chamber, where she received her confidants; sometimes, when she was in a very condescending mood, the ministers were also admitted to an interview there. This room, where her private audiences were held, was lighted by four windows and contained a magnificent silver toilet-table, covered with costly lace. In a bow-window was a desk; in each corner of the room a large Venetian mirror extending to the floor, and various small tables covered with books, pictures, and ornaments, ready to be rolled at convenience from one place to another. No tabouret or seat was seen, except the arm-chair of the marchioness, lined with sky-blue damask interspersed with golden lilies; the walls were decorated in the same style, with borders, festoons, and draperies of white lace. No one was permitted to sit in the presence of this lady. Sweet perfumes loaded the atmosphere; and from a bronze bowl near the hearth ascended the smoke of frankincense, ambergris, and fragrant essences.

The Marchioness de Pompadour, about forty years of age, was sitting or rather reclining in her chair, looking dreamily into the large mirror, and watching her maid, Madame de Hausset, who was putting the last touch to her mistress's head-dress of red roses.

The marchioness now and then exchanged a few words with Mesdames d'Hautecour and de Vilaille, or passed her hand over her white brocade dress. She was born to be a sultana. It would have been difficult to find a more lovely or captivating woman, with her rich light hair shining in gold dust. It is true she was beginning to lose some of her youthful charms. The freshness of her complexion had withered; the blush on her fair cheek was not natural; the blue veins ou her temples were prominent, and there was something hectic in her countenance; she often suffered from shortness of breath,—plain signs of a disease she endeavored to hide even from herself. Her arms and neck, which the fashion of the day uncovered, were as beautiful as ever, and the inevitable traces of age were carefully concealed by the arts of the toilet. She sought to supply what she had lost in physical attractions by dress, energy, and intellect.

"Then you think, Hautecour, that Choiseul urged me to grant an audience to the Duke d'Orleans, because the minister finds him useful in the Chamber of Peers, and hopes to succeed in the question against the Jesuits?"

"Certainly, gracious lady, and because he thus gains a means to render the most restless family (those standing nearest the throne) dependent and submissive, and to strengthen the royal party especially against the dauphin."

"But I do not like the business. The king entertains a silent but real dislike to all the Orleans. They are very wealthy; their object in attempting a reconciliation must therefore be some higher ambition. I shall be polite, but I must not concede any thing."

"It is said, madame," interrupted the Chevalière de Vilaille, "that the duke has equivocal designs, but is incapable of any serious intrigue on account of his frivolities—his gambling, and fashionable follies. His son Chartres has much more mind."

"Chartres? Nonsense, a boy of fifteen! Old Orleans had spirit enough to ally himself with the party opposing us in the Parliament; he has always avoided me either from the pride of a prince, or coquetry with the mob. All his actions indicate a premeditated plan."

"Perhaps a mere appearance of having some plan!" smiled Madame d'Hautecour. "He keeps aloof from the dauphin as well as the queen, and opposes Conti in the Parliament. His ambitiou consists in producing a sensation."

"That makes me only more suspicious. He may wish to establish a separate party—a sort of coalition, and speculate on the future," she sighed, "as others do. The question is, Which is more cunning, he or Choiseul?"

"I think the minister?"

"Very well, dear Vilaille, but Heaven forbid that M. de Choiseul should be too shrewd! The best thing is to balance one by the other." A slight knock was heard.

"It is Chevalier de Salvandy—let him enter." Madame d'Hautecour opened the door and the chamberlain of the marchioness entered.

"Their royal highnesses the Duke d'Orleans and Prince de Chartres."

"He has brought his son! That is either very prudent or very foolish! Has Beaumarchais arrived?"

"Not yet, it is not quite time."

"It is always time for a commoner. See to it that no one meets him. Repeat my orders to Binet that he is to take the professor of music up the back-stairs, and let the duke enter alone. You may talk any nonsense you please with young Chartres, and D'Atreuilles may assist you; it is always well to learn the character of the father through the son." She laughed,

and was about to raise her hand and dismiss the chevalier.

"One moment," whispered Madame de Vilaille; "does your grace bid us go or stay?"

"You will stay. Place yourselves so that you can observe Orleans without looking at him.—Admit his royal highness, chevalier."

The ladies had scarcely taken their positions near one of the mirrors, when the duke entered. His costume glittered in unusual luxury. He was scarcely forty, of good figure and graceful manner; his well-formed countenance bore an expression of deceit mingled with dissipation, and he only made himself more repulsive as he assumed an appearance of frankness and amiability.

"Allow me to salute you, my goddess!" he said, kissing the hand of the marchioness. "I hasten to offer you the homage that I have long silently felt for you."

"A very pretty compliment, your royal highness, but such speeches are made every day, and an intellectual prince like you ought to have presented something new. I am surprised that you bring your homage so late. Why not *sooner*, if you desired to come; and why *now*, if before you had reasons to keep at a distance? I like to know on what footing I am with my people."

The duke smiled, looked around and noticed that he was watched. "You are pleased to question me so closely, gracious lady, that I can only answer sincerely when we are *tête-à-tête*."

"That is not important enough for a private audience, your royal highness. Mesdames d'Hautecour and de Vilaille are my confidantes, who do not deserve your suspicion; besides, this interview must not be too secret, or it might be mistaken for a conspiracy; it certainly is not intended to have a political bearing."

"As you please, fair lady. The position of my family is independent; and, as we are so nearly related to the king, but have always been unjustly accused of an ambition that has never been proved—"

"Ah, your royal highness, am I to give you a list of all the intrigues against the Bourbons since the time of your ancestor Gaston?"

"Well, if all were made answerable for the sins of their ancestors, none would be either fish or flesh." *

"You are pleased to be witty, prince; but a person not having illustrious ancestors, and belonging to a lower race, is responsible for no one but himself. You were never friendly to his majesty in the Parliament."

"And his majesty was never friendly to me or mine. I was excluded from all participation in the government, and was therefore forced to seek it through my position as first peer."

"Which was made uncomfortable enough to you by Conti, Aiguillon, and Richelieu. Well, I will not dispute with you; I have still some feeling. I am, however, glad to see you, and to have received the assurance from M. de Choiseul, that in future you intend to use your influence in favor of the king's party. Since we appreciate your great gifts in the management of affairs, the step you have made to-day will probably be a pleasant surprise to his majesty."

"Ah, but will you resolve, madame," he smiled, "to meet the nation and the Parliament, whose voice has become so loud since the attempt of the assassin Damien?"

"One never meets the nation!"

"Ah, madame, but that does not prevent us from voluntarily acting in a manner to please it; you ought to spare the poor people some of your etiquette."

"In what way could this be done?"

"By repelling the Jesuits."

"Ah, that is plain speaking!"

"It would put an end to most of the difficulties between the Parliament and the clergy, and—"

"Philosophy would gain the day!"

"In order to deprive it of such a delusion, I propose the condemnation of this book in my hand. It is written by Rousseau, and entitled, *Emile*. It has just been issued, and openly prophesies a revolution."

"A revolution?" She seized the volume. "I will read it, and send it to Maupeau, the president of the Parliament. It is said that a blow aimed against the Jesuits will also strike the dauphin. He is a very—pious prince, a sort of secret miner, and, since the attempt on the king's life, maintains a very ambiguous position."

"That is true, and perhaps more complicated than you imagine. One thing is certain: he hates your politics as well as your person, Choiseul, and my humble self, because we do not love the Church. Besides he is busy about matters that agree neither with the Jesuits nor our policy."

"How so?"

"He sleeps with Locke under his pillow."

"Locke? You seem to know what passes in his chamber, monseigneur! Can he have joined the philosophers since 1757?"

"Not such as Raynal, Holbach, and Diderot. But it is said that strange actions take place at Trianon. At all events, we must fear that he will overthrow the old order of things. He is quiet, grave, pretends to patriarchal citizen virtue, and has a distinct object in view."

"And you think you have discovered all that?" said the marchioness, in

* "Ni de poisson ni de viande!" Madame de Pompadour's maiden name was Jeanne Poisson (Jane Fish),

some excitement. "Orleans, you knew of this long ago, and only come now—" She covered her face with her hand, and a feeling of terror took possession of her.

"Dearest lady, you are ill!—Permit me." He drew forth a small phial, and presented it to her.

She started, looked first at it and then at the duke. "I thank your royal highness, I have a preference in perfumes; those to which I am not accustomed might do me no good.—Epinay, give me my vinaigrette!" While the marchioness took it from her attendant, she looked at Orleans fixedly. He turned pale.

"I did not know," he said, in a wavering voice, "that your nerves were so delicate; however, as the attack has passed, allow me to tranquillize your mind, assuring you that we can settle with all our opponents at the right time. I hope you will consider me as having the best intentions. I am the most devoted servant of his majesty!" He kissed her hand.

"I thank your royal highness; I shall not forget one word of this conversation, and weigh it well."

"Then will you permit me to present you my son Chartres? He is a madcap, but ingenuous as Nature herself. He will be a good subject as soon as he has outlived the follies of youth."

"With great pleasure.—Will you ask M. de Chartres to enter, dear Vilaille?" The lady withdrew, but returned almost immediately.

On the threshold appeared a boy dressed in rose-colored satin, about fifteen years old, very much like Orleans, though handsomer and of brighter eyes.

"My son, the marchioness." Madame de Pompadour turned smilingly toward the new-comer.

Scarcely had the young man looked at her, than he threw himself at her feet, covering her hands with kisses. "Ah, how lovely, how angelic she is, papa! You are right—she is dangerous to young hearts."

"Why, my little fellow, you are very gallant for your age!" laughed the marchioness.

"Can I help myself, in your presence, gracious lady?"

"How dare you!" said Orleans, drawing the boy away. "You stand before the greatest woman in France! Pardon the 'good-for-nothing child, your grace!" begged the duke.

"Indeed," smiled the marchioness, half frightened, "the poor boy ought to associate more with ladies, so as to learn better manners.' Bring him again, he must become accustomed to me. — Adieu, dear duke." Orleans kissed her hand, Chartres bowed profoundly. While both were moving toward the door, Madame de Pompadour saw through a corner mirror that the father was staring at the son, and the latter making a grimace of disgust.

"One moment, duke." The marchioness rose and turned. "Prince de Chartres, I wish to say another word to you." Chartres hastened to her with a beaming face. "That is for your falsehood!" She gave him a box on the ear. "You will become the greatest knave of your house, and that is saying much. — M. d'Orleans, our accounts are settled; as long as I live, Versailles sees you no more; I am a little too old to take part in a comedy!"

"I shall act accordingly, madame." He took the young man's arm and drew him away. When they reached the carriage, the father lowered the blinds, and gave his hopeful son a slap on the other ear. "These two exclamation points, my friend, may tell you that you have compromised your father, and ruined your own prospects. I must take you from St. Sulpice, and send you to the Marchioness de Venta-dour; she will teach you something of self-possession and propriety. It is in my power to make a beggar of you, boy—to incarcerate you for life—yes, I will even do more than that, if you do not mend your manners!"

"I suppose you intend to let *me* smell your phial, that—"

"Silence, *she* did not smell it!"

"Now I comprehend both the blows given me!"

"I hope you also see that you have acted very stupidly. If you have not enough self-restraint to be prudent, you will never be worthy of the brilliant future for which I have educated you."

"Oh certainly, I was a fool. But I was so disgusted with her, I was obliged as soon as possible to give vent to my feeling."

"You must have aversion for noth-ing that may be useful to you. I will introduce you to some places in the Temple, that you may become accus-tomed to every thing. Unless you have strong nerves you will be ruined when the spirit of the age begins to dispose of the Bourbons."

While this remarkable paternal lec-ture was given by a prince of the royal blood to his only son, the marchioness paced the floor of her apartment in great excitement, disturbed by various senti-ments. She was half angry at being deceived and insulted, half satisfied that the son had so exposed the father. Experiencing a painful emotion hither-to unknown to her, she looked silent-ly at her perplexed ladies, and then laughed bitterly, murmuring execra-tions and fears. Her condition indi-cated mental anguish, that rendered her alarmingly nervous. Suddenly a noise in the adjoining room aroused her, and her frame seemed to be convulsed. —"Call Binet!"

Madame d'Hautecour hastened to summon the royal chamberlain. In the mean time the countenance of the mar-chioness expressed her gloomy resolu-tion.

Binet, an old confidant of the king's love-affairs, and first cousin to Madame de Pompadour, entered with his head bowed, accompanied by the lady of honor.

"Is Beaumarchais here?" whispered the marchioness, pointing to the por-tière.

"Certainly, madame, according to your orders."

"When did he come?"

Binet drew out his watch: "Immedi-ately after the dukes, about half an hour ago. I thought your grace would re-ceive Monseigneur d'Orleans in your chamber, as he belongs to the royal family."

"You erred, my friend, and I had forgotten the professor by means of this Orleans. What an unfortunate day! Order the captain of the guard to have four men prepared to take Beaumarchais to the Bastile. I will write the warrant; but the captain must not enter until specially com-manded. It is possible that things are not so bad as I imagine. Is the king out hunting?"

"He mounted his horse as soon as he returned from Paris, and will dine at Choisy."

"Well, give my instructions to the guards." Binet, retiring, bowed with the same indifferent gravity; his va-cant face concealed both emotion and thought.—"Enter my chamber, ladies. I must be alone with this man. I will ring when I want you." The mar-chioness seated herself before one of the mirrors, assumed a picturesque attitude, and gave the signal with a small bell. The portière separated, and Beaumar-chais stood before her.

"I suppose, sir, the time has hung heavily on your hands?"

"I SUPPOSE, SIR, THE TIME HAS HUNG HEAVILY ON YOUR HANDS."   p. 92.

"Oh no, marchioness. An acute observer never finds time tedious."

"I have long had you in my mind, and it amuses me to see you now."

"I can hardly think you intend to make me vain, but such must be the effect of your words, whether they are friendly or not."

"You know how to understand people very well, M. Beaumarchais. But, I am told, you sometimes fail, however correct your calculations in financial gambling."

"Calculations, marchioness? Admitted that luck and a little intellect gained me a fortune, I really do not see what a musician has to calculate, except to keep good time. You wish to hear me play the harp; permit—"

"You do not escape me so, sir! You belong to a class of persons who seek importance by circumlocution and figures of speech. I do not like that sort of skirmishing, and I tell you, plainly, you are a parvenu and an intriguer! What do you say to that?"

Caron smiled quietly. "Ah, madame, I know I am. It is no disgrace in these days. Intrigue? what is it, but to maintain my position—to defend myself against my enemies, and serve my friends?"

"Ah, you can be malicious, and attempt to elude me! But suppose I tell you, M. Professor, that formerly you exerted yourself to win Choiseul by secret means to the cause of the queen and the dauphin, and plotted against me, how will you excuse yourself?"

"Madame, you are pleased to be surprisingly frank with me, instead of simply annihilating a man against whom you have any proofs of his unworthiness. That is remarkable."

"I wish to interrogate, not to answer."

"That is to say you acknowledge that you are puzzled?"

"Impertinent!"

"You are greatly embarrassed, and I will tell you why: Choiseul told you a long history about an intrigue of Beaumarchais, to impress you with the value of his own friendship. In this he greatly deceived you. You would decidedly ruin me, madame, if you possessed indisputable facts—if the servant of the princess could so unceremoniously be imprisoned in the Bastile."

"I think," and Madame de Pompadour was highly excited, "that you have cultivated impudence as a special virtue. Since you called the prime minister a hypocrite in my presence, and cannot deny that you conspired against me, you comprehend that I can easily sign a *lettre de cachet* against you, can I not?" She rose haughtily, went to her desk, drew out a warrant, and prepared to write.

"Oh, do not trouble yourself, madame! I can fill up the blank myself; have the goodness to dictate!" He approached, and politely offered to take her pen.

"Sir!" she exclaimed, staring at him. "Your audacity is beyond belief!"

"Not at all, marchioness. I am a parvenu, and such persons are always audacious. Until now I have been simply fortunate; you are about to bestow on me the highest fame."

"I, sir? You must be a fool!"

"Do you not believe that the Bastile will make a martyr of me? Voltaire and Diderot were of no consequence whatever until they had been imprisoned. A few years in a dungeon is a small price to pay for immortality."

"It might be for life!"

"During *your* life! Very well, noble lady; for no one can tell what will happen afterward."

"Do you mean to say, Beaumarchais, that I have not long to live?" she exclaimed, almost beside herself.

"If I am incarcerated, certainly not!"

“ Man ! ” she murmured, turning pale, “ you are either a demon, or the greatest charlatan on earth ! ”

“ No, marchioness ! I confess that I was very foolish in acting against you. I would never have done so, had I known M. de Choiseul or you better. I am seldom frank, and least of all where I see danger ; but, madame, I will be so now, as an exception, if you wish to make a compromise.”

“ On what condition ? ”

“ I am really sincere. But whatever I refrain from telling must be considered a secret, to reveal which would be a baseness ; in return, I demand that no power on earth shall send me to the Bastile so long as you live ; for, to speak the truth, I am not desirous of the immortality it may bestow.”

She threw down the pen. “ This is the strangest affair that has ever happened to me ! Very well, you have my word. So long as I breathe, no one shall trouble you. What do you know of my death ? ”

“ In future keep aloof from certain *phials !* ”

“ You are a man of honor, Beaumarchais ! ” she whispered, taking his hand. “ You—you observed it also ? ”

“ As well as the grimace of the son ! Be silent as the grave, madame ; forbid your confidantes to speak of it, and banish all perfumes.”

“ I shall do so. But explain your behavior to me. You are a servant· of the party that hate, and yet you warn me ! You slander Choiseul, who is my friend, after endeavoring vainly to gain him for the queen. How can a man act thus and yet remain honorable ? ”

“ I was poor, marchioness, and oppressed by wicked men, when the princesses received me into their favor. Would you have been less grateful, and venture nothing for your deliverers ? ”

“ Granted.”

“ I hated you, as one does the person about whom all his friends complain ; is that wicked ? ”

“ No, but you disliked what you had no positive knowledge of, and undertook what you did not understand.”

“ I was a novice.”

“ And the Jesuits had not schooled you ? ”

“ The Jesuits school me ? I have never met one, either at the residence of the princesses or at the dauphin’s, and I possess means to keep them at a respectful distance—but that is my secret.”

“ But, I pray you ! What of the people that surround the dauphin— those from St. Sulpice, the Molinists ? ”

“ Of course, Choiseul has persuaded you and the king into that belief. You may consider your opponent in any light you please, but you must not hold monseigneur and the princesses as devoid of all honor. You might miscalculate ! ”

“ But they are bigoted ; it is well known what persons—”

“ Formerly had access to them—formerly ! The dauphin was intrusted to the elder Marchioness de Ventadour and the Jesuits, to be educated. His real piety prevented him from perceiving the character of those around him ; but he has been disabused since 1757, when his name was so shamefully taken advantage of in the attempt of Damien. He is religious, but no Jesuit ; on the contrary —however, that is the prince’s secret.”

“ And is monseigneur so very different from what I thought ? He and his party would not object to the fall of the Jesuits ? ”

“ Scarcely.”

“ And what do you expect of him after the king’s death ? ”

“ That I shall not tell you. It must be more indifferent than the question : What are you to expect from him ? ”

“ Oh, the greatest degradation—the most humiliating disgrace that a victor can inflict on his victim ! ”

"Madame, I doubt that. He will spare in you the companion of his father; at least, he will respect his father's memory. The dauphin has feelings, marchioness, and will show, at least, some outward decorum."

"Are you quite—quite sure of that, Beaumarchais?"

"I could procure you a written promise to that effect."

"You? merciful Heaven! If you speak the truth, how my heart would bless you! I—I am not quite so bad as people say!" Tears were streaming from her eyes. Suddenly she looked searchingly at Caron. "The prince, I am told, is not in very good health; he often has attacks similar to those from which I suffer; suppose he should die before his father!"

"Then, madame, I would hide myself in private life! But no! It is possible to look at things in too dreary a light. You could do much to preserve him for us all. Only do not trust Choiseul; I need not repeat my warning against Orleans."

"Choiseul — and again Choiseul! Speak plainly."

"Well, he is unworthy your friendship, though only the dupe of Orleans. He has obtained the premiership, and through you. Now he will aspire to govern alone."

"Beaumarchais, that is not true! I am at the king's side."

"And should you—die! Choiseul has a sister, Madame de Grammont. Beware of strange smelling-bottles!"

"You give me an insight into a terrible plot. What is to be done?"

"I will tell you," he whispered, "when I have seen the dauphin. Use all your efforts to reconcile the king with his son; attend to Terray and Maupeau; they are in alliance with Madame de Ventadour, the Jesuits, and Orleans. Let Choiseul never have a private interview with his majesty. In all this there is but one thought: Bourbon or Orleans. A day may come when that boy will return you the blow you gave him."

"You will not mention the scene?"

"So long as you do not force me, when by doing so I might avert some calamity threatening me."

"Are we, then, friends in future?"

"That is our secret. I advise you to publish me as a most malicious and intolerable person."

"But I was intending to propose you to the king as a proper man to be ennobled, on account of the phial."

"That is a trifle!"

"No, it must be done, that you may have an entrée here. I must clothe you in some dignity, that you may have the right to see me as often as it may be necessary."

"Well, as you please, marchioness. Say that you could purchase from me an awful pamphlet against you and Choiseul, only by bestowing such honors on me. You are aware that I could easily write one, and have it printed in London."

"That is a good idea. I think you like to frighten people."

"It is a good way to rise in this world. Will you now hear me play?"

"Not to-day! You would make me sad. I am often very sad."

"I believe you, dear madame! Perhaps the consciousness of having done one good action may give you pleasure."

"I will try, but I do not believe in any thing good.—Enough!" She offered him her hand and rose. "I shall see you soon again." At her summons, the captain of the Swiss guards entered, leaving the door open. "Marquis, accompany the Chevalier Caron de Beaumarchais to the grand portal, and let the sentinels present arms. He has been appointed Chief Master of the Huntsmen at Varenne du Louvre, on account of his merit, in place of M. de Cabran, recently deceased."

The officer made a military salute, and the lackeys rushed forward to open the carriage-door for the professor. As his equipage drove through the court-yard, the Swiss presented arms.

"What has passed between you and that woman?" exclaimed Duverney, when Beaumarchais arrived at the "Red Horse."

"A great deal. Let me be silent about it—it is better. But what will you say, papa? I am a nobleman, and have the titles of Chevalier and Chief Master of the Huntsmen at Varenne!"

"Are you insane?"

"No, indeed! That is the price of a pamphlet I was about to have published in London against the marchioness and the new prime minister. We can always talk best when we hold the whip!"

CHAPTER VIII.

CORALIE RAUCOURT.

As it has already been mentioned, the first floor of the Pigeonnier, toward the Rue Bertau, was occupied by the all-admired actress of the royal opera, to the no small vexation, envy, and scandal of all the other inhabitants of this large building. She was the aristocrat among them, and always in danger of being assailed, as a strange bird among a flock of sparrows. Mlle. Raucourt had formerly been no better than a Paris beggar-girl—a kind of female *gamin*, who possessed nothing besides her rags, her pretty face, and a silvery, flexible voice, with which she accompanied the shrill treble of her mother in the streets of the capital. At an early age familiar with the vices usually attending a wretched vagrancy, she would probably have become but a chorus-singer in the operas of the celebrated Rameau, which, like the *Fêtes de Ramire, Hippolyte, Princesse de Navarre*, and *Temple de la Gloire*, required kettle-drum choruses, and a very full company. She continued her itinerant life unobserved, except by a young clerk, who fell in love with, and would have married her, if he had been able to give her a support.

About this time, the old French music, as well as much that had hitherto been considered classic, was succeeded by the Italian buffo operas, which were the masquerade pieces of Gerardi thus rendered. They displaced a natural and rough style by higher art, and the heaviness of Rameau's recitative by a wild gayety. Paris was electrified! As Madame de Pompadour, however, protected Rameau, and the queen the buffo operas, they almost became a political question; the public patronized the queen's taste, and the Italians gained the day. This enthusiasm lasted from about 1753 to 1756. The foreigners finally withdrew, for, how well soever their music and acting may have pleased, after the first fashionable intoxication it was discovered that their language could not be generally understood.

The lover of Mlle. Raucourt could not offer her a brilliant future, but he earned sufficient to assist her and take her several times to the opera. She could sing the principal airs after hearing them but once, and imitate the Italians in their pantomimes. Passing into the street, she performed the favorite popular pieces, which attracted the crowd, and mother and daughter found a lucrative business. One day they were singing under the windows of the young musician Duni, who sent for the girl, made a contract with her, and she acted in Rousseau's *Devin de Village*, as well as in Paesiello's operettas in the Palais - Royal. In Duni's celebrated *Milkmaid*, specially written for Coralie, she gained both for the composer and herself a great triumph. She had surprising skill in her coquetry, uniting a subtle impertinence and boldness with an appearance of thoughtless naïveté. Inviting questionable attentions, she would suddenly flee her admirers, of whom she had many, being considered a person of unusual attractions, with the voice of a siren, but of little cultivation, a fault which she concealed by comic acting. Any one, however, who had attempted to rival her would have been laughed at for her pains. In the scene of the *Milkmaid*, where, in pumping water into a tub, she so modulated the creaking of the handle as to jeer at the love-making of an old abbé, the theatre shook with applause, and she became a favorite.

In her popularity, Mlle. Raucourt was not bewildered; she had an object in view—future independence. She could have resided in the best part of Paris, but she had her own reasons to do otherwise. She was a very dangerous acquaintance for a careless person, for her extraordinary talent in gaining a knowledge of secret information made her visitors dependent on her, and forced them into innumerable intrigues. For these reasons she chose to dwell in the muddy and disreputable Quartier du Temple, in the roomy Pigeonnier, where there were so many entrances and exits at all hours. Her windows were often lit during the whole night. Music and dancing, song and wine, held high carnival there; and to be permitted a share in her revelries was the ambition of dissipated courtiers and rich men's sons.

Such a life naturally excited the curiosity and envy of the neighboring poor, and induced them to institute a plan of espionage that often threatened to result disagreeably to Coralie Raucourt. To prevent this, she was benevolent — extravagantly so. She gave work to those who might become dangerous to her, or made presents to people with babbling tongues, having it understood that they must be silent and blind. In short, she had made herself a kind of queen of the Pigeonnier, by means of reward and punishment. The landlord yielded her the greatest privileges in order not to draw upon himself the hatred of the aristocracy that visited her.

This was the lady on whose account a gentleman one day, about noon, left a hired coach in the Rue St. Martin, muffled himself closely in his cloak, and, hurrying down the little alley Clairvaux, disappeared inside the west gate of the building. He did not go to the principal staircase, but, through the court-yard, reached the back-stairs that led to the garret formerly occupied by Beaumarchais and Morelly. He knocked at the side-door of the singer's dwelling, and was admitted by a good-looking, well-dressed man of about thirty, who, as soon as the visitor showed his face, bowed silently and profoundly.

"Is Coralie at home?" asked the gentleman, taking a seat.

"She is at home, your—" The young man would undoubtedly have uttered a title, if the other had not raised his hand in a forbidding manner.

"I have told you, once for all, Debrelou, that I desire my titles to be ignored; here I am simply M. Cloud; that is a very innocent name, and will cost your weak memory no effort. I expect this command to be strictly obeyed. If Coralie is at home, what is she doing? Has she any visitors, or is she practising?"

"She is alone, M. Cloud. I will announce you."

"I have not much time to stay." Debrelon bowed, and left the cabinet by a tapestry door that closed noiselessly.

The gentleman who called himself "M. Cloud," seemed to be lost in profound meditation. He was of medium height and strongly built, wearing a citizen coat of coarse gray cloth, his linen, on the contrary, being very fine and white. A well-powdered bag-wig of flax covered his head, and a walking-stick completed his patriarchal appearance. But what rendered him mysterious, and even an object of fear, were the nonchalance and contemptuousness of his manners, something in his countenance commanding reverence, and at the same time recalling a certain resemblance, together with an expression of heartless calculation. His small fiery eye seemed to enlarge when he was animated, and glared like that of a beast of prey. He was deeply engaged with the memoranda in his pocket-book, when Debrelon returned and politely announced that Mlle. Coralie would receive M. Cloud. Without saying a word he rose, made a gesture to Debrelon to remain where he was, and, entering a luxuriously-furnished chamber, passed into a small drawing-room, where Mlle. Raucourt sat before the instrument on which she had been playing.

"Ah," she exclaimed, laughing, "I am pleased to receive M. Cloud again. I always thought St. Cloud was a pious man, and if he were your ancestor, godliness must have sadly diminished in your family, since you appear in the Pigeonnier in broad daylight! I would give all masses for my soul, if I could see M. St. Cloud in this dress at Versailles, in the Luxembourg or Palais-Royal, among princes, dukes, and counts."

"All very well, Coralie, but M. Cloud is a man whom I hope you will respect in any dress. Dispense with these fooleries, I am not in the humor for them; I came to talk of business. When was La Blache here last?"

"Yesterday at dinner."

"Not in the evening!"

"He avoids our little gay circles since he has returned from exile, on account of his jealous wife and austere father-in-law."

"You allowed yourself to be deceived if you believed him."

"Why should I not believe him? He is generous with his presents, and comes none the less often. Do I lose by it? It would be different if mere suspicion brought in any thing."

"Your confidence may cost you my favor, if you are not more watchful."

"Why, I pray you?"

"I will tell you presently. He was here at dinner. What was his object?"

"Why do you ask, St. Cloud?"

"I wish to know whether he made any discoveries to you, or said any thing that is worth mentioning. I know, Coralie, Mammon is your deity; therefore, be serious and sincere. I could prepare unending repentance for you, if you thought this count could enable you to dispense with my protection."

The little woman, who had hitherto been in so gay a humor, now reddened with anger. "Monseigneur Cloud, La Blache has other reasons for not passing his evenings here. He has attached himself to Minister de Choiseul, and commenced a love-intrigue with the Duchess de Grammont, Choiseul's sister. I had a great deal of trouble to get him to confess it, and had to use all my art."

"Very well; you see, that is something! Count Falcoz de la Blache wishes to succeed at court, and must give up improper companions. Choiseul is prime minister, Madame de Pompadour's health is failing more and more. She will die, I tell you, very soon, and the Duchess de Grammont wishes to take her place. Count de la Blache hopes to be elevated by her means to a position near the king's person, and will then care little for you. His whole party, the St. Albins, Ventadour, Maupeau, and Terray, are on the point of abandoning the Jesuits and swearing to the standard of Choiseul."

"But what use is that to you, monsieur?"

"To me? You ask ingenuously? I wish to hold the wires of these puppets of France in my hands, so that they may dance to *my* tune. That is not difficult to comprehend, is it?"

"Oh, holy St. Cloud, I believe it! but, as you are the premier's friend, you could find out every thing from him much better than through your humble servant."

"It suits me to work in this indirect way, and it will bring you a thousand francs. Is that a sufficient inducement?"

"For my interest, but not for my understanding. I doubt that you would act as you do merely from choice, if the interview with Madame de Pompadour had succeeded better. Ah! that unhappy blow given your son, brings Coralie Raucourt a thousand francs!"

M. Cloud rose impetuously, his countenance changed color. He looked piercingly at the speaker. "I do not think," he said dryly, "that you know exactly what you are talking about, but you are, however, shrewd! Tell me, how did you hear the history of that blow?"

"Dear me," she laughed, "Count Falcoz told me himself; several other friends, Chevalier d'Atreuilles and Captain de Troquade also spoke of it. That slap turned a certain useful acquaintance of mine forever out of Versailles. The friendship of Choiseul has also become lukewarm. That is the reason why I am to reunite the broken threads—a labor certainly worth more than a thousand francs."

"Ah, you wish to enhance the value of your services! Suppose you judge correctly, will this kindle your zeal?" He placed two thousand-franc bills and a diamond bracelet on the table. "In case you refuse, he added, gloomily, "I will ruin you, publicly and privately. What is your decision?"

"I await your commands, and will obey them."

"Then you must use all your skill to induce La Blache to show you the love-letters he receives from Madame de Grammont. I know she writes to him. You will use your art to procure them for me."

"And when he finds himself compromised, he will leave me! Monseigneur, it is no trifle to lose a lover who is heir to the court banker Duverney; and who has promised me in writing a landed estate and a villa."

"I leave it to your prudence and cunning to prevent such a misfortune. Besides, I do not believe he will abandon you, since he is ridiculous enough to love you. You might return a good imitation of the originals to him. When he demands his letters, you could produce the false ones, and, in a feigned jealous fit, fling them into the flames."

"A pretty *coup de théâtre!* When you have the originals, what use will you make of them? I must know what consequences to expect."

"The letters will force into my unconditional service the Duchess de Grammont, the La Blaches, and Ventadours. These good people think that Choiseul might also possibly fall some day, and the king would be left entirely under their control. I must have their fate in my hands. Remember one thing, Coralie: it was I who gave you a professional reputation, and advanced your pecuniary interests, and who will one day royally reward you; but who, if necessary, can also condemn you to your old obscurity.—Do you know whether La Blache has any more such plans? Does he employ spies or reporters? for a man watched by his wife and father-in-law needs such agents."

"Nothing worth talking about. In the fourth story lives a musician, named Batyl, good at his profession, who often helps me to study my parts; otherwise he is a knave. Formerly La Blache was rather intimate with him, and employed him in several matters in which I was not particularly interested. For a long time the count was very angry with the musician, accusing him as the cause that his old enemy Beamarchais had ruined him with the princesses. But yesterday Falcoz again visited Batyl, and they had a long and secret conversation."

"You are wrong to consider such facts trifles, even if they are only love-affairs. Watch La Blache closely, he is of importance to me. We must find means to advance him or render him harmless, according to circumstances. Bribe Batyl, promise him every thing: it is necessary that I know what happens in the society of Choiseul, in the Hôtels St. Albin and Ventadour; for that purpose I have located you in the Pigeonnier. Apropos, does the musician inhabit a room by himself in the fourth story? Has he connections with any one?"

"You know how difficult it is to control people in a house like this. Sometimes transient lodgers come, stay a few days, and disappear again. Such a hole is the garret above. One side is occupied by Louise Duchapt, my milliner, who is reliable; the other, by Batyl. Formerly Beaumarchais lived there also, on account of whose very pretty wife La Blache fell into that well-known difficulty. The third tenant there was an old school-teacher of St. Lazare, called Morelly, half a beggar and half a philosophic dreamer, who has written a fantastic poem, the *Basiliade*. One of Louise Duchapt's girls spoke about it and brought it to me. I never have read any thing more absurd."

"Coralie, does the author of that poem live here?" Cloud walked the floor in the utmost excitement.

"Well, what of it? You look as if I had discovered for you a Voltaire or a Marmontel."

"You have decidedly made a discovery as to a man who will outlive those gentlemen. This fourth-story garret is invaluable! You must instruct Duchapt, Batyl, and Debrelon. What has become of Morelly?"

"I do not know. He suddenly gave up his situation and dwelling. Batyl says that the old man returns now and then and passes a night here. It seems he has a living out of the city."

"The musician and Debrelon must follow him, when he comes again, and find out where and how he lives. I have reasons not to lose sight of that man. Can I depend on you, Coralie?"

"You may, monseigneur, as certainly as on yourself."

"Then you will place your fortune on a sure foundation.—Adieu! I will send a safe man to whom you may deliver your notes to me in well-sealed envelopes."

"At your service!" They shook hands. The visitor walked out, muffled himself in his cloak, in which he was silently assisted by Debrelon, and left the Pigeonnier by the Rue Bertau. Scarcely had his footsteps ceased to be heard, when Debrelon locked the door and hurried to Coralie.

"What did he want?—he seemed to be intent on mischief."

"So he is. You and Batyl are to watch Morelly when he appears again, and to find out where he goes. I have also my instructions about the love-affair of Madame de Grammont and La Blache. Do not ask any more questions, I will tell you all to-night; for I am expecting Falcoz every moment. M. St. Cloud has two faces. He is playing two games, and in both we obtain advantages—therefore we must keep on good terms with him. There!" she pushed the money and bracelet toward the young man; "he is good pay. Ah, I shall not always be pretty and have a good voice. When we have possession of our property and a good income, we shall care very little whether the Orleans or Bourbons are ruined."

"It would scarcely trouble us if both were!" laughed Debrelon. "I believe we are among the very few who have wisdom. If you should by chance discover that I carry on a little private business of my own in political espionage, consider that I am only imitating M. St. Cloud. Since the time of Noah, there is but one useful article in the world—money! Do not endeavor to find out how I earn mine."

"I suppose by the remarkably stupid face you always assume!" Both laughed.

—————

CHAPTER IX.

THE TEMPLE OF THE SUN.

FÉNELON, as early as the Spanish war of the succession, remarked, in reference to the condition of France, "We exist by a miracle; the government is a dependent machine, moving only from habit, and that will be destroyed at the first accidental jarring. I fear that our greatest evil consists in the fact that none regards our real condition—all resolutely shut their eyes!" This truth had taken root not only in the mind of the pupil of the immortal author of *Télémaque*, the Duke de Bourgogne, who died during the regency, but in that of his grandson, the dauphin and son of Louis XV., not-withstanding his Jesuitical education and the influence of the elder Madame de Ventadour.

From the day when the king's life was attempted, the prince had energetically freed himself from the disciples of Loyola, and prepared for the throne, as few heirs of a crown have ever done before or since, by cultivating the quiet and austere virtues of private life. Other persons of quality experienced also gloomy forebodings that affairs would not remain as they had been— that the "jarring" must come, sooner or later, and the "machine" cease to work.

The people were still suffering from their usual obtuseness—satisfied at first with the spirit of the new philosophy, but, by means of it, as well as the Jansenist ideas, slowly acquiring an inconsiderate and unpitying selfishness, that would at last put into their hand the torch to destroy the temples of their native land. In the mean time they avenged themselves on the existing order of things, and those whom they hated, by bon-mots, and particularly by ironical couplets, first adopted as political irritants by Minister Maurepas. This man was void of principle, without a shadow of statesman-like ability or object, but a witty and skilful courtier, belonging to the school of the intriguing Cardinal de Fleury (the tutor of Louis XV.), who early inculcated into his pupil's mind that "love for humanity, frankness, and kindness, were any thing but estimable qualities in a monarch!" Maurepas knew that public opinion was a mighty power, and that the French people were happy if they could only laugh and sing; he therefore sacrificed all his opponents, among them many an honest patriot, by making them subjects of ridicule in some street-satire, which he himself composed and taught the women of the market to sing.

The *Dames de la Halle* were the residents of that structure of cellars and shops, situated between the Rues Tournellerie, Chaussetrerie, Lingerie, and the Maison Pillory, in the centre of the old town, at an equal distance from the Tuileries and the Hôtel de Ville. The female fishmongers, greengrocers, and hucksters of all kinds, had always the privileges of a corporation, one of which was the right of sending a deputation to the king at seasons of rejoicing or sorrow, in order to express their sympathy. They were very insolent and assuming, in many instances wealthy, but as rough in manners, and especially in the use of their tongues, as their sister contemporaries in other cities. These persons, each of whom was an archive in herself of old national songs, M. de Maurepas raised by his verses to the rank of a powerful political institution, and Fleury encouraged him. He gave them such songs as "*Quand Biron voulut danser,*" "*Marlborough s'en va-t-en guerre,*" "*Barbari, mon ami,*" "*A l'allure, mon cousin,*" "*La Turlurette;*" and finally, when Madame de Pompadour was enraged against Maurepas, and his fall imminent, he added the following:

> "Les grands seigneurs s'avilissent,
> Les financiers s'enrichissent,
> Les *Poissons* s'agrandissent,
> C'est le règne des vauriens!"*

Maurepas was banished; but his successors, the Abbé Bernis and Choiseul, continued the same business, and the *Halle* was never in want of poetic effusions, nor the people of subjects for laughter. The blood that was afterward shed in France is not to be ascribed so much to the mob, or the abused Jacobins, as to the dissipated aristocracy of that period. The shallow Maurepas little imagined that, by his frivolous verses, in which royalty and nobility were ridiculed, he was systematically educating rude and remorseless women to be the Megaras of Versailles—the fearful knitters, who sat down by the guillotine and made socks, while before their eyes flowed the blood of whole families, whose names for many a year they had learned to hate! We shudder at such consequences, but forget how very natural they were, and how industriously they were designed.

The justices, intendants, and magistrates (although all authority was losing its power over the public mind), were servile enough to accede to the wishes of the ministers in 1763, and erect a statue of the king, first in the provinces and then in Paris itself, on the Place Louis. To complete the sarcasm, Louis XV. was represented on a low pedestal, supported by the symbols of justice, power, wisdom, and clemency.

At the consecration of this monument the fishwomen, as on all public occasions, took a prominent part. When the veil of the statue was drawn aside, one of them exclaimed: "See, the king has his four mistresses with him; he could not be without them! That one is Mailly; this, Vintimille; there is Chateauroux, and, at his side, Pompadour." This explanation was received with shouts of laughter. Thus the people honored their sovereign!

While the Parliaments were waging a long and fruitless war against the higher clergy, the tithes, and numerous forms of arbitrary power, and in favor of personal liberty and the right of common trial, the *Encyclopédie* was prohibited, after the seventh volume had been published. The philosophers who had united in its support were not at all times unanimous in their opinions, but now they separated, each taking his own path.

---

* The "grands seigneurs" degrade themselves; the financiers grow rich; the *Poissons* (fishes) become great; it is the reign of rogues.

On the other hand, the fate of the Jesuits was sealed. How much soever had been done to cover up the attempted deed of Damien, to guard the assassin from betraying his accomplices, and to punish him most barbarously, in order to spare the originators of the crime, yet his first expressions in the moments of fear had sufficiently revealed that the plot was hatched by the Jesuits and their aristocratic abettors. Notwithstanding all effort to compromise the name of the royal heir, it was impossible to make manifest their own innocence. Many scandalous actions of the order were discovered ; the lower clergy, the pastors and lay-priests, who were nearest and dearest to the people, rose against the Jesuits. The dauphin, in disgust and anger, dismissed them from his household ; and Madame de Pompadour and Choiseul saw that but one means remained to tranquillize the public mind, to intimidate the higher ecclesiastics, and satisfy the Parliament, at least on one point—the abolishment of the whole order.

In 1761 the government commenced by destroying the extensive and dangerous commerce of the brotherhood with India; by declaring all Jesuit houses in France judicially responsible for their foreign connections and debts, placing their operations under the control of the state, and permitting the Parliament to investigate their correspondence. In 1762 they were declared by a royal decree dangerous to the common welfare. In consequence they were forbidden, after a short but violent struggle, to give public instruction, receive novices, obey their general, live in communities, or wear the dress of their order. Their convents and churches were closed, but so far no punishment had been personally inflicted. Now, however, preparation was made to strike the last blow—to confiscate their possessions for the benefit of the state, to declare the brotherhood extinct, and exile its members. There was a general agreement in this disposal of the Jesuits.

There are moments, when, against our will and without premeditation, we see something terrible in what is apparently of little consequence, and become impressed by a presentiment almost too shocking to think, much less to express. Beaumarchais had said to the Marchioness de Pompadour, " Banish all perfumes ! " and she understood what he meant, as well as the way he pointed out as her only escape. This woman had obtained, by the most objectionable means, an ascendency over Louis XV. such as none had ever exercised over any sovereign. She stood on the pinnacle of that power of which she had dreamed ; but in Caron's presence she felt her weakness and danger. The marchioness had long been aware that she never possessed the real love of the king, even had he been capable of loving any one besides himself. She had made a slave of him by truckling to his evil passions and refining his sensual pleasures. Enchained by her penetrating and variable intellect, he yielded to her the management of his government—a burden odious to himself. Louis XV. did not love her, and yet he would sooner have sent every minister of his court and every member of his family to the Bastile before he would dare to deny her a privilege. She knew that he would never dismiss her—that she could not be ruined, but might be assassinated ! Having converted all around her to the mere creatures of her will, there was none on whom she could really depend, and so much the more was her fear of political convulsion or domestic trouble. With a quick instinct of danger, her energetic mind at once accepted the assistance offered by Beaumarchais—the possibility of the dauphin's good-will. The woman who in her fresh beauty surrendered it to dishonor as a price for court influence, at length seemed to yearn after something better—something that might atone for her sins, and save her old age in a new and purer epoch. Bold as she was in vice, could she prosper by being bold in virtue?

The marchioness's desire for a reconciliation with the dauphin was granted. Caron brought her a secret written assurance, that she need not fear for herself after the death of the monarch; that every thing unfavorable was forgotten, and all the esteem and favor should be shown her that a woman merited who had so long enjoyed the confidence of the king. This invaluable document Madame de Pompadour pressed tearfully to her lips. A reaction of her long-suppressed emotion followed, and in a letter, full of sincere repentance, she prostrated her soul before the prince. Beaumarchais was provided with all means and opportunities to drive the opposing party from the field, and to reunite the king with his family. She also followed Caron's advice in reference to perfumes; used her influence with the monarch to prepare him for a meeting with the dauphin; rendered him less cordial with Choiseul, and strengthened his dislike to Orleans. In all this she struggled but for her own security.

Cabals and systems of espionage were an indispensable part of the court machinery in that age. From the monarch to the lowest police agent, all employed spies with greater or less secrecy. Mlle. Raucourt and her friend Debrelon were no exceptions. They loved each other, prospered, and worked for the future. All they cared for in others was their money, and they exercised great skill in the management of their business. When admiring cavaliers, or her principal patron, the

Duke d'Orleans, paid her a visit, Debrelon appeared the most insignificant person on earth—in fact, nothing but a lackey of Coralie; but his eyes and ears were remarkably keen, while his expression was dull and his conduct stupid. He was so awkward at times, and yet so devoted, as to awaken pity. Whatever important affairs were transacted by her visitors, she always honestly mentioned them to Debrelon after their departure. And he also had similar business on his own account. He was a spy of Beaumarchais, who controlled him, and who knew all that occurred in the Pigeonnier by means of the porters and other lower employés. Coralie and her friend had therefore each an opposing party whom they served; and could sometimes exchange important secret information, when they were certain of being paid, without much exposing themselves to suspicion. The money thus earned fell into the common treasury for their future independence. It sometimes happened that one party demanded discoveries the other was not willing to betray. In such cases, Batyl was used as a dummy; certain hints were given him and he executed what they considered beneath themselves. As the musician was a very respectable rogue, such commissions well suited him. But since his employers were more cunning and calculating, and never lost the guidance of their own affairs, he became dependent on them, and could never quite understand their designs. They often deceived each other, by false reports, and then laughed at their attempts to cheat.

While Batyl, then, was ordered to discover Morelly's present residence and manner of life, Debrelon gave Beaumarchais a circumstantial account of all that had taken place between Orleans and Coralie. Caron immediately fathomed the duke's plan. First the marchioness, then Choiseul, and finally the sister of the latter, were to fall; Maupeau and Terray were dependent on Orleans, through Diana de Ventadour. The old king would necessarily fall into the hands of his arch-enemy Orleans. Could such a state of things exist during the dauphin's life?

"Banish all perfumes!" Caron could not forget the phial. He ordered Debrelon to let him have the letters of the Duchess de Grammont for one day, in return for five thousand francs. Beaumarchais had the advantage of Orleans; for Debrelon never knew any of the former's plans, nor did he fear the duke, while he loved his purse, and was aware that behind Caron was the party of the dauphin, who, when king, could hang all spies. Orleans could offer only money; Beaumarchais, money, safety, and even favor. As the latter invested the funds of Debrelon, he and Coralie were entirely in Caron's power.

Scarcely had Beaumarchais heard these new revelations, than he hastened to the dauphin, and at a private audience described to him the scenes at Madame de Pompadour's, and the far-seeing calculations of the foe of the Bourbons. The prince was greatly disquieted, but his pure heart could not believe in such dishonorable plans, such criminal intentions of Orleans, who, though worthy of distrust, was the first prince of the royal blood and the king's cousin. He refuted all the reasons offered by Beaumarchais—such vice he thought could not find culture in a man of his blood—but he resolved to thwart the plots of his enemies. He sent the Chevalier Machault to Morelly, ordering him "on no account to go to Paris, or visit the Pigeonnier, before he had seen monseigneur and received an explanation." Then the prince resolved to have a personal interview with the marchioness, and arrange

with her a complete reconciliation with the king. Tears stood in his eyes; he placed his hand on his heart, and looked upward, saying, "I do this only for France and my children!"

Louis XV. was decidedly the most vile and wretched monarch in the world. Was he, however, naturally so wicked? Did he possess the tyrant-soul of a Nero, Caligula, or Tiberius? Was he a fool and a brute at the same time? No! His father, the Duke de Bourgogne, was a noble man in every sense, and the son had in his figure and manner something of the majesty and *bonhomie* of the great Louis; but Fleury, first his preceptor, then his all-powerful minister, like a second Richelieu, had stifled in the pupil all his better nature, sense of independence and faith. Choiseul himself said of Louis that he never had courage but when he was angry, and only then he felt that he had a soul!"

The queen, Maria Leszinska, was beautiful and loving when Louis married her, but scarcely did she obtain real influence, when Fleury, trembling for his position, exposed the monarch to the seductions of conjugal infidelity. Perhaps this would not have grown into immeasurable criminality, if Maria Leszinska had not herself been the cause, at least, in some measure. She had been educated so piously, that she considered she had almost been guilty of crime in becoming a mother! A monarch, whose youth had been so slavish, and whose will so circumscribed, required a cheerful wife who knew how to interest and amuse him; But the melancholy spirit of the dethroned Polish king descended to the daughter. She was strictly devotional; but at Choisy the pleasures of the world, and the fascinations of Madame de Mailly and de Chateauroux, converted Louis into a mere sensualist. His family was a secondary consideration; he had no affection for his serious son, and could scarcely bear the presence of his daughters. He was so inexperienced in government business, that the death of Fleury would have left him in abject helplessness, if Madame de Pompadour had not been at his side, who knew how to direct him and control the state.

Choiseul, formerly ambassador at the court of Vienna, was made minister, after Bernis and Maurepas, to assist the marchioness with his intriguing mind. He brought with him the so-called Austrian policy, that is, the allying of the houses of Hapsburg and Bourbon, which was unpopular since the days of Richelieu, Mazarin, and Fleury; but the Marchioness de Pompadour accepted it as the means of maintaining herself through the influence of Maria Theresa. Choiseul, however, was ambitious of greater power; he wished to be prime minister, and, after an earnest but fruitless struggle, the favorite mistress of the king was forced to concede that position to him. He became every day more dangerous to her by an authority gained through the parliamentary party, whom he brought to his support by means of Terray, Maupeau, and Orleans, and who yielded in the questions concerning the Jesuits. The king — always satisfied if affairs seemed to go smoothly—if his family did not annoy him, and he was undisturbed in his pleasures —noticed the growing ascendency of his premier with distrust, which the marchioness strengthened, and endeavored to render that policy suspicious which had at first advanced her, but which became so unfortunate in the war with Prussia.

Since that time Louis XV. used his private purse to enlarge the system of espionage which he maintained at Paris, in the provinces, and at all foreign courts, in order to watch his own ambassadors, to work against his own ministers, and discover their plans and connections. The differences existing between him and the dauphin would have rendered it impossible even for the marchioness to bring the king to a reconciliation with his family (who had always appeared as a tribunal that reminded him of his shame), if at the right time there had not been a secret ally, deciding the monarch in a most extraordinary manner, and awakening feelings in him that had hitherto lain dormant.

In the household of the Duke d'Orleans, the place of governor to the pages was held by Chevalier de Bouilli. The latter had a daughter of extraordinary beauty and intellect, and possessed of those virtues in which the French ladies of that time were so deficient. She was retired, as some sweet blossom hidden in the foliage. Her parents, who were blind partisans of the wily Orleans, did not love her, for she was a quiet but fervent friend of the dauphiness, as well as the princesses, to whom she remained attached, notwithstanding the parental displeasure. In order to save themselves from the inconveniences and dangers of such intercourse, as well as to disencumber themselves of an unloved child, M. de Bouilli and his wife married her to M. de Seran, whose personal appearance was very repulsive. He was a generous man, and, aware of her dislike, resolved to renounce a union that to him was all his happiness. Adelaide de Bouilli was touched by his magnanimity, and cheerfully gave him her hand. The esteem of parties apparently so unsuited to each other, soon changed into a reciprocal and enthusiastic love, rendering their marriage an example of unusual felicity. Chevalier de Bouilli retired to his estates, and the office of governor devolved on his son-in-law Seran. It was a court position, and could be granted only by the king after an official presentation.

Louis XV., who had revelled to satiety in the pleasures of his court, was not blind to the fast-vanishing charms of the Marchioness de Pompadour—time and disease were stealing away the bloom of her beauty, and he became melancholy, which the consciousness of his own approaching age did not relieve. He accidentally saw Madame de Seran, and fell violently in love with her. As a sort of irony of his past life, the royal sensualist, in his degraded decrepitude, was condemned to a ridiculous passion. He made the appointment of Seran dependent on the condition that, after the audience, the lady should consent to a private interview, to which she agreed. The king—always timid iu making new acquaintances, and until now surrounded by none but vicious women who knew how to conquer his natural pusillanimity—was the more bashful, because his affection was sincere. Madame de Seran kept him at a respectful distance by the gravity of her virtue, and the charm of her intellect. She told him plainly she could not love him, and would assuredly never dishonor herself or her husband; but, if he desired a true and disinterested friend, she would become such in all fidelity. The influence of a pure woman over his desolate mind, together with a longing to be delivered from the disgrace and wretchedness of his life, induced the king to institute such relations with Madame de Seran, that, on her side, was a most respectful friendship, while on his, a Platonic tenderness that never thought of venturing beyond the boundaries of chastity and honor. No mail-day passed, that the monarch did not write to her, and expect an answer. In the interviews she granted him, she obtained the promise of a reconciliation with his family, long desired by her, and in which she succeeded by the noble qualities which affected his mind and heart. The Marchioness de Pompadour knew this, but had sense enough to tolerate a rivalry she could not destroy, and which specially served her own present purposes. A meeting of the king with Madame de Seran, the dauphin, and herself, was secretly arranged, after the marchioness had previously paid a visit to Trianon, the results of which greatly pleased monseigneur, though at first he had difficulty in conquering his repugnance to her.

The first advances of Louis XV. toward his son were concealed in mystery. One November afternoon, the king pretended that he was not very well, in order not to be burdened by the presence of his ministers and courtiers, and accompanied the marchioness to the "Temple of the Sun," a villa situated at the edge of the gardens of Versailles, and offering a fine view of the Vale of Arcis, Trianon, and Marly. Dr. Quesney, physician in ordinary, followed in a second carriage, the only other person in attendance being Binet, the head valet de chambre. About the same time there arrived from Trianon the dauphin, escorted only by the Chevaliers de Machault and de Beaumarchais. At the hedge, monseigneur and Caron descended from the equipage, leaving Machault behind; and approached the "Temple of the Sun," where they were expected by Madame de Séran and her husband.

The dauphin was deeply moved. He seized the lady's hand and pressed it to his lips, saying: "You are not the good friend of the king and myself only, but the protecting spirit of France. May Heaven reward the courage which not all the treasures in the world can worthily repay!"

"Monseigneur, you are to be that protecting genius. I am sufficiently happy in having aided in accomplishing this blessed meeting. Will you permit M. de Beaumarchais and my husband to await his majesty?"

"I pray you, do so, chevaliers." Both withdrew to the antechamber.

"Monseigneur, let me seize these few moments and beg you to lay aside all constraint, all painful reserve toward the king. The first word often decides all. Act as if you did not notice how distressing this effort is to his majesty. Let him not feel ashamed before his son, forget the past, and think only of your children—of France.—I believe I hear the carriage."

"You will be satisfied with my conduct, gracious lady."

The Chevalier de Seran entered: "His majesty is arriving, accompanied by the marchioness, his physician, and Binct. Beaumarchais is receiving him."

"Let us go into the cabinet; I will introduce you, monseigneur," whispered the lady. They left the drawing-room.

During this time Caron met the sovereign at the gate, and was presented by Madame de Pompadour. Louis XV. cast a sharp side-glance upon him, nodded, and walked on, the marchioness walked after him, while Binet opened the doors. As the king appeared in the pavilion, Madame de Seran advanced, smiling, and holding the dauphin's hand: "Your majesty, I present you your best friend."

"My royal father," said the prince, "my first sentiment at this moment can only be gratitude to these two disinterested women who obtained for me the favor of an interview with you. Allow me," and he seized the hand of Madame de Pompadour, "to tell the marchioness in your presence that she disarms whatever unhappy feeling I ever entertained toward her, and that Madame de Seran has long had my unbounded reverence. Whatever may happen, your majesty, both these ladies have claims on my gratitude, and

which I shall always be ready to pay in memory of this hour."

The king, at sight of his son, inclined his flushed countenance, and, during this address, raised his eyes slowly and uncertainly. Something like emotion trembled in his glance, but he did not trust himself. "Very good, monseigneur," he replied, nodding. "You will only be doing justice. What do you wish to say to me?"

"Your majesty," said Madame de Seran, stepping between them, "let the marchioness and myself take the king and the dauphin with us, and leave here the father and son. Will you permit us?" She offered her hand to the monarch, fixing her bright eyes on him.

"Certainly, my dear Seran." The king smiled in an embarrassed manner, and extended his left hand toward the dauphin.

Monseigneur kissed it: "My dear father!"

Madame de Serau offered her arm to the marchioness, and both ladies departed. Louis and his son were alone.

"Your dear father? That name is new to me? You did not always consider me so!"

"Tell me frankly, sire, with what you have to reproach me; I am strong enough to hear it, and to answer in sincerity."

"I have always been told you were my opponent. I must also remind you of the unheard-of disgrace you made Madame de Pompadour suffer at the great levee, and of the mischievous connection of your name with the dark attempt of 1757. I do not believe the latter; but who can assure me, that you are otherwise changed, that in your breast you do not despise your—" His face flushed, and turning he walked to the window, and drummed on the panes.

"My father, it is not enough that we

suffer like common citizens, from family sorrows, false friends, and malicious enemies; kings and princes have the misfortune to be systematically deceived by those who creep into our confidence, and whose object is to control us more than the meanest in the land. The education I received was bigoted and servile, directed by Madame de Ventadour, whose family are now allied with Orleans and Choiseul, for the purpose of saving themselves from the fate of the Jesuits. My eyes were opened on the day when that most terrible occurrence took place—when I was on the point of losing a father, and France a king. I call God and Nature to witness, whether there can exist a son, himself a father, and loving his children, who can entertain such thoughts as my enemies accused me of, for their own purposes in creating divisions in our family. Madame de Pompadour will acknowledge to you, sire, how greatly she erred to her own hurt when she allowed herself to be persuaded that I was guilty of actions of which only an Orleans or a Choiseul is capable."

"But you criticised my manner of life severely. You judged of my relation to the queen like a person who does not understand what he says; nor know how she herself—yes, you spoke like one who does not feel that he—was not himself the offspring of love, and—"

"I only judged as a son who loves his mother, sire. I am well aware now that I did you injustice, for if Fleury had never lived—"

"There, that is sensible! Fleury was the bane of my life. I tell you affairs are not as they should be—I feel that; Madame de Seran—"

"My dear father, let us forget all." They embraced each other. "I neither have the right nor the will to listen to that which only confirms the fact that the misfortunes of kings originate in the selfishness of servants. I beg you for your confidence only; that will increase your happiness, lengthen your life, and ameliorate the evils of the age. I fear that I have not very long to live, that since 1760 a growing and ineradicable disease is at work within me. Conscious of this, ambition for the crown would be very hasty. Imagine yourself, sire, alone—an old man—that you must leave this country in its present condition to a child, your grandson! Shall I, the father, not tremble for my poor boy, who may fall into the hands of a second Fleury?"

"You are right, quite right! Oh, every thing is in a miserable condition! It will last during my lifetime—but my grandson! You will not die, however, before me. Heaven cannot so afflict the Bourbons! Retirement has made you gloomy. Do you agree in the abolition of the order of the Jesuits?"

"Unconditionally, sire."

"You consider Choiseul an intriguer?"

"Certainly, and a fool besides, who serves Orleans involuntarily."

"I will investigate that. We can do nothing before the publication of the edict against the Jesuits. But I wish to be freed from Choiseul. Austria has brought us nothing but unhappiness and debt. Whom do you propose in his place?"

"I am not prepared for that question, your majesty. The marchioness, however, is of our opinion, and Madame de Seran has a clear mind. It is true, she is partial," smiled the prince; "she is a friend of the dauphiness."

"I am glad, my son, that Josepha loves her," replied the king. "We can arrange all else at Trianon or in the *Œil de Bœuf*. I will take care that Madame de Pompadour sends you daily all the official papers, to give your opinion on them. Will you visit me at Fontainebleau?"

"Very gladly. When do you command it?"

"No, without commands! Come with the dauphiness and the children. I should also like to see Madame de Seran with you—with her husband, of course; I do not desire any misinterpretations."

"I shall invite them immediately, sire."

"Very well, my son. And ask your mother, the queen, whether she will receive our visit."

"My father!" The dauphin kissed him.

"Very well! I will observe all conventionalities, my friend, but—what married persons have once been guilty of toward each other cannot well be forgotten! Be content that Josepha is all in all to you, and kiss my grandchildren!" He pressed his son's hand, and, opening the door, smilingly beckoned to those waiting without. "We must end the conference, ladies and gentlemen. In order, however, to enjoy your society longer, and, as the weather is fine, I beg you to accompany us a short distance."

"With great pleasure, your majesty," said the dauphin. "Will you accept my arm, marchioness?"

"I have never supposed," replied Madame de Pompadour, blushing, "that I could ever merit this attention."

"But, in addition, I beg you for the first dance at Fontainebleau."

The king smiled, gave his arm to Madame de Seran, and preceded monseigneur. The Chevalier de Seran and de Beaumarchais, as well as Quesney and Binet, followed. At the first fountain the party separated. His majesty, the marchioness, the doctor, and the valet de chambre, entered their equipages, and the rest slowly returned.

"My friend," said the dauphin, "this is the happiest day of my life; it will bear fruit. Each of you, faithful ones, has sacred claims of gratitude, which he can always assert. Chevalier de Seran and consort, I invite you as my guests to Fontainebleau. M. de Beaumarchais, tell my royal sisters that I am quite satisfied with the meeting."

No reliance could be placed generally on the word of Louis XV. He repented in the morning of what he promised in the evening, and repeated the next, and gave assurances that he never intended to regard. But on this occasion two women united in strengthening his good resolutions, and fear and suspicion aided in prejudicing him against Choiseul, whose fall seemed certain. The dauphin received, through the couriers of the marchioness, all documents, and gave his opinion in a note. The premier's ambition was checked by the increasing coolness of the king and the marchioness, and the former granted him no audience at which the favorite was not present. He rejected Choiseul's opinions, and rendered them void by instructions that were, however, neither the monarch's nor in accordance with the former policy of Madame de Pompadour. This was the more remarkable, as scarcely a year had elapsed since the conclusion of the Bourbon family treaty which sanctioned the minister's future policy. The unfortunate audience of Orleans resulted in many severe expressions toward Choiseul, from the sovereign and the marchioness, and exposed him to the suspicion of a secret alliance, from which he could not free himself even when he withdrew from the duke's party.

The key to all this the premier did not discover until he followed the king to Fontainebleau. After his return he sent a confidential note to Orleans, urgently demanding a private interview. The duke, informed of the position of the minister, by Mlle. Raucourt, Maupeau, and Terray, laughed aloud, and offered him a supper for two at Saint-Cloud. Choiseul was at that point where Orleans desired him to be —he had become dependent on him from necessity. "He wishes to maintain his place at all hazards, and so he applies to me," said the duke, ironically; "well, he shall not get rid of me again so easily!"

CHAPTER X.

"BANISH ALL PERFUMES!"

THE leaves had fallen, and the days were short and cold. The wind whistled through the trees of the park; and the hunting-lodge of the Duke of Orleans, at Saint-Cloud, looked uninhabited and dreary. The only signs of life were the wreaths of smoke faintly issuing from one of its unsightly chimneys, and the light in two windows of the principal story, as if some visitor were present. As a hunting rendezvous of that time, the proprietor and his guests remained there only a few days. On this occasion the duke had sent his steward and cook to announce that he was coming without attendants, and he gave strict orders that his presence there should not be mentioned. About dark he arrived on horseback. Throwing the reins to the manager of the household, he said that a gentleman was soon expected, probably in a carriage; that the servants were to be well cared for, but kept in sight until their departure. Then he hastened to the dining-room, and paced it thoughtfully, while his steward laid the cloth. Suddenly he halted and remarked: "You have an unaccustomed office to perform to-day, dear Sillery; it scarcely suits your rank, but do not forget that I will reward your present humiliation, and procure you the cross of St. Louis.

—Silence! You know much, but all must not be told you now; I am to sup with a gentleman with whom you will merely fancy that you are acquainted. When he is here, you must take the trouble to bring in every thing yourself, and then leave us alone. When I ring the bell, it is for the carriage of the stranger; immediately afterward I will require my horse. Your devotion induces me to demand a very important service from you."

"Your royal highness, you can command me in any respect. But though I shall not know the person you expect to a private supper, will you permit me to speak of what I do know?"

"Yes."

"It is in reference to your son and his education. What is the reason that, after the scene at Versailles, you first placed the disgraced prince for several months under the tuition of Madame Diana de Ventadour and the Jesuits; then introduced him into the brilliant circles of the Palais-Royal, at the same time directing him nightly to certain houses, and strangely letting him finish his pious studies at the Pigeonnier, in the apartments of Mlle. Raucourt? Such preparations hardly qualify him for a—throne."

"I might reply by another question; Is it a proper study for your son, who is to be the confidant of mine, that he admires the philosophers?"

"O certainly, your royal highness. If we are convinced of the instability of the present, and that a political revolution is inevitable, it is indeed necessary to know whither the future will bear us."

"Very well, and therefore my system of education is preferable. Let your son become acquainted with the doctrines of the times; mine, with actual life. Chartres has talent and wit, but he cannot control himself; of this we have proofs. He is to learn from Diana and the Jesuits to keep up appearances; to despise sensual enjoyments, and gain an insight into the passions and follies of the people, in order to rule well. He must practise four things!—Cunning, hypocrisy, presence of mind, and power; everything else is as nothing to a king."

"That I concede, monseigneur, but all these are vain, unless he have courage. Such an education will rather weaken him."

"No fear! The blood of Henry IV. flows in his veins. His energy just now has something in it of the wild-cat, but does not the lion belong to that genus? —Our visitor approaches." M. de Sillery bowed and hastened away. The duke resumed his walk to and fro.

The door opened; Choiseul appeared, greeted the prince, and threw his fur robe on a seat near the fireplace. "Your pardon, monseigneur, that I announced myself without ceremony; but necessity and want of time left me no choice. The king may return any day to Versailles."

"Then you would be compromised by your intercourse with me," laughed Orleans.

"Your royal highness seems hurt at a caution that alone can save us, since an imprudence has already done us great damage—"

"Hurt? No, indeed, M. Prime minister! In my own circumspection you may see that I approve of yours. If you are ready, I will order supper at once." He rang for Sillery, who brought in the dishes and retired.

"Your steward, your royal highness?"

"M. de Sillery, yes. No one is near us besides him. Help yourself. You come from Fontainebleau?"

"Where I saw something very curious. The dauphin danced a minuet to-day with Madame de Pompadour."

Orleans put down his wineglass and stared at the minister. "You are jesting!"

"Would to Heaven I were!"

"The dauphin—reconciled with the king!"

"A month ago. That is the secret work of the dear marchioness. And monseigneur had the goodness to bring Madame de Seran to his father."

"That is why the Chevalier de Seran asked leave of absence! I must dismiss him."

"That he may become private secretary to his majesty, or, maybe, something worse."

"Surely! But how do you explain this miraculous change in the father and son?"

"It would not have taken place had not Prince de Chartres made that ominous grimace. I cannot comprehend what distrust entered the mind of the marchioness after we had come to a good understanding. In short, one month ago, Binet accompanied the king and Madame de Pompadour to the 'Temple of the Sun,' and a complete reunion took place between him and the dauphin, and at my expense."

"And because your fall is certain, and you have no other resource, you think it necessary to call on me for assistance!"

Choiseul's countenance darkened. "All I need do, would be to make a decided movement—"

"Toward the dauphin's side? Very good, a man does any thing to maintain his position. But who will believe you? I might just as well give my homage to the dauphin."

"The distrust of the house of Orleans by the Bourbons is historical. If you remember that it has been increased by that unhappy incident with Madame de Pompadour—"

"As you are continually returning to that subject, do you know what happened at the interview?"

"Enough to insult the marchioness."

"Then you think that the impertinence of a half-grown boy is a sufficient indication of a well-weighed plot of his father? Nonsense! Especially when you consider that both are princes of the royal blood! The marchioness would have treated that childish prank in a more prudent manner, if something else had not happened between us, so that she seized that opportunity to strike my son and mortify me. You will give her credit that she would not have gone over to the enemy's camp without strong reason."

"I do not understand your royal highness. What else occurred between you and Madame de Pompadour, that—"

"There are circumstances, you know, in all our intercourse, which do not bear expression, and which are generally of great consequence. Silent motions, for example, often reveal innermost thoughts, alarming and separating friends forever. Can you imagine such a case?"

"You remind me of something of the kind which took place between the marchioness and myself the day after your visit. There was a moment in which she started, changed in her expression and manner, and I understood her no longer. From that time she became my opponent."

"I will aid your memory. After my adventure, I wrote a note to you, stating that Madame de Pompadour had dismissed me very ungraciously, and that I must see you. You did not answer, but thought it right to avoid me who had been so unfortunate at Versailles. How did you hear of it?"

"I confess that your note alarmed me. I paid a visit to the marchioness on the following day, after the king had addressed severe words to me, on your account, at the afternoon audience."

8

"You were received coldly!"

"More than that, your royal highness. The deportment of the lady had something in it anxiously expectant. She related to me the incident with your son, but in that deliberate way which betrayed too well that she wished to read in my features the effect her communication would have. She seemed also to suffer physical pain more than usual, but endeavored to conceal it. I sought with all the eloquence at my command to excuse the affair."

"That rendered you suspicious; ha! ha! What before was only a presentiment became an assurance."

"Your royal highness!" and Choiseul stared at the prince, "what became assurance?"

"Well, that you participate in all my good plans. Did you not observe any thing unusual?"

"What do you mean?"

"Well—I mean—were you sensible of any perfumes?"

The countenance of Choiseul expressed fearful astonishment. "Monseigneur, I do not know what to answer!"

"Dear me, were you never aware of the presence or absence of perfumes?" Orleans drew a case from his pocket, opened it, took from it a phial of pale-blue glass, and handed it to him.

"What a shocking idea! On that day her apartments were certainly free from the fragrance that usually filled them! She called you a low intriguer, the demon of France, and other complimentary names. A feverish flush accompanied her words, and she seemed to be suddenly ill. While Madame de Vilaille was absent for water, I offered her my smelling-bottle. She appeared terribly frightened, and turned away her face with a bitter smile, rudely ordering me to go, as I could see she was suffering, and that my presence could be dispensed with. From that moment she was changed in her manner toward me; even iu the royal council she avoided speaking to me."

"The same thing happened to myself on the previous day with this phial."

"But is not all this very foolish?" He took the bottle from the hand of Orleans.

"Are you insane? Do not open it! It is too strong for those who are well!" The prince took it away.

Choiseul rose, pale as death. "Monseigneur, permit me to return to Paris."

"As you please, M. Minister," smiled the duke, slowly returning the phial to its case, and then to his pocket. "To save yourself you might, out of all these circumstances, forge a parliamentary process against the house of Orleans; ha! ha! But, remember, we both presented a perfume, both are exposed to the same suspicion! What can you do? You are ruined! Iu the mean time, those against whom you have hitherto been acting, will assuredly conquer. Why did you wish to see me? I am providing you with an elixir, and you run away!"

"Prince, prince! Are then those monstrous reports about your family true? Just Heaven! Are all your thoughts bent upon—"

"On what? My dear Choiseul, either your moral alarm is merely a comedy, or such cowardice that you do not deserve to be minister of France. The marchioness is diseased already—incurably so! She has had her share, but will still have time to ruin you and imprison your sister for life in a convent. How can you prevent that? By simply assisting the departure of your enemy, of which eventually there is no doubt whatever."

"She has truly had her share, your

royal highness!" replied Choiseul, resting his head on his hand.

"Yes, since the judgment pronounced against the Jesuits, her over-excited nerves have helped her to absorb many deleterious substances!"

"The Jesuits?"

"Why, yes; it is rather popular, and the easiest thing in the world, to accuse them of every thing evil."

"When she dies, Madame de Seran and the dauphin will govern the king."

"The dauphin is predisposed to consumption, and—"

"Monseigneur," cried Choiseul, in the utmost terror, "I believe it must be Satan who has assumed the form of Orleans!"

"Then you prove that a man may be an atheist, and yet as superstitious as a negro. That is not reasonable. Consumption is a disease no physician has yet been able to cure, and no science has fully discovered its origin. Do not trouble yourself on that point. When Madame de Pompadour is dead, the king will soon turn, from his platonic ennui with Madame de Seran, to your beautiful sister. We must leave it to the art of the duchess to neutralize the dauphin and his party. If we do not succeed we must have another private supper!"

"And what advantage does your royal highness expect from all this?"

"Advantage? What are my purposes to you! Do you think you are my confidant? Either you save yourself, or you attempt do so without me. I allow you to imagine that what has passed is an illusion, or believe at every moment that you smell, taste, or feel something that might effect a rapid decline in you. The naked thought is—poison! However, our plans may be turned to our own injury, according to the manner in which we manage them."

"Suppose, monseigneur, I offer you

my assistance at your service, what would you reply?"

"That the king as well as yourself shall live and reign as long as it is in my power to permit you. I will make my wishes known to you in private; and, in return, I will support you both in the Parliament and among the people."

Choiseul sighed. "Very well, I agree." He gave his hand to Orleans.

"You are acting wisely. As Binet, the grateful cousin of the marchioness discovered to you the new alliance, I suppose he fears to lose his lucrative situation?"

"Certainly."

"The faithful fellow will be glad, then, soon to be freed from his relative Poisson?"

"We must place it in a proper light before him."

"No time is to be lost. She must hasten to die, or Binet loses all consequence. Here is the elixir, it is well closed. One drop on a piece of sugar every three days, and in a few weeks we have innocently reached all we desire. Do not hesitate, but take the phial. The contents will lay out as natural a corpse as could the most ordinary disease." He handed the case across the table, smiling.

Choiseul raised his trembling hand, seized it hastily, concealed it in his breast-pocket, and sadly muttered: "It is the only safe means!"

"Did Binet tell you who else was present at that secret scene of reconciliation?"

"The king, the marchioness, and Quesney, the physician in ordinary. With the dauphin were both the Serans and the upstart Beaumarchais, professor of the princesses. I remember also that the valet de chambre told me that the latter was at the same time with you at Versailles, and had au audience of Madame de Pompadour immediate-

ly after you left. No one knows what was transacted at that interview; it is only strange that he left the palace a nobleman, and the reunion between father and son followed very soon."

Orleans rose, turning pale. "And you say that as if it were child's play?"

"Why, you must know he is the agent of our opponents."

"But I have considered him of less importance than he really is. He saw the marchioness alone immediately after my departure! And this reconciliation! Are you aware that certain persons among us are in his power? I begin to understand many circumstances that until now were inexplicable to me? If this phial does not soon act—if the dauphin is not rendered powerless in some way—if this Beaumarchais is not soon set aside—the son of a Parisian watchmaker will know so much about us, that all we have left will be a pistol to send us out of this evil world! Oh, do not question me! Wherever I turn he has spread his net. He has discovered that a man becomes terrible only when he has no conscience."

"You surprise me!" exclaimed Choiseul. "Well, you will know best how to put the man out of the way; I have enough to do with my own task."

"Be sure to instruct your spies; I will set mine in motion.—And now, to the health of your fair sister!" They raised their glasses with a smile full of meaning. Choiseul wrapped himself in his fur, and Orleans rang the bell. A few minutes later, the minister left the palace, and soon after him the duke.

The court had assembled again at Versailles. Christmas had passed, and the beginning of February, 1764, had come, bringing no change in the position of the different parties. The confidence of Louis in his son, and the influence of Madame de Seran increased, as well as the illness of the Marchioness de Pompadour. The violent and fitful palpitation of her heart and her repulsive meagreness baffled all the skill of Quesney. The phial was continually remembered by Beaumarchais, and though the marchioness avoided all perfumes, he was convinced that some effective means had been used slowly to destroy her life. But how and by whom? He noticed that Orleans kept away from court, and seemed to renounce aristocratic society, remaining long on his estates at Dauphiny and Brittany. The clique of Ventadour and La Blache appeared also to have broken off all intercourse, devoting themselves to the honorable and universally venerated family of Penthièvre. On the other hand, Caron became aware that his own movements were watched. Debrelon warned him, and revealed the fact that Orleans had shown some distrust of himself and Coralie.

Notwithstanding his many connections and acquaintances, Beaumarchais continued to live in his accustomed quiet style. He never dined from home, and was accessible only to his friends, whose familiar society had been diminished, eighteen months before, by the decease of the Chevalier de Piron, to whom Caron and Susanna were indebted for having brought them from the obscurity of the Pigeonnier. "Do not leave my wife," he said, as he was closing his eyes in death, "and take some advice from me. It is natural for you to ruin your enemies, and that very speedily—to disgrace them publicly by a single blow, and then forget them. Be moderate in this style of warfare, for what is too often repeated loses effect—but always remember your enemies!"

Madame de Piron could find consolation only in Susie's society. She ac-companied Caron and his wife (after the king had domiciled his daughters at Versailles), to the residence assigned them there, and the three were rarely seen at Paris. There was, however, one suspected person from whom Beaumarchais could not free himself—Batyl, who visited him under all kinds of pretences, and whose attachment seemed to have no bounds, though Caron knew well enough that the harpist was again in the pay of La Blache. To forbid his intercourse altogether would have seemed strange, and Beaumarchais preferred to understand his spy rather than be surrounded by unknown and more dangerous persons. All his opponents counted on Batyl's intimacy, who was commissioned to find out all the professor's plans, and to silence him whenever he was about to make use of the proofs he was supposed to possess against the Choiseul-Orleans party. By this means Madame de Ventadour and Terray would also be relieved of an old and troublesome apprehension, and La Blache's revenge satisfied. If Caron had estimated the whole influence that might be brought against him and the undying hatred of his enemies, he must have trembled to think of that hour when the marchioness would cease to live. An unexpected occurrence called him suddenly far away from his usual routine into a new world.

About two months after the private supper at Saint-Cloud, the aged father of Beaumarchais and his daughters came weeping to Versailles.

"But my dearest father, what is the matter?" exclaimed Susanna, as she met the old watchmaker. "Why, you seem to be in great affliction!"

Caron led his father to an arm-chair. "Have you had great losses, or is your honor endangered?"

"Yes, our honest name is attacked by a profligate wretch!"

"Who in Paris could vent that hatred on the father which was intended for the son?"

"Would to Heaven it were that only, and in Paris!" the elder Beaumarchais sighed. "We are men and can protect ourselves, but a villany that is perpetrated on defenceless women—"

"At a distance? On women?" exclaimed Caron. "You must be speaking of my sisters at Madrid! What has happened to them?"

"You are aware that, since the death of my son-in-law Gilbert, they have been living in retirement, esteemed by all; and that the keeper of the royal archives, Don José de Clavigo,* has been visiting them for years as Marie's accepted lover. How often have we read his ardent letters—"

"And the knave is faithless to Marie!"

"Faithless, and a slanderer. After having deceived the poor girl for a long time, he exposed her to the scorn of the community while she was making preparations for the wedding. Since he can give no good reason for his conduct, he endeavors to defame her publicly. Sorrow and shame have brought Marie to a sick-bed. Read these letters. We are far away, and can give her no assistance."

"Calm yourself, my father. If Clavijo is a worthless fellow, Marie shall be avenged, and I will not remain idle one moment. She is my sister; but the position of Clavijo in Spain is too important to attempt any thing against him without strict investigation. We can do little in such cases by violence, or vengeful intention, and if we can place them both in an honorable position, I am certain their estrangement would be more pleasant to all concerned."

"Dear Caron," said Susanna, "use all your influence for these deceived women; go and save them from the calumny and the disgrace of having been abandoned by a faithless man, where it is impossible for them to assert the rights pledged to them. In your absence I shall be consoled by the thought that you are preserving our loved ones from despair. Tell the princesses of your purposes at the audience."

"I thank you, daughter of my heart!" said the father, embracing her tenderly. "We as well as all our friends will watch over you, and God will be gracious to my son in his noble undertaking."

"Await me here after the audience, father; for not a day must be lost." Caron hastened to his royal pupils, related to them Marie's affair, and read them the letter of Madame Gilbert, his oldest sister. "In view of these circumstances, your royal highnesses, I have only to make the request, that you give me immediate leave of absence. My presence is not necessary here now, as the reunion of his majesty's family and the confidence of all true patriots have been attained. The time for mystery is past, and I shall soon have the happiness to know that my only duty consists in aiding to entertain your highnesses."

"Your leave of absence is granted," replied Adelaide. "Not for a moment, dear Beaumarchais, must your sister remain without a protector. We will procure from the king the best recommendations for you to our ambassador at Madrid, the Duke d'Ossun, in order to give you importance, and render your undertaking successful. This is only a part of the gratitude the royal family owe you. We are, however, anxious on account of the illness of the marchioness, and the perplexing thoughts that naturally associate themselves with her death. It is a strange

* The name is Clavijo, like Montijo; not as Goethe has it: Clavigo.

justice that this woman approaches the term of her life just when she is about to make amends for the harm she has done. Do you think that the Duchess de Grammont is dangerous?"

"Your royal highness, she would be, if my observations were less penetrating. If the marchioness should die, be pleased to hand to his majesty the letters I shall leave in your charge at the farewell audience. Madame de Grammont will then be quite inoffensive."

"What letters are they?"

"The original correspondence of the duchess with Count Falcoz de la Blache, where can be read the ambitious views of the lady, as well as her liaison with the count."

"Madame de Grammont with La Blache?" exclaimed Victorie.

"That decidedly ruins her prospects!"

The information which Beaumarchais obtained in reference to his sister and Clavijo, given by two Spanish merchants, acquaintances of Duverney, who had just arrived from Madrid, and had business relations with Madame Gilbert, decided Caron to start. The banker gave him letters of credit; and the king, influenced by the princesses, the dauphin, and the marchioness, ordered his ministers to supply the professor with ample recommendations. Of course, Choiseul was informed of every thing, and took counsel with himself what he was to do with Beaumarchais. It was most painful to the premier to feel that he was in the hands of Orleans, who forced him to crime, in order to have him thoroughly under his control. If Caron was really dangerous to the duke, for reasons which he concealed from Choiseul, why could not the latter, if he showed himself a friend, make use of so skilful a man as Beaumarchais? Besides, the absence of the professor during the time an

attempt would be made upon the life of the marchioness, would make it impossible for him to plot against the party seeking to destroy the influence of the dauphin and Madame de Seran. Choiseul therefore concluded to use all means at his command so that Caron might succeed at Madrid, and detain him there by diplomatic missions which the minister knew how to render plausible.

Beaumarchais, therefore, received commissions that appeared too honorable and important to be refused, and that could also assist him in his principal object. Whether he had any idea of Choiseul's intentions, or was anxious about the events that might occur during his absence, he informed the dauphin of the sources whence he drew his intelligence respecting the opposing party. Debrelon was requested to send his reports to the Chevalier de Lavarde, an attaché of the Prince de Conti; the latter then was to forward them to the dauphin. The same arrangement having been made with Duverney, while Turgot and Malesherbes were in communication with monseigneur through Morelly, matters went on as well as if Caron were personally on the spot. During his absence, the dauphin had invited Susanna and Madame de Piron to take up their abode with Morelly; there they would be unnoticed, and safe under the guardianship of monseigneur, Conti, and Richelieu.

Madame de Pompadour dismissed Beaumarchais with a smile and the words: "I will recover before your return! This summer I shall be released from my suffering—ask Quesney." But death was in her features.

The dauphin gave his hand gravely to Caron, saying: "May Heaven help you to finish your affairs quickly and favorably! When you come back, you will find great changes. Whether for the better, who knows? Think no more of us, but of yourself. Let the assurance accompany you that I shall appreciate your fidelity as long as I live."

Beaumarchais again embraced Susanna as well as the rest of his relatives, visited Morelly at Trianon, to dream away one more hour of their ideal paradise for man on earth; then he hastened to Marseilles, where lay the vessel in which he was to embark for Spain.

On the 22d of February the Jesuits were banished—an event important to France as well as all Europe. The same proscription that they had often influenced the pope to decree against the Jansenists, was decreed against them, and received with popular gratitude, as a first blow against a domineering Church, the profligate clergy, and the power of the confessional. Jansenism avenged itself on Molinism, the people on the black cowls; and the charge of Jesuitism was sufficient to deliver any priest into the power of the magistrates, who fancied they became more important, the more victims they had. The motto of the order, " *Vestra fides nostra victoria est,*" * which Voltaire had satirized by the interpretation, " *Votre bêtise est notre force,*" † was illustrated by all the " *bêtise* " that revenge can imagine. Many innocent and pious priests were driven from their homes into wretchedness and disgrace. Venerable men, who had passed their lives in the service of religion, were imprisoned, and subjected to the most painful trials, because they had in some manner incurred the dislike of an official; and the means employed to uproot the order were as contemptible as those that had elevated it to respectability and power.

The dauphin, who certainly had most to complain of a society that as-

sociated his name with a most foul crime, was shocked at the disregard of every sense of equity, and the authority given to private enmity, for the ruin of the innocent, under the merest semblance of justice. The urgent representations he made on this subject to the king and the marchioness, and the encouragement he gave Madame de Serau to do the same, discredited him again with the people, who found pleasure in persecuting the black - coats. The real Jesuits were unharmed. The most cunning had sought a shelter before the tempest came, and laughed at Loyola's followers. They preached atheism, and no longer showed their heads; they derided the holy offices, and swaggered in fashionable costume, but expecting, some at home, and others in distant lands, the reëstablishment of their order.

France experienced yet another triumph. The Marchioness de Pompadour was near her death. There was a report that something mysterious was occurring in her apartments during her last days, but both her ladies assured inquirers that no one but Binet had been near her, and, as her illness had been long known, her decease was expected.

The princesses, the dauphin, and the queen, secretly visited Madame de Pompadour the day before her death, but his majesty manifested a strange equanimity at the approaching loss of one who had so materially aided him in the management of state affairs. On the 15th of April, the unfortunate marchioness—so long the curse of her country—was reclining in her easy-chair, breathing heavily; but she smiled as if she had resolved to leave the world with a bon-mot on her lips. The king visited her in the morning, asking after her health.

"Very well, your majesty!" said the

* Your fidelity is our victory.

† Your stupidity is our strength.

dying woman. "The spring air affects me a little, that is all."

"I believe it is true, my dear madame. — Adieu!" He did not even offer her his hand, but merely nodded and left, locking the door of communication to his private cabinet. The rattling of the lock in the profound silence suggested a rude and merciless heart in his majesty. Mesdames de Vilaille and d'Hautecour sat at the window with Quesney, while the marchioness stared with wonder after her old lover. Bitter thoughts darkened her countenance, but she folded her hands on her bosom and cast down her eyes. *This woman prayed!* Her whole life passed before her. Sad and joyful memories alternated through her mind. She seemed to experience a profound contrition, and again an exhausting contempt of herself. Finally, in a melancholy voice, she called, "Dear Hautecour!"

"Madame!"

"Take from my pocket the key of my secretary, and open it. You will find three sealed papers. Place them on the table before me. Do not forget to lock the secretary again." Madame d'Hautecour obeyed. "Now call Salvandy — and retire, all of you; the doctor also. I will ring when I want you." The ladies and Quesney withdrew, and the chamberlain entered. She beckoned him to approach. "Bend close to me, so that you may understand; I have much to say to you. — Chevalier de Salvandy, you were poor and despised when I took you into my service, and obtained for you a position, a salary, and the cross of St. Louis. Is not all this true, Salvandy?"

"As true as my gratitude."

"But I was a hard mistress. I tormented you in many ways; I often took pleasure in slighting you by preferring the smooth, versatile D'Atreuil-les, and in scolding and insulting you. Is that also true?"

"Madame, you were often excited, and this pained me; but I have forgotten all. You introduced my old mother into the religious house of St. Quentin."

"He has forgotten all!" she said, musingly. "If others could only speak thus!—Salvandy, I hear that you have long loved Mlle. de Rouverais. Is that so?"

"Marchioness, I have no hope! We still love each other—but my salary! I once petitioned you to increase it—"

"And I refused!"

"But you were so kind to my mother, and—"

"Silence, my friend! I did what I could. You know that the king could not bear you; he once nearly sent you away. In unimportant matters I was always obliged to let him have his way; he calls that economy! But listen! I feel that I shall die to-day! — Be calm; do not become alarmed. It is for me to fear death, not you. When I am dead, you will be dismissed. You were my servant; take this document with your name on it, and put it into your pocket; it contains the title-deeds to an estate of ten thousand francs a year. Leave Versailles; do not look back at this vile place, and on your wedding-day do you and your wife pray for the repose of my soul.—No, no, do not thank me; I command you not to thank me. You are to pay me for this present by a last service.—Place your ear close to my lips, for no other person must hear me. Do not start, or cry, but remain self-possessed. If you weep in my presence, my heart will break. I shall die more easily, because all around are so happy.—Well, then, when I am dead and buried, go to the Duke de Richelieu. Tell him I send him my greeting, and am sorry I hurt his feelings, and prevented him from gaining influence at court; that, by the just Judge, before whom I shall soon stand, I assured you that I had been poisoned —slowly but surely poisoned! Tell him that he must warn the dauphin against Orleans and Choiseul!—Now, take your inheritance, and perform my last request, and may you die more happily than poor Jeanne Poisson!" She held out her hand, which Salvandy kissed, bathing it with his tears. She turned her head in order not to witness his grief, and her bosom heaved violently. "Away, if I am not to curse you! The doctor—the ladies!" Salvandy rushed out. The others entered hastily, supposing that her hour had come. The marchioness smiled, "Ah, I have to endure yet many a struggle before I arrive yonder."

"But why do you suppose, gracious lady, that death confronts you?" asked Quesney.

"Doctor, surely you do not take me for a child? You are a great physician, and a state economist besides, but, believe me, you have greatly mistaken the nature of my disease! Do not feel mortified about it. Take this document as an acknowledgment of the friendship you have always shown me; it secures your future independence. While laboring for the good of the government, you have neglected your personal prosperity. The other paper is for Madame d'Hautecour. The rest are wretched parasites, who may apply to the king. I command you to have no *post-mortem* examination of my body. I have a horror of dissection.—And now, I am ready to depart."

For two hours the marchioness sat silent, lost in prayerful meditation; then her breathing became oppressed, and her neck, arms, and hands, suddenly swollen. The change in her condition was announced to the king. In

a few minutes the rotunda was filled with courtiers, and the ministers arrived. His majesty stepped into the audience-hall, and the apartments of the dying marchioness were opened; but no one entered, except the confessor, who had been sent for. When she saw him, she made a contemptuous gesture. "What can *you* forgive me?" she said, ironically; "I have never injured you! Send some one whom I have ruined—call all France to administer to me the viaticum!" The priest turned toward the door. "One moment!" she continued. "Wait; we shall go together!" All was silent.

Quesney entered the reception-room. "Your majesty, the Marchioness de Pompadour—"

"Is she dead? Very well, doctor!" The king bowed and went down the large staircase. He was soon riding to Choisy, on a hunting-excursion. The ministers could scarcely conceal their joy at the insensibility of the king and the death of their tyrant.

Doctor Quesney, Salvandy, and Madame du Hausset, the waiting-lady of the deceased, remained near her body. She was buried without display; but at Versailles and Paris great rejoicing took place. She was dead who had once expressed the wish, "*Après moi, le déluge!*" ("After me, the deluge!") The people avenged themselves by satirical epitaphs written to her memory. "But," Beaumarchais had said, "she is not the worst"—words afterward repeated with a full conviction of their truth.

On the day of Madame de Pompadour's death, while the king was hunting, and all were curious to know what his majesty would do, Choiseul, the Duchess de Grammont, Orleans, Maupau, Terray, and Diana de Ventadour, held a council at her Hôtel in the Luxembourg. That Louis had departed for Choisy, and did not intend to return in less than a week, accompanied only by those most indispensable to him, proved that he was wavering in his future plans, and trying to come to some certain resolution. He appeared to be making a weak effort at independence. A counteraction was determined upon, and his humor, whatever it might be, should be taken advantage of. The conclave decided to make a bold step. The fair sister of Choiseul, who had already, if only temporarily, obtained a victory over the king, was to surprise him at Choisy. He liked such *coups d'amour*. The place of Madame de Pompadour was to be filled before her remains had descended to the grave! A courier, therefore, was sent to Binet, the chief valet de chambre, and the duchess followed in the afternoon alone in her carriage, entertaining a confident hope that she would soon be able to inform her friends in Paris of her success in supplying the place of the deceased marchioness.

The forest of Choisy reëchoed with the horns and hounds of the chase. The king hunted all day, endeavoring to divert his thoughts by the excitement. It was getting dark, when the signal to return was given, and he entered the beautiful chateau where he had first seen Mesdames de Mailly and de Chateauroux. Advancing into the antechamber, he dismissed his attendants, and gave his whip, hat, and cutlass, to Binet, who whispered, "I have some news for your majesty."

"What is it?"

"The Duchess de Grammont has just arrived, and alone."

"Grammont? Where is she?"

"There!" Binet pointed to the royal cabinet.

A blush suffused the king's face as he stepped quickly toward his chamber, leaving the door open. On his entrance the duchess started in assumed confusion, and advanced to meet him.

"You, duchess! What do you wish? Probably you expected to find Count Falcoz de la Blache here, or your coachman has lost his way."

"Your majesty! you mistake me!"

"Your correspondence with him is in my possession; Binet will hand it to you, that you may be convinced how well I am informed. Your ambition is rather rude, and if I had never felt dislike toward you, I would now!" He rang, and Binet came. "Take this lady to her carriage and see that she arrives safe in Paris. I do not wish to meet her again.—My writing-case; and have the supper served." Love did not modulate the king's voice; it was authoritative and severe. He made an impetuous gesture, and, before the duchess could recover herself, she was in the first entrance-hall, where the cavaliers paid her sarcastic compliments. Louis wrote to Madame de Seran.

The Duchess de Grammont returned to her brother, and toward morning stood at his bedside, in anger and tears.

"Do I dream? You here! For Heaven's sake, what—"

"He sent me away like a servant-girl! In the anteroom his attendants laughed at my disgrace. At the same time a courier departed with a note to Madame de Seran."

"Seran? The dauphin? Impossible! But why—"

"Hush! the king is informed of my correspondence with La Blache."

Choiseul sank in alarm on his pillow. "I would say this is the work of Beaumarchais, if he were not four hundred miles away. It certainly comes from the dauphin. Then we must go a step farther and— Retire; I assure you we shall not fall!"

CHAPTER XI

FAREWELL TO TRIANON.

THE family of the dauphin were again at Trianon to enjoy the spring, and the princesses came on a visit, for a May-tree was to be planted and a festival held, as usual, assembling all in the vicinity. Grand levees always ceased on the appearance of the prince at this favorite country-seat, and he very seldom granted audiences while there. Even the king respected this custom, and when he surprised his son by a visit, he was generally accompanied only by three or four cavaliers. At this fête no one was specially invited, but all were welcome. From among those who thus volunteered their presence, the dauphin selected the persons whose society he most desired afterward, and the inquiry, "Shall we see you again at Trianon?" was understood as an invitation at any time. Those who did not appear at this May festival were excluded not by others but themselves.

The woods and meadows had just donned their first verdure, and not a cloud darkened the sky. The bell of the village church echoed in the valley; and, on the upper terrace of the palace, the musicians of the body-guard of the dauphin, in shepherds' costumes, played a morning serenade. In the square the villagers were assembling, the women dressed in white, with red ribbons on their shoulders and bodices, and green wreaths in their hair. Crowds from Arcis, St. Cyr, Marly, Fontenay, and Villepneux. In the park, upon the terraces, and in the arcades, many cavaliers and ladies assembled who wished to pay their respects to the prince, and the old custom of the day.

As the clock struck eleven, the dauphin appeared, having on one side his consort, and, on the other, holding the hand of his eldest son, the Duke de Berri. His sisters Adelaide, Sophie, and Victorie; the governesses of the "children of France," Madame de Marsan, followed with the young Provence and Artois; a nurse carried the Princess Elizabeth. In the suite of the royal party, besides a few servants, were only Captain d'Aumont, Count de Mouy, Sieur de Romanet, the secretary, and the Duke de Vaugyon, the adjutant. The band immediately left the plateau, and proceeded to the church, while monseigneur and his family moved among the visitors, conversing with all. However affable the prince was, his eyes glanced restlessly around, as if in search of some one, and when by a gesture he intimated that those present should follow him, he appeared to be displeased. While the guests were arranging themselves according to rank, in the procession that was to be headed by Cardinal de Luynes, he whispered to the dauphiness and his sisters: "I do not see Richelieu and Conti. What does their absence mean?"

"They visited us yesterday at Versailles and promised to come," replied Adelaide.

"Then they are detained at Paris by something very important," said Josepha; "probably they will be here at dinner."

"As I am not accustomed to be neglected by them, I feel somewhat anxious. But let us go; the cardinal is waiting." He made a motion to Luynes to take precedence, and the cortége moved through the left arcade, across the village street, where the peasants were crowding toward the church square. Here, at the head of his festively-arrayed congregation, was Father Morelly. Thousands of rejoicing voices received the dauphin, who again became cheerful when he perceived Malesherbes. He greeted all, and the dauphiness accepted a myrtle-wreath from the daughter of the mayor.

It was the custom that the pastor should hand the breviary to monseigneur and madame, with the prayers marked. When Morelly was offering the book to the dauphin, he said in a low voice: "The first prayer is very important, monseigneur!" then, bowing, he walked into the church porch, followed by the surprised prince, his suite, and the people. While the organ sounded and high mass began, the dauphin opened the prayer-book, and was greatly astonished to find a note between the leaves of the first prayer. He gently touched his wife with his elbow, opened the paper and read:

"*Monseigneur:* We have arrived secretly, and are at Father Morelly's. Chevalier de Salvandy is with us, who has a message from the deceased marchioness to you—very urgent and serious.

"CONTI and RICHELIEU."

"Let us exchange books, dear Josepha." He handed her the breviary with the note.

The princess glanced over the writing, and was also greatly perplexed. She bent slowly toward him: "When and where?"

"During the fireworks; at Morelly's."

The dauphiness traced these words with a pin on the margin of the book, and hid the note in her bosom.

After the high mass the pastor delivered the May sermon. Some of the courtiers considered it too philosophic, others too agricultural, but the congregation understood it.

"When," he said, "our forefathers ceased to live by hunting and began to use the plough, they annually planted a May-tree, as a sign of public spirit and of pastoral happiness—as a sort of pledge that they would regard the cultivation of the soil as the source of freedom and contentment. It is well, indeed, thus to celebrate anywhere the Spring in her green robe of hope—to renew our covenant with a bountiful God, and, while sowing the seed which Autumn gives us back in fruit, to rejoice in the divine dispenser of sun and rain—the fountain of light and love. Only the solitary man lives by intrigue and crime; but the members of a well-ordered state flourish best by agriculture. They rejoice in the anniversary of the May-tree, which is always a poplar,* the emblem of a people advancing in prosperity."

In his discourse, Morelly spoke of the inhabitants of Trianon, as to their increase in charity and brotherly kindness, under the protection of the dauphin, closing with the prayer: "That some day all France may live in gratitude and hope, under the rule of him who had made a paradise of the village!"

The picture of the future happiness of France impressed all the hearers, but the dauphin and his wife were deeply moved. After the last hymn all rose, and the festival began.

At the side of the mayor and the pastor, the chief members of the royal family walked at the head of the peasants, among whom were the courtiers, according to custom. On the square in front of the church a place was prepared for the planting of the tree, whither a band of maidens, preceded by music, brought the young poplar, which had been taken from the palace park, amid songs and rejoicings.

The dauphin approached Morelly, sprinkled holy water on both the tree and the ground where it was to be planted. Then the princesses, court ladies, peasant-women. and girls, dec-

---

* Le peuplier, from peupler, to multiply.

"LET US EXCHANGE BOOKS."

P. 124.

orated it. In the midst of a chant of blessing and thanksgiving, monseigneur seized the trunk, and, assisted by the women of the village, lowered the roots into the earth, while slowly the branches rose into the air, fluttering with ribbons.

He said: "I, Louis, Dauphin of France, Lord of Trianon, in the name of God, plant this May-tree, the poplar, in the consecrated soil of my land, as a sign of liberty, order, and prosperity, for this village! May felicity and virtue ever dwell here! May all France be happy! Long live the king!"

"Long live the dauphin and his family!" the crowd replied, and the trumpets sounded.

The youngest members of the royal family threw the first earth upon the roots. The mayor, the pastor, and the maidens, filled up the pit, and, amid music and song, a May king and queen were chosen from among the youth of the people. Monseigneur danced with the May queen, and the dauphiness with the May king, once round the tree. The maiden received a gold chain and cross, and the young man a ring. The royal party and suite then returned to the palace, accompanied to the entrance of the park by the mayor, the pastor, and the newly-elected royal pair.

When the prince returned the breviary to Morelly on the way, he remarked: "The first prayer appears important; I have marked it on that account. Take my compliments to your guests."

The day passed pleasantly. The aristocracy celebrated the festival in the park, and the villagers on the square. When the sun was sinking behind the distant towers of Nauphle, the people were permitted to enter the park, and witness the fireworks to be displayed on the middle terrace. After the dauphin had given the signal, and the first

rocket rose, he pressed Josepha's hand, and quietly disappeared. In his apartment he found the Chevalier de Mouy, and both hurried through a side-gate to the parsonage. In the back room toward the garden, they met Conti and Richelieu.

"What have you to say to me, my friends?" exclaimed the prince, uneasily. "You have almost spoiled for me the happiness of the day. While I was lowering the poplar, I felt indeed as if burying my heart. You cannot imagine how sad I was at that moment of general joy. What message have you from the deceased marchioness? Where is Salvandy?"

"In the next room, dear sir," replied Conti, gravely; "Father Morelly, Malesherbes, and Mouy are with him. Before we present the chevalier we wish to prepare you for bad tidings that require energetic measures."

"On account of the marchioness? Marshal, do not conceal your news any longer from me."

"Gracious prince, Madame de Pompadour died of *poison!*"

"How can this terrible accusation be proved?" said the dauphin, horrified.

"A few hours before she died, she made Salvandy solemnly promise that, as soon as possible after her death, he was to come to me, her old enemy, and reveal that she had died by a system of slow poisoning. I am charged to warn you against Orleans and Choiseul."

"'No perfumes!' Then Beaumarchais was right? That scene at Versailles between Orleans and the marchioness was no illusion, and we have again the old watchword, 'Bourbon or Orleans?'" He paced the room in the utmost consternation and anger. A profound anxiety for his family occupied his thoughts.

"No other motto than that, my royal cousin," said Conti, in a melancholy tone. "The reports I have lately received from the husband of Mlle. Raucourt demonstrate that the plans of the duke are inimical to you; that Choiseul is his instrument, and that they have complete control of Binet, the king's valet de chambre. The love-correspondence of Madame de Grammont with La Blache, and which was betrayed to Beaumarchais, has destroyed the hopes of these people."

"Binet, who was probably used to accomplish the death of his relative," added Richelieu, "is zealously employed to estrange the king from your highness and Madame de Seran, by some new love-intrigue."

"All this must be finished at a single blow, my prince!" exclaimed Conti. "Now is the favorable moment. The king will not always be happy in his relations with Madame de Seran; and being incapable of holding the reins of government, either you or Choiseul will rule him. Have no hesitation, for every day brings us nearer to ruin."

"Oh, these reasons are more than sufficient to rouse me. It shall not be said that I was negligent when danger approached in so undisguised a form. I will demand the dismissal of all the ministers, as well as the banishment of Orleans."

"And the estates of the kingdom, your royal highness!" exclaimed Conti. "Without their assistance we cannot remedy the public misery."

"Malesherbes says the same thing. —Let Salvandy enter."

Conti and Richelieu retired to the adjoining room, and sent Salvandy. The dauphin demanded a circumstantial account of the death of the marchioness, and, receiving the chevalier's word of honor to be silent on the subject, dismissed him. Conti and the marshal returned.

The dauphin was pale and gloomy. "My friends, to-morrow you will accompany me to the king. Either Choi-seul and Orleans will then be nothing, or—I have planted the last May-tree." He preceded them into the next apartment, where, pressing the hands of Morelly and Malesherbes, he said: "Let us be prepared for a strange change in our affairs. This is a decisive day in my life!" He returned to the palace with his confidants, just as the names of Louis and Josepha shone in the last fireworks. He was no longer the reserved prince, who concealed his resolutions, but the royal master, for whose brow a crown seemed not far distant. All remembered the words he uttered on that day, and comprehended that the determination of his fate was at hand.

On the next morning there was great excitement at Versailles. The king countermanded the session of the council, as he intended to grant a special audience to monseigneur. Strange reports were abroad about the May festival of the preceding day. Choiseul returned full of uneasiness to his dwelling, and, after a conference with Maupeau and Terray, sent a messenger to warn Orleans.

The dauphin was accompanied by Conti, Richelieu, and the Cardinal de Luynes, but entered the royal cabinet alone. Something uneasy and undecided marked the reception the monarch gave his son—a manner contrasted by that of the prince.

"According to your note, Louis, which Mouy was ordered to hand personally to me, something important in reference to state matters must have led you here. As you have brought Conti, the marshal, and the cardinal, you must be prepared with extraordinary news. These gentlemen are your confidants."

"Indeed, my royal father! my appearance here concerns not only the state, but the well-being of our whole family, who are very dangerously threatened. And this hour will decide our prosperity or destruction."

"That is saying a great deal! Who dares to plot our ruin?"

"Your majesty, do you remember our meeting in the "Temple of the Sun?" I owe the happiness of that day to Mesdames de Seran and de Pompadour. The conference was secret, and yet it was betrayed."

"By whom?"

"By Binet."

"I do not believe that!" cried the king, violently. "Binet is my faithful servant; he has never deceived me."

"Nevertheless, Choiseul hated the marchioness from the day you began to be kind to me."

"That is possible, even without Binet. The minister saw you dance with Madame de Pompadour at Fontainebleau, and, of course, divined that a reconciliation had taken place between us."

"I will not dispute that, your majesty, but what do you say to the fact that Choiseul, on his return from Fontainebleau, had a secret interview with Orleans at Saint-Cloud?"

"How do you know that?"

"Through my agents, sire; you make use of such people yourself. They heard young Chartres talk about it, and so it is certain. At that time you spoke against Choiseul, and gave me your word to dismiss him as soon as possible. If I now solemnly assure you that he is a confederate of Orleans, and that Diana de Ventadour is his friend, while she influences the financial minister and the chancellor, you must own, your majesty, that those persons should be discharged who conspire with the treacherous head of a house so nearly related to the throne, and interested in the destruction of the Bourbons. Suppose I reveal to you that Madame de Pompadour did not die of consumption, but of a slow poison; that two hours before her death she confided this secret to Salvandy, ordering him to in-

form Richelieu of it, who was to warn me against Orleans and Choiseul; that, besides her two ladies, no one but Binet and Quesney were near her—Binet, who now enjoys the minister's friendship—then all I have to propose is, that you should exile Orleans for life, order Chartres to receive the tonsure, instead of consenting to his projected marriage with Mlle. de Penthièvre, dismiss Choiseul and the other ministers, and arrest and try Binet."

"What proofs," exclaimed the king, "have you for such terrible accusations?"

"My word of honor, the reports of Beaumarchais and his agent, and the declarations upon oath of Conti, Richelieu and Salvandy." He opened the door leading to the audience-hall.—"Come, gentlemen, tell his majesty all you know, for the dauphin has no credit!"

Before the king could signify his dissent, the prince's companions entered. His majesty, however, gave them no indication to speak, but walked about, uneasy and suspicious. "You wish to have a scene, Louis; to force me to extreme measures, and I do not like such a mode of proceeding. The marchioness is dead. Deprived of her intellect and assistance, you wish to make me despise those who may be ambitious and intriguing, but are nevertheless experienced in business. Whom am I to trust? Rogues usually have sense! I cannot make much use of integrity and virtue in politics. Choiseul sketched the Bourbon treaty—a proof that he loves our house. I do not believe in his alliance with Orleans. Who can replace him, or undertake the management of the disordered finances, complete the army and navy, and control the restless Parliament?"

"If you really wish to have the public misery ameliorated, I can find the right persons for the right places.

Make Marshal de Richelieu minister of war, and Conti prime minister; place Cardinal de Luynes over the Church, let President de Malesherbes control the finances, and convoke the Estates-General! I demand this in the name of a dishonored France, of my children, of God, who will hold you responsible for the future of our country!"

"Estates-General!" Louis XV. passionately seized his son's arm. "I would kill my own brother if he uttered that word a second time! It means republicanism and abdication!"

"The Estates-General, sire, constitute an old French institution, by whose aid Henry IV. and Sully reigned well."

"Oh, I understand you! You wish to deprive me of the sceptre! Richelieu, Luynes, and Conti, would be your ministers; not mine. Perhaps I ought to be thankful should you allow me the means of subsistence! In order to satisfy your ambition to govern, you endeavor to frighten me by suggestions of poison and death! Hypocrite! your favorites are your witnesses—men who will rise by Choiseul's fall! If I need ever tremble for my life, it is in view of him who cannot patiently await his coronation!" His anger mastering him, he gave the dauphin a violent blow.

"For Heaven's sake, your majesty, what are you attempting?" cried Conti, stepping between them.

"You will not," exclaimed Richelieu, with proud indignation, "insult your son and yourself, sire! Take the dauphin away, Prince de Conti, before the worst happen!"

"No," said the crown prince, very pale; "the worst has happened! You, sire, have pronounced sentence of death on your son! The danger you need not fear will be mine, because you will be Choiseul's slave, as you were Fleury's and Madame de Pampadour's.

When I am dead, think of this hour, when you gave my enemies the signal for my murder, and allowed the Bourbons to be destroyed through weakness and cowardice! I bewail nothing but the fate of my children!" He cast a bitter glance at the king, and withdrew. Conti and Richelieu followed.

When the party were driving back to Trianon, the dauphin said, sadly: "It is decided! All I ask of you is never to mention what you have just witnessed." From that day, he secluded himself more than ever. Formerly, he could not account for his bad health, though he expected to die early. Since his conversation with Salvandy, he felt that he was the victim of his enemies, and concealed from his family and friends his mental and physical suffering. His ideas of morals, religion, government, and the glory of France, he condensed into memorials for his son Berri, and recommended by name those whom he confided in and honored. The papers were sealed, and delivered into the hands of the Duke de Vaugyon, his adjutant, who was ordered to give them to the prince's eldest son as soon as he was old enough to govern. He never voluntarily approached Versailles again, living as a private person. The education of his children, and the improvement and society of Trianon, occupied his mind.

The new rupture between the king and the dauphin was too serious not to encourage Choiseul in his attempts to possess himself of all power. But however dull the king was—however great his indignation at the idea of changing his policy and convoking the Estates-General, his indecision and fear did not permit him to place himself again under the control of the premier.

An incident one day frightened both Orleans and Choiseul. While the king was dining with the minister, he said to Binet, who was waiting on them: "Listen, fellow: it is publicly reported that Madame de Pompadour died. of poison—you ought to know about it!" This remark was so unexpected, that the trembling valet dropped the dish. "You are becoming awkward in your service; therefore, begone! I shall give you a pension, but I do not wish ever to see you again." His majesty rose, cast an angry glance at Choiseul, and left him to finish his repast alone.

This affair induced Orleans and his accomplice to change their tactics. The king seemed warned, for the secret was betrayed. They were obliged to be at least polite to the dauphin on the few occasions of meeting him, and even praise him to his father; but this was for the purpose of destroying him the sooner. The monarch, still under the influence of Madame de Seran, alarmed by Binet's suspicious fear, and worked upon by Choiseul, gradually forgot his anger, and again inclined toward his son, who maintained a serious and reserved behavior.

When it was noticed that the king regarded with satisfaction any effort to please the young Louis, the premier proposed to have him nominated commander-in-chief of the army, and to give him a public proof of confidence, by directing him to move to a military encampment. The dauphin felt little inclination to accept a favor obtained through Choiseul; but to refuse would be to offend the king, and so the prince's party urged him to take that opportunity of gaining influence, at least in one branch of the state government. He consented, with the understanding of having with him Richelieu and Conti; and of being responsible, not to the minister of war, but to the king alone. These conditions were bold, but Choiseul took care that they should be granted. Again a reconciliation was

effected between the monarch and his son, though the latter retained his sadness and distrust.

In July the troops moved to the camp at Compiègne, except the Swiss regiment, the light horse-guards, and the Paris garrison. Choiseul had omitted nothing to render the reunion of the king and his son as prominent as possible, as well as the honor bestowed on the dauphin. The higher officers were to meet the commander-in-chief at Versailles, and accompany him, together with the dauphiness, the princes, and his whole suite.

It was the last day at Trianon to be passed in quiet, for the military reviews were to last until the end of the autumn, when monseigneur and his family, on the king's invitation, were to visit Fontainebleau, and thence remove to the winter residence, the Hôtel St. Louis. Again the dauphin assembled around him the limited circle of his friends who favored his ideas and plans. Turgot had come from Limoges at a wish expressed by his patron. They sat under the elms near the grotto, and visited every place dear to them, enjoying the happiness of unrestrained friendship and of hope in the future.

The dauphin was thin, but he jested at the anxiety of Josepha, saying that the camp at Compiègne would render him robust, as the exercise on horseback would be beneficial. A sad irony was in the words, and a peculiar thoughtfulness made their conversation involuntarily grave. After dinner he remarked: "It may be long before I again see you, Morelly, Turgot, and Malesherbes; but my other loved ones remain with me. I beg you, then, to accompany me to the heights. Let us once more recall the happy ideas of former times.—We shall not tarry long, dearest Josepha."

The three gentlemen rose and left the

dining-room with the prince, slowly walking up the winding-path leading to the ruin on the hills.

"My friends, this upward road resembles my own life's labor! If I ever reach the summit, I shall see nothing but the remains of an edifice whose ruin I could not prevent. You are more to be envied than I am! Voluntarily you could devote yourselves to the good of your fellow-beings—unhindered and assisted by honest auxiliaries. The heir of a throne, even when at the age of manhood, is but a guarded and watched child; so much the more troublesome will be the pressure of a crown, as it will find him unprepared. He should learn in time how to govern, and be a master before the real period of his authority."

"It is no wonder, then," replied Malesherbes, "that there are so many bad kings—how are they to become capable? But good and great monarchs do sometimes exist, and óne of them makes amends for the misery caused by ten of his predecessors. Whence do those obtain the virtues in which the others failed? They originate in an oppressed youth; from their own sufferings come the blessings of their government. Are not Henry IV. and Frederick II. historic examples? And the same discipline will make you, my prince, a good king!"

"Perhaps, Lamoignon, when I have passed through such a preparatory trial. But every one has not that iron nature which endures to the end."

"Should you not find pleasure, your royal highness," interrupted Turgot, "in the thought that your virtues have gained the love of the oppressed people, who see in you their only hope? I will not mention the happiness of your private life, for thousands of excellent fathers enjoy that, but you are aware that every good seed you plant in the heart of your sons will bear fruit for a whole nation, and that your example and favor encourage your friends to walk in the path of duty. Yonder ruin may be untenable, but has it not material which may serve for a new edifice?"

"And now, look down," added Morelly, gently, "into our sweet Trianon —how peacefully it rests at your feet! Cheerfulness and industry dwell in those cabins formerly filled with poverty and vice. The May-tree flourishes in a village that you have turned into a paradise. It is something of the *Basiliade* dream that you have realized. Can any prospect be more charming?"

"Yes, it is fair as all my wishes and hopes! Our whole life is a dream, from which we awaken only after death! Perhaps my presentiments are foolish, and I will not sadden you by repeating them. I have accustomed myself to regard my own life as very transitory, and to make a friend of death. I would like to speak to you on that subject, without giving you an impression that I actually feel myself near my end. But suppose I die as dauphin? I wish to impart to you my unchangeable will. This ruin, an image of my France, is before our eyes; the earth lies silent at our feet, and the eternal heavens are above us. Give me your hands, as men of a pure conscience —as friends of him who loved you in life as in death!" The prince extended his hands with an unusual melancholy, and tears filled his eyes.

"Do not leave my children while you live, even should they prove unworthy! I have left a memorial for my son Berri; Vaugyon has the original, and the dauphiness will find a copy of it. Your names are mentioned, and how I regard you. You, Turgot and Malesherbes, must be his immediate reliance, but Morelly will remain with my Trianon. Do you agree?"

"It shall be as you say!" replied the three, greatly moved.

"Now I ask you not to speak of this conversation as long as I live. Two persons I would like to have seen are not here. Piron is dead, and Beaumarchais is abroad. When Caron returns tell him of my wishes, and receive his promise, should I be—prevented! He is skilful and honorable. Though he cannot enter the lists with great politicians, he can always warn my children against their enemies. If I were king, I should make him lieutenant of the Parisian police." He smiled, and, making a hasty motion, intimated to his companions to remain where they were, while he walked farther on, and looked down for some time with folded arms. "Oh my Trianon, farewell!" he said, as if in pain, and extended his hands. He turned quickly and advanced toward his friends with an agitated countenance. "Let us go! I should like to see all the villagers before I depart!"

"To-morrow, your royal highness, at starting?" asked Morelly.

"Yes!"

The party descended in silence toward Little Trianon, each engaged with his own thoughts. Shortly before their arrival the prince spoke in a more lively manner, asking information about the condition of affairs at Limoges, and the business of the Chamber of Taxation.

On the following morning, when the long travelling-train stood before the porch, the inhabitants of Trianon assembled in the court-yard. The dauphin and the princesses were personally acquainted with each individual, and his circumstances; they had a sympathizing word for every one. Many tears were shed, and a feeling of sadness pervaded the minds of all present.

"But, children, we are going to return! I shall send you word, by your pastor, how we are!" Monseigneur hastily conducted his wife to the carriage. "Farewell, farewell a thousand times!" he whispered to the people. His equipage rolled away; Madame de Marsan, with the children, the ladies and cavaliers, followed. For a long time the peasants, together with Morelly, Turgot, and Malesherbes, looked after the departing retinue.

CHAPTER XII

THE CAMP AT COMPIÈGNE.

THE son of Louis XV., though he was thirty-six years old, for the first time forsook the obscurity in which royal jealousy and intriguing politics had designedly kept him, and entered a public career. He was now the leader of an army—a fact received by the Parisians with joy, and with suspense by the soldiers. Any one who wished to be presented to monseigneur hastened in advance to Compiègne and Versailles. After the king, surrounded by his ministers, had delivered the command to his son in the grand audience, introduced him to the generals, and dismissed him and his family, the dauphin departed on horseback, with a military escort, in order to reach the camp by passing through Paris, St. Denis, and Senlis.

Though the last audience was the only official ceremony, and Choiseul intentionally avoided any thing like an ovation for the prince, his progress through the capital was a voluntary and universal triumph. The indignation against the king and his councillors was for the first time clearly expressed in the enthusiasm of the people for his successor. The disposition of the inhabitants of Paris reflected itself in those public bodies always in conflict with the government, and they secretly resolved to make a demonstration. These were the Parliament, the Châtelet, with the lawyers, the Chamber of Taxation, and the Communes. All was arranged so speedily, that the son of the king, had left Versailles before the ministers knew any thing of the intended movement, or they would have prevented it. At the head of mounted commissioners came the lieutenant of the Parisian police, M. de Sartines, who, disquieted by the crowds and the excitement, met the prince at Vaugirard.

"What do you mean, sir, by your police guards?" asked monseigneur.

"Your royal highness, the Parisians are crowding at the barrières and on the streets. Various corporations wish to address you, and the greatest disorders—"

"M. de Sartines, I command you to return immediately, and post your men at the street corners, that no accidents may occur. I will answer all who address me; besides, I do not fear the Parisians, and a view of my person will not create disturbance. It is scarcely suitable for a French soldier to be protected by the police, and I come as such!"

Sartines had to depart unwillingly. The trumpeters of the dauphin's regiment opened the procession, followed by himself and madame on horseback, attended by Richelieu, Conti, Mouy, Vaugyon, and a suite of generals. After them came the carriages containing Madame de Marsan with the Princes de Berri, de Provence, d'Artois, and the Princess Elizabeth, the ladies of honor, the physician Dr. Bouillac, and the travelling equipages, and finally the troops from the vicinity, with their bands. At the Barrière Vaugirard the mayor and elders of the community received the procession, surrounded by a multitude of rejoicing people, who, understanding the purport of what the prince had said, treated Sartines with contempt.

"Will you permit," began the mayor, "that Paris may see her beloved dauphin, and wish him a happy return? We desire to take advantage of this opportunity, to express to you personally and voluntarily the hope, love, and reverence of the capital."

"I thank you and the loyal inhabitants of Paris," responded the dauphin, "who are my friends, and among whom my family and myself have always felt happy. I will return love for love, and your respect toward me by a hearty desire for your good, which every man owes to the capital of his native land. Your hope, greater perhaps than it ought to be, I will endeavor to justify as far as I am able, and only demand confidence in return, for the confidence of a people is the security of the throne. Distribute among the poor of Paris, at my expense, what you may consider reasonable, and do me the pleasure of accompanying me as far as the Barrière St. Denis—the mayor alone shall be my protection in the capital!"

Amid thunders of applause, the procession entered the city. When the prince was crossing the Pont Neuf, and had arrived at the statue of Henry IV., he stopped, and, reverently taking off his hat, said: "Gentlemen, that was a great monarch! God grant that we may follow in his footsteps! Cousin Conti, let my sons see the face of this great man, who never caused but one sorrow to his country; and that was when he died!"

As the deputations from the Parliament, the Châtelet, and the Chamber of Taxation, moved from the old palace of justice, the prince covered his head...The three presidents, in their addresses, assured him that the opposition of the Parliament was founded on love and care for the royal house and the well-being of the country, but that they entertained the best wishes for him wherever he went.

"I am glad to hear that," replied monseigneur. "Justice requires no bed,* for it should always be awake. You have ever been the advisers of the crown, and honest opposition is your attribute, which I honor. But never belong to any party opposing mine, which is that of our native land. I wish you all, especially the Chamber of Taxation, joy in your duty, and may you endeavor to diminish the oppression of the people!"

In the Rue St. Denis, near the Place Innocence, the crowd was very great, for there the "Dames de la Halle" had posted themselves. The oldest among them, with white locks straying from under her large lappeted cap, advanced, and, seizing the bridle of the prince's horse, offered him her hard right hand.

"Monseigneur, the fishwomen wish that you may return in good health, and live to be so old that my great grand-daughter may be as gray as I am, before the good God sends for you!"

"That, dear madame, is a very beautiful and pious wish. It affects me above all others. Give your faithful hand also to the dauphiness, and let Marshal de Richelieu present you my children. I am sure they will love in you, fidelity, industry, and the old Parisian sincerity. Farewell, ladies, and greet from me all wives and mothers!"

"Long live the dauphin and his wife!"

"Long live the dauphin's children!" cried hundreds of shrill voices, in which the people generally joined. Thus the prince left Paris by the gate of St. Denis. He returned the same way, but more quietly.

---

* "Lit de justice," the court of justice held by the ancient French kings, reclining on a couch.

"I do not fear the Parisians! The people's confidence is the throne's security!"—"The mayor shall be the only protection of the dauphin in the capital"—"Justice requires no bed, it should always be awake,"—were expressions repeated by the people, and the scenes at the statue of Henry IV. were remembered throughout France; they startled the king and his ministers at Versailles.

When the dauphin arrived at Compiègne, and held the first review, he walked along the ranks with the hand of the dauphiness on his arm, stopped before each regiment, and said, "Soldiers, let me present to you my wife!" He developed his military views with great modesty, and his intimacy with Richelieu, the victor at Mahon, as well as with the noble Conti, gained him the hearts of the officers. His simple manners, his cordiality with all who addressed him, his daily visits to the bivouacs, and his care for the sick, made him beloved among the privates.

The evident popularity of the dauphin occasioned Choiseul much uneasiness. He did not expect that, suddenly emerging from retirement, the prince would have been so successful with the troops. In all his remarks, however respectfully the king was referred to, there was something criticising the condition of the country. Such a man, on his return from camp, and as chief of the army, would take a threatening attitude, and who knew how far his decision would go? These thoughts the minister instilled into the mind of his majesty, and he was ordered to follow the dauphin.

The Duke d'Orleans and Chartres had preceded the commander-in-chief to Compiègne, in order to present themselves, as was customary, at the head of the duke's regiment. Orleans, however, was treated with coolness, and never invited to headquarters. This neglect extended even to the regiment itself, which the prince visibly slighted, taking no trouble to point out their failures in discipline, or giving any evidence of interest in their soldierly bearing. Perhaps this was unwise, but his personal feelings conquered him, and on prominent occasions his behavior toward the duke was very marked.

Choiseul appearing a few weeks later (who had control of the war department), and having been treated in the same manner, it was the signal for the officers to withdraw from these two obnoxious persons, and the privates generally treated their comrades of the regiment Orleans in a similar way, who in consequence became discontented, looked askance at their colonel, and repeated old anecdotes of the mutual hatred of the houses of Orleans and Bourbon.

One afternoon the minister Choiseul dined alone with Duke d' Orleans. "He works into our hands," said the latter. "Believe me, he is too inexperienced to govern France; he cannot conceal his feelings and intentions. After his conduct toward me, I consider myself justified in leaving Compiègne without leave, and returning the command of my regiment to the king. I leave you to inform the dauphin of it, unless you prefer also to depart."

"I can neither blame you nor repress the desire to follow you; but I have been ordered to observe the prince at his first appearance in his new character, and, it seems, he forces us to make an end of him, but how?"

"I have already provided a very experienced fellow, who trembles at no danger—one of those madcaps who consider a quick death by the rope as compensated by a life of wild enjoyment. He has already acted for me, and will not fail again. Should I name him, you would be surprised."

"Monseigneur, if you are sure of the matter, I will follow you in a week. It would be advisable then to resign your commission into the hands of the dauphin, who is an independent commander-in-chief, responsible only to the king, and deliver the regiment to your successor. It will give you an appearance of loyalty and of unappreciated honor."

"Very well, though it will cost me some self-command to concede this precedence to my opponent. Now, I will name my agent to you—Belot!"

"Belot? The sub-officer in the provost guards, whose suspicious relations with Damien—"

"Hush! do not name either again. Think what you please. The man's name now is Trubaine, recommended to me by Sillery; his papers are in order, and I have placed him in my regiment. Before the affair is made public, he will be on board a vessel at Calais."

On the following morning at parade, Colonel Brian de Sully, commanding a regiment of the troops Orleans, handed the dauphin a sealed note, with the report that the duke had departed during the night, and left this letter to be delivered by M. de Sully. The prince opened and read it. "The Duke d'Orleans," he said, "has forsaken his post and sent me his farewell.—I hear, M. de Choiseul, that you dined with him yesterday; did you know any thing about his contemplated resignation?"

"He mentioned to me the reasons for it, and as it was not my duty to make representations to you, all I could do was to induce him to communicate with your highness, and not directly with his majesty."

"I am much obliged. In this case it would have made little difference. Such mere form-commanders, who regard the profession of arms an amusement, cannot be useful to the army, and can never obtain my esteem, even if they are princes; I feel the same toward ministers of war who would not have much to do with gunpowder. For the relinquishment of his post the duke must obtain the king's consent, and justify himself in that quarter. Colonel de Sully, I give you the regiment; it shall henceforth be called 'Sully'—a name immortal in the service of the Bourbons. I nominate you general. My son, the Duke de Berri, shall enter your corps when he is old enough."

"Then I would request permission, on account of the decided opinion expressed by your royal highness, to return to Versailles and report to his majesty," said Choiseul, bitterly.

"I have no objection. Go when you please—adieu!" The minister withdrew angrily. The honor of the troops Orleans, now called Sully, was reëstablished.

Nothing in nature is more inexplicable than the workings of the human heart. And it is remarkable that some characters display their highest functions when death is about to snatch them away, leaving a profound impression of qualities that were supposed to be originally absent. Such often die early, and the dauphin belonged to their number. His whole life, since he had left Trianon, was distinguished for noble aspirations and purposes. His activity, his desire to learn, his efforts to prevent suffering, and to administer justice, were extraordinary. He never spared himself, physically or mentally. His custom, even in the most inclement weather, was to visit regularly the posts, and he was often seen at the camp-fires, chatting with the soldiers. Perhaps there never lived a French prince so generally respected and beloved.

On the evening of the day in which Orleans had sent in his resignation, and Choiseul was treated with such un-

disguised contempt, the dauphin threw around him his field-cloak and prepared for his usual walk.

"Do not go this evening, dear Louis; it is cold and damp," said his wife.

"Do not hinder me, Josepha; you know I am on my usual round to regain the hearts our family have lost. I have acted so openly, that I must not neglect any thing to make my position secure, so that when I return to Paris, Choiseul and the old policy must fall, if the king does not wish to hasten a revolution in the state. I am determined to abolish abuses, lest the people violently demand their rights; for misery will make them rebellious. I am acting for the good of our children, dear wife. It is very necessary to make an inspection of my troops to-night; for I wish to make amends for an injustice into which I was forced in order to disencumber myself of Orleans."

"You are about to visit his old regiment? That makes me anxious. Orleans and Choiseul will do all they can against you."

"Do not be disquieted; we know how to meet them. They are accustomed to my resistance, and what is good cannot triumph without conflict. I know that the soldiers feel unhappy at my coldness, and I must visit them to-night. Sully will dine with us to-morrow, and present Berri to the men; they expect me. I only satisfy my own heart in not deceiving their expectations. In two hours I shall be back."

"Will you not ask Conti or Richelieu to accompany you? At least take your physician."

"You are singularly anxious to-night, dear Josepha. If you really desire it, Bouillac and my master of the horse may attend me." He left the town with them.

The camp occupied the right side of

the river. A quarter of a mile to the northeast, where the Aisne joins the Oise, a five - angled battery had been erected, manned by the regiment Orleans, and which they were to defend on the days of their battle evolutions. Loud merriment reigned there, for Colonel (now General) de Sully had informed his corps of the favor of the prince; other officers had come to wish them joy, and all expected the dauphin.

In front of one of the tents the soldiers were particularly gay. Sub-officer Trubaine, who had lately entered, and had plenty of money, was treating his comrades, who, from harmless merriment, were verging toward riot. Only Bedoyer, the second sergeant, and two privates, kept aloof, sipping their wine and keeping their own thoughts.

"I cannot banish it from my mind," said Bedoyer, "that I have seen this fellow before."

"As a soldier?"

"I am certain of it, Landry. I will wager my head that he was at the same time with me in the provost guards at Paris."

"No, sergeant, you must be mistaken," exclaimed the other private. "I remember the names of all that were there during the three years you served, but no Trubaine was among them. I have another idea, however."

"What is it, Favras? Perhaps it will lead us into the right track."

"Do you not remember a fellow resembling him, who acted wildly in Paris about 1758, and afterward deserted?"

"Belot! Yes!" exclaimed the sergeant. "He was implicated in the affair of Damien! A dissipated wretch?"

"Sergeant," said Landry, rising, "if you wish it, I will go and ask him; we can tell, by his manner, if he is the same man."

"We will go with you!" said the others. They were about to approach Trubaine, when the cry arose. "The dauphin!"

The prince with his attendants entered. The soldiers leaped up and greeted him with a shout. Sully and the rest of the officers hastened from their tent. Among the group the bold, broad-shouldered Trubaine was prominent; he was just uncorking a fresh bottle and filling his tankard. All were silent.

"Soldiers!" began the prince, "you have lost a chief under whom you could not obtain my approbation. I have now given you a new name, to show you that my objection was not against you. As my son Berri is to enter your corps, you will know how to appreciate that honor by good conduct as men and soldiers. I will present him to you to-morrow at parade.—General de Sully, you and your staff will be my guests to-morrow. Let me drink to the health of the regiment!" Many tankards were offered from all sides.

"Take mine, monseigneur!" said Trubaine, stepping up to the prince. "No one has yet drunk from it, and never shall. It must be called the dauphin's tankard. His royal highness the Duke de Berri will some day also drink from it, and it will become a sacred relic of the regiment."

The dauphin looked smilingly at the speaker. "Very well, my friend; that is an excellent idea. But do you drink first."

"Long live the dauphin and his illustrious family! I drink this in the name of the regiment Orleans!" Trubaine made a pretence of drinking, and handed the cup.

"Long live the dauphin!" echoed the soldiers.

"You meant Sully, my good man! I drink to the health of this regiment, its renown, its discipline in war as well as in peace, and its fidelity to the *fleur*

de lis. Long live the regiment Sully!"
—The prince emptied the cup to the bottom, and gave it to the general. "Have it bound with silver, and the date of this day engraved on it.—Good-by, children! acquit yourselves well on parade to-morrow." He departed from them with a farewell gesture, and the officers accompanied him to the battery, while the shouts of the privates resounded in the stillness of the night. While he was walking through the fields, he felt unusually ill; he shook with ague and his teeth chattered.

"Your royal highness, you are not well!" exclaimed Doctor Bouillac, approaching and taking his hand. "What does this mean? Your pulse is at high-fever heat!"

"It is nothing, doctor. Do not frighten any one on my account. Take me quickly home. The night air is damp and cold." They continued their way, the prince being supported by his two attendants. "I have taken," he said, "a violent cold, that is all." He had a bad night. The dauphiness sent for Conti and Richelieu. He felt better in the morning, but the parade and dinner had to be postponed.

General de Sully was rather glad at not immediately meeting the commander-in-chief, for he had a disagreeable report to make—Sergeant Trubaine had deserted during the night, and left no trace that could lead to his capture.

In the course of the next week the dauphin's condition was a little improved, but great weakness and loss of flesh were evident. He was well aware of the cause of his sudden and fatal illness, but no complaint ever escaped his lips, and he constantly endeavored to remove the fears of his family. In September, when he was considered past all recovery, and could appear among the troops in a carriage only, the king recalled him to Fontainebleau, and

placed him under the care of the royal physicians. The sorrow of the soldiers and the consternation of the citizens, were indescribable, especially as dark rumors were current as to the cause of his indisposition. The king had latterly become less cordial toward his son, and, agitated more by fear than love, was gloomy but calm. The dauphiness could not endure the idea of losing the father of her children, and still believed in his restoration. Conti and Richelieu alone had no doubt of the approaching calamity.

The village of Trianon was busy, for the ripened grain had called all to labor. Loaded wagons were moving, and men and women at work among the sheaves. Nature seemed to sympathize with this activity. The yellow forest rustled, for a breeze swept along the valley, bringing with it swift clouds that darkened the harvest with their shadows and returned it to the sun again. Flocks of pigeons passed from field to field, where the cattle were rejoicing in the new-mown pastures, and all seemed glad in the triumphs of human industry.

Little Trianon, however, looked as a half-buried tombstone in the scene of happiness. The palace of the dauphin was deserted, save by some sleepy gardener binding up the vines. The May-tree stood before the church, but its leaves had long withered and passed away, while the faded ribbons still fluttered in the autumn wind.

Father Morelly was sitting in his study, preparing his harvest sermon. Alas, he never felt less inclined to write! He was to give thanks to the Creator for the fruitfulness of the season, while his heart was filled with grief, and his thoughts were far away, with the suffering dauphin, the hope of the old man's life. In the adjoining sitting-room, near a window, were Susanna and Madame de Piron, engaged in their embroidery, and by the stove was the housekeeper, a matron with a gray and trembling head, who was serving the third pastor. She sang in a low voice to the humming of her spinning-wheel.

The two ladies were whispering together about the protracted absence of Beaumarchais, though he had been on his way home since last March; and about the changes of life—how hope was disappointed and happiness turned to sorrow. But the lark, amid the flowers of the garden opposite them, did not cease his notes on that account.

In the mean time a travelling-carriage was approaching at a rapid rate from Nauphle; it was drawn by four horses, and stopped before the parsonage. Susanna rushed to the window of the front room. "Caron, it is my Caron, God be praised!" and she hastened out, followed by Madame de Piron and the pastor. Can that haggard man on whose bosom Susanna is resting her head, and who is covering her with kisses, be Beaumarchais, so long expected and so welcome? "Where have you been? Why are you so pale and wan?" she asked.

"You promised to return four months ago, my friend!" said Morelly, half reproachfully, seizing the traveller's hand.

"Look at me, and you will be answered," replied Caron. "I was ill, and in fact am now little better. Even if longer absence had not endangered my safety, the desire for home would have killed me."

"During the four months that we received no tidings from you, you were ill?" said Susanna, "and you would not let me go and nurse you!"

"After you had successfully ended all your business, was your life threatened?" asked Morelly, hastily.

"It was!" Beaumarchais entered the sitting-room with his friends.

"Our opponents, especially Choiseul, set their agents on me in Spain. I knew it from the beginning, for I found difficulties notwithstanding my papers. Nevertheless, all was finished early in the spring, and I am happy that Maria never became the wife of Clavijo. Her honor is reëstablished in the face of all, her health improved, and her deceiver deprived of his office by the king. My diplomatic missions were all completed, so that I left Madrid on the 16th of March. My journey to Valencia, however, was but one series of accidents, delays, and vexations, evidently intended to retard my return. I had proof that I was to be imprisoned at Marseilles on any possible pretext."

"The reason for this is very plain!" cried Morelly.

"After the death of the marchioness, and the unfortunate meeting between the king and his son, which you announced to me, the adverse party feared my presence. While in Valencia, surrounded by spies, and prepared for all, I wrote to Bardoulin, the correspondent at Marseilles of my partner Duverney, and who is also the mayor, and owner of a vessel; I revealed my position to him. A small schooner took me away in the night and brought me safe to France. The sea-voyage, my home-sickness, and anxiety, together with the effects of what I have passed through, made me ill, as you may suppose. I remained three months in Bardoulin's house, time enough to bring my persecutors on my track, and they very soon found me. That I am with you I owe to a false passport of my friend; I shall not be safe except in Paris, in the presence of my patrons."

"Or when the atrocious deed is accomplished!" said Morelly, "for both you and he will then certainly be harmless."

"What atrocious deed?"

"Caron," said Susanna, gloomily,

"all Paris whispers it. The dauphin is dying."

"The dauphin? Die?" Beaumarchais wrung his hands in agony.

"It is too true, Prince de Conti said so. Something happened in the camp at Compiègne."

"That is to say, the vile scoundrels compassed his life there! Then all was useless—the hope and labor of years! In vain the dangerous work of rending that web of cunning! Morelly, all is over! Let us not think of the future, it will be sad enough. It will soon come, dark and wretched. We were fools in devoting our thoughts and feelings to mere possibilities—in meddling at all with that insane fantasy called the regeneration of France! The present moment is every thing; I seize it and press it to my breast!" He drew Susanna sadly toward him. "Oh, let us hold it fast, and never look back. I shall henceforth live only for myself, and believe in nothing but your love, my friends, and my own heart. Come, my love; come, Madame de Piron, let us go to our dear asylum at Paris. Morelly will have to follow us, and we must have a chamber ready for him."

The dauphin suffered dreadfully, but bore up with a greatness and piety universally admired. After having lived virtuously, done all to prove his love for the people, he died as a just man who falls a victim to treachery and murderous designs.

On the 20th of December, at noon, the king visited his son for the last time. He left the room in great emotion, ordering the confessor to be sent for. What was transacted between him and the dauphin was never revealed. It was not until the arrival of the priest, that Josepha became fully aware of her approaching sorrow.

"Be of good cheer, Josepha," said her husband, as she wept; "had I a choice between life and death, I would give a thousand lives for my desire to be with God. You will be reunited with me. Educate our children for the happiness of France, which I loved so much. Sooner or later, the Sovereign Judge will reward the good and punish the wicked. Farewell!"

Josepha was about to reply, but fainted. The attendants carried her away. An hour later the dauphin was dead!

When the confessor entered the cabinet where the king sat lost in grief, to announce the decease of the prince, the old man started, tore his gray hair, and tremblingly ordered the servants to bring the Duke de Berri. When the boy came, he exclaimed, despairingly: "Oh, my son, my son, you prophesied this! My poor country, all your hope now is myself, and a child of eleven years!" He kissed the young duke sadly, and took him to his mother. "Announce the king and the dauphin!" he said to the chamberlain in the anteroom.

"My daughter, our hero, our martyr, is no more. I bring you the dauphin. Nothing shall again separate me from you and your children. I will myself watch over your well-being, for that is the least I owe my departed son."

The widowed princess cast herself at his feet. "Then grant that I be not deprived of the education of my children; I have no other object now in the world."

"Your will is sacred! Calm yourself sufficiently to accompany the remains to St. Denis, and then you must dwell with me at the palace of Versailles."

To St. Denis? Not to be crowned amid the triumphs of a happy nation —but to be committed to the tomb with universal lamentation. Sorrow darkened the land. "There is no hope for us!" was the wail of all patriots.

The lines of the poet, in reference to the death of Britannicus, were inscribed on his tomb:

> " Connu par ses vertus, plusque par ses travaux,
>   Il sut penser en sage, et mourut en héros." *

Turgot, Malesherbes, and Beaumarchais, hastened to Trianon, to announce the dismal tidings to Morelly. A commissioner of Choiseul was there before them, who took possession of all, as reverting to the crown, and displaced the pastor because "he was suspected of being a Jesuit." Morelly a Jesuit!

" Say no more," exclaimed the venerable man, tearlessly. " The dauphin is dead; the dream of the *Basiliade* is over. Let me awake in the Pigeonnier!"

Silent and gloomy stood the villagers, when their friend, teacher, and consoler, departed. Low murmurs against the officials were heard on every side. The old housekeeper appeared with a hatchet in her hand. "Come with me!" she said, and they followed her to the May-tree. Cutting it down, she exclaimed, "There lies France!"

CHAPTER XIII.

" CARPE DIEM."

The death of the dauphin was the heaviest national calamity that could befall France before the revolution. From that time the state plunged into ruin. It was neither cowardice nor selfishness that caused Beaumarchais to say, " The present moment is most important!" This sentiment was gradually adopted by the people of the times. The interest of to-day excluded all thought of to-morrow.

The king, in his repentance and anxiety, made arrangements, near his own apartments, for Josepha, the Duke de Berri (now the dauphin), Provence, Artois, and the Princess Elizabeth, with their reduced suite. There the widow lived in harmony with her sisters-in-law, who had lost their usual cheerfulness after the death of their brother. The monarch's care increased for the well-being of the dauphiness and her children. He had a night-bell communicating with their chambers, so that his presence might be instantly summoned, and in various ways manifested deep concern in their safety and happiness. He also became reconciled to the queen. He was like a cowardly penitent, who assumes an extraordinary piety to atone for the consequences of a wasted and sinful life. On the other hand, he did not resolve to dismiss Choiseul or Orleans, or change his system of government. He could not agree with the virtuous, while he had no difficulty with the dishonest. He imagined that any effort to improve the condition of his country would produce a revolution.

Under these circumstances Beaumarchais could not gain access to the dauphiness; he scarcely obtained permission to speak once more to his patronesses. Shrugging his shoulders on leaving the palace in company with Richelieu, he remarked that the king's anxiety had severe results, and that it might be very possible to shorten people's days by an excessive and cruel attention.

" What do you mean? Surely you would not say that, even under the eyes of the king,—"

" Oh, my dear duke, I have no longer an opinion. If matters continue thus, I shall not have one idea left. But I intend to live! We learn to value life in these days."

Beaumarchais bade farewell to the court and its intrigues; he took off his

---

* Known by his virtues more than by his works,
  He thought as a sage, and died as a hero.

mask, and felt well again. Turgot buried himself in Limoges, his little reformed world. Malesherbes, in view of approaching storms, united himself with parliamentary circles, but his favorite rendezvous was at Morelly's, where he sometimes met Caron. Morelly's heart had received an incurable wound. At Trianon he left the best part of himself—the realization in part of his ideas; sadness and resignation occupied his mind, but he was incapable of happiness. Life had lost its meaning for him. He hid himself again in the old garret of the Pigeonnier, a gloomy companion of Batyl. His visits were now few at the Hôtel Piron. Thus the friends of Beaumarchais became diminished, only Duverney and Caron's family being his usual visitors.

This retirement, however, was useful, for Beaumarchais was lost sight of by his opponents. During his absence, and when the illness of the dauphin was known to be fatal, Debrelon, convinced that the influence of the professor was at an end, demanded his money from Duverney, and gave no more reports. He still feared Caron, but expected nothing from him. Batyl alone continued the same person—friendly, sly, and watchful, but he did not force himself upon Beaumarchais as formerly, for the professor now appeared harmless to his enemies. The houses of the great were closed against him; he was an *homme passé*, and it was difficult to remember him. Yet he was of such an elastic nature, that while he could confine himself in a very limited compass, he did not lack expedients to regain at a bound his former authority. But he cared nothing about that. His great wealth gave him and Susanna all the enjoyments he desired, and he laughingly turned his back on those who knew him no more. Only one nobleman retained a friendship for him—this was the Prince de Conti.

Beaumarchais now sought other society—the theatre and opera. Having become a man of the world and a wit, he received actors, and managers of public amusements. His poetical talent, at rest while he was engaged in politics, awoke with renewed energy; he wrote songs and composed airs adapted to them, gave concerts to his friends, and the long-forgotten manuscript *Eugénie*, once given to Piron, was re-read, and pronounced worthy of the stage. He appeared like a different being, and never did he make a remark that could remind one of former times. He revised his old work, made it more popular, and yet more thoughtful. Diderot and D'Alembert, who had become his friends, were enthusiastic in their praise of it, and Gauchat printed it.

New public troubles were at hand. Josepha, suffering in body and mind, sought consolation in the education of her children. Madame de St. Marsan was dismissed, the Duke de Vaugyon was nominated tutor of the royal children, and a certain plan was followed with rigid exactness. The Duke de Berri received a serious and simple training, while more liberty was permitted to Provence and Artois. The constraint of their mother's sorrowing life, and the severe piety of their aunts, together with the pedantry of a courtly mentor and an intolerable guardianship, made an unfortunate impression on the minds of the sons, and the result was any thing but what their deceased father would have desired.

Berri, the eldest, afterward the unfortunate Louis XVI., a good but rather dull and diffident child, instead of growing up in physical and mental strength, became timid and distrustful. He was early taught that mankind are wicked, and that Choiseul was the cause of his father's death. His faculties seemed to fear development, on account of the dangers to which they might invite, and in which he had been abundantly instructed. Provence was gloomy, reserved, and crafty. He determined to adapt himself to circumstances, until age or opportunity freed him from control. He had a better mind than his older brother, but a worse heart, and felt little of the humanity of his father, which Berri especially inherited. The third, Artois, was excitable and covetous, resembling his grandfather, Louis XV. He was sensual, and his ambition preferred splendor and intrigue. Habituating himself early to dissimulation, the restraint in which he lived corrupted his honor and ripened his passions.

Living so near the king and fearing Choiseul, whom the former thought he could not well discharge, the dauphiness gained great influence over his majesty (in which she was assisted by Madame de Seran and the princesses), and sought to carry out some of her deceased husband's plans. She was, therefore, dangerous to the minister and his party.

The relation between the government and the Parliaments was not simply unsatisfactory—it fostered reasons for a perpetual hatred and conflict. After the fall of the Jesuits, other abuses were exaggerated and attacked under the leadership of Malesherbes, and in Brittany a rebellion arose against the oppression of the military governor, the Duke d'Aiguillon. When remonstrances were found to be of no avail, a lawsuit was instituted against the duke by the Brittany courts of justice, assisted by those of Paris, and the public commotion was extensive and dangerous. Choiseul could have spared the king this trouble by displacing M. d'Aiguillon, but he desired to control his master, and kept him in fear and perplexity. Both Parliaments were thus addressed by the angry king, holding a *lit de justice* on the 3d of March, 1766: "I have received my crown from God alone; who will dare touch it?"

When this expression was repeated to Beaumarchais, he remarked: "If it were true, it would seem as if Providence sometimes erred!"

Nevertheless, no punishment was inflicted on Aiguillon. The Parisian Parliament was about to pass sentence of death on him, when the king quashed the whole process. Finally, the duke was recalled in 1768. From that time the province of Brittany hated the sovereign, and all the high courts of justice in the land entered into a coalition against him. During this dispute other events interested the popular mind.

The Dauphiness Josepha died on the 13th of March, 1767, in consequence of a cup of chocolate she drank on the 1st of February! The woman so feared by the court ministers had gone. Her children were sent to Marly under the guardianship of Vaugyon, and the princesses removed to the Hôtel Bourbon. Beatrice de Grammont was again presented to the king, and Choiseul hoped to eject Madame de Seran from the authority she had gained. Conti went over to the adverse party; all the partisans of the dauphin retired to their estates, and the queen herself was attacked at this time with symptoms of disease similar to that which caused the death of Josepha.

Again, the Indian commerce of the Jesuits resulted in dishonor and confusion. To put an end to their despotism, a soldier, Count Lally de Tolendal, was sent to the Eastern colonies in 1760. He had neither mercy nor prudence, but he certainly meant to be honest. His justice, however, was not impartial, and his obstinate will was cruel. His first blows against the fathers were so severe that the country suffered with them, and they avenged themselves, notwithstanding their fall, by startling accusations which, unfortunately, facts corroborated. The general was recalled, and on various complaints, more or less true, at once arraigned. Imprisoned in the Bastile from 1763, his case remained undecided. Madame de Pompadour and many of the younger members of Parliament desired to ameliorate his fate, but Choiseul, acting a double part, as his practice was, intended to make him a victim of the clergy, and at the same time strike terror into the people by the extreme punishment of a count. Tolendal was sentenced to death by the sword, a judgment executed on the 9th of May, 1767, on the Placé Grève.

"Every one," wrote Voltaire, "was entitled to lay hands on Tolendal, except the executioner." It was a thrust at the aristocracy, if he bled in the same public place where Damien died —if the lower classes witnessed a man dragged to his death whose breast was decorated with the cross of St. Louis, and who could not be reproached with dishonesty, but with the resolution and cruelty of the rude soldier, and with hatred of the priests. He was criminal in the sight of humanity, but before that tribunal the king and his minister were greater culprits.

Vast crowds hastened to this horrible spectacle, and, what was curious, they were composed of the highest nobility and the lowest outcasts of the Quartiers St. Martin, Temple, and Antoine. The middle classes were not present, for they pitied the count. By the side of the old man, who even to the last never expected to end his life in this manner, walked his pale and sorrowing son, a youth of fifteen years. Murmurs of indignation were heard, and all were sorry for him who at one

blow was to lose father, honor, and future hope. The count's wife had died insane during the lawsuit.

"Theophilus," said the father, "I give you my last command; henceforth you are your own master. You must not weep. Spare yourself for the day when you can vindicate our honor and avenge my blood. May God have mercy on you!" He kissed the boy with deep emotion, and walked toward the block. A moment of silence—a blow—a sigh, as if uttered from one heart, of the multitude present. Above all was heard the shrill cry of the son, who fainted at the foot of a scaffold red with his father's blood.

Two persons, unknown to each other — one, old, thoughtful, and poorly clad; the other, a young man of apparent intelligence and wealth— stood side by side as the criminal crossed the Place Grève. Both saw the son of the general fall, and felt the same emotion when they heard the heart-rending scream of the orphan.

"Will no one have pity on the poor boy?" exclaimed the younger in a sympathizing voice.

"Let me pass; let me go to him!" said the old man, pressing through the throng, who opened a path for him. He took the youth in his arms, where he soon awoke to consciousness.— "Weep not, young man, you are not quite despised and abandoned. I will be your father, in the name of disgraced humanity!"

"And look on me as a brother, Lally!" said the other, ardently. "Let us pass, my friends—let a bereaved child hide his grief in solitude until the day of vengeance."

"The day of vengeance?" exclaimed Lally, "I will live for it, and restore the honor of my name. I go with you! Whither?"

"Where you will be safe. Let us hasten, for the police may hear your threats. I am taking you to the Pigeonnier!"

"And I will accompany you," said the other, "if for nothing else than to save for our country a heart that hates tyranny as I do." They supported the youth between them, and departed. The people, deeply moved, looked after them, and the police let them go unhindered. They were three representatives of the future—Morelly, Condorcet, and young Tolendal. They had met on the Place Grève!

On the evening of the same day, Morelly visited Beaumarchais. "Caron, I never asked you for any thing. You were always obliged to force me to take money from you. Now I demand it in the name of charity. I have adopted young Tolendal as my son!"

"My dear friend, two hundred francs monthly are at your command. Is that sum sufficient?"

"More than sufficient for both of us!"

"Then I beg you to receive the first amount immediately, but on condition that you never mention the subject again."

The garret in the Pigeonnier was the favored haunt of those embittered men who afterward formed the club, *Amis du Peuple*—who saw salvation only in the fall of the monarchy and the establishment of a republic—silent and cautious miners, who laid the train to destroy the old France of the Bourbons. Sometimes Beaumarchais came among them, but they despised him secretly as a wit, a former intriguer and courtier, but Morelly dared not betray that he was their benefactor. The old gentleman was involuntarily influenced by younger and more daring minds; and there was much pleasure to him in hearing the assumptions of youth promising to verify his dreams.

Beaumarchais cared little for politics and public conflict; he had renounced them. He enjoyed life with his Susanna, and taught the actors his play; for he had received permission to have it represented. It is true, the police first asked Maupeau and Choiseul, knowing them to be inimical to the author, but the premier said: "If M. de Beaumarchais does nothing but write dramas, do not meddle with him. If he has literary ambition only, he is harmless."

Eugénie pleased the people greatly, for two reasons. They were tired of the tragedies of Voltaire, who was growing feeble—of his tirades against intolerance and the priests. The philosophy of the Encyclopædists had also been served up too often. A drama descriptive of the passions was more to the taste of the multitude: to justify and ennoble a deceived maiden—to illustrate the claims of a woman on her husband was something new to a public not ignorant of neglected wives. On the following day Beaumarchais was the idol of Paris.

Choiseul had obtained his object—he was the actual and sole ruler. The queen died in the summer of 1768. The tears of repentance which the king wept at her tomb were his last. He became insensible toward his family and subjects. The *Parc aux Cerfs* and Madame de Seran became tedious to him; and, as she had lost the object of her intercourse with Louis XV. by the death of his son and daughter-in-law, she accepted the position of lady of honor in the suite of the Princess Adelaide de Penthièvre, who was about to be married to Chartres, the son of the Duke d'Orleans. Choiseul succeeded in isolating the king, and all the wishes of the premier were fulfilled when his majesty consented to receive Madame de Grammont, who, with her brother, jealously controlled the aged Louis. No one was permitted to approach who might withdraw him from their influence; wherever he went he was accompanied by either one or the other, and they soon incurred the hatred of all the courtiers and attendants for their pride and severity of manner, which knew no bounds, especially as Orleans could do little injury without endangering himself; and Count Falcoz de la Blache, inconstant and unfaithful as he was in all his relations, acted as a spy in his own and the Orleans family.

“Nothing is more desirable than independence and quiet comfort, united with the charm of an artist’s renown,” said Beaumarchais one day, when he was walking with Susanna along the shady paths of his garden, pressing her small, soft hand to his lips.—“This world is beautiful, but human beings make it a sad abode.”

“And you tell me that so complacently, while kissing my hand! Why, Caron, it is unreasonable and ungallant of you. So you think this world would be more agreeable, less the human inhabitants? I had an idea that it would be nothing to you without me!”

“If you argue in that style, my love, I acknowledge myself defeated. Without you, indeed, all things would lose their interest to me—without you my happiness would be incomplete. Men make the world good or bad, for they are its masters; but as evil-disposed persons prevail, the virtuous can live happily only in a narrow circle, far from scandal and dispute. That was the meaning I intended to express just now. Have we not learned how often the noble-minded are disappointed and miserable, how baseness triumphs; and is it not reasonable to prefer a hermit’s life?”

“Especially when the hermit has me for a companion, and congenial friends to visit his cell. Oh, we are very happy! Far from excitement and intrigue, and having nothing to fear but —pardon me, one thing is wanting!” She became grave.

10

Beaumarchais looked curiously at her. “And what, my child, can you wish more than to walk by my side thus quietly through life?”

Susanna shook her head. “That is self-complimentary! Besides, you think only of to-day, and forget that to-morrow all may be changed.”

“Just because I do think of to-day— because I know the instability of human affairs—I appreciate the present and think little of the future! But you have other thoughts. You mean that our daily happiness is not sufficient. What can you desire?”

“Do not be angry! I often mused over it when you were so long in Spain, and oftener now that we are away from the manners of the court, and have time to indulge in other thoughts than those of intrigue and rivalry.”

“Well, let me know what those thoughts are.”

“But you will not laugh—that would hurt my feelings. We have been united thirteen years, and—” Susanna blushed and tears stood in her eyes—“God has denied us children. It was very well the first three years, when we knew not whence the next day’s food would come; but now we have all we desire, except one of our own blood to inherit our fortune. As long as we are young we may not think so much of this, for many years of life and hope are before us; when we are old, however, and friends now around us begin to pass away—when we have neither ambition nor enjoyment, must it then not be very sad to live in solitude, and to anticipate sickness and death unrelieved by tears that we know would be natural and sincere? We have no offspring, and I believe it is a curse upon us that I, whose mother never loved me, should have no child to love!”

“You seem to be in earnest! But how can you torment yourself with foolish thoughts? Do you consider

Providence so unjust as in such a case to punish you for the sin of your parents? I cannot recognize my sensible Susanna in these words, and am afraid some person has been agitating your mind in this respect. Is it so?"

"Oh no!" she said; "the thought occurred to me without suggestion from any one."

"And how long have you been trying to discover your parentage, which will give you no pleasure, but rather destroy your peace? I pray you, be warned. The revelation of such a secret would bring dangers which you cannot even imagine, and—"

"You know my origin! I have felt, indeed, that you were concealing something from me. Answers once given me by Duverney convinced me that he himself brought me to Passy—that he is somehow involved in the sin of my parents, and—"

"And thus, my only love, you poison your life, which otherwise would be happy. I have long feared this. On the day when you know all we shall perhaps both be very wretched! I married you without troubling myself about your parents; for true love makes no such inquiries! And now, have we gained so much of the world's goods in order that you should make yourself unhappy? Listen to me, your best and only friend: be satisfied with the reasons I give you, and make no further investigation; forget what can never now be changed. I am acquainted with your birth, and have all the papers—"

"And who—who are my parents?" cried Susanna, in great excitement.

"That I shall never tell you, my wife!" exclaimed Beaumarchais, gloomily. "No; for I love you too much! Your origin is such that you can never be recognized. Your parents yielded to unlawful passions, and under circumstances that render them great criminals, whose discovery would break your heart and ruin us both. They would never forgive you—they would perhaps avenge themselves, if you dared to inquire who they are. Ask me not; think not about them! I have never refused you any thing, but in this I must be firm, or on my death-bed I could not forgive myself!"

"I believe it all, and have often, as I have said, felt it. Providence punishes my dishonorable birth by a childless old age. As my cradle was solitary, so shall be my grave!"

"By Heaven, Susanna," exclaimed her husband, angrily, "I really believe that I was a fool in considering the present moment every thing, renouncing for it all hope of the future, for you embitter the cup of our contentment. What unreasonableness, to grieve over a secret whose knowledge would bring you profound sorrow! Thousands are orphans, or have never known their parents, and enjoy a life of honor and virtue, without ever attaining to our independence. The times are serious, dear wife. Every day is characterized by injustice and violence; the virtuous are oppressed and the worthless triumph! Every man of feeling and intellect foresees the fearful epoch approaching, and who would wish to leave children as its victims? A time might come, Susanna, when perhaps you would bewail the hour you became a mother. What we wish for so earnestly is not always the best for us. Let us be contented, and not war with the dispensations of Povidence. We have far more than enough to live comfortably, and have many friends; we love them, and are loved. Why should we repine at what to many is a curse? Let us die merry old people. Many a year lies yet between us and the first furrow on our brow, and who knows what may happen!" He laughingly embraced her, and kissed away her sad thoughts.

“I am very silly, Caron, but I will endeavor to be reasonable, as you call it.”

Beaumarchais would have continued his exhortations, when he noticed his valet de chambre Gomez, whom he had brought from Spain, approaching from the terrace.

“His royal highness the Prince de Conti, señor!”

The prince appeared at the other end of the walk. “Very well,” said Caron, “ask him to come here.” While Gomez was hastening away, Beaumarchais whispered: “I beg you, Susie, to control your emotion. I do not wish to make excuses for you. It seems we have lived peaceably too long, since you are so anxious to indulge in unnecessary grief. I hope Conti’s presence does not indicate new trials for us.”

Susanna found neither time to answer nor altogether to remove the effects of the conversation; for the prince soon stood before her and her husband, kindly offering his hand to Caron: “As you never give us your presence in the Hôtel Conti now, dear Beaumarchais, you see I come to you.”

“You embarrass me, prince, for I still owe you an acknowledgment of thanks for the favor you bestowed on my *Eugénie*. I would certainly have waited on you, if I had not feared to recall sad memories without being able to be of any more service.”

“You are right; and I envy you that you could withdraw from this comfortless court society, and live for love and poetry.” Conti took Susanna’s hand and kissed it. “How happy you two must be! And yet, madame, I hope sorrow has not dared to enter even this elysium—” He dropped her hand.

“Permit me, gracious prince, to retire!” Susanna, scarcely able to restrain her tears, bowed and disappeared in a side-path.

“What is the matter, Caron? I came at an unseasonable hour, I fear, and interrupted perhaps—”

“A man so noble-minded as your highness can never come to my house at an unseasonable time; and, as you remark something wrong, I do not see why I should conceal it from you. A day may come, when your assistance, at least your esteem, may be my only consolation.”

“Is your mind also disturbed? You, the lively, intrepid Beaumarchais? Well, so far as you may think it right, reveal your trouble to me, it will not be the first-secret we have shared together.”

“And, as far as you are concerned, not the most important. Yet, as it is the only and highest one in reference to myself, I need not assure you of its consequence. There may come a time when all cause for secrecy will be removed. Do you remember our first meeting at the residence of the princesses, my scene with La Blache, and the strange withdrawal of the Marchioness de Ventadour?”

“I have not forgotten, in fact, that you still owe us an explanation of that affair, and that you were then more agitated than perhaps you are now.”

“Because I made a very painful discovery, and from that moment gained control over certain persons whom I might ruin, but who in return could destroy all that is dearest to me.”

“Your wife has much anxiety about this?”

“She does not and never shall know it. The only and very foolish trouble with the little woman is simply in not being informed of that which would render her wretched.”

Conti, in great astonishment, looked piercingly at Beaumarchais, and laid his hand on Caron’s shoulder. “Either you are incomprehensible to me, or I understand you only too well. At your appointment as professor to my cousins the princesses, some of your envious enemies reported that your wife is illegitimate. Now I understand thoroughly what once seemed to me rather strange: Madame Susanna greatly resembles the Marchioness de Ventadour."

"Good heavens!" Caron's hands fell powerlessly at his side, and his face grew ghastly.

"I see all the rest, and you need not explain how you kept our opponents in check so long. This secret is so dangerous that it may really destroy your wife. You were wise in going into retirement. You will use your weapons against those persons, only if other means fail; and I am glad to know enough about the affair to be able to assist you when that day arrives. I feel uncertain now whether the object that led me hither will be welcome to you."

"Your highness, I am ready to do any thing that has no connection with plotting. You never found me tardy when our hopes rested on the dauphin; now I should endanger myself for nothing."

"Very true. But I have not come to the political agent of the Bourbons—he died with the only prop of that house; I have come to the poet Beaumarchais. I am endeavoring to imitate you and force myself to forget our loss."

"The poet is at your service, monseigneur. What is it you require of him?"

"Perhaps you have heard that the grand-admiral of France, the Duke de Penthièvre, is about to marry his only son, the Prince de Lamballe, to the beautiful Princess de Savoy-Carignan, the daughter of my sister!"

"The report has been current for some time, your highness. But in this way the family of the Contis would become closely allied to the house of Orleans, for I hear that Mlle. Adelaide de Penthièvre is to marry the Prince de Chartres."

"That fact, alas! embitters my joy, which would otherwise be unalloyed at having the child of my deceased sister always with me. It is, however, not the first time that these two families were united; my divorced wife was Diana d'Orleans. You see what results that connection has had. Lamballe is an amiable, noble - hearted youth, and my niece lovely and of a superior intellect. I wish to have a festival on the day following the wedding, and beg you to compose something for me. Will you refuse?"

"How can you think that I would refuse you what is not only honorable to me, but gives you pleasure? Yet anxiety and fear trouble me. I shall have to meet Orleans and Chartres— perhaps even the Ventadours and La Blaches. I wish to avoid them as they avoid me."

"Can you not practise the same skill in your own cause that you employed in that of the dauphin? Pretend not to know any of these persons. I hardly think that even Orleans would then care about violating the hospitality of the Hôtel Penthièvre. If the grand-admiral invites Chevalier de Beaumarchais, a friend of Conti, officially, I should like to see him who would dare interfere!"

"I make no further excuses."

"Then I will present you to-morrow to the Duke de Penthièvre, and you can survey the apartments appropriated to the amusements. May I be sure of your presence?"

"Certainly, your highness."

"You know, Caron, that I shall always be your friend. Compose something pretty for the festival of my niece."

Beaumarchais accompanied the prince to the gate, and returned slowly and gloomily. "O Fate! Thou art no fiction! I withdrew from all court intrigues, resigned myself to poetry, and now poetry leads me back to the tumult. Shall I again escape? There is a shadow on my mind that will not depart; there is a spectre moving in my path with threatening gestures, and —very well! I must disperse these fancies."

CHAPTER XIV.

THE WEDDING FESTIVAL OF THE PRINCESS DE LAMBALLE.

In the Rue St. Honoré, formerly the pride of Parisians, between the Place Louis and the convent of the "Filles de la Conception," was the old Luxembourg, better known in those days as the Hôtel Penthièvre. This was the centre of the French marine, the grand admiralty, whence decrees were issued concerning harbors, fleets, and colonies. The principal building, fronting the street, was built in the style of Francis I. It had but two stories, with a high, heavy and obtuse-angled roof. Above the carriage entry-way, on each side of which were towered projections, and between which the ornamented railing of the balcony could be seen, glittered two gilt crossed anchors, and above them the royal coat-of-arms of the Bourbons, and that of the allied house of Penthièvre. The lower floor of the edifice was in Florentine taste, used for offices and servants' dwellings. Above this rose the splendid apartments of the duke's family and the reception-halls.

The Hôtel Penthièvre was interesting to Parisians, not only account of its imposing aspect, but for the Japanese Pavilion, at the end of the garden, where it touched the wall separating it from the nunnery. It was constructed of variegated wood, had a pointed green roof, from which were pendent numerous small bells that sounded at every breath of air. The many-colored materials of the building, the grinning idols and fabulous animals decorating it, and the no less strange contents visible when the windows were opened, always excited the curiosity of the inhabitants of the capital; and, though this edifice had been built many generations before, and its singularity had become familiar, no Parisian would fail to point out to the visitor the Pavilion of the Penthièvres with as much pride as the Louvre or Notre Dame. It was really a treasure, for it contained a select though unclassified collection of all foreign rarities, brought by voyagers to the grand-admiral as testimonies of esteem.

Many anecdotes were related of the grave and whimsical duke, who sometimes seemed to personate the Brahmin or Mandarin, but who in truth cared for little else besides his official business, the strictly aristocratic education of his two children, and his pavilion. He liked to indulge in his dreamy studies there, or in the evening pace the adjoining plateau with his hands behind him, or take his tea in public, to be stared at by the wondering crowds. In wet weather he could reach his Oriental paradise by the colonnade underneath the terrace.

In the same line with this pavilion, was another, lofty and massive. The back wall formed a half crescent, and the flat copper roof rested on two stone pillars. This seemed to have been intended for a theatre, and here Beaumarchais was to contribute his share toward the amusements of the festival.

Caron, according to the arrangement with Conti, was presented to the Duke de Penthièvre, who was greatly pleased with him, not only as an admirer of his curiosities, but for proposing to arrange the most interesting, so as to display them to the best advantage to the guests. Conti saw with pleasure that the duke soon considered Beaumarchais as an indispensable person at the wedding celebration. Every thing was done privately, in order to produce surprise, and the admiral did not spare his purse.

The festival lasted three days. On the first, the bridal pair were presented to the king at Versailles, and in his presence the marriage articles were signed. On the second, the ceremony was performed in the royal church at Versailles, followed by a reception held by the newly married in the grand apartments of Penthièvre. The last day was devoted to a family reunion, at which no one was to appear without special invitation. A fortunate circumstance heightened the brilliancy of the entertainment.

Admiral de Bougainville, the first Frenchman who had sailed round the world, returned at this time from his three years' expedition. In his company was the most gallant soldier of his day, Prince Otto von Nassau-Siegen, as well as Chevalier d'Oraison, a sportsman and a sailor, who felt nowhere so well as in the chase or on the sea. They hastened to present themselves to the duke, the king, and Choiseul, and of course were invited to the wedding feast of the grand-admiral's son.

The nuptial ceremony and the banquet at the monarch's palace were over, and the relatives of the young couple drove to Paris. The anterooms of the Hôtel Penthièvre were already filled with a large company ready to do homage to the newly-married pair. Beaumarchais, busy with his final preparations for the entertainment, had scarcely seen the prince, and the princess not at all. Casting a last glance on his work, he left to witness the levee from the gallery of the large hall, and especially to see the bride in whose honor he had composed his verses. He was thinking how he was to deport

himself in case he met his enemies, when he heard the voices of two men approaching from the other side of the walk. As the garden was closed to all except Penthièvre and Beaumarchais, the latter was somewhat surprised at the presence of strangers. He stepped aside unseen to discover who were the intruders.

"I wish," said one, in a violent tone, "the Sahib of Madras had cloven my head, and ended a life robbed of its joy, its last hope! I am resolved not to return to the army. Since I cannot be what my birth claims, I will remain what I am—an adventurer!"

"Then, poor prince, you are really in love with the fair Princess de Lamballe, and had to return home just when the lady of your heart is married to a royal blockhead, who wears an admiral's uniform without ever having seen the ocean? And you are formally invited to witness the climax of your misery! That is too bad of the lady!"

"I beg you, D'Oraison, not to accuse the princess. She knows not that she is loved by me any more than she is aware what flower her foot treads upon. You remember that in the spring 1766 we had to wait for equipments at Marseilles, and that Bougainville, as well as myself, was invited to Chambery for eight days by the Duke of Savoy, her father. There I saw and conversed with her long enough to love her my whole life."

"I remember having heard Bougainville relate how the lady sympathized with your adventures. I could almost affirm she entertained some love for you."

"Love! Chevalier, then she would not have married Lamballe."

"A princess! Was ever one of her rank permitted to choose according to the dictates of her heart? Such a person is hidden in a convent, and takes a bridal veil according to her diplomatic value. It is not until these poor women are widows that they are at all independent. Madame de Lamballe might love you as well as you—"

"Will you comfort my heart, D'Oraison, and tell me of impossibilities, in order to make life tolerable? Fortunately I always remember that I am a prince without property, a gentleman-beggar, who is pursued by creditors with unredeemable bills. I must away to some place where I may lose the last and most foolish of possessions—life!"

"I agree! Let us throw dice upon the compass, to see whither we go. But for our new undertaking we require money, and neither of us has any. The royal treasury is empty, and instead of reimbursing us for our outlay, we shall be sent off with compliments."

"If I am to fight for pay, I shall take foreign service, in Russia or Spain—not where I would be near her and an object of pity!"

"Then nothing remains to me but return with good-humor to the arms of the royal widow Wavrateva!" laughed D'Oraison; "and become King of Otaheite—Oraison I.! Oh, let me be your chief fan-bearer, sire!"

Beaumarchais had heard all. He was at once interested in the prince, whose knightly deeds and magnanimity he had so often heard praised. Affected by the position of a man whose circumstances resembled his own while living in the Pigeonnier, he suddenly made his appearance. The conversation of the sailors ceased.

"Who is here?" cried Siegen, placing his hand on his sword.

"I believe the fellow has overheard us!" D'Oraison grasped Caron by the collar.

"Your Otaheitan majesty, how can you act so cowardly!" replied Beaumarchais. "Heroes do not fight two against one."

"You have been listening to confidential conversation," said Siegen, angrily, "and have obtained possession of secrets never intended for your ears! You shall not leave this spot alive, lest you should destroy my honor!"

"Who tells you, my prince, that I am a spy? Suppose I should be a friend, and would rather assist than harm you!"

"I know all my friends, sir! Not one would force himself into my confidence!"

"And I, your highness, force my benefits on few. Only persons under my orders had a right to enter this garden to-day, and it is natural that I should be concerned at the presence of strangers. I shall be silent about what I have heard, not from fear, but esteem for the illustrious hero Nassau-Siegen, as well as from reverence for a lady whose uncle is my patron. If you will take a walk with me in this direction, I will convince you that I am able and ready to be useful to you in any way you desire."

"That is remarkable enough!" said Siegen, in surprise. "Then I have no choice but to grant you the conference you ask."

"I will suffer no such thing," exclaimed D'Oraison, violently, "if I do not know who he is!"

"My name is Beaumarchais. We can walk this path so that the chevalier can watch over the safety of your serene highness, without hearing us. The moon is bright."

"Are you insane, D'Oraison? It is Beaumarchais, the author and musician, the financier and politician, whose influence prevailed in all circles previous to our departure, and whose good fortune embittered the minds of many blockheads. Come, sir, perhaps I may learn from you how to be a conqueror." D'Oraison muttered a seaman's curse, but stayed where he was, while the others disappeared. "What have you to say to me ?" Siegen began again after a pause.

"First, I must confess having heard all you and the chevalier talked about. I would not have committed such an indiscretion, if it were not my ardent desire to serve you. A man who has had such a checkered life as myself, who has felt how tormenting it is to be exposed to cares and even degradation, notwithstanding talent and tact, must be sad at your fate—a high-born man, of magnanimity and lofty endowment, and yet condemned to roam as an adventurer, while knaves and fools govern empires! I have been wishing to acknowledge my own prosperity by an act of friendship, and offer myself to you as your banker to the amount of four hundred thousand francs. It is no present, prince, for you will repay me as soon as you can. And no doubt you will be able to do so, because France will need your fidelity and courage."

"M. de Beaumarchais, you do not speak thus of your own impulse! You have been commissioned to make this proposition, that—"

"You are mistaken, if you think I act as agent for the Princess de Lamballe. I cannot suffer you to remain in that delusion, for the sake of her honor, as well as Conti's, to whom I owe gratitude. I have not yet seen the lady, for she arrived only the day before yesterday, and if I offer you the use of my strong box, no other condition is required than that you succeed in your undertakings either here or elsewhere. Would you rather be indebted to others—perhaps usurers—and attribute at the same time degrading thoughts to the princess ?"

"No, not that !" cried Siegen. "Does not the flower borrow light from the sun ? Is not Nature a vast loan-office ? Why should not I, a soldier of fortune, borrow from my colleague Beaumar-

chais ? Pardon an unhappy man who, in a moment of despondency, could suppose that the Princess de Savoy-Carignan, a descendant of the Bourbons, would lower herself so far as to endeavor to compensate him for her loss by a paltry sum of money."

"Prince! many a brave man has been ruined by perverse delusion and foolish love. I conjure you to discover your real sentiments. Do you think that the princess is even aware of your love for her ?"

"I do not know."

"Do you believe yourself beloved in return ?"

"I doubt it."

"Do you wish to know it, your highness ?"

"Is it wrong to desire the knowledge of truth, especially if it heals a wounded heart ?"

"Would you feel happy if you were convinced that you are not loved, but that you had disturbed the tranquillity of the lady of your choice ? Or would you rather believe yourself loved in secret, while she could never be yours without dishonor ?"

"You lacerate my heart! I wish to know neither !—to hear nothing ! Thirty thousand francs are sufficient to secure my departure. I will go without wishing to see again either the princess or France, and the god of war must decide whether or not I die your debtor."

"My prince, the people call you the last knight, the Bayard of our day, and they are right. And shall we be deprived of our hero ? Must he expose himself to distant dangers when he might wield his arms for fair France, where his love would rouse him to great deeds ?"

"I do not understand you, M. de Beaumarchais. Aid France here ? Ha! ha! In a state as vile as it is poor, whose universal wretchedness—"

"Will probably lead to a revolution. And could you see the princess sink under the evils to come, without using your sword for her deliverance—without releasing your Andromeda as Perseus did his?"

The Prince von Nassau-Siegen shook Caron's hand. "Ask of me what you will. To fall in such a conflict, with my last glance on her, would be worth more than life. What am I to do, what sacrifices do you demand of me?"

"That you meet the princess calmly, without betraying yourself, and then leave Paris for a time, in order to escape temptation. I will arrange your financial affairs in the meanwhile. Keep me informed of your residence, that my letters may reach you. Every day brings forth something new here; what exists now may be changed in a few months, as if it had never been."

"I promise to do all you enjoin me, and you may rely on the word of one who cannot forget his origin though in a beggar's garb—I promise it by the chaste love I bear her who was torn from me before I could express to her my sentiments."

They returned to D'Oraison. Nassau made a sign to the chevalier, and they advanced toward the brilliantly-lighted palace.

"I beg you to pay me a visit to-morrow, your royal highness," said Beaumarchais, "at the Hôtel Piron, Rue des Ormes. Here we must separate." Caron bowed, and the others continued their way.

The festive hall was sumptuously decorated. In the galleries were the marine and ministerial officials with their wives, and persons of rank and distinction, but who were not familiar enough with the friends of the family of Penthièvre, to have any claim to a formal presentation. The middle balcony window was hung with a red drapery of heavy brocade, on which were wrought the royal *fleurs de lis*, with the coats-of-arms of the Penthièvres and Savoy-Carignans. On either side were flowers, flags, and naval symbols; and in front, upon a platform, two seats for the newly married, who were to receive the homage of the aristocracy. On the bride's side stood the Prince de Conti, the Dukes de Noailles, de Luynes, de Broglie, old Richelieu, and the daughters of the king; these were the members of what had once been the dauphin's party. On the side of the Prince de Lamballe were his father Grand Admiral de Penthièvre, his sister Adelaide, the Duke d'Orleans, Prince de Chartres, Duke de St. Albin, the Count and Countess de la Blache, and the Marchioness de Ventadour. Behind this group were many ladies and cavaliers. Those to be presented were ushered in by the main entrance, passing up the left side of the hall, and, after paying their respects, returning down the right.

All eyes were turned to the young bride, coming from an obscure court to this brilliant but intriguing circle. To Beaumarchais she was specially an object of interest, as for her he had written his verses; she was, besides, Conti's niece, and, above all, the secretly beloved of an unhappy prince, whom the army worshipped as their ideal of warlike romance. It seemed almost miraculous to Caron that he should be led to the assistance of Siegen just at the moment when he could also be of service to the house of Penthièvre, in guarding the princess and Nassau from a false step that might have evil consequences. The conversation around him prevented the poet from understanding what was said at the introductions between the young couple and their visitors. All appeared as a theatrical pantomime, but so much the more he endeavored to draw conclusions from the movements and bearing of those in whom he was particularly interested.

A maiden of eighteen in her bridal costume is always an object of admiration to young and old; but the beauty of Louise de Savoy-Carignan, now Princess de Lamballe, was of that rare and pure type which we admire so much among the statues of those ancient divinities that yet remain to us. Hers was not the soft and rosy charm of Venus, but the regularity of feature and serious brow of a Minerva. Her large, expressive eyes, and arched brows—her rich dark hair, sprinkled with silver powder, and the gentleness and yet decision of her profile, were of ideal beauty. In her light-blue velvet brocade robe, sparkling with diamonds, she resembled a queen who unconsciously conquers all hearts. One scarcely knew which to admire more, her thoughtful brow, or her enchanting smile. Besides, she had a peculiar expression of cheerfulness mingled with melancholy. It almost seemed to Beaumarchais that he was called upon to protect her from some danger of which she had a presentiment. He understood how Nassau-Siegen must love her.

The princess listened now to some friendly remark of her uncle or her father-in-law, now she would quietly exchange a few words with her husband, or reply politely to the salutations of those approaching her, and presented by Penthièvre, sometimes she would smile at a jest of her sister-in-law.

Orleans, with reserved haughtiness, looked searchingly at every one, studying each word and gesture, while his son Chartres, who seemed to have profited by the education he had received, whispered sarcastic remarks to his father, with the adroitness of a courtly roué, sent flattering compliments to his future bride, Adelaide de Penthièvre,

or uttered a bon-mot to his future brother-in-law, the youthful husband. Sometimes Orleans would turn to the Marchioness de Ventadour, who, with her usual solemnity, seemed to regard the whole ceremony as an unavoidable task. The most insignificant among them was the bridegroom himself. He was good-looking, but effeminate; his countenance manifested benevolence, yet also much imbecility of mind; he seemed born to be under guardianship. The best feature of his conduct was the timid reverence with which he regarded his wife.

Beaumarchais, noticing his old opponents, and among them the pure and lovely bride, was anxiously awaiting Siegen's presentation and her behavior on his arrival. As yet the Swiss guard had not announced the prince; and Caron leaned over the railing, regarding all present with his lorgnette.

While all was proceeding according to the programme, the Marchioness de Ventadour approached Orleans. "There is some one here, duke, whose acquaintance you will like to make."

"I, marchioness? It must be an enemy."

"Who is it? In what direction is he to be seen?" interrupted Chartres, who had overheard the words.

"It is Beaumarchais. Count de la Blache has drawn my attention to him. The gentleman in the gallery to the right, in violet moire, who is engaged with a gold glass. I should think he ought to be remembered by the house of Orleans since the audience at Versailles."

"And you, chaste Diana," said Chartres, ironically, "seem to be concerned about him, notwithstanding all your efforts to hide the fact; is he unforgotten?"

"So long as I am not avenged, yes!"

"Ah, is it on account of La Blache?"

"Something of older date than that. Count de la Blache is man enough to settle his own matters whenever the time comes; I shall also have my turn."

"That is very good!" laughed Chartres. "I hope Beaumarchais will defend himself with his usual skill, and return every blow you aim at him."

"The wound I will give him will be worse than death!."

"Have you such cause for hatred?" replied Orleans. "Well, Diana, you shall do no harm to that man; La Blache must not dare to raise a finger against him until I give my permission."

"Monseigneur, what do you mean?"

"I am in earnest. I am sure I have reason enough to ruin him, and if he were only an unprincipled rascal, like a great many of my acquaintances, I would leave him to your tender mercy. But, fortunately for him, he has one of the wittiest, keenest, and most remarkable minds, and that makes him of some account. Such people are useful to me; therefore, I repeat it, no one must attack him before I give the signal."

The marchioness cast a dark glance at Orleans, and then smiled ironically. "Monseigneur, my revenge permits its victims to live—it only renders them wretched."

"You are right, marchioness," said Chartres, "to call that worse than death; it is the vengeance of the Jesuits." Diana started.

"And I would repay you, Ventadour, mercilessly repay you," said Orleans, turning his cold and piercing eye full on her, "if you disobey my command. You do it at your own peril."

"Your highness must have some special object in view!"

"Certainly, and remember your family is dependent on me."

"That is right, papa," and Chartres laughed mockingly. "I learn to ad-

mire you more every day. What is the use of friends, but to hold them until your purposes are attained?" Orleans smiled; the marchioness stepped back hastily, making an abrupt bow.

A commotion in the mean time occurred among the guests. The usher announced Admiral de Bougainville, Prince Otto von Nassau-Siegen, and Chevalier d'Oraison. As they entered, the attention of all was directed toward them. By the side of the meagre, sun-burnt hero, in the admiral's costume, walked Nassau, wearing the uniform of a French naval captain, and followed by the "wild D'Oraison," as he was called, of a short and compact figure, with a swaggering gait, his toilet, though brilliant, showing his fantastic taste. He wore a costly Persian scarf instead of a belt; but what excited the most surprise was a jewelled scimitar, and a gold-wired basket adorned with emeralds, containing shawls, Indian perfumes, and trinkets, borne on a cushion by the admiral's Malay.

Penthièvre turned to Lamballe: "My son, my dear daughter, I present to you our greatest naval hero, Admiral de Bougainville, as well as his gallant companions, his serene highness Prince von Nassau-Siegen and Chevalier d'Oraison, who returned yesterday from their voyage round the world."

Prince de Lamballe bowed. The bride, in her confusion, forgot the customary salutation.

"Permit me, grand-admiral," Bougainville began, "to take this opportunity of wishing happiness to you and this young pair. As a sailor, I am perhaps too rude in offering the prince and princess a few trophies, that are at the same time a memorial of French renown and of your happy union. This sword was taken from the Sahib Rakschasa of Madras; for, after we had shown him friendship, he insidiously attacked us. When some time after we took reprisals, the widow of the Sahib, Apsarasa, sent us this basket as a token of subjection. May it find a more suitable place in your jewelry-case, madame!"

"I heartily thank you, admiral," said Lamballe. "This present shall inspire me to become worthy of your example, though I can never hope to win such fame as yours! What is the name of the brave man who took this weapon from the Sahib and so humbled his widow?"

"He stands before you," said Bougainville, indicating Nassau. "He saved my life by the same act, cutting down Rakschasa, while Chevalier d'Oraison led forward the reënforcements."

"Oh! admiral," exclaimed Nassau, quickly, "the honor is not that of a single man, it was French courage that triumphed. Our men were always of one heart, one arm, one mind! I wish, madame, that I could add some trophy of my own to this basket, in order to express the profound emotions with which I again see France. Will you permit me to believe that you will accept a present from my next adventure?"

"Prince," and the voice of the bride trembled slightly.—"France has not so many heroes that she can spare their blood to be shed in distant countries."

"My only happiness, illustrious lady, consists in activity and danger; in what else could I find it?" The princess was silent.

"Do you intend to leave the French fleet and service, your highness," said Penthièvre, "as you are speaking of new and hazardous enterprises?"

"Certainly, duke! To-morrow I shall send in my resignation to the minister. But, be assured, if serious troubles arise in France, I shall be soon at hand."

"But will you not honor us with your presence to-morrow, prince?" asked Conti, eagerly.

"I can refuse nothing to a Conti."

"Ah," said Chartres, "we were informed yesterday of an interesting relation you bear to the Queen of Otaheite. Perhaps it is gallantry that leads you back to her." A smile was visible on the countenances of all, and Princess de Lamballe blushed.

"If what your highness says is intended for a jest, be kind enough to inquire to whom this honor belongs. The Indian I slew was rather more of a man than is usually found in the Palais-Royal! But if you are repeating a certain anecdote, Admiral de Bougainville will tell you that it has no reference to me. I leave the service because I do not wish to remain here, and, to satisfy your inquisitiveness, I tell you plainly I am going to Africa."

"To Africa?" asked Penthièvre.

"To hunt tigers, grand-admiral! And I hope you will permit me to bring your daughter-in-law a skin for her boudoir. If we should meet with a few ostriches, my dear D'Oraison, we must send their plumes to the Prince de Chartres for his masked balls!" He bowed and retired, mingling with the rest of the company.

Scarcely had this curious scene passed, when Orleans gently touched his son, who was looking at the bride.

"Did you observe?" whispered the elder.

"How the princess was confused at the salutation of Nassau-Siegen?" replied the son in the same manner.

"And he talks of going away immediately to bring her a tiger-skin from Africa!"

"It is really droll; we are, however, accustomed to such follies from Siegen; but she turned pale, and at my anecdote blushed deeply—besides, her diamond clasp, as it trembled, was a tell-tale. Lamballe will assuredly be disappointed in his wife."

"So much the better for us. If

beneath the blushes of the fair lady there is something more than coquetry, we ought to be thankful to Nassau-Siegen, and you must endure his insults into the bargain! Do not forget what we arranged in reference to Lamballe."

"I shall find some one to compensate him for the indifference of his wife."

"How about the enterprise undertaken by Leblanc and Binet? Have they found Du Barry's little angel?"

"They have. Coralie Raucourt will spare no trouble to execute that matter, but I shall hear more to-morrow afternoon."

"Very well, be reserved toward La Blache; and we must overlook Diana de Ventadour's anger in reference to Beaumarchais. Apropos, if you should see the elder Sillery, send him to me; he must know what business Beaumarchais has here; at any rate I shall not let the opportunity pass for throwing a bait to him." Chartres nodded and disappeared in the crowd. M. de Sillery soon came, who whispered for some time with Orleans, and remained the rest of the evening near the duke.

Though Caron did not understand one word of all that was said by the principal actors in this ceremony, he knew enough of court conduct to feel that he was an object of remark by La Blache, Madame de Ventadour, and both the Orleans. He noticed the duke making him known to a tall cavalier. The bearing of the princess and Siegen had not escaped his notice, as well as the eagerness with which Chartres watched her. Beaumarchais felt himself unintentionally in the midst of new plots, and anxiety warned him to great caution. As he was receiving his cloak from Gomez in the corridor, the same gentleman who had spoken to Orleans quickly descended the stairs, evidently seeking a conversation with Caron; but the latter hastily turned and left the mansion, followed by his servant.

"Where is my carriage?"

"It was here half an hour ago, these equipages must have driven it aside."

"Then let us proceed on foot."

Master and valet without delay went up the Rue St. Honoré. Quick footsteps were heard behind them. Caron folded his cloak on his left side in order to leave his right arm free, placed his hand on the hilt of his sword, and turned. "It is only one man," he said, and continued his way. When he reached the Place Louis he heard his name called. Beaumarchais stood. "I find it strange, sir, that you should select the street as the most suitable place to honor me with your attention."

"I beg your pardon. As I know that you will not be at home to-morrow afternoon or evening, and, as my business is pressing, I am thus compelled to ask whether I may wait on you to-morrow before dinner."

"You improvise a rendezvous, in order to appoint a second one, the object of which is probably a third."

"That may be the case."

"And, as I am aware you belong to the Duke d'Orleans' suite, you will not be surprised that I know for what this three-fold meeting is intended. I am not at liberty to-morrow; besides, I have withdrawn to private life. If you are curious about my appearance in the Hôtel Penthièvre, the mystery may be solved very satisfactorily in the evening. I have written a play for the festival, that is all. I wish to be forgotten, and as I do not trouble others, I care not to be troubled. Good-night, sir."

"You seem to be afraid of the duke!" replied the cavalier, sarcastically.

"Only the weak and unprincipled have fear; I am neither. I do not love M. d'Orleans, and am satisfied with the courtier experiences I have had already."

"You will probably have sufficient courage, then, to repeat all this to the duke at the festival to-morrow, for which you must find a little time. My commission is executed. If you will avoid M. d'Orleans, you do it at your own peril, besides indicating a fear that will drive you the sooner into the net you are endeavoring to escape. At the worst the duke will surprise you with an invitation, and then you cannot refuse."

"I do not understand you, sir. I do not fear your master, and have the necessary means to defend myself against my enemies. If the duke insists on an interview, he can find me to-morrow evening, after the play, and before the masked ball, in the grove to the right of the garden theatre, near the arbor; the disguises will favor our meeting. It will be his fault if it should not satisfy him. I shall wear the yellow gown of a Persian, with a green dragon on my breast."

"Very well, chevalier. You will find your equipage near the Palais-Royal. Pardon me for obliging you to walk so far." The stranger bowed and left.

Beaumarchais was very thoughtful as he entered his carriage, which was found at the place designated. He was vexed at himself for having acceded to Conti's request, and thus finding himself in a society which his prudence imperatively demanded him to forsake. On the other hand he felt interested both in Louise de Savoy, on whose countenance he could read not one trace of happiness; and in the brilliant but poor Nassau, for whom, it seemed, she felt some sympathy. He was not also unconcerned in the new complications in which Orleans wished to involve him. As he could not avoid the duke, he resolved to take a bold position. But, in order to become fully informed of the situation of affairs, and to control as much as possible the intrigue now contemplated, he decided to take advantage of his knowledge of the locality, the change of disguise, and the courage of Siegen and D'Oraison.

On the following day the Prince von Nassau made his appearance in the Hôtel Piron. "Prince," said Beaumarchais, "the checks drawn in your favor on my partner Duverney are ready; I do not think that your presentation to Madame de Lamballe will change our plans."

"No, indeed! Delicacy and honor command me to avoid her. I must go again into other regions and breathe foreign air. My destination is Africa, for I have promised her a tiger-skin."

"Prince, you jest! If you really intend to do any thing so foolhardy, I must reproach myself for assisting you. I desired your happiness, and you rush into dangers to escape which would be a miracle."

"If you take back your promise, Beaumarchais, of course I cannot go on this adventure; you may possibly prevent me from falling a prey to wild beasts, but my honor will be wounded in sight of the court and the lady of my love. I become henceforth nothing but a miserable boaster! I know, notwithstanding my rashness, that my life is worth more than to throw it away in such a manner, but M. de Chartres so irritated me while in presence of the princess that I made the promise in public. But D'Oraison will be of the party."

"Prince de Chartres! I pray you, conceal nothing from me. All that the Orleans do, father and son, can bode no good to Madame de Lamballe."

"While standing before her, Bougainville mentioned an act of mine performed before Madras, and I said that I would again leave France, when Chartres referred to a ridiculous anecdote about D'Oraison, but maintained publicly that he supposed I intended to return to the arms of the Queen of Ota-heite. The deep blush on the counte-nance of the princess told me how she felt this infamy, and I replied by the abrupt proposal of a tiger-hunt."

"I see from this how narrowly her behavior toward you was watched, and that the object was to compromise the lady and make you a laughing-stock. You must, unfortunately, keep your word. Perhaps your good star is in the ascendant. Your knightly deeds have preserved you from the immoral atmosphere these persons breathe, and in which the noble lady will perish if some true heart does not guard her. In this society, my prince, you would find beasts of prey in comparison with which those of the Indian jungles lose their terrors. If you wish to know in what labyrinths of wickedness you leave your beloved, I will show you it this evening at the festival. You may be taught to be more cautious with all your courage, and reserve it for the day when the princess may need it."

"My friend, I will follow your direc-tions. Tell me what must I do first?"

"What disguise will you wear?"

"That of a templar, black and red."

"Very good. As at the beginning the face is not masked, you will be recognized. The first meeting of the company is near the fountain. Make yourself very conspicuous. When it becomes darker, hasten unobserved to the groves between the Japanese house and the theatre. Call my servant Go-mez by name, he will conduct you to me. Understand, you are not to know me, and mark well the costumes of the company. Tell Chevalier d'Oraison to stay near the elder Orleans, and watch him as a hunter does his game. After the representation he may await us in the middle aisle in front of the stage. Then you may depart enriched with experience, and knowing why you must be careful of yourself."

The conversation ended by Beaumar-chais handing the money and letters of credit, and writing down the names of Nassau's creditors. They made the ne-cessary rearrangements as to the voy-age, and Susanna was then presented.

"Gracious lady," said the prince, "fortune has led me to make your husband's acquaintance, and I am his debtor for life. It would scarcely be-come me, who from my cradle have been the football of misfortune, to speak of returning his benefits; many things in life can never be repaid. But accept the assurance that there is no case in which you cannot call on me for my services, as far as I can possibly render them."

"I thank your serene highness," re-plied Susanna, "I will certainly re-member your promise. Since my hus-band was forced to return to court so-ciety, from which we seemed to have happily escaped, I feel as if some great calamity is menacing us. Permit me, therefore, seriously to look forward to the assistance of a cavalier known as the model of all knightly virtues.—But I have another petition, do not call me 'gracious lady!' I am not of that rank, but, as people would say, of low origin, the wife of a man who has ob-tained his fortune and title by his mind and heart, and who never forgets that he was once poor and despised. Call me Susie, or Madame Susie; that is an honorable appellation given to me by my husband's friends."

"Certainly, my dear Madame Susie," said Nassau, pressing her hand, and smiling, "I will call you so, and when-ever you remind me of my duty, I will obey your behest as proudly as if a queen beckoned me to her banner. This charming frankness greatly in-creases my esteem for you. I envy Beaumarchais. Whatever evils may be in store for him, he has you, and can laugh at the freaks of fortune."

"And as to your presentiments, my dear child," added Caron, "no evil but what we ourselves cause will make us really wretched."

The evening of the festival at the Hôtel Penthièvre was very favorable; a starry August sky shone over the shady garden. In the Rue St. Honoré, a gaping multitude assembled, to admire the splendor of the aristocracy in their varied and fanciful costumes entering in a long row of carriages into the court-yard. The place around the fountain was soon crowded with the visitors. Prince de Conti, Penthièvre, and Orleans, were the only persons in ordinary ball-dress, carrying their masks on their arm. While Penthièvre did the honors, Conti and Orleans seated themselves on either side of the newly-married couple, who appeared as an Arcadian shepherd and shepherdess. Behind the chair of the princess stood the Countess de Gorzka, a lovely blonde of seventeen, a native of Poland, educated at the court of the deceased king Ladislaus Leszinsky, and one of the princess's ladies of honor; she was dressed in Turkish costume. Adelaide de Penthièvre represented Flora; Chartres, a negro; Madame de Seran, a fisherman's wife; La Blache, a marine divinity; his wife Rosa, Luna; Diana de Ventadour, the queen of the night; Bougainville, a Chinese; D'Oraison wore a red domino, and the others many-hued and brilliant disguises. In the midst of so much splendor, where fair women and chivalrous men were conversing beneath the trees and along the flowery paths of the garden, who would have supposed that the cruel sacrifice of a young and beautiful girl was celebrated?

The etiquette of the preceding days was banished, giving place to the freedom of a family reunion, which embraced about three hundred of the highest nobility. Nassau-Siegen and D'Oraison accompanied the admiral. The prince avoided Madame de Lamballe, except at the salutation on his entrance, and conversed with Orleans, Conti, or young Lamballe, who made many inquiries about his sea expeditions. Tea, confectionery, and wine, were served, and, as it became later, there appeared in the foliage, as by a fairy's wand, colored balloons, torches, and variegated lamps. The company formed themselves into numerous small groups, and Nassau took advantage of this moment to seek Beaumarchais, but before he reached the rendezvous he was stopped by a masked Turkish lady.

"Sir knight, lend me your ear for a few seconds."

"Certainly, fair odalisk! But is it not half a betrayal of your religion, for a Mohammedan to speak to a templar?"

"I have an excuse. I must beg your serene highness not to undertake that wild voyage. Your friends will be very anxious, and many hearts tormented on your account. Remain in France. A man of your fame will find sufficient at home to employ all his energies. Do not expose your precious life!" She seized his hand in her excitement.

"I did not know until this moment, fair lady, that so many hearts have any interest in me. If that is the case, my expedition would be the means of making them apparent. Are you one of my well-wishers, or do you speak in the name of a lady near whom you are usually found?"

"I—I am not authorized to answer that question."

"Then pardon me if I say that I have given my word as to this voyage, and in the presence of a prince who was slandering me. Does there really exist a heart that trembles for my safety—that shares my own painful feelings? Answer me!"

"There is such a heart, your highness!—a heart that would break in case of your death."

"Then this precious conviction will bring me back unhurt. Farewell, console her who sympathizes with me; at some future time I will kneel before her and ask whether my hope was too daring!" He disappeared among the trees.

When the Countess de Gorzka had returned to those still chatting around the princess, two gentlemen, as if by accident, separated themselves from the rest, and glided toward the colonnade under the terrace.

"Well, my dear brother-in-law, how do you like being a married man? You certainly have a handsome wife!"

"Don't talk to me about her."

"Pshaw! do you play the bashful?"

"Do not trouble me with your sarcasms! I pity my sister that she must become your wife, as I pity mine for having been obliged to marry me. Yes, she is fair and virtuous, and so far my superior that I tremble before her! I could be happy with her if your pernicious example had not blunted my respect for female dignity, and disqualified me for domestic bliss!"

"Ha! ha! You mean to say that you cannot gain her heart, because she pretends to be immaculate. Is it so?"

"Your prying talent has discovered what I do not care to confess. Since yesterday I have learned to hate you as my seducer, and Louise cannot despise me more than I despise myself."

"From the moment she placed her foot in your father's house you have become a fool! Is that gratitude for my friendship? Who saved you from the tedium of your paternal education? Who gave independence to your mind by merry nights that compensated the slavery of the day?—Virtue, domestic bliss! I almost fancy I hear a Paris trader speak, and not the Prince de

11

Lamballe. That you should fall in love with your wife was natural; that she should be reserved is mere coquetry. Make her jealous. Pass your time in the Pigeonnier, as formerly, and she will soon be devoted to you."

"Do you really think so, Philip?"

"Of course, I shall act in the same manner toward Adelaide, and she will be deeply in love with me, whereas now she is only polite and cool. Make an attempt. I am expected in the Pigeonnier. Accompany me, amuse yourself, and, if you find Louise with tears in her eyes, tell her calmly that it is all her fault."

"I have made a vow never to return to Coralie Raucourt's dwelling."

"Such weakness is beyond comprehension! I see you cannot forget your pedantic and bigoted governor. Is not the drawing-room of Coralie the best place of amusement for the court aristocracy? Besides, you will find my father there to-night in an exclusive circle, and expecting you. Do you think I shall be believed when I tell them that you could not come because of melancholy on account of your wife's reserve? Imagine the ridicule! To-morrow you will be the greatest simpleton in all Paris."

"Your father at Mlle. Raucourt's!"

"You are surprised, because it is new to you? Well, my father himself introduced me into that house; he is a free-thinker, a philosopher, like most of our intellectual men. You cannot comprehend how the Pigeonnier is the rendezvous of intriguers, and what mysteries find a solution there. We are going to see the new Circe to-night who is to overthrow Madame de Grammont and Choiseul! You have therefore three objects in going—you subdue your wife, dispel your low spirits, and become informed of a political secret that gives you some influence. Every thing must turn out at last as my father and I desire it ; and, you will also have your share ! Will you come with me after the ball has commenced ? "

" *Ma foi*, I believe I must ! " replied Lamballe in an uncertain voice. Both stepped out, looked cautiously around, separated, and returned to the company.

Silence succeeded, and then a noise as of the breaking of twigs and whispered conversation. Two men as shadows passed out of the dark colonnade and vanished in the garden—Nassau and Beaumarchais.

"Do you now understand why you are to take care of your life ? " whispered Caron. "Have you now a conception of the society around this poor lady, torn from the patriarchal peace of Chambery, for the arms—"

"Do not utter a name so hateful to me ! I have had a glance of the creatures calling themselves the French aristocracy, and I shudder ! I must live to save the beloved one, or at least avenge her ! What are we to do now ? "

"Let us also pay a visit to the Pigeonnier. First, however, I have a meeting with Orleans, and you are to be present."

"With your old enemy ? "

"I am forced to it. You may judge whether I can grapple with him."

An hour later, and the assemblage were summoned to the play by the music of the orchestra. The light partition that had excluded the garden disappeared, and the large rotunda with its red curtain, lighted by lamps and chandeliers, was visible. The play began.

The festival drama of Beaumarchais was *A Tale of Savoy*—an idyl, representing the monarch of the ocean searching in all the zones for the highest good promised him, and which he at last finds in Savoy under the protection of the lilied banner. The fair lady was intended who was to be his bride. It was a graceful compliment to Louise de Lamballe, closing with the following words, spoken by the celebrated actress Dumeuil, in the character of a disenchanted princess :

> "O stolzes Frankreich, Dir
>   Weih' ich hinfort mein Leben,
> Dem Helden der mich durch
>   Die Lilien bezwang !
> Ich folge ihm, er soll
>   Ein süss'res Glück mir geban,
> Als einst im Vaterhans
>   Mein junges Herz durchdrang !
> Ans sanftem Kindertraum
>   Zum lieblichen Erwachen
> Der Braut ward ich geführt !
>   O wacher Hoffonngstraum,
> O Liebo, zieh' mit mir
>   Auf duft'gem Rosennachen
> Durch Sturm und Sonnenschein !
>   Am fernen Küstensanm ,
> Erglühen schon im Grün
>   Die stillen Sonnenmatten,
> Wo Glück und Frieden sich
>   Mit Ros' und Myrte gatten ! " *

The Princess de Lamballe grew pale and cast down her eyes. Her husband, gloomy and embarrassed, bit his lips ; Orleans and Chartres exchanged an ironical smile. Not a dozen of those present seriously believed in the happiness of the newly married. After the curtain had fallen amid great applause, the bride took her husband's arm and turned toward Conti : ".May I ask who composed the poetry containing those well-meant wishes ? "

" Caron de Beaumarchais, to whom our family owe many obligations."

---

* To thee, proud France ! and to thy princely son,
  For whom home's happiness I flee,
Who sought me, and my pure affection won,
  My days shall consecrated be.

From childhood's fairy visions I awake,
  Fast in Love's silken fetters bound ;
Day-dream of Hope ! be with me, nor forsake
  A bride with virtue's garland crowned.

I step into thy flowery boat, O Love !
  Nor fragile let its promise be ;
As in the sunny calm so may it prove
  When tossed upon a stormy sea.

Our haven glows beneath the western beam,
  Where roses and the myrtles twine ;
Bright are the skies, and fair the valleys seem,
  Where peace and happiness combine !

"Does he no longer live at court ? "

"Not since the death of the dauphin. He is our guest to-day, quite as an exception."

"I would be glad, dear uncle, to thank him personally."

"I shall not fail to present him to you, Louise."

The company put on their masks, and passed across the terrace, now fully lighted, into the ballroom. The last that entered were Orleans and Chartres.

"Have you spoken to him, Philip ? "

"Under the colonnade. It is as we suspected."

"Then I am certain she has an inclination for Nassau-Siegen. I am glad you led him into that tiger business. I hope one of the beasts will be kind enough to dine on him. Is the poor husband coming ? "

"Yes, for I have persuaded him that it is the only way in which he can make Louise jealous."

"You are at last beginning to do credit to my style of education. We must not let Lamballe come to his senses, and so make the breach between him and his wife complete."

"The Pigeounier will do its duty. When he is once excited he is like one insane, and will dispose of himself without our aid."

"Go to Adelaide until it is time ; I have some business to attend to."

Chartres hastened to the company, and Orleans walked slowly through the forsaken garden toward the grove where he was to meet Beaumarchais. The latter was there already, dressed in his yellow robes, with a mask concealing his face. Nassau and Gomez were with him.

"Has D'Oraison taken care of the elder Orleans for the evening ? "

"The chevalier understands his business."

"I hear footsteps. There he is. I will remain near in the shade, that you may hear all."

When Orleans approached, he beheld the figure of the Persian ; the moon was shining upon him, and silvering the foliage with its full brightness. "Son of the green dragon, why so lonely ? "

"I am waiting for a friend."

"One who offered you a rendezvous yesterday ? "

"Near the Place Louis, when I could not find my carriage."

"And have we met at last ? "

"Contrary to my desire."

"That I believe. But you have often interfered in my affairs, and I would now ask why. If you are really as skilful as you are said to be, you must know how little advantage all your manœuvrings were, and that your opponents are at present so situated that they could ruin you, unless you join their party."

"The latter I doubt. You can do nothing by endeavoring to frighten me. My plans failed because I did not know the use of the—*phial*, as some do ! "

"Ah, you insinuate that you may become very dangerous to me, thus heightening the value of your friendship. If you really intended to adopt certain means, you would not thus talk about them."

"If I do speak of those I possess to injure you, I have said nothing of the mode in which I shall use them."

"Nonsense, my good fellow, I am acquainted with the extent of your information ; and I do not fear a parliamentary process."

"Preserve that conviction. If, however, you did not fear my knowledge of certain facts, you would not have exposed yourself to the night-air on my account. You are aware that I have given up all such matters, and have no cause to compromise you, unless you force me to it. What do you want of me?"

"I wish to engage your excellent talent in my favor; and, if you refuse, destroy you."

"Destroy! In what manner? The phial will hardly serve your turn, if I know nothing. And if I do know something, my death would communicate the secret to the public in a printed form."

"Your secret! Let us hear what it is. You can accuse me of nothing, for what you saw at the Marchioness de Pompadour's is no proof. On whom, then, will suspicion fall? On Choiseul? He gave the phial to Binet, he was last near the dauphin at Compiègne. The dauphiness died under the eyes of the king, and any cause to which her decease may be ascribed can only be traced to the Hôtel Choiseul. What therefore, would be the consequences of your threats, but that the premier would fall, and not a thought of suspicion rest on me? And who is not suspected in these days? Let me tell you, further, that I am of your mind in reference to the downfall of Choiseul. I wish to make use of you in effecting it. You are as egotistic as I am, and, as you are wealthy, name the rank that will satisfy your ambition."

"And you would raise me to it when you are *king!* Choiseul is a mere instrument, but I like him better than you and your vicious family. Your degenerate mind seems to have no other idea than to reap advantage from the graves you have opened for the good; but I tell you, neither you nor your son will ever be king!"

Orleans murmured an oath, and gnashed his teeth. "Ah, and so you insist on playing the virtuous? You declare war against me! Well, then, I assure you, that you shall not escape either me or my son. We do not mean to kill you, for you are very useful, but to subdue you, so that you cannot help serving us blindly but willingly; and, when we have done with you, we shall dismiss you as a valet."

"I thank you for your sincerity, duke, and, in return, I will endeavor to be as frank. I know that you can array my enemies against me; and I do not doubt that you will cause me many sad days, but you have no conception how a pure conscience can sustain a man under all vicissitudes. Perhaps you will understand me better when I say, that, to overthrow a dynasty and raise your own, you require at least an insurrection, do you not?"

"Go on."

"That you must have the people on your side?"

"Well!"

"But there is no historical precedent that a man branded as you with vice, was ever chosen by any people as their ruler. I will describe your actions, doctrines, and manner of life, in a pamphlet; and it will have its effect. Even if the Parliament does not condemn you, there is such a thing as public contempt, and which will drive you even from the steps of the throne, leaving your head behind! Now we stand emphatically unmasked before each other; let each therefore go his own way."

"Orleans stood confounded. He passed his hand over his brow.— "Chevalier, I have been deceived. I confess I cannot fathom you. Let us make peace."

"I thank you for the honor. I ask nothing. Follow your instincts, and forget that a Beaumarchais ever lived. I shall not hinder you, for I will not anticipate the misfortunes of my country; my hopes lie buried with the dauphin. But respect my feelings, for the sake of your family, duke! Should you ever reach your hand toward the crown of him whom I consider as your victim, then you shall hear from me again."

"Let us agree not to molest each other."

"I can make no bargain with you. I shall live quietly, as I am accustomed to do, and await your future action. Have not the least trouble about me."

"Very good, sir! You think you have the advantage, and are skilful in its use! I hope we may meet again."

"I neither hope nor fear it."

Orleans returned slowly and musingly to the ballroom. He was pale and agitated.

Two men, in civilian dress, silently left the other side of the grove—Beaumarchais and Nassau. The third, D'Oraison, joined them in the middle walk.

"Have you your arms, chevalier?" asked Siegen, abruptly.

"I have."

"Well, then, to the Pigeonnier!" whispered Caron; "we must go across the terrace, and escape secretly. They ascended and passed toward the pavilion, fastened to the balustrade the ropes with which they had provided themselves, and, being assured that the coachmen were quietly sleeping on their carriage-boxes, they descended, and hastened to the equipage of Beaumarchais, where Gomez was awaiting them. "To the Rue St. Martin, near Clairveaux!"

"Just Heaven," said Nassau, in a low voice, "what have I heard!"

"A fragment from my courtier life!"

BOOK III

CHAPTER XV.

THE EMPIRE OF THE ANGELS.

THE carriage of Beaumarchais rolled swiftly through the deserted streets. D'Oraison related to him and Nassau the conversation of Orleans with his son Chartres. Then all three were silent, each thinking of the coming danger. When they reached the Rue de Tournellerie, Caron suddenly asked: "What weapons have we?"

"I have my pocket-pistols," said D'Oraison, "they are my indispensable companions."

"Are they loaded?"

"With as good lead as ever entered the body of an enemy."

"Give me one, and the prince the other. Gomez has his knife, and you must use your sword. The persons with whom we shall come in contact, do not know you, prince; you will therefore represent the officer of the Versailles police, commanded by Choiseul to arrest the singer Raucourt and her friend Debrelon, provided they refuse to accede to my demands. When we enter and I accost the man, we must surround him. Gomez knows his part, and the chevalier will be your sergeant. Let us not use our arms except in case of extremity."

The others were satisfied with this arrangement, and the rest of the way was again passed in silence. At the Cour de la Mer the coach stopped, the party descended, and arrived in front of the old Pigeonnier. Beaumarchais knocked in a peculiar manner, and the face of the porter appeared at the small window.

"It is I, good fellow, your lodger and patron," whispered Caron. "You can earn a hundred francs."

"Dear me, I would scarcely have known you, dear M. de Beaumarchais. I am coming directly!" The bolt was withdrawn, and the four men entered.

"Is there much company with Mlle. Raucourt?"

"Not yet, unless some came by the other gate. But what do you mean with so many companions? Formerly you did not like to be seen in her apartments, and since Debrelon has turned traitor against you, I thought—"

"We have no time to talk. Here are a hundred francs, I am acting by order of Minister de Choiseul; these gentlemen belong to the Versailles police-guards, and are engaged to watch Debrelon. You are not to hear us; know nothing if questions are asked, and leave your gate open. Are they quiet above?"

"Yes, dear sir. I do not think there will be many passing to-night; for we have been ordered to refuse entrance to all visitors that have not the watch-word."

" What is it ? "

" ' Has the angel come ? ' Ha ! ha ! They seem to be bent on some special mischief."

" That is why we are here."

" Shall I light you ? "

" No ! "

The conversation ceased. Beaumarchais took Siegen's hand; the four glided noiselessly through the passage into the inner court. Lights were in the windows of Coralie's rooms, but, from the silence reigning, the company had apparently not all assembled. They walked near the wall, that their shadows might not be seen in the moonlight, and ascended the staircase which had so often led Caron to his garret. Beaumarchais requested his companions to keep close behind him, advanced to the door of Coralie's apartments, listened, and knocked gently.

" Who is there ? " asked Debrelon, in a suppressed voice.

" Has the angel come ? "

Debrelon opened. Beaumarchais seized him, held the pistol to his face, and whispered : " Be still, or I fire ! Not a breath ! "

Nassau, D'Oraison, and Gomez, followed. D'Oraison stood at the entrance, Gomez stepped between the two doors leading to the inner chambers, and drew his knife. Debrelon was speechless and trembled. " What —what do you want ? " he stammered.

" We have come to pay you a visit ! After the death of the dauphin you thought I could no longer injure you, and you sold yourself, soul and body, to Orleans. But that you may see how you are in my power, pay attention to what the captain of the police-guards of Versailles has to say. Reveal his fate to him, sir."

" Debrelon," said Nassau, " if you utter a sound or show the slightest disobedience, I will stab you as I would a wild boar. I am ordered to arrest you and Coralie Raucourt, and impris-on you for life at Loches. If you wish to escape, you must obey M. de Beau-marchais."

" Heaven," murmured the wretched man, " it is betrayed ! "

" So it is," said Caron. " By your treachery you have gained nothing, but lost my patronage, besides giving me a chance to put the minister on your track. You were a great fool."

" I was ! I will do all you wish, sir ! "

" Be so kind then to lead us to your private room, where, as you have often told me, can be seen the conduct of your company. We shall remain there until we know what Messrs. Bi-net, Orleans, Chartres, Lamballe, Le-blanc, and others like them, are con-cocting. Do not dare to give warning, for you would only cause unnecessary bloodshed, and yourself would die on the Place Grève. Attend well to what we tell you. Orleans and his companions will be here soon."

Beaumarchais released Debrelon, who in the utmost terror took the light, advanced softly toward the tapestry por-tière in the corner, opening it by a secret spring. They entered a small cabinet. The walls seemed to be very thin, for male and female voices could be distinctly heard and understood. Caron took the light from Debrelon, and directed his attention again to the pistol, in a very significant manner ; he then made a sign to Gomez, who took his position at the door as guard, while Debrelon retired in silence. When they were alone, Beaumarchais pointed to two sliding panels in the corners on one side of the cabinet, and extinguished the light. The room was dark, except that a pale ray passed through the tapestry opening where Gomez stood with his knife. Noiselessly they drew back the panels, and surveyed two apartments, each containing a different set of persons.

The room into which Beaumarchais looked was sumptuously furnished. On the table were wine-glasses, decanters, and writing-materials; before the latter sat a small, thin, lynx-eyed man, playing negligently with a pen. He was dressed in the exaggerated style of a dandy, and his fingers were covered with rings. Opposite him sat (for Caron immediately recognized them) Binet, the discarded valet de chambre of the king, and his friend and colleague Leblanc, who now occupied his place. —Debrelon entered and sat down with them, hastily swallowing several glasses of wine. He turned his face furtively toward the panel, and as quickly averted it again.

"As I was saying, Leblanc, the little girl will please him. She is different from any lady he ever knew. She is capable of urging a demigod into any follies for her."

"Surely you do not expect me to make a contract, without seeing the ware?"

"And I will not present her to you, unless you consent to my conditions. Do you suppose I care who has her, so long as I am well paid? There are people in Paris who have more money at their disposal than can at present be found in the purse of the eldest son of the Church."

"The Duke d'Orleans, for example!" laughed Binet. "I would not like either him or Chartres to see our angel, for she would soon be bespoken. I mentioned her to them, and they will come to see her. You must therefore be prompt before the count becomes impatient."

"Orleans!" exclaimed Leblanc. "Does he know I am here? You have purposely brought me into this dilemma, you old rogue, that I may have no choice but to dance to your whistle."

"You are a fool, Leblanc. What is your object? You wish to find a successor to Madame de Grammont, and send her and her brother to the mischief! Do you wish to lose your place by betraying your tricks? The little girl will be grateful to you, and you can make your own conditions with her. It cannot matter to you, if any one else is served. Do you wish to become a politician, or would you not, rather lay by something for a rainy day, or when you can no longer work? You will find it to your advantage if Monseigneur d'Orleans, Chartres, Aiguillon, and the ministers, assist the pretty child with their influence. I think that, for the last four years, you have had neither pleasure nor profit."

"It is all the same," replied Leblanc, "if she only please the old man.— Write your agreement that I may lay it before the king."

The little thin man, who had been listening contemptuously to the conversation, dipped his pen in the ink: "I, Count Robert du Barry, will deliver Manon Vaubernier, also called Mlle. l'Ange, eighteen years of age, to M. Leblanc, that he may present her to the king. If she does not please, I am to receive thirty thousand francs for my service; but if otherwise, then an annual life income of a hundred thousand francs, and M. Binet a hundred and fifty thousand francs as commission, and—"

"Count," exclaimed Leblanc, "your terms are unreasonable. If the agents receive so much, what remains for myself and another party?"

"That I leave to Mlle. l'Ange, my friend," said Du Barry.—"Debrelon, my carriage!"

"Are you insane, Leblanc?" asked Binet. "Will you lose all your prospects? I know the old man better.

You will be astonished at the favor with which the king will receive her."

"Well, then, I will venture it."

Du Barry's pen passed rapidly over the paper. "What does she demand for herself?" Leblanc interrupted him.

"That is nothing to you," smiled Du Barry. "She will make her own terms with her royal lover."

"You really make me very curious. I thought most persons cared only for pecuniary profit."

"Your Versailles beauties certainly were of that coarse quality, and had no confidence in their blandishments! " Gentlemen, sign!"

Debrelon went into the anteroom. Du Barry hummed an air, while Binet and Leblanc read the contract. The chief valet de chambre then wrote his name, followed by Binet. It was a strange moment, when the future of France was decided by a lackey's pen! The count was signing the paper when the door opened, and Orleans, Chartres, and Lamballe entered.

"Am I too late?" exclaimed Orleans.

"A little, your highness!" said Binet, respectfully.

"Did I not tell you to wait for me?"

"I was obliged to give the preference to his majesty," replied Du Barry, bowing.

"But the contract dates from to-morrow, does it not?" Du Barry nodded. Chartres laughed.

"Then I will order supper to be served," said Debrelon.

While Beaumarchais was witnessing this scene, another was passing before the eyes of Nassau in a boudoir hung with pink silk, the curtains at the windows and portières being of the same color and material. It was small and square, containing a richly-carved sideboard and a large round table, at which about fifteen or twenty persons could sit, but so low that at first it was incomprehensible how any one could conveniently eat at it. A heavy red-silk cover was spread over it, and it might have been taken for any thing but a dining-table, were it not for the silver dishes, decanters, and glasses on it. Before each plate stood a vase with a fragrant bouquet, so that the flowers formed a circle in the middle of the table. The floor was covered with a light-green carpet, very rich and elastic. Instead of chairs, cushions were arranged, so that the supper might be partaken of after the manner of the Orientals. Numerous wax-lights in crystal chandeliers burned near the walls, and the ceiling was composed of plate-glass mirrors, so that this Lucullian company could behold themselves reflected.

In this apartment were two ladies, reclining near each other, engaged in lively conversation. The one was Coralie Raucourt, wearing a violet dress of silk moire, and her powered hair adorned with a wreath of evergreen. Her neck and arms were overloaded with ornaments, and what her complexion lacked in natural brilliancy was supplied by art. Whatever impression this woman intended to make, it was surpassed by that of her neighbor, who was in the freshness of her youth, without rouge, powder, or jewelry, and who relied on the charms which Nature had lavished on her. She was dressed in a flowing tunic of rose-colored gauze, fastened on her shoulders with satin bows; in her light toilet she recalled the idea of a seaborn Aphrodite. Her dark-brown hair, interwoven with a wreath of water-lilies, fell negligently on her shoulders and arms, and her countenance, expressing a mingled naïveté and boldness, would have forced a painter to confess that in her beauty she had few rivals. This was Mlle. l'Ange, or Manon Vaubernier, soon to favor France as the beautiful Countess du Barry.

"Did you understand me, little witch?" Coralie continued. Kings are like other men in their emotions, and Louis is the greatest simpleton alive. The wilder you are—the more you assume your natural manner—the surer you enslave him. Provoke him by your coquetry, make him embarrassed and angry, and turn his displeasure into merriment; give him no rest—that is the way to secure your footing. He will feel miserable and stupid when you are not near him."

"O good Cora, I understand you as well as a dog his master's whistle. I see through it all. You say that I am certain of the influence of Orleans, Chartres, Maupeau, and Terray?"

"Chartres himself told me so, and you will be informed of it to-night, Should the princes act as if they were dissatisfied with you, do not mind them, but be assured that they work secretly for your elevation. They must not know, however, that you are prepared. When you are established at Versailles they will tell you how you can effect the downfall of the Choiseuls. The Duke d'Aiguillon and the ministers will declare themselves your adherents. But then you will forget your friend Coralie, you will become a woman of rank, moving in a sphere inaccessible to me, and yet it was I who received you in my house, made you acquainted with Binet, and prepared the way for your great fortune."

"You distrustful creature, you believe that, and your face seems to say that you really do. No, my dear, we remain the most intimate friends. You must pay me a visit at least twice a week. Do you think I could bear the old man of the Œil-de-Bœuf * without any change of society? Indeed, no!

* The king's apartments at Versailles.

You must manage new intrigues with me, arrange our amusements, and repeat to me the scandal of Paris, that I may have something to prattle about; and I hereby invite you to our little reunions! In short, pleasure is the watchword; innumerable eccentricities shall distinguish me, and, if I really succeed, I will enrich you, Cora, should I have to overturn even the state treasury, and the Abbé Terray lose his last sou."

"My angel!" exclaimed Coralie Raucourt as she embraced her friend, and overwhelmed her with caresses, which were interrupted by the entrance of Debrelon.

"Leave off your nonsense, ladies! Manon, retire; the princes are here, and Du Barry and Leblanc have come to an agreement. The latter sends word, that you may anticipate the whip, unless all turns out well."

"Well," said Manon, sulkily; "let him take care I do not turn the tables on him." She disappeared.

"Did you impress it on her mind that she ought not to forget us?" Debrelon whispered to Coralie.

"Certainly, and all that Orleans commanded us. Let the affair proceed."

Debrelon turned, cast a glance toward the hiding-place of Nassau, and opened the door. Orleans, Chartres, Lamballe, Count du Barry, Leblanc, and Binet entered. The duke welcomed Mlle. Raucourt with a bon-mot, while three young women brought in the dishes; and the gentlemen reclined negligently on the cushions. Here the valet de chambre sat next to the duke; the spy by the side of the prince of the royal blood. Six well-dressed women appeared from an opposite door and seated themselves, laughing and jesting. The supper commenced.

"I do not see the queen of our feast, for she was the object of our visit," said Chartres. "Is she to be retained until the end of the banquet?"

"Not quite," laughed Du Barry, "but if she is the queen of our little party, as you say, you are also aware that sovereigns always let others wait for them."

"In this case," said Leblanc, "I desire no delay, for I must return this night with my report. I hope, count, you do not intend to aid our judgment by wine."

"No," exclaimed Orleans, "we shall not be deceived; I will not touch my glass before I have seen her."

"Deception is not necessary, monseigneur!" Du Barry rose and approached the portière. "We are waiting for you, Manon."

Delicate hands pushed aside the curtains, and Mlle. l'Ange stood laughing before the guests, who rose in surprise, while in the mean time a little Moor of twelve years, in a red garment, and bearing a basket of flowers on his head, walked rapidly from behind the lady, and took a place cross-legged on a cushion. The beauty glanced around with a consciousness of her charms, and seated herself near the young Moor, who sprinkled his flowers around her. She smiled, and drank a glass of champagne.

"Leblanc," exclaimed Orleans, "your treasure is found."

"So I think!" returned the valet with a sparkling eye. "I do not return to Versailles without her. Choiseul is lost."

"Do you think so?" said Manon.

"Yes, my angel," said Chartres, "his empire is at an end."

"And the empire of the angels begins!" she added exultingly. "Pleasure is its crown, and folly its sceptre; let love rule."

"Then let us drink to the empire of the angels!" Orleans arose laughing, and held his glass high.

The Prince von Nassau-Siegen and Caron heard and saw enough. With embittered minds and full of disgust they quietly passed from the dark room to their carriage near the Rue Clairvaux. They had seen the beginning of a new court government. It was not long before it was established.

Mlle. l'Ange succeeded so well in the part assigned her that, a week after her first appearance at Versailles, Madame de Grammont had to leave. Choiseul was quite unprepared for this blow, but he sacrificed his sister in order to maintain his position. Manon was married to the brother of Du Barry, who immediately disappeared from Paris with a large revenue assured to him. Louis presented her with a diamond set worth four hundred thousand francs. Soon the low birth of the new favorite was known everywhere, for Choiseul did his utmost to render her contemptible in the eyes of the people. Her freedom with the monarch and courtiers was unprecedented, so that the aristocracy did not know whether to be shocked or amused at the new countess. The princes and princesses of the blood avoided the court, Choiseul made advances to the Parliament, and a conflict involving the whole land seemed inevitable. Powerful accomplices supported the new mistress, and seemed prepared for any extreme. Aiguillon, who had every thing to fear from the Parliament, was the first to fall at her feet. Chancellor Maupeau, who wished to obtain the premiership in place of Choiseul, declared himself her cousin; and Terray, who desired to unite in himself the offices of financier and head of public worship, pressed harder on the already-exhausted resources of the country, in order to make himself necessary to the countess in supplying her with money. "I take all, wherever I find it!" he said. "That is stealing," replied a financial intendant. "Very well, then let us steal!"

A few days after the wedding festival, that ended so seriously in the Pigeonnier, Nassau and D'Oraison started for Africa. There was no necessity for any more explanations between the prince and Beaumarchais. They had seen Lamballe degrade himself far beyond their expectations, they knew the misfortune menacing the nation, and they felt that no human power could avert the consequences. Conti, who had vainly searched for Caron after the representation, wrote him a note on the following day, reproaching him with having withdrawn without receiving the well - deserved thanks of those whom he had obliged, and asking him to accompany Conti to the Hôtel Penthièvre. Beaumarchais went to the residence of his old patron, but only to unburden his heart of what he had seen at Coralie Raucourt's; he was, however, silent about the presence of Siegen. Under these circumstances, the grieved prince had no disposition to present Beamarchais to Madame de Lamballe.

Secrecy concealed from all but those nearly related to the young couple, the destroyed happiness and hopes of the wife, who had been taken from the quiet home of her youth to find a husband demoralized by every vice of Paris. Her pure dignity scorned to reproach him, or complain to her father-in-law Penthièvre, who adored her. From the beginning she had considered herself as a victim to family interests, and, finding her husband so far beneath her in every respect, she proudly hid her disappointment and misery. Lamballe was not honest enough to confess that he could not abandon a life to which he was accustomed; and the princess, instead of becoming jealous, only treated him with more coldness and contempt. Fearing his austere father, he did not dare to say any thing of Louise's conduct, and after fruitless endeavors to awaken in her an interest she never possessed for him, Lamballe plunged headlong into all the iniquity the refined arts of Chartres could imagine; this made him quite dependent on Orleans, and completely ruined his health.

Adelaide de Penthièvre gave her hand to Chartres in 1769, and the king made Madame de Seran her lady of honor. The latter was the only virtuous woman of the court who made a fortune under his reign.

Choiseul, on his side, resisted his adversaries as far as he could. The Austrian policy, rendered permanent by the Bourbon family treaty, had, even in Madame de Pompadour's time, led to secret negotiations with the court of Vienna, aiming at a marriage between the Duke de Berri and Marie Antoinette, the second daughter of Marie Theresa. The ratification had been delayed on account of the deceased dauphin's dislike to such a daughter-in-law, and by the reluctance of the dauphiness; nevertheless, the Abbé Vermont was sent to Schönbrunn to instruct the future queen in all regal virtues. After the death of the crown prince and his consort, the minister hastened to conclude the marriage, through the ambassador Abbé Prince de Rohan; and Choiseul hoped, by the speedy union of these mere children, to bring the Austrian influence again to its former importance. He did more: he sought to disarm Madame du Barry at one blow, by proposing to the king, as a second wife, the Archduchess Elizabeth, Marie Antoinette's older sister. But his foes, especially Orleans, had some knowledge of these projects.

"Ah, my dear," said the Countess du Barry one day to the king, in presence of Aiguillon, Maupeau, and Terray, "it is said the silly Choiseul intends to burden you with the Archduchess Elizabeth! Are you not alarmed? I should think we had enough already of the thick-lipped Hapsburgs. Should you walk between two such princesses, their protruding mouths would be likely to conceal you."

Louis XV. was silent and embarrassed; the rest burst into laughter. On the following day the bon-mot was in the *Mercure français*, all Paris talked of it, and the minister's project was defeated. He was thankful that the young dauphin's marriage, and the favor of the future queen, seemed assured.

Debrelon's fear of falling into the hands of Choiseul's police, and of being dependent only on the favor of Beaumarchais, was so great, that at first he did not dare to move, or even to inform Coralie of the supposed danger. But when Manon reached her ascendant at Versailles, and Madame de Grammont was dismissed without his being molested, he revealed all to Mlle. Raucourt, and she mentioned the conduct of Caron to both the Duke of Orleans and his son Chartres. They were highly indignant at the audacity of their opponent. They inquired of Maupeau, and learned that Choiseul had never had any idea of taking official measures against Debrelon—that, in fact, the whole affair had greatly surprised him. Orleans immediately drove to the Hôtel Ventadour.

"Marchioness," he exclaimed, on seeing Diana, "I permit you to do whatever you please against this vile Beaumarchais. Let your hatred deprive him of every thing except his life."

"Except his life, monseigneur! You could never have harmed him without me!"

CHAPTER XVI.

FROM THE DESERT.

MORE than three-fourths of a year had passed since the festivals at the Hôtel Penthièvre; winter and spring had passed, and the summer was in full beauty, with its banks of flowers, and the sweet evening air whispering among the acacias and chestnut-trees. The grand-admiral was on a tour of inspection to the northern and western harbors. Rumors were abroad of an expedition against England, which, taking advantage of the weakness of France, had deprived the latter of a number of her most important colonies in the West and East Indies. By the admiral's order, his son Lamballe accompanied him, whose health was completely undermined by the vices in which he indulged, though the unsuspicious father did not even dream of his son's conduct, nor of the coolness existing between him and his wife Louise. He considered their deportment toward each other as aristocratic. Penthièvre hoped to strengthen his son's constitution by this voyage, present him to the fleet as their future grand-admiral, and permit him to begin the inevitable year of naval service.

When the prince was taking leave of his consort, he whispered to her: "Louise, either I return worthier of you, or never!" She bowed silently.

The Princess de Lamballe was now mistress of the old mansion, could at least diminish her constraint, and abandon herself to the dreams of solitude, and the society of her friend and lady of honor, Countess Charlotte de Gorzka, whose cheerfulness and sympathy made retirement tolerable. She was often visited by her uncle, Prince de Conti, and she sought a balm for her heart in the conversation of this worthy man, who had retained his amiability, though he knew well the fallacy of human hopes, and had a large experience of mental suffering. Her father-in-law Penthièvre was ceremoniously tender, but very pedantic, and sometimes foolish in his desire, especially for foreign curiosities. While she endured his disquisitions about other nations and customs, she became gradually and unconsciously interested in navigation, ancient history, and travels. He had confided to her care before his departure, the Japanese Pavilion and its curiosities, and she there passed much of her time, amusing and instructing herself. The reports, day-books, and ship-journals of Bougainville, the events that occurred during his voyage round the world, the recorded deeds of Nassau and D'Oraison, gave her great pleasure, and she followed with renewed interest the story of the past dangers of a man who, to satisfy a mere whim of gallantry, was exposing himself to new perils. In all this, Charlotte de Gorzka was an indefatigable assistant. Passionate and fanciful, the countess easily expatiated on all the adventures, and this mutual sympathy united in frendship persons of opposite temperaments.

One day Prince de Conti greatly surprised both ladies by delivering to his niece a letter from Siegen to Penthièvre, just received by means of Beaumarchais; it was a report from the "desert," in which Nassau announced his success in having killed a tiger. Both women were forced to control their feelings in presence of Conti, but they gave way to them the more completely after he left.

"Quick, dear Gorzka!" and Louise's heart beat violently, "let us go to our dear Pavilion; there we have everything to aid us in understanding better the description of Siegen's hunt."

"Yes!" cried the countess. "Ah, I never before wished his highness away!" She hastened forward with the key in her hand.

The princess looked after her lady of honor. A strange thought passed through her mind; then she smiled at herself and crossed the terrace, carrying the letter in her hand.

Countess de Gorzka was already in the Pavilion, had placed the seats, turned the globe, and spread out the maps of Africa, besides several copper-plate works on Algiers, Tunis, Egypt, and the eastern portion of Sahara.

"Really," smiled Louise, "the wives, sisters, and betrothed of our ancestors, who went to Palestine bearing the cross on their breasts, could not have been more ardent than we are to live in thought through the dangers of heroes." She sat down before the charts.

"But among all the deeds of those knights, your highness, there was not one like this!" said Charlotte with sparkling eyes. "They took the field and suffered for the cross. To be faithful to their vows, was their highest renown. Is there, however, an example in history, that a brave nobleman—nay, a prince—went to Africa, from mere gallantry, to bring a tiger-skin for a lady, whom he saw but for the second time on her wedding-day, to whom he is related in no way, except as an admirer of virtue? If Nassau can do such great things for a lady with whom he is scarcely acquainted, what miracles would he not perform for one he loves, who can inspire him with passion, with whom he might rest from his active and perilous life, and who could crown him at once with the laurel and the myrtle?"

Madame de Lamballe turned paler while listening to the fair Pole. Something like irony trembled on her lips. "Indeed, you are quite imaginative while thinking of the prince, dear Gorzka. Your enthusiasm makes you partial. The fact that our ancestors went to the East in defence of the cross — that a sacred pu: rose urged them to danger and death, makes them immortal. If the history of knighthood can show no similar case of devotion, it is probable that our forefathers had something nobler to do than to visit the sands of Africa to capture robes for ladies. I would call Nassau's undertaking unpardonable, if Prince de Chartres had not maliciously bantered him, and endeavored to compromise him at a moment when he was conscious of a gallant action, aud of having borne away the palm of French glory."

"And can you, for whom he has hazarded his life, find his conduct unpardonable, your highness? So the noble fellow has endangered his life uselessly—"

"Do not be so concerned about it, my dear friend," interrupted the princess, smilingly. "This letter tells us that the action is performed. Until now I reproached myself with being the cause of such foolhardiness, and involuntarily I was anxious about a man who certainly has no right to claim any interest in me, other than that which courage usually inspires. Heaven be praised, fear and expectation cease, as well as a more profound feeling; aud I think only of an insane daring, that neither my understanding nor my morality can excuse." •

"Oh yes, your highness!" said the countess, bitterly; "your proud and cold nature cannot comprehend the poor prince's despair, that drives him restlessly into dangers. Action diverts his feelings; the desert makes him forget that his own life is void of woman's love—of all those calm resources that give a man contentment, strength, and happiness! You forget that France has been a false and thankless mother to him; no loved one greets him here;

uo congenial mind understands him; he vainly seeks some loving heart to bless him, and bid him fight for something nobler than a tiger-skin." The little lady rose, and turned away her face to conceal her tears.

"If, as you say, I do not understand him," replied Madame de Lamballe, in a trembling voice, and with a forced smile, "it is probably because I am a married woman."

"Certainly, princess! And a married woman with a broken heart!"

"Gorzka!" exclaimed Louise, rising. "O Charlotte, I never could have expected this from you! You are right! Such au unfortunate being as I am has lost the privilege of judging the worth of men.—Be kind cnough to lock the Pavilion when—when you have finished your studies." She was about to withdraw.

"Princess, dearest lady, pardon my worthless words; I would rather shed my blood than wound your poor heart!" The countess weepingly threw her arms around Louise's neck, pressing her head on the duchess's shoulder. "Can you believe me to have beeu intentionally malicious, so as to wound you in the most vulnerable spot? It was only a momentary indiscretion that made me tamper with the sacred bond of our confidence and friendship, and to forget, in my selfish fcelings, your grief, and that virtue which my own violent nature would long since have disregarded, or under which I would have sunk! You are noble and good! You cannot be irreconcilable. If you will not make me quite wretched, you must pardon the folly of a girl who has no one to guide or love her but you. Oh, forgive me!"

While these repentant words were uttered, a great change took place in the appearance of Madame de Lamballe. The pain occasioued by the countess turned to gloomy sadness; yet she silenced her own emotions in order to sympathize with her companion—she was one of those who could forget her own heart, and sacrifice herself for others. She pressed her friend to her bosom and kissed her forehead:

"Tranquillize yourself, my dear Charlotte, and believe me, I love you none the less for this little commotion. What would friendship be worth, if it dissolved at the first thoughtless word? You acted unwisely to wound where you would really least wish; and I to forget that a more violent spirit than usual was actuating you at that moment. Ah, it is a privilege of love that we pardon each other—that the most grievous words cannot destroy a union which has given us so many delightful hours. Dry your tears, silly maiden! Be sensible, and smile again. Confess to me what it was that made the whimsical heart of my little Gorzka overflow in that manner." She attempted gently to push away her friend in order to look into her countenance; but Charlotte would not move, she only pressed her blond head closer to Louise's shoulder. The latter could not but notice how the fair neck of Charlotte was suffused with a crimson glow, and she felt a slight shudder agitate the frame of the maiden. "Dearest Charlotte, have confidence! You love Nassau-Siegen!"

The countess slowly raised her head. Her blue eyes looked steadily at Madame de Lamballe. "Yes, I love him more than life—more than my future happiness!"

The princess turned her face, she became pale, and a painful emotion pierced her heart like a dagger. She led Charlotte to a seat and placed herself opposite. "Poor child! and this you have so long concealed from me! Let us talk like sisters who are perfectly frank toward each other. It required more self-control to confide to you, an innocent girl, the misery that I a woman suffer, than to speak of happiness and hope, for these fill the soul, renewing its life and aspirations. You love the prince! Have you any idea of a return? Have you any thing proving to you that your love is reciprocated—that it is not a dream, from which you must awake to perpetual sorrow? I wish to see you happy, and to assist in creating for you an elysium, which I might appreciate better the farther I myself am removed from its enjoyment. Alas, love without possession is as a flower without perfume! Do you think you possess the heart of the man you love? Have you spoken to him? What certainty have you?"

"Alas, princess, why must a magnanimity like yours be unanswered, or senseless persons like myself hurt you!"

"Pray, do not speak of me. If God has given me power to bear wretchedness, He has also destined me to a life in which my faculties may be used, and I only fulfil my duty. He will not burden me with more than I can endure. It would be, however, as a beam of light to see you happy—to witness the justice of destiny fulfilled in you. Perhaps, Gorzka, love was denied me that I might the more enjoy friendship. Therefore, child, confide your secret to me."

"When, at your wedding reception, I saw the prince for the first time, and heard him reply to the insult of Chartres by his proposal to hunt tigers, I felt irresistibly that I loved him, and that I could follow him for life through all privation and danger. I felt like one awakened from a sleep by the sound of his voice and the proud glance of his eye. I cannot tell you how I suffered when I heard him speak of accomplishing his resolution. I could not rest the next night, and eagerly sought an opportunity to entreat him to give up his enterprise. How happy

"LET US RE-READ THE PASSAGE TO WHICH WE REFER."   p. 177.

was I when you shared my anxiety, and ordered me to beg him to desist. I met him at the entrance of yonder grove, where you see the red blossoms; we were alone, and the evening was near. I hardly know what I said to him, I only remember that with difficulty I repressed my tears. I assured him that his friends would be inconsolable at his projected voyage, and—"

"You did not mention my name, I hope!" interrupted the princess quickly.

"Oh, my inclination was much too selfish! I told him it was a lady that begged him, and whose heart would break at the knowledge of his death. Ah! that you could have witnessed his surprise, and in what a tone he exclaimed: 'Is there really one so interested in me?' He told me of his unloved existence—and gravely refused to desist from the adventure he had publicly undertaken. Pressing my hand passionately to his heart, he said, that the thought of a lady anxious for him would be a talisman in the hour of peril, and that I was to console her by the promise that he would some day kneel before her and ask whether his hopes were too bold."

"Did he really say that? You are not deceived as to his words?"

"I am certain of what he said. Every syllable is engraven in my breast. Had you witnessed the mingled sadness and joy with which he abruptly departed, you would believe he loved me. To whom besides could he have given his heart?"

"Yes," said Louise; "he loves you! I know no one else to whom his conduct could apply!" She seized the letter of the prince, and her voice trembled. "On reading these lines, after what you have revealed, I am convinced of his tender sentiments toward you."

"Is it not so?" cried Charlotte. "Surely they are intended for me! Alas, the delight of knowing him to be

safe, and his daring task completed, so confused me that I insulted my best and dearest friend."

"Do not let us think any more of that. Let us re-read the passage to which we refer: 'And thus, grand-admiral, I have returned from the desert. I entered Cairo on my charger, surrounded by a crowd of brown Bedouins in white burnous, with the dead animal before me, gazed at by the motley multitude, and respectfully greeted by the Aga. My mission is finished and my honor redeemed! I am sitting here looking down upon the Nile from the roof of my dwelling, and toward the palms of the Delta—toward my northern home. I fancy I hear lovely lips speak affectionately to me. Sweet thoughts lead me back to her, and I have vowed to persevere! I will wait, but not in inactivity. A sybarite's life disgusts me. My Arabian steed neighs in the court-yard; my friends of the tribe Beni Hassan are breaking up their camp, and I must go with them! From desert to desert! I leave D'Oraison with the sultan, who intends to raise him to the dignity of Mamur of the Province of Fayum. This restless life must continue until she who bade me farewell recalls me, or—there are graves even in the desert! The simoom heaps up many a *castrum doloris!*' He meant you and no one else," added Louise, after a pause.—"Pray, dear Charlotte, bring me my vinaigrette from the table near the window in my sitting-room; I feel somewhat exhausted. You may also tell the valet de chambre to serve the tea in my chamber. You and the others may bring your cards and books there; I must retire earlier than usual."

"You are very pale, your highness! You are concealing from me the fact that you are seriously ill!" exclaimed Charlotte.

"No, no, only a little faint! I became rather too much excited just now. It is nothing else."

"I shall certainly not let you sleep alone-to-night, I—"

"As you will; we may then talk of your bright prospects. Only do as I request you." Countess de Gorzka hastened away to the apartment indicated.

Louise de Lamballe pressed her hands on her brow and sighed. "He loves her, it is too certain! Oh, not to you, Nassau-Siegen, does the motto 'From desert to desert!' apply, but to me! And art thou quite broken, my poor heart? has your last hope vanished? But what right had I to suppose such a thing? Was it his glowing eyes, his trembling lips, as he saluted me at Chambery? Dare I, a married woman, think of him without dishonor? Does my husband's baseness give me any reason to feel freed from duties I vowed before God? What fancy was it that led me, a princess of the Bourbon blood, to believe in the devotion of a man whose love fluctuates as the sea that bears him—as uncertain as the sand of the desert that slips beneath his feet! Oh, shame on me, to endeavor to degrade the greatest, the noblest man in France, that I may not envy my friend her possession! This ignoble sentiment, not at all justified even by misfortune, requires penance, and I will make amends to him and her.—Air!—air!" She opened the window of the Pavilion, and stood gazing down the Rue St. Honoré, where curious groups were gathering and wondering at her haggard and wild appearance.

"That is an idol of the savages," cried a *gamin* aloud. "It is made of wax!"

"No," said a poor woman with a child in her arms; "it is an angel standing by some one's grave."

The blood rushed to Louise's face, and her pulse beat violently. She threw a gold-piece to the woman, who picked it up with joyful surprise.

"Ah, if she is an angel, she is already glorified!"

Madame de Lamballe closed the sash, and the countess stood behind her. "Charlotte," said Louise, seizing the maiden's hand, "I swear to you that I will myself adorn you with the bridal wreath and veil!"

"And how can I ever repay you for thinking of me thus in the midst of your grief?"

"Adorn me with the crown of death!" She left the Pavilion.

Caron returned to privacy; he knew enough of what the country had to expect, to make no further researches. He wrote a new drama during his leisure, entitled: *The Two Friends; or, the Merchants.* The disorder of the finances and the decay of public credit, the oppressive taxation, the unprincipled game with paper of imaginary value, as well as the universal social misery, seemed to him worthy objects for representation. All the great and small *littérateurs* and the financial world, who envied the ascendency of an ennobled parvenu as much as did the numerous lower aristocracy, who concealed their poverty by borrowed splendor, were aroused by the piece. *Les Deux Amis* was condemned, and hissed from the stage, for no one wished to see represented there the ruin of his own fortune; all were offended that the poet had dared to look into their purse, or to expose the wretched machinery by which they kept up appearances.

A gradual change had also taken place in Paris Duverney, the partner of Beaumarchais, forcing the latter to dissolve the partnership existing for so many years. Paris was growing old and dull; a morbid piety became apparent. Countess Rosa de la Blache, daughter of the Duke de St. Albin, visited the banker frequently, and the result was a reconciliation with his nephew; for who would die while not at peace with the world? The old man's mind was soon in such a condition that the injustice he had endured seemed as nothing in view of eternity.

Beaumarchais understood it all.— First, their friendly intercourse ceased, and then it was easy for Duverney to make propositions as to their business relations, and Caron was the more ready to accede to a dissolution of their firm, as he cared not to have any collision with La Blache, who was the heir of his uncle. They arranged their affairs so that they separated on the first of April, Duverney still owing Beaumarchais fifteen thousand francs. It was not a large sum, but as the old gentleman would have lost a great deal by exchanging paper currency into gold, he gave a note for the debt to Caron. He would gladly have taken back the documents in reference to Susanna, but Beaumarchais, already distrustful, said: "I am sorry, my friend, that I must refuse you. Those papers are of use to no one except myself; they belong to my wife."

"But you were bought off with five hundred thousand francs, sir!"

"'Bought off?' a fine expression from you! My character, I should think, vouches for my silence, as well as my love for my wife, to whom I would spare so painful a discovery. I know the persons who wish to have possession of those papers, but I will not deliver them into their hands by your means."

"Oh, I see that you cannot appreciate the feeling of a noble family as to its honor! Very well, after my death, come what may!"

"Formerly you thought differently about this family honor. I do not blame you for your change of sentiment; nor will I be so imprudent as to tempt your weakness by giving you possession of what you cannot claim. Tell those interested that it will be their fault if I make use of the documents."

This was the last conversation between the former friends. In the mean while public life wended its way. No demand of the Parliament was granted. Aiguillon lived near the king, and Madame du Barry absolutely governed Louis. The scandalous scenes that occurred at Versailles, the orgies, the shameless jests of the favorite, went beyond the conception of the most depraved imagination. Maupeau and Terray, who surpassed all others in malice, hypocrisy, and every baseness, united with her in making the king a complete slave. Though the administration had never conceded any thing to the Parliament, they pursued their old quiet policy, and knew how to legalize oppression; but, from the moment that Choiseul's power was broken, Maupeau, Terray, and Madame du Barry, obtained the upper hand, and the true meaning of this "Empire of the Angels," as it was called, became obvious. The use of *lettres de cachet* was excessive; every one who merely seemed dangerous was sent to the Bastile; the manner in which Terray filled the treasury resembled the results of a continual raid of robbers; Aiguillon mocked at French justice, by being made a companion of the king's revelries, who lived like Tiberius on Caprera. One last blow was to be struck at the Parliaments.

Madame du Barry had a painting brought into her apartments—the execution of Charles I. of England. With this she threatened Louis XV., representing the death of the unfortunate Stuart, in all its horrible details, as the destiny of the King of France, if he did not destroy every germ of patriotism; and, in Choiseul's absence, it was decided to change the public tribunals of justice. The beginning was made in the *lit de justice* of the 27th of June, when the Parliaments were ordered not to consider themselves any longer as united, indivisible corporations, but to remain separate, nor yet to cease their action or refuse to register royal decrees. It was a command to dishonor themselves, and the tempest came. Led on one side by Conti and Malesherbes, on the other by Choiseul, the Parliament protested, the Châtelet refused criminal jurisdiction, and in Brittany and Limousin rebellious scenes took place.

Four months after the last interview between Beaumarchais and Duverney, on the 20th of July, the latter died. Caron was most disagreeably surprised at this event, as he was obliged to obtain his money from La Blache. He did not wish to appear pressing, and therefore waited patiently for the count voluntarily to attend to that duty, when suddenly the following note was sent to the Hôtel Piron:

"M. Caron Beaumarchais is informed by the undersigned, and in presence of his lawyer, that, from the books of his deceased uncle, M. Paris Duverney, it appears, according to an arrangement made between M. Beaumarchais and the deceased, on the 1st of April, the former owes the firm of Duverney one hundred and fifty thousand francs. As legal heir of the banker, the undersigned demands full payment of that sum by the 1st of October, to be handed to his lawyer, No. 13 Rue des Hirondelles, or judicial proceedings will be instituted.

"Count Falcoz de la Blache.

"Dormain, Lawyer in the Department of the Seine."

Beaumarchais rubbed his forehead while Susanna was reading the note. "What!" he exclaimed, "instead of receiving fifteen thousand francs, I am to pay one hundred and fifty thousand ! Does the little count really mean war, and enter upon his strategy in so wretched a manner ? Judicial proceedings! Very well! I will see what tribunal in France will deny the handwriting of the deceased ! "

"He wishes to entangle you in a lawsuit, because he can in no other way attack you. As he is on good terms with Maupeau and Terray, men who have no shame, it will be easy enough for La Blache to get a decision in his favor."

"It may be so, my child, but that I should lose this process before a French court of justice is simply impossible."

"Oh, do not let it go so far. Right cannot always maintain itself against might. We are rich enough to bear the loss of one hundred and fifty thousand francs."

"And I am to pay such a sum as that against my conviction ? To an enemy, too, who cares less for my money than the humiliation he occasions me ! If he dares thus to publish me a debtor, when I know I am a creditor, he can burden me with new debts, and my fear would only increase his audacity. I shall not concede one hair's breadth, and if he dares attack me, after twelve years of rest, I will treat him as I did formerly."

"You forget that at that time you were powerful, but now you do not live at court."

"I require no protector against such swindling."

"Where all are treated unjustly, will you insist on your right ? "

"At least, I will first be sentenced before I pay. The Châtelet will not expose themselves to the curses hurled on unjust judges, and if M. Falcoz drive me too far, I will put instruments in motion against him that will deprive him of the little mind he has."

"Ah, dearest Caron, if we had only remained unknown, unenvied, had eaten our bread peaceably with our family and friends, we should be happier! All around us is changed. The courtiers avoid you, you have been unfortunate in literature, and now they are after our wealth. When in trouble, you will see how your enemies, high and low, will attack you like vultures."

"Let us quietly await the end, dear wife. Our conscience is right before God aud man, and our riches will not be so easily taken away."

"You have received your money through Duverney, and La Blache knows this as well as we. He will find means to make us lose it by degrees, until—"

"—We return to the Pigeonnier, to Morelly?" laughed Caron.

"Laugh, but in these days all things are possible."

"Your faint-heartedness has no bounds. Where is your cheerfulness, the energy with which you suffered the misery of the first years of our married life? Is happiness so hard to be borne? In order to tranquillize you, let me inform you, that our fortune does not originate with Duverney. I brought him five hundred thousand francs, and with equal capital we had equal gain."

"You invested that sum in his business? And where did you get it?"

"From your parents!" he answered, violently. "And now enough of that!"

"My parents! And I am living by your side in ignorance of what so nearly concerns me, and you say you love me?"

"It is on that very account, dearest wife! Do not think of such old affairs. Are they who do all they can to disown you, worthy of your thoughts? When I came to court, and, by means of the ring, discovered your parents, they bought from me the promise of never revealing to you your origin!"

"Is it possible for parents to act thus?"

"Thus they did act, and I took the money because it was all they could offer; they had no love for you, and thus performed at least a part of their duty, by securing your future independence. Go one step further in your curiosity, and you invite the misery I have so long been trying to prevent. Life makes of us what it pleases, and we cannot help it; but our heart, our honor, our courage, are our own, and let them suffice to secure our happiness." As he drew her toward him, unusual tears came to his eyes.

All was quiet in the Hôtel Penthièvre, even more so than when, two months previous, the princess, holding Siegen's letter in her hand, had exclaimed, "From desert to desert!" The grand-admiral had returned, but the Pavilion was solitary. Before the mansion in the street, straw was spread to prevent the rattling of passing carriages. Penthièvre was seated near the sick-bed of the young prince, on whose countenance death was visible. The old man shook his head helplessly, at times holding his hand to his brow, as if to detain some fleeting thought. The princess sat with eyes cast down, while she held in her own the fevered hand of her dying husband. The physician had announced the fatal nature of the disease, but, being urgently requested, concealed the cause. It was easy to deceive the venerable admiral, who had never supposed that his son had led a dissipated life; but Louise knew better, and had silently watched its inevitable effects. At the age of nineteen she was a widow, without having enjoyed the happiness or dignity of a wife.

In the silence of the sick-chamber, as

the ticking of the clock told how his moments were passing away, Lamballe suddenly said : " My dear father, send for the priest, and permit me to be half an hour alone with the princess. I have a few words for her whom I leave so young."

"Her greatest sorrow, my dear child, is, that she loses in you such a noble husband ! I cannot love her more than I do already ; but when you are taken away, she shall be my all, and her happiness my constant care." Penthièvre rose, kissed his son's forehead, and walked totteringly away.

A painful pause ensued. Louise did not raise her eyes. The wretched young man gazed sadly at her. "Princess," he began, "if I dared speak to you now of my profound repentance and my great love, you would be right in saying that a vulgar fear of death or mere hypocrisy suggested my words. I have no right to ask for your forgiveness, since the day of reformation has passed. You cannot pardon my sins against you; but is he not at least worthy of commiseration, who through his own folly leaves this world so young, and who did not appreciate his opportunities until too late."

"Prince," she replied, "I sincerely pity you ; I believe in your repentance, and, if I refuse the assurances of your love, I yet wish to give you more of my esteem at this last hour than I ever could during your past life. I do not desire to burden you with reproaches, for God is our judge. I would not increase your torments by permitting you to make revelations that would only lower you further in my eyes. You are to me now a sufferer, whom I would soothe to the utmost of my power—a husband for whom I have never failed to perform the duties I vowed."

"You have faithfully fulfilled them, Louise. You have nursed me in sickness, and watched at my couch many a long and dreary night, and I—I—" He pressed his hands to his weeping eyes.

"I pray you, my husband, do not abandon yourself to needless despair."

Lamballe raised himself by a great effort, and again took his wife's hands. "Louise, even though the priest administers the last sacraments to me, God will never pardon me, if you will not hear and forgive me; but at least in death believe in my love, my repentance, and last words. Oh, fold me but for a moment in your arms, that it may be a sign of love still dwelling in your heart for a fallen man."

The princess shuddered. She knelt beside his bed, placed her arms round his neck, and held his head upon her beating bosom. "I confide in the sincerity of your emotions as I confide in heaven. Believe me, I will keep your dying words as the most faithful of wives."

"Yes, Louise ! I must think of you, not of myself. I only wish that the philosophies I tried to consider truth were so—that in reality there existed no God, no future life, no retribution, and that death were an eternal sleep. Louise, you may consider all else I say falsehood, but believe one warning from me in these last moments. *Beware of the Orleans family !* There live on earth no surer destroyers of body and soul, no worse enemies of our native country, of the royal family, as well as ours, than the malicious Chartres and his dark-minded father. Oh, I pay this late and bitter conviction with my life, with a hatred of both of them, and with your contempt of my character and conduct. Neither my father, nor any other friend, can protect you, poor lady, if you do not arm yourself against them with a profound aversion !"

"The Orleans ? My husband, that is incredible !"

"OH! TELL ME ALL!"

"If it is incredible to you, I die the death of the damned, for I leave you defenceless, and you will surely be ruined."

"Oh, tell me all!"

"I am by nature effeminate. The rigorous education my father gave me, robbed me of what little strength and independence of mind I had, and which alone give dignity and security to manhood. I was scarcely fifteen when Chartres introduced me to all the secret haunts of iniquity. There is a house in Paris, called the Pigeonnier, where the youthful aristocracy are morally and physically ruined; it is the fountain of all the vice that floods the land, and Orleans and his son are the princes of that pandemonium. Though I am guilty, I had no idea that there lay concealed in those orgies a plot, so that a word uttered in a moment of intoxication was remembered and used, to render the victim dependent on Orleans. When I married, I hoped to recede from this abyss; and when I saw you, I felt you could not love me, degraded as I was. You were cold and haughty, and could be won only by manly virtue. Could I gain your heart? Chartres persuaded me, on the day of the wedding festival, that I could awaken your love by making you jealous; I followed his advice, and you became aware of my unworthiness. But you do not know that I also met the elder Orleans in the Pigeonnier, and was a witness of the scheme by which the woman Du Barry was traded off to the king. I abandoned myself to revelry, to still the upbraidings of my conscience; I played the hypocrite, in order not to betray my share in a crime that would blot my name from the list of peers. Now, when I am awaiting death, my mind seems enlightened as to many things, and it is very clear to me that Chartres seeks the title of my father, for my decease makes him heir in my place. That is the solution of my early death, Louise. I cannot fathom their intentions as to you, but you will either serve them, or die also! Listen, my wife, receive my last warning—it is a sacred sacrifice of love. I release you from your vows; you never loved me—forget me! Take the hand of a strong, heroic man; give him your purest affection, and reveal to him these—my dying utterances. I have read Siegen's last letter from Cairo, and I understand what our unsuspecting father does not. This letter, and the glance Nassau cast on you, as he left on our reception-day, prove that he loves you. If you can return this sentiment (and why should you not?), he will console you for the misery of having been my wife. Be happy! If on your way you meet those reptiles, Orleans and Chartres, tread them into the earth; then shall I be vindicated, and a just God will grant me eternal rest."

"He already takes you in his arms!" cried Louise, sobbing. "In His name I exonerate you! Who will condemn, if I forgive you? who hate, if I declare that in your last hour you won my heart?" She pressed him to her bosom, and kissed his pale forehead. He sighed—a smile moved his lips, and in a moment he was dead.

When the prince's remains were lowered into the vault of the Penthièvres, Louise remembered her husband's words, and she said to herself. "He directed me to Siegen! From desert to desert!"

On the same day Beaumarchais wrote to Nassau at Cairo.

After the appointed time, Count de la Blache really commenced a lawsuit at the Châtelet, by his lawyer Dormain, a person well skilled in legal strategy. He disputed the authenticity of the note which Caron presented, and perplexed the judge, the witnesses, and the accused, by a vast array of plausible precedents. The court, however, regarded them as weak and trifling. A revision of the inheritance was ordered, and, as Duverney's accounts had disappeared, those of Beaumarchais were compared with the remaining papers of the deceased, and the testimony of the book-keepers. The complainant lost his suit, though he determined to renew it, and even to appeal to a higher court, encouraged by the persevering Dormain. In the mean while, however, this higher court, the Parliament, had ceased its functions.

To obtain an absolute recognition, as a lady of court authority, and to force Choiseul to extremes, Madame du Barry demanded an acknowledgment at a grand audience. All the peers and courtiers assembled, for to be absent was considered an insult, and the only one who dared this was the fearless Conti. When the countess appeared, she was saluted by the king, who addressed her with all her titles, and complimented by Maupeau, Terray, and Aiguillon. Orleans was the first who kissed her hand, and called her, half ironically, "My cousin!" The homage of the princes and notabilities followed. Choiseul alone did not approach, and was avoided by every one. Instead of taking advantage of this opportunity, and kissing the hand that humiliated him, he turned his back on the lady, and left. His fall was decided upon. On the very same day he was banished to Chanteloup by the king's command. Elevated by a woman, a woman degraded him! But his dismissal caused a great excitement. However criminal the intentions attributed to him, his administration had been comparatively mild.

The people in Paris crowded to receive the exiled minister, the members of the Parliament hastened to assure him of their sympathy, and his fall was turned into an ovation, to spite the favorite; for, to aim a direct blow at the nation, Aiguillon was made minister, who had been condemned to death by the high courts of justice, while Tolendal's head fell, because he had at least been honest in India—an injustice of which the brilliant memorial of his young son Lally (published from the Pigeonnier), was a sad commentary. The Board of Censure became really intolerable. The Duke de Brissac was made commandant of Paris; his son, commandant of Versailles; for they were amorous rivals of the king. The capital was burdened by an unmannerly and menacing soldiery, by patrols of various kinds, and their incessant demands upon the citizens. Alas, the rule of Madame de Pompadour appeared as a golden age!

"I hate you more than I love my pleasures!" La Blache once said to Beaumarchais, on leaving the Hôtel Bourbon on the morning of that unfortunate audience. For years he had bridled his hatred for the sake of Terray and Diana de Ventadour, as well as for his inheritance of Duverney's fortune, and the wish of Orleans; but this had only increased his aversion, so that it became a disease, and his vengeance an unforgotten idea, urging him to its dark fulfilment. When, by the enormous wealth left him, he became independent of his wife and father-in-law, and had the means to satisfy all his desires, at the same time that his party were gaining the upper hand, he had recourse to a lawsuit to harm his old opponent. He brought his complaint, assisted by the crafty Dormain, to the second tribunal, producing the books and some accounts of Duverney, by which, strangely enough, it seemed proved that Caron owed the sum stated. This was too much. Beaumarchais had remained in the background, and employed his lawyer, Gudin de la Brunellerie, to plead for him; but now he appeared himself, and led his enemies into repeated contradictions, ending his speech thus: "These are the facts, judges, founded on testimony and the contradictions of the adverse parties. The result of this investigation is, that a count, a man of the oldest and highest nobility, has permitted his hatred to blind and mislead him, and to endeavor to reverse a decision by means of false documents, *known to him as such*. The first result ought to have convinced him of the weakness of his cause. It is not necessary to say more; the case speaks for itself. But I may remark, gentlemen, that I have no other tribunal to vindicate me at this moment. The administration of justice is with you. Neither I nor my accuser can appeal to the Parliament; they have laid aside the sword and scales, for equity has forsaken the earth! However insignificent my cause may be in comparison with that of the whole country, it will at least be an example that justice has yet one altar in France!"

The judges consulted, and Count Falcoz de la Blache was again defeated. He was beside himself, and about to give rude utterance to his anger, when Dormain his lawyer seized him by the arm and brought him to his senses.

"While demanding your indulgence for the excitement of my noble client," said Dormain, "I have the honor to announce to you that he does not recognize your court as the highest tribunal, and that his grounds of litigation against the accused are by no means exhausted. The Parliament will decide the case, and I ask a return of the documents."

"That cannot be granted," replied the presiding judge. "If you wish so to appeal, the Châtelet has no objection. We announce to you, however, count, that if the Parliament do not receive your complaint within six months, and demand from us the papers relative to it, the sentence rendered to-day becomes valid, and the officer of this court will receive orders to collect the costs of this suit from you, Count Falcoz de la Blache!"

The case was as good as ended, for the Parliament could listen to no appeal, so that the decision of the Châtelet was to be executed in six months. With a light heart Beaumarchais returned home, embraced his Susanna laughingly, and related to her and Madame de Piron the last session of the judges and the disappointment and impotent malice of the count.

"God be praised," said Susanna, "that this matter is settled! I do not fear the Parliament in case of any subsequent process. The gentlemen of the red robe know the count's party too well, and hate the administration too much, so that his appeal would do him no good."

"If it really comes to that," replied Caron, "I can give the Prince de Conti, Malesherbes, and their friends, the facts of the case beforehand."

"How unfounded were all your fears, dear friend!" said Madame de Piron, smilingly touching Susanna's shoulder. —"That is the result of borrowing trouble. Be cheerful, confide in the caution of your husband, who has so often proved himself equal to all emergencies, and let us laugh at the storms that rage without. You require diversion and a change of scene. When your husband is away, you hang your head like a flower languishing for the sun. Why do you not give one of those charming little suppers, when we used to be so merry with Morelly, Malesherbes, D'Aumont, and other old friends?"

"Our old friends are scattered or dead," replied Susanna.

"The death of the dauphin dispersed us all; and each of us is borne far apart from each other in the whirl of destiny. But you are right, madame, if death has taken old friends, life has given us new ones. I am expecting the Prince de Nassau; Malesherbes must find a moment's leisure for us, and though Father Morelly has attached himself to the extreme fancies of Lally and Condorcet, the times are so wretched he would be glad of a renewal of former thought and hope. I really feel a desire for some change!"

"My dear husband, that is a good idea. Let us ask them to come to-night. Each will have something to say, and thus we may revive a little of our animation; and when the prince arrives he will have much to tell us. I see already that more cheerful days are dawning for us."

"So I hope, Susie. We need not fear Lally and Condorcet's maxims, either. The former has gained renown by his memorials; the latter, a seat in the Academy, and however misanthropic a man may be, honor and office make him milder. To render our circle complete, I will at once invite Diderot and D'Alembert, personally."

"Then, dear chevalière, we must immediately go to work at our invitations and make out a bill of fare."

"While I hunt up D'Alembert." Caron took his hat, kissed Susanna's hand, and hastened away.

Beaumarchais passed through the Rue des Fauconniers, in order to reach the Rue d'Antoine. As he was about to cross Barrez Street, an old coach in the form of a dark, ungainly leather box, surrounded by mounted police, slowly passed him. Its destination was well known to all Parisians. "A victim of oppression is wanted! Some poor fellow who has disturbed the rest of the 'Angel' or her companions!" he murmured, and continued his way.

"That is the official wagon of the Bastile," laughed a laborer; "it will drive till some bright day we place the police officers themselves within it!" Caron did not notice that the coach stopped, for he was occupied with pleasant thoughts, believing that Nassau must now be on his way back. He was soon, however, awakened from his reverie by the trotting of horses, and by voices shouting, "Arrest him in the name of the law!" Suddenly a policeman rode close up, turning his horse so that it stood before Beaumarchais. "Halt!" thundered the officer.

"You mistake me for some one else, sir."

"We shall soon see. What is your name?"

"Caron de Beaumarchais."

"Then it is all right. Here he is!" The crowd pressed closer, and the carriage advanced.

"But what warrant have you to arrest me?" exclaimed Caron.

"Our horses, as you see, are warrant enough. Why did you run away? We would prefer to take you most respectfully out of your golden nest. But here is the lieutenant himself."

The coach stopped, and M. de Sartines, lieutenant of police, alighted, followed by Dormain, La Blache's lawyer. "There he is," said the latter, mockingly. "Take our bird to his cage."

"Oh, I know him; we are old friends, M. Beaumarchais, are we not? You are no more at court, and can no longer insult magistrates!"

"Spare your witticisms, sir! You cannot arrest me without a warrant. I take these citizens as witnesses. Besides, I wish to know of what I am accused, and what Lawyer Dormain has to do with it."

"I see you know the forms," said Sartines, sarcastically. "Here is the order of Minister Maupeou. You are accused of having charged Count de la Blache with falsifying during a lawsuit at the Châtelet."

"I did not! I—"

"Seize him; he will have time enough for the exercise of his memory. The Bastile has long been waiting for you. Not another word, or we shall use the gag. You are a slanderer, a disturber of the peace, and an intriguer, and we are only spoiling your trade, that is all."

Beaumarchais bowed his head and suppressed his anger. It was useless to talk with such persons. He entered the coach without reply. Sartines took a seat beside him. The people hooted the police, and the street-boys threw mud at them. On they drove toward the Bastile. The outer gate quickly opened, both draw-bridges fell Commandant de Launay with his officers received the prisoner, Sartines delivered the warrant, the commandant put a red mark on it, and turned to a savage-looking fellow who stood near, playing with a bunch of keys.

"Santerre, take the prisoner Beaumarchais to the fourth tower, No. 70. You may treat him well."

"Very good!" said the jailer, seizing Caron by the collar, "We treat all our guests well. Come, my boy!"

Beaumarchais was taken to a cell almost under the roof. "Am I to enter this stifling hole?"

"No objections, forward!" Santerre pushed Beaumarchais before him. "You ought to be glad of your location. This is one of our best lodgings; underground you would have no prospect."

"That is very philosophic, my friend. I thank you for your sincerity—take these ten francs."

"Hem! Is that the amount for your week's board?"

"No, my good fellow; it is for you.

As on going out, however, I did not anticipate the honor of a visit to the Bastile, I have not enough money with me. If you wish to earn ten more francs, go to my residence and take a note to my wife."

"I will do it this afternoon, after the second round."

"I see you seem worse than you are. How long have you had your office?"

"My father had it before me. I was born in the Bastile."

"No wonder that you are unacquainted with liberty, and gentleness of conduct. Have you a family?"

"I should like to beat out your brains for that question! Do you think I want children to grow gray like me in such a place as this?"

"Santerre, perhaps I can do something for you when I am free again. Bring me writing-materials."

"Ha! ha!" Santerre turned to the door. "Oh, how many have told me that! Those who were liberated forgot me; those who did not, died here. In the Bastile there is no memory!" The ponderous door closed with a great noise, and the bolts were fastened. Caron, almost deprived of his reason, threw himself down on his litter of dirty straw.

CHAPTER XVII

A FEUDAL RIGHT.

BEAUMARCHAIS, an inmate of the Bastile, the most fearful of all state prisons, with no friend near to succor him, in the power of an enemy who now had time and opportunity to wreak his vengeance, and knowing Susanna defenceless, did not, however, abandon himself to violent grief or deceptive hope. His first business was to discover some influence which might be employed against the man who had brought him into his present condition, and to choose the safest means of deliverance, as well as the protection of his wife from persecution. He had no one on whose sympathy and assistance he could at all rely, but Santerre, the jailer. Caron wrote to Susanna, enclosing in the letter the key to his secretary, which he always carried with him. His wife was to be the instrument of releasing him—the woman who in other days had shown her fidelity, decision, and strength of mind. He placed in her power the only means at present at his command, with the firm conviction that her love and anxiety would induce her to make every effort in his behalf. About five o'clock in the afternoon Santerre appeared.

"Well, my bird, how do you like your cage?"

"Open it, and I will answer you."

"Ah, do you take me for a madman? But there are about a dozen iron gates between you and the street. Since the day of its structure no one has escaped from this prison!"

"I was not thinking of any thing of the kind. I wish to be liberated legally, and will soon be free, if you will have the kindness to take this letter to my wife."

"I have reflected since this morning," and Santerre laughed maliciously. "Why should I endeavor to release any one? No one cares for me! My only pleasure consists in seeing persons like you struggle against your imprisonment, especially when they are very rich and of rank. You said something about philosophers this morning. We have had several here, and from them I have learned what I am to believe and hope."

"Be so kind, Santerre, as to tell me your philosophy; one can learn even in the Bastile."

"If I were beyond these walls or before the commandant, I would take care in uttering what I think, and I would perhaps deny what I did say, and on my official oath too."

"Then you consider an oath nothing, though you took it in the presence of God, and in view of eternal judgment?"

"Ha! ha! that is just the point! What kind of oath is that which a man takes to torment his fellow-creatures? It is well that I believe no Deity exists. With our last pulsation life ceases, and we are as if we had never been. A priest was once imprisoned here who clearly proved this to me. He was taken to some other place, Bicêtre, I think; for he acted strangely, as if he were insane. I believe the fellow pretended madness. If there were a ruling Providence, could there exist kings that impoverish the land, as caterpillars a tree? And, on the other hand, beggars, who do not know where to find a crust of bread; or persons like myself, who are treated as brutes, unless they are even more cruel to their prisoners? Patience and money can effect every thing. Human flesh is the commonest article in the country, and we are all bondsmen unless we have a coat-of-arms! What a Creator that must be, who has made us all so miserable! What is the world? A herd of beasts, The larger are the worst, the smaller are intended for their prey!"

"If you were one of the larger beasts would you be as savage? Santerre, I believe not. I am sure you have a heart, and if you were happy yourself, you would not find pleasure in rendering your fellow-creatures miserable."

"Heart? Why, yes! I have such a thing, which indeed often causes me sleepless nights and makes me weep; but I drown it in brandy! It is a folly, and the only fault I have.—Happy! I cannot say whether I would be different, for I know nothing of happiness!"

"But I can give it you! You will take this letter to my wife, and receive a thousand francs for it; you could then leave this place, enter some respectable business, and marry." Beaumarchais looked piercingly at the jailer, who was walking up and down, sighing, and in apparent anxiety.

"And why would you wish to establish me in business?"

"Only to prove to you that you are no brute, and that your degraded views are false."

"Oh, I would like to risk it! No, no! I might become more tyrannical. Here in prison, dreading the whip, I have just a tolerable existence, and no more. I do not know whether life beyond these walls would suit me. My father and mother were incendiaries; they behaved pretty well in prison, and were made jailers; my birth vouches for my propensities!"

"Fie, who would think so meanly of himself? Would it not be better if you turned the bad name of your parents into a good-one? If people said: 'No poor man passes the house of the rich M. Santerre, without receiving something! He has a heart for the poor, and despises the nobility!'"

"That would be well! But, how would you accomplish this? Are you so wealthy?"

"Perhaps."

"But why would you throw away your money on me? It will cost much, I should think."

"Well, I would get you to learn a trade, and finally to become your own master. If you are industrious, I would lend you money. You might make a fortune, and—"

"Hem! Sir, I did not think that there were such good men—"

"Brutes, you mean!"

"No. You would make a man of me, and I would have to regard others like myself. Yet who will marry the son of the incendiary Santerre; who will be his friend? Even had I money,

I would not be released from the Bastile, for I come from an evil stock, and the police would always be on my track, right or wrong."

"Why, you have never committed a crime!"

"But my parents did, and it always clings to a man. However, give me your letter; I will take it without a reward, because—" the jailer turned away.

"Well—beeause what?"

"Because you are no brute, sir!" Santerre's voice quivered with sudden emotion, and he hastily departed.

Susanna, who had cheerfully parted from her husband, and, tranquillized as to the result of the lawsuit, had no presentiment that any misfortune had happened, was giving directions with Madame de Piron for the supper that was to reunite their old friends. Gomez was sent with the invitations; the chevalière took the carriage of Beaumarchais to pay a few visits, while Susie with her maid Minette was busily engaged in making preparations for the evening's entertainment. The hall bell rang.

"Ah, my husband has returned early Quick, open the door!"

Minette left, and returned immediately. "It is not M. de Beaumarchais, but two gentlemen, apparently of quality, who wish to give you some special information."

"Me? Two strangers? Have you inquired their names?"

"No, gracious lady. As I was expecting the master, I opened hastily. They entered without ceremony, and were so urgent that I took no time to ask questions."

"How awkward to let in people when we are alone! Since I cannot avoid it, admit the gentlemen; remain, however, in the hall, in case I should ring for you."

Minette again left the room. Some

words were exchanged in the anteroom, the door opened, and, to the terror of Susanna, Count Falcoz de la Blache and Batyl appeared.

"Sir, what do you want? My husband is not at home, and I—"

"I know that, my charming little friend. He is well taken care of, and will not soon return."

"Not return? Minette!" Susie was about to take up the bell. The count quickly seized her hand; Batyl bolted the door, and put the bell into his pocket. "This is a premeditated attack, count! If you do not at once release me, I shall call my servants, who are near."

"We know better. Madame de Piron has driven out, your valet Gomez is also away, and the maid not very formidable. If you make an alarm, our *tête-à-tête* will be variously interpreted, and you will not have liberated your husband from prison."

"My husband from prison!" cried Susanna, trembling. "Count, I know too well that your lawsuit ended in our favor; you cannot induce me to believe your falsehood."

"Falsehood? How can you believe I would approach you unless my threat were serious? Be assured he is a captive, and for a longer period than will please him. I have come to make your time pass agreeably."

The poor lady almost fainted, but her determination, arising from an instinctive fear of extreme peril, gave her strength to resist. She felt greater presence of mind than ever before. She considered that Madame de Piron, Gomez, and her husband, could not remain away much longer; that assistance must come, if she could only delay her oppressor without irritating him too much. "You have well selected your opportunity to execute your revenge. As you do not scorn, though a nobleman, to take advantage of my defence-

less position, I suppose I must listen to you."

"That is right, my fair opponent capitulates!" La Blache released her hand. "Be kind enough to take a seat near me on this sofa, that I may explain myself."

Feeling herself free, Susanna rushed to the window, saying bitterly: "I can stand here, count, and hear your conversation. If you dare to lessen the distance between us, I shall call on the passers-by for aid! You are the oppressor of a defenceless woman; you may be her assassin—a proud triumph of your courage!"

"You are really so lovely in your anger. little lady that I feel disposed to ruffle your temper still more. But, fear nothing, such a victory does not suit me. I wish to have the pleasure of seeing those lips appeal to me—those blue eyes ask me for mercy! I will force you to bow at my feet as a slave; that is much more interesting, and will become you better."

"I have nothing to answer."

"Nothing? Very well; listen. My aversion for Beaumarchais is as old as my—my love for you. Perhaps I might have forgotten that, and the insults he has heaped on me, if he had not ruined my position at court, rascal as he is, but one too dangerous to escape exemplary punishment. I swore revenge, and to-day I hope to square accounts with him. You are as pretty, as charming, as you were twelve years ago—nay, more so—"

"Count, cease such words; they are more out of taste than you imagine."

"You desire proofs of my love? You may have them!"

"I would rather hear why you delayed your conduct until to-day; such hatred seems incredible to me. You come only to gain some advantage in reference to the lawsuit."

"Very business-like, madame; but I

hope to prove to you the contrary. Hatred never dies!"

"Then you were only deterred by fear!"

"It is unnecessary to talk of that. The principal reason for my patience is, that I waited until I was sure of my enemy. The lawsuit was only a means."

"You lost it in two courts."

"But I shall gain it in the third—the Parliament. As M. Beaumarchais was so kind as to accuse me to-day, in open court, of forgery, I have sent him to the Bastile by a *lettre de cachet*; and there he may remain as long as I please, and reflect on the folly of injuring the reputation of persons of quality, unless you resolve to purchase his freedom."

"Since when did hatred sell its victim! You do not seem quite sure of your retaliation."

"Perhaps only too much so, and it is an act of generosity if I offer you a compromise—perhaps it is a weakness; but I like to be accommodating with your tender sex! You were my first love, and that a man never forgets. Beaumarchais became my rival, he withdrew you from my possession; I shall therefore be contented if I can, after all, out-rival him."

"You really tempt me to ask how you intend to do that?"

"I will liberate your husband, and refrain from all further judiciary proceedings—I will even pay him one hundred and fifty thousand francs as damages, if you will accompany me. My carriage is in attendance. An income of twenty thousand francs and a landed estate, will soon make you forget that you ever belonged to a watchmaker and a vulgar spy."

Susanna laughed mockingly. "How small must be your understanding, if you expect to succeed in such a manner. It is too amusing to permit me to give full expression to my contempt."

La Blache sprang up, his countenance glowing with anger. "Ah, well, madame! You do not believe that Beaumarchais is incarcerated—you find my proposition, my love, ridiculous! But I will forget indignities that a person of low birth like yourself cannot comprehend! Do you know, vain puppet, who you are?"

"Now, sir, you have assumed your real character! Now you show your deep depravity, but I would rather have that than your forced and false flattery. Not a step nearer, or—" She raised the window.

"Do not trouble yourself. When I want you I can have you. You do not believe me? Well, wait for your husband. Let me, however, give you some information. You were born in Passy on my estate, an illegitimate child of one of my bondwomen, raised by my uncle at Garnier's house, on account of a mere whim of his. You could not marry without his consent or mine, for you belong to me, on whom I intend to assert the rights of a master! I shall reclaim you through the police, delight myself in your sufferings, and then let you go as a dishonored and degraded wretch. That is my revenge, and I have the law on my side. Even if you are possessed of millions, you will always remain the runaway peasant-girl of La Blache! Think of all this until my return; you will find that M. de Sartines, lieutenant of police, is much less gallant than I am!"—He made a sign to Batyl, who unlocked the door, and both departed.

When Minette, anxious on account of the violence of the conversation, hastened toward her mistress, she found her senseless on the floor near the window. Susanna at length awoke to a consciousness of her condition. Her servants were faithful, but were not suited for confidantes or advisers. From the bold and taunting threats of the count, she understood too well that

Caron must be in the Bastile. She did not comprehend all the rights the lord of a manor had over his bondwomen; but she never doubted that by birth she belonged to her worst and bitterest enemy, and that her honor and her conjugal peace were endangered. She thought of flight, but rejected it as foolish. Whither could she go? The arm of public authority could reach her everywhere. She was recalled from this painful uncertainty between anxiety and hope by Gomez, who had just returned, and announced a jailer from the Bastile.

"Quick!—admit him! Merciless Heaven, he brings the assurance of my husband's imprisonment!"

"The master imprisoned?" exclaimed Gomez, and he hastened away. The colossal frame of Santerre, with his savage face, made Susanna shudder.

"You bring tidings of my unfortunate husband!"

When the jailer saw the lady and the splendor of the apartments, he took off his fur cap. "Yes, madame, or gracious lady (one of my class has not much manners); yes, your husband is in the Bastile."

"What has he done, and when will he be free again?"

"The commandant de Launay alone can tell you that!—Be free! Madame, that is not so easy from the Bastile. Here is a letter, and I am to wait for an answer. You have half an hour; I must not remain longer."

"A thousand thanks! Do all you can to ameliorate his distress; I will reward you. Take care of him, that God may in future have mercy on you!"

"Read, madame. Let me be torn to pieces by horses, as Damiens was, if I do not do my utmost!"

Susanna went to the window, opened the letter, and read: "My dear, dear wife—I have no time to enter into explanations or complaints about the misfortune that has just befallen us. You have been with me in evil as well as good days; and when I tell you that you alone can save me, you will be strong and fulfil my wishes. If our enemies cannot break our courage, they are conquered, not we! I enclose the key to my secretary: send me by Santerre four hundred louis d'ors, which you will find in the left drawer. He is honest, and I have promised to be his friend when I am at liberty. Make him a present of a thousand francs, for he is of importance, and will do all he can for me. I fear that La Blache will profit by my captivity to intimidate you; perhaps strangers will force themselves upon you, but—*be on your guard!* The documents pertaining to your birth, that I so long concealed from you, can alone save us. At the back of the middle drawer you will find a knob—press it, and you will discover a secret receptacle enclosing a small iron casket; it contains the papers, the key is in the lock. If you wish to add to the horror of these days and satisfy your curiosity, look at them; of course, I cannot prevent you. But you must immediately take the box to Prince de Conti and relate the whole matter to him. I never accused La Blache of forgery, as the records of the Châtelet and the testimony of Brunellerie, my lawyer, will prove. The prince can free me and protect you; he will do so without being reminded of the deceased dauphin. Show him this letter. Lose not a moment. Write me an answer, and hasten to Conti. Do not weep; be strong, my darling wife. The malevolence of the whole world cannot destroy our love. Farewell!

"Your faithful BEAUMARCHAIS."

Susanna began to read with sobs;

but as she continued she became more composed. Her husband's spirit seemed to take possession of her and rouse her energy. Notwithstanding her terror of La Blache, she felt some consolation, and, writing to Beaumarchais, imparted to him a knowledge of the scene between her and the count, assured her husband of her courage, and that his orders should be punctually obeyed. She delivered her letter, with the louis d'ors, to Santerre.

"My friend, my husband tells me you are poor and unhappy, and he will improve your circumstances as soon as he is at liberty. Do not doubt but he will redeem his promise. Take these thousand francs as a present, and remember that you will ameliorate the distress of a solitary woman if you are kind to her husband."

"Blessed saints, madame, I will do that!" cried Santerre, with emotion. "Your husband says he will make a man of me. If I am now only a poor down-trodden cur, I know how to be faithful! Oh, madame, I will earn these thousand francs; farewell!" He took the soft hand of Susie, pressed it to his breast, and then bowed and departed.

"Gomez," said Susanna, "remain in the anteroom and admit no one. When Madame de Piron returns, ask her to come to me; I must wait on his royal highness Prince de Conti." She was alone. With trembling hands she opened the concealed drawer and drew forth the casket, hesitating whether to open it and reveal her origin, though against the express warning of Caron. But had not La Blache told her she was his bondwoman? Might not the knowledge the papers contained be of the utmost importance to her at this moment? Should she remain in ignorance of their contents, though Conti was to be put in possession of the secret? She opened the box, read the

13

papers hastily, and exclaimed in joyful surprise; "Heaven be praised, I am no bondmaiden, nor subject to the base La Blache! I am the daughter of the Marchioness Diana de Ventadour and of the Abbé Terray, the minister!" Suddenly she continued: "And this woman, whose hypocritical piety, power, and alliance with the Jesuits and the Orleans, Caron so often mentioned, is my mother, who bought my husband's silence with five hundred thousand francs! My father is the most evil-minded and godless man in existence; my mother, a heartless intriguer, concealing her iniquity by a religious exterior. She hates me because she bore me, and will annihilate me when her disgrace is made public. O Caron, you were right! It is misery to know what should ever remain a mystery. My lips shall never speak of it!" She returned the papers to the casket, and placed it in her reticule, with the letter from Beaumarchais. "To Conti—I must be in advance of them all!" She rang the bell.

At this moment Madame de Piron appeared: "Good heavens, what have I heard! Is it true? Your husband—"

"Is lost, unless I wait immediately on the Prince de Conti. Accompany me.—Not another word! Gomez will attend us." Susanna ordered Minette to bring her cloak and hat, locked her husband's secretary, and hid the key in her bosom. She was preparing herself for her drive, when Gomez rushed in.

"The Police-Lieutenant de Sartines, his myrmidons, and Count de la Blache, are at the door!" The valet hastened away again across the terrace.

The distressed woman rang her hands despairingly. "Must I then suffer all that can degrade a woman? Is there no way of escaping an act of barbarism, for which language has no word, reason no conception? Have mercy, O my God, and let me not lay violent hands on myself!"

"Dear friend!" said Madame de Piron, taking Susie's hand, "do not lose confidence in the justice of Heaven. I shall not leave you; only tell me what these persons want, and—Oh, too late," she added in a lower voice, "here they are!" She pressed her pale friend in her arms.

Sartines, La Blache, and the officials, now entered. "Which of these is it, count?"

"The younger, of course! Surely you give me credit for some discrimination and taste?"

"Do you call yourself Madame Beaumarchais?"

"I am the wife of Caron de Beaumarchais."

"Very well! You are the same he abducted from Passy, in 1755, where you were nurtured, at the expense of the lord of the manor, by the steward Garnier, and were known as the illegitimate daughter of the laborer Gomart and of the bondwoman Nini Falou. You are, consequently, the serf of Count de la Blache; you ran away and are playing the part of a lady—a position that does not belong to you. You will obey your master in every respect; and these people will take you to Passy, where the count will detain you as long as he pleases, or dismiss you, as it may suit him. Neither the Parliament nor the philosophers have yet abolished the old laws and prerogatives of the French nobility."

"Be of good cheer, my dear," added La Blache, "I will accompany you. You shall be well treated."

"M. Lieutenant!" exclaimed Madame de Piron, stepping in front of Susanna, "in my veins flows as noble blood as in yours, and I will not suffer this inhumanity. Whatever pretensions that count may make to a lady I call my friend, he may prove them in a court of justice! You shall not drag a woman from my roof who lives respected by the world, and whose husband enjoyed the favor of the most illustrious persons; nor shall you violate the hospitality of my house! I have influence enough to prevent that, at least!"

"Madame, you trouble yourself needlessly. If M. Beaumarchais were the nabob of India, he could not erase the blot defaming the birth of his wife! She is a woman over whom Count de la Blache has all the rights of a lord of the manor. He need call on no tribunal, for he is the judge in his own territory, whose power I must respect.— Accompany us, therefore," turning to Susanna, "or worse treatment may subdue you!"

"I will not! His pretences are false. I declare solemnly, and can prove it, that I was not born on the territory of the count, nor do I belong to his serfs! I swear to the truth of this!"

"Oaths are of no consequence in such matters—the documents only are necessary. Who, then, are your parents?"

"Well, Heaven pardon me for revealing them!" exclaimed Susanna, frightened. "I am the daughter of the Marchioness de Ventadour and the Abbé Terray! I was brought by M. Duverney from the Ursuline Convent to Passy, when only a few weeks old!"

Sartines and La Blache stepped back in the utmost astonishment, while the chevalière uttered a terrified exclamation.

"What!" cried La Blache. "The daughter of Terray and the marchioness?"

Sartines cast a curious glance on La Blache. "Well, my beauty, better and better! Even if the count had no claims on you, you have insulted a servant of God, and done dishonor to an old aristocratic house; I shall imprison you in the Salpetrière!—Here, men, seize her ! ” He rudely pushed the ladies apart, and several of the officials caught Susanna, who screamed wildly, and sought to elude their grasp. The lieutenant was suddenly thrown to the ground, aud two officers and several dragoons of the queen's regiment released Caron's wife.

“ He that moves is a dead man ! ” thundered the voice of Nassau, who stood with a drawn sword in the middle of the apartment.

Sartines rose, and advanced toward the liberator. “ And what audacious intruder dares to restrain judicial—”

“ Prince Otto von Nassau-Siegen, M. Policeman—that is my name, and I command you to depart with your attendants, or I will lead you a dance such as no Paris bailiff ever performed before.—Comrades, draw ! If you leave not the field in two miuutes, your blood be on your head ! ”

“ That is unusual gallantry,” said Sartines, bitterly, “ whose object is a woman with whom you are unacquainted. This Susanna Beaumarchais is a runaway bondwoman from the estate of the Count de la Blache, who demands his rights through the guardians of the public law.”

“ You are no guardian, but a criminal, morally and legally ! I swear by a nobleman's honor that this poor lady, whom I recognize as the virtuous wife of my friend Caron de Beaumarchais, shall not be subject to your violence, nor to that of this so-called count, who is the greatest scoundrel on God's earth ! He had the husband incarcerated in order to dishonor the wife, but I will engrave his *jus primœ noctis* on his back, and in such a way that a galley-slave shall be a happy man in comparison with him, if he ever dares raise his eyes again toward this lady !—Forward, dragoons ! ”

“ Hold, your highness ! ” cried Sartines, “ do not insult me ; I wear the king's coat. I will go, but to insist on my right by means of his excellency the minister.”

“ Seek it from His Excellency Satan, who more probably is your minister. You can inform me of your success at any time, and should M. de Maupeau share your views, I should be glad to take a walk with him.”

“ We shall see about that, your highness ! You take excessive liberties on account of your rank.”

“ The king will understand this matter.” Sartines, La Blache, and their attendants, withdrew.

“ O my noble prince ! ” said Susanna, weeping and offering him her hand, “ I have to thank you for more than my life. Let us hasten to the Prince de Conti, he can and will save Beaumarchais.”

“ Calm yourself, dearest lady, I am near you. I will guard you like a brother. All that is possible shall be done to liberate your husband. Take courage !—Madame de Piron, accompany us to M. de Conti's.”

“ In reference to the security of the ladies, prince,” said one of the officers, “ we could quarter our dragoons with the servants, after obtaining permission of our commander.”

“ Excellent, Marquis d'Aliaga ; and I know that each of you dragoons feel, as well as the highest nobleman in France, that to protect a woman is the proudest privilege of brave soldiers.”

“ Gentlemen, consider my house as your own ! ”, said Susanna. “ The service you have rendered me cannot be fully rewarded, but public opinion will bestow honor upon you.”

The officers bowed. “ I will remain here, gracious lady,” said D'Aliaga. “ Lieutenant de Lorges will be kind enough to report to our chief.”

“ Then, ladies, let us hasten to his royal highness,” said Nassau.

“ Allow me first to send Gomez to

our lawyer, M. de Brunellerie, and ask him to wait on Prince de Conti." Susanna gave the necessary instructions to the valet, while Madame de Piron ordered her servants to attend to the officers and await the friends invited for the evening, acquainting them with what had transpired. Before they left, Susanna took a diamond cross from her bosom. "Prince, do not fancy that I intend to reward you with this. You are too far above me for that. But I hope you will regard it kindly if I offer you this trinket as a memorial of your conduct! It is nothing but a token of respect for French chivalry by a woman delivered from the vilest persecution."

"Dear lady, I accept it, and will ever remember the meaning of your costly gift.—Dragoons, you are witnesses! Marquis, M. de Lorges, each of you, take one of these bars; and the third is for you, brave Marmutore." Nassau separated the cross-pieces, giving three to his companions, and then accompanied Susanna and Madame de Piron to the carriage.

After the departure of Nassau and the ladies, De Lorges stared at the marquis, as if awaking from a dream. "By Jove, this prince is like the magician in a fairy tale! He sails round the world, kills tigers, and, wherever his presence is, there is no lack of adventure. Tell me how all this has been done!"

"I was walking through the Rue des Ormes when an equipage drove from this house. It stopped, and I heard my name called. I turned and saw Nassau beckoning to me. 'To the barracks of the queen's dragoons, near the arsenal!' he exclaimed, and we rapidly drove off. Without giving me time to speak, he said that he had arrived but an hour before, and was about to visit his friend Beaumarchais, to whom he was under many obligations. When he came to the hôtel he observed the police, and a servant to whom he was known informed him that Caron was in the Bastile, and his wife surrounded by the myrmidons of Sartines. Of course, he did not hesitate as to his duty. When we reached our quarters, you were the first man we met.

"'Ten dragoons, comrades, for a noble deed, and Siegen is your debtor!' cried the prince. In an instant the fellows were on their horses, and, with him at our head, we dashed along, to the great surprise of the pedestrians!— But what do you say to this La Blache and his feudal right? It will make a good parade anecdote!"

"No nobleman will associate with him again."

"He can do nothing but challenge Nassau."

"The prince had better order his groom to a duel with such a man. Good-by, good-by, D'Aliaga; the commander will be delighted with the story!"

It was about eight o'clock in the evening. Terray (both minister and abbé) was about to put on his cross of St. Louis, in order to attend a supper at Madame de Ventadour's, when the Prince de Conti was announced. This unexpected honor startled him joyfully, and, supposing the visit to have reference to some political movement, he had the prince shown into his private cabinet.

"The pleasure I feel, noble prince, at an honor—"

"I pray you, abbé, do not be too pleased. I come on business that is not altogether agreeable."

"Is Paris in disturbance?"

"It is sad enough that, under your administration, you expect such a thing. Apropos, I believe you are acquainted with Caron de Beaumarchais."

The minister was embarrassed.— "Somewhat; I have heard he is an adventurer."

"Less so than you are! I think either you or M. de Maupeau has sent him to the Bastile."

"Ah, yes, I remember! The man dared to accuse Count de la Blache of forgery before the Châtelet."

"Count de la Blache *is* a forger, but it is false to say that M. de Beaumarchais was so imprudent as to express this. He merely said that it was evident the books of his deceased partner had been tampered with, as to a debt due Beaumarchais."

"I do not trouble myself about such suits, and am astonished, prince, that you come personally to me concerning such a trifle."

"Are you surprised, abbé? Well, then, you may also fear! You will immediately dispatch a courier with a warrant of liberation for Beaumarchais, and take care that La Blache never again endangers the honor of this man, or his wife; or, abbé, I shall make use of certain documents relating to an event in the Ursuline Convent. An atheistic priest and a lady of quality are the parents of a woman whose husband they hate, because he served the dauphin, and despises certain persons as much as I do. To-morrow morning Caron must be free, or, by my honor, you march from the ministerial chair into the penitentiary! As yet the Parliament stands! It cannot cease more brilliantly than with your condemnation!" His highness departed.

Terray sank into his chair, as if annihilated. His perfumed wig fell to the floor, and he passed his hand over his hair, as if searching for the tonsure he had dishonored. He felt, more deeply than ever before, what a terrible reality is remorse.

———

CHAPTER XVIII.

FIGARO.

THE condition of Beaumarchais, when he received Susanna's letter through Santerre, and learned the conduct of the count, was very deplorable. The only hope left him was, that Susie would immediately hasten with the casket to Conti, and place herself under his protection. He was expecting his freedom every moment, but the approaching evening increased his anguish. Santerre came and went, and in his rough way spoke encouragingly. He seemed to have become milder since his return from Susanna. He was not avaricious — in fact, unacquainted with the full value of the present he had received, and knew that it was difficult for him to make use of it; but he found to his surprise that a promise made to him, the son of a criminal, had been kept—that a human being was really interested in him, and his heart was touched. With the shyness and simplicity of a slave, to whom the world beyond the prison walls was as a foreign country, he sought the advice of Beaumarchais as to the best means of investing his treasure. Caron was diverted and interested in raising the hopes of another, though he himself was so sad. At length, night came—night, the terror of the captive, writhing in his agony, and haunted by feverish fantasies, Beaumarchais no longer counted the hours—only two thoughts burned in his brain: "Susanna in the power of La Blache, and himself a captive!"

The day was dawning when Caron was aroused by the sound of voices and jarring of doors. His cell was opened. Santerre entered, carrying a lantern.

"Rise, sir, and hasten! The order has come for your liberation. Do not delay! I have known persons who had a letter of deliverance in their pocket, but before they reached the open air, there was a new order of arrest."

"Enough, my friend!" Beaumarchais sprang up and seized his hat. "Be assured that I will remember you. We shall meet again!"

"I believe you, sir," replied Santerre, seizing Caron's hand. "I do not see, however, how I can ever repay you; but yet it may be. Do not remain a moment longer." They hastened down, and across the inner court into the governor's office. De Launay announced to the prisoner that he was liberated by a ministerial warrant, and the official coach was ready to take him home.

Beaumarchais signed his dismissal, and, accompanied by Santerre, entered the same leather box that had conveyed him to the Bastile. He shook the jailer by the hand. The wheels rolled over the drawbridges, the fresh air fanned his face, and the grim prison was soon behind him as he was driven rapidly through the quiet streets toward his home. The Hôtel Piron was before him, and a light burning in his chamber. As he alighted, the window was opened.

"Caron, dear Caron, is it you?—have you indeed come?"

"Yes, I am coming; I am free!" He rushed through the yard, while Gomez, who had been on guard with two dragoons, threw back the gate; Susanna ran to meet him, and husband and wife sank weeping into each other's arms.

On the following morning, while Susanna was relating all that had occurred, Nassau-Siegen came, bringing a note from Conti, in which Beaumarchais and his wife were requested to come to the Hôtel Penthièvre, to be presented to the Princess de Lamballe. In considerable excitement the three went to the mansion of the grand-admiral.

While Nassau had been absent in the deserts of Africa, and Mlle. l'Ange became the ruling genius of both king and country, a new set had entered the complicated scenes of court life, little calculated, notwithstanding their high position, to exert a very beneficial influence.

The young dauphin, formerly called Duke de Berri, was educated at Marly, by the Duke de Vaugyon; and Madame de St. Marsan obtained, by means of flatteries and plottings, the place of governess to the young Princess Elizabeth, and a partial control over Provence and Artois. Vaugyon was honest but pedantic, and not suited to be the instructor of a future king; he was capable of nothing but executing the plans of his former master, even to the point of exaggeration and caricature. Unfortunately, the dauphin was quiet, dull, and reserved, and the discipline to which he was subjected affected him greatly. He was mentally inferior to his younger brothers, who were continually brought before his mind as remarkable examples, thus increasing his natural timidity, and destroying his ambition. His heart lived in the distant but enchanting dream of his childhood, passed at Trianon; and the sweet thoughts of love and hope that sanctified the memory of his parents, made the lad melancholy. Nevertheless, he was obstinate and determined on certain points. Whenever he said, "My deceased father did this, or had such a habit," it was useless to resist him, so that his will was at length obeyed without contradiction. The intelligence that it was arranged for him to marry Marie Antoinette, the dauphin received as a command which he should obey, though with the utmost reluctance. He was informed that his bride was lovely and amiable, but an Austrian, selected for him by Choiseul, who, as well as Austria, had been the foes of his parents, and therefore he could not love her. The Parliament and the nation were also opposed to the marriage.

Hatred and suspicion, greatly increased by the Seven Years' War, the Jesuits, and the prime minister's policy, awaited the daughter of the Cæsars, then scarcely fifteen, at Strasbourg, and at Compiègne, where the king was holding his court, and the dauphin with his brothers appeared for the first time in public. The German bride, however, conquered her adversaries by her beauty, and her charming naturalness of manner; all admired her except the chosen husband of sixteen, whose heart remained closed against her. He was constrained and awkward in his manner, stupid in his words, sulky and irritable, whenever near Marie Antoinette. She seemed isolated and disheartened, notwithstanding the respect generally shown her, and betrayed no expression of happiness as a wife. There was, in fact, none to whom she could confide her thoughts, but the Abbé Vermont, her preceptor, who had accompanied her from Vienna.

After the preliminary marriage ceremony had been performed at Compiègne, the court returned to Versailles, where the public nuptial rites were to be celebrated by brilliant festivals. All who had been attached to the father of the present dauphin, hastened to them, and placed their hopes in the son. Aiguillon, Maupeau, Terray, and the clique of Madame du Barry, detested Marie Antoinette as much as did Vaugyon, Madame de St. Marsan, the Duchess de Guemené, and the old French party. It was not to be wondered at, therefore, that the young princess longed for a friend—for some relief from silly compliment and the burden of the etiquette and pomp surrounding her. Among those who waited on the young pair, at the great levee at Versailles, were Orleans, Chartres, Prince de Conti, Penthièvre, and the widowed Princess de Lamballe, the last bearing on her countenance all the traces of a melancholy destiny. Marie Antoinette saw and loved her; heard her history, and recognized her as a congenial spirit. The dauphin met Conti again for the first time after many years; he remembered well that tall and stately man, wearing a white cross on his breast. The prince and his niece were received with a courtesy generally very different from the manner of the dauphin.

"Madame," he said, turning to his bride, "the Prince de Conti is a noble man, whom I learned to love when I was a boy, and I honor him as a friend of my unforgotten father. You will oblige me by being very friendly to him and his niece, as well as to the Duke de Penthièvre."

"There is no wish, my husband," replied Marie Antoinette, "that I would fulfil more gladly. His highness Prince de Conti, who was acquainted with your mother, will teach me to follow her example, and Madame de Lamballe will strengthen me in suffering.—May I rely on your friendship, dear princess?"

"As far as my heart can entertain such a sentiment, madame," replied Louise, in emotion, "it shall be the greatest happiness of my life."

The dauphin cast a glance of pleased surprise on Marie Antoinette. "That will be agreeable to me, dauphiness." Turning to Conti, he said, "I shall see you often now, dear prince."

When the reception was ended and the newly-married couple withdrew, Louis remarked more ardently than usual: "You have acted very well indeed, and I am glad of it!"

"Who can approach the Prince de

Conti without feeling reverence and confidence in him; and who can see Madame de Lamballe without loving her? I am happy that I have discovered parties unobjectionable to both of us. May I express but one wish?"

"What is it, madame?"

"That you will permit me to have Louise de Lamballe always near me. I am so young, and have so much to learn, in order that you need not be ashamed of me."

"Certainly, I give my permission, Antoinette. We are both young, and know little of life. We stand alone in a critical position. Yes, her society will be good for us both. The Princess de Lamballe shall be your friend; Conti, mine—that is (you do not know the court and its constraint), so far as my grandfather and his party suffer it."

"There are wicked people among them; they ruined Choiseul."

"Do not mention him! You know not what he is, nor what he did when —No, no, I must not talk to you about politics; we do not agree about them. Perhaps you may hear all hereafter."

It was the first time that the dauphin conversed so long with his young wife, and called her Antoinette. His feelings were sluggish, and his good qualities revealed themselves but very slowly.

Conti and his niece often appeared at Marly, where the young couple had established their court, and there soon existed between the dauphiness and Louise de Lamballe a most enthusiastic friendship, becoming in time a sisterly familiarity. Two camps were now organized; one was under the direction of Madame du Barry at Versailles; the other (the small and insignificant one at Marly), under that of the dauphin, to whom passed all those who hoped for the future, but some of them not always of the best character.

This was the condition of affairs when Nassau-Siegen returned.

On Conti's invitation, Nassau, Beaumarchais, and Susanna, drove to the Hôtel Penthièvre. They were accompanied by Gomez, who carried a morocco case of considerable size, belonging to Siegen. Louise blushed when she saw the latter.

Conti met the visitors. "Pardon me, Prince Nassau, for receiving you here, but the duke and my niece, on whom you also intend to wait, desire to see a man who is careless of danger, and who appears wherever honorable deeds are to be performed."

"I greet your serene highness heartily!" exclaimed Penthièvre. "Believe us, that, though we have had much sorrow, we yet had heart enough to feel anxious for you. We have often spoken of you, have we not, dear Louise?"

"Yes, my father," replied the princess, "and our Gorzka invented a thousand romantic tales about you. We often followed your movements on the map, and dreamed ourselves near you. I hope you do not intend to give us any more anxiety by seeking new adventures."

"Are you not to remain in France?" asked Penthièvre.

"I hope to stay if opportunity is given to distinguish myself. Before my departure I was told that France might need what little valor I may have, and that I should spare myself. I will endeavor to obey.—Princess, if you do not consider it indelicate that to-day I redeem a promise made on a more joyful occasion, permit me to offer you the booty I have taken in my hunt." He advanced toward Gomez, who was waiting at the door, opened the box, and, kneeling down, spread out a splendid tiger-robe before the feet of Louise. The claws were of silver, and the eyes large rubies, surrounded by small emeralds. All approached with expressions of surprise, while the prince cast a passionate glance at the young widow.

"Your serene highness," said Madame de Lamballe, stepping upon the mat and giving her hand to Nassau, "I feel proud to stand on the skin of the monster to which you exposed yourself on my account. But I also know that Heaven favors the daring and magnanimous, and that injured innocence will always find a protector in a man who could do so much for so small a reason. In this sense I accept your present."

"And as often as your foot touches it, illustrious lady," replied Nassau-Siegen, kissing her hand, "may you remember that it needs but a sign from you, and Otto von Nassau is ready to perform any deed that may gain your applause!"

"This assurance, dear Louise," said Conti, "is proved by Siegen's first action after his arrival in Paris: he saved the honor of a woman, and thereby the happiness of our brave Beaumarchais."

"Oh, do not mention that," smiled Nassau, leading Susanna to the princess, "for I ask you, noble lady, whether I could have seen this woman insulted without assisting her, even if her husband were not my friend?"

"Ah, you remind me," cried Conti, "that in my admiration of you, I have forgotten to present M. Caron and Madame Susie, as we are accustomed to call them. We passed together a bright and hopeful season at Trianon, and sometimes I think I hear again the harp of Beaumarchais resounding of a summer's twilight in the garden, when we all dreamed of a loving and happy future. Louise, ask the dauphin whether he remembers the flowers blooming in those days of his boyhood. Penthièvre, here is personification of French dexterity, chivalry, and naïveté,

—a trio whom I recommend to your good-will."

"Well, papa," said Louise, "if we had not already reason to be interested in them, the recommendation of my uncle would be irresistible."

"Indeed!" replied the duke. "And we are ready to serve them. If you can find the household of an old man and a widow attractive, you will always be welcome. I am, as it is, under obligation to Beaumarchais.—Let us go to a collation in the Pavilion. I must take possession of you, prince, for I want to hear how you attacked and killed the tiger, and what has become of your brave companion D'Oraison."

"Then Madame de Beaumarchais must take my arm," said Conti, "and relate her experience to me, that she may be convinced how little true merit need fear the disadvantages of birth."

"I would be jealous of you, dear uncle," exclaimed Louise, "if I thought I should not see madame again." Bowing to Caron—"Will you accompany me, sir, that I may thank you for the pleasure your poetry once gave me?" The Countess de Gorzka was superintending the arrangements at the Pavilion, while the rest entered the garden.

"You think too highly of my effusions, princess," said Beaumarchais, continuing the conversation; "they really do not deserve special praise. The merit of the piece to which you refer consists, perhaps, in my devotion to the lady for whom it was intended."

"You are unjust toward yourself, sir. If your verses contained no real poetic sentiment, why should they recur to me in solitary hours, and their melody come to my heart as a sweet solace?"

"Is that so, gracious lady?" exclaimed Caron. "And dare I be so vain (we poets are all vain) to ask, which lines you prefer?"

The princess was embarrassed. "Sir, I acknowledge that at this moment—"

"O madame, unless you wish me to believe that you only intended to flatter me, allow me to assist your memory:

'Aus sanftem Kindestraum zu lieblichen Erwachen
Der Braut ward ich geführt! O wacher Hoffnungs-
    traum,
O Liebe, zieh mit mir auf duft'gem Rosennachen,
Durch Sturm und Sonnenschein! Am fernen
    Küstensaum
Erglühen schon im Grün die stillen—'"

"Finish! You know not how you agitate me."

"It is the privilege of poets to read the human heart."

"But do all desire to be read? Should we not fear the eye of the inquirer?"

"A noble mind becomes more beautiful by being understood."

"Not all our concealed feelings should be revealed. If it is a poet's privilege to read them, he should—" Louise hesitated.

"He should translate his language into music, felt by every one, and appreciated especially by the congenial. Song is the true and only messenger of the heart."

"Do poets then purposely make us tremble?"

"Perhaps, your highness, when their intention is not misunderstood, and they are regarded as friends whose sympathy awakens the soul to the sweet sounds of music."

The princess walked at Caron's side with bowed head. "But I am told that you are also a diplomatist, and a very expert and dangerous one. How can you unite both, how can you gain the confidence of others, where they cannot look into your heart, nor fathom its fidelity? How can we help being suspicious when we see you so often purposely exchange your roles, playing the intriguer where you ought to be the poet, particularly when you appear before both friends and foes?"

"Ah, your highness, now you induce us to take up a very different position, and speak in another language. You are right; the part of poet or diplomatist, minister or confessor, financier or soldier, is a mere mask and attitude, which we assume, or into which we are forced, in order to be or gain something. The disguise is worn with vanity, and we are very careful to have it suit well, that the world may not suspect us; we lay it aside in privacy only when we are among real friends."

"And what does it conceal?"

"In my case, your highness, a man, in the majesty of his mind, with his joys and sorrows."

"And may I ask who are the friends before whom you lay aside your mask?"

"Those for whom I also gladly wear it."

"I mean, would you name them to me?"

"I have no mask in the presence of myself and my wife, of my old friend Morelly, whose misfortune it is that he never wore one. When the noble dauphin lived, he never needed it, though often enough I have had to wear a mask for him. I am also undisguised before your uncle the Prince de Conti, and before my dear friend Nassau-Siegen. Should your highness desire me to appear as myself, then you will always be able to distinguish the poet from the intriguer."

"If I inspire you with so warm an interest, and you presume to read me by your poetic magic—in fact, if you will count me among your friends, you will never wear a mask before me. You will express yourself in all sincerity and simplicity."

"Princess, I am serious—perhaps you may even think me rude, but I speak the truth: *Beware of the house of Orleans!*"

"That was the last petition of my poor husband! I feel that you know more of this faithless court than others, and you comprehend the malicious plots to ruin us. Your enemies will leave no means untried."

"Am I too bold to ask your confidence?"

"We shall certainly be friends, M. de Beaumarchais; yet my father-in-law—"

"I understand. I will ask him as a favor to let me practise duets on the harp with you. The royal princesses were my pupils."

"Oh, that is an excellent idea! But with the understanding that Madame Susanna does not forget the Hôtel Penthièvre."

"Of course not, your highness."

The conduct of Count de la Blache in reference to Susie had very disagreeable consequences. Though the feudal right by which he acted was valid in the provinces, and practised by many a sensual nobleman, it was ridiculed and abhorred in Paris; and the attack on Madame de Beaumarchais, as well as her rescue by Prince Otto von Nassau-Siegen, was the newest and merriest topic of conversation.

About the same time that the liberated Caron was driving to the mansion of the Duke de Penthièvre, La Blache was called to the Hôtel de Ventadour by a threatening letter, where the ministers wished to see him. He well understood the cause, and that he could not evade the command; he therefore went, arming himself with all his insolence. He noticed Maupeau and Terray whispering together, while Diana was pacing the apartment in violent excitement. Greeting them smilingly, he said:

"Did you desire to see me, marchioness?"

"Falcoz!" Her voice trembled with anger. "I have been too lenient to your follies! It was I who protected you when you were in disfavor with the princesses, and reconciled you to your family. I defended you from Choiseul's vengeance when you thought it necessary to present to your mistress your correspondence with Madame de Grammont. I think I have been criminally indulgent. What possessed you, after we had managed to send your opponent to the Bastile, to make attacks on his wife? How could you dare to be so hasty and absurd in retaliation, knowing that it was in our power to give you all the aid you needed?"

"Marchioness, you talk to me as to a school-boy. Moderate your indignation. I do not see why any longer I am to be moved according to your orders. I hate Beaumarchais and his wife, and beg you not to interfere with me."

"Listen to him, abbé," said the lady, sarcastically; "the gentlemen feels himself above us since he has inherited Duverney's money! When a man hates another, he ought to have the prudence to work skilfully. What have you gained by your stupidity? You have made yourself the laughing-stock of Paris, and forced the ministers to liberate Beaumarchais!"

"Liberate him? Well, that is revenge! So you have quashed my accusation against him of having insulted my honor?"

"Do not excite yourself, my friend," said Terray; "your complaint could not be proved."

"And why, you wise ministers, did you not proceed with your judicial reformations before I twice lost my suit? You assume a menacing language toward me, while you act kindly toward your own enemies. My rights as a nobleman I must exercise."

"Would you venture to act contrary to our decrees, count?" said Terray, rising as if in anger.

"We can, if necessary, transport you to St. If," said Maupeau, "or give you a voyage to the colonies!"

La Blache was startled, but soon recovered himself. "Ah you seem very careful not 'to disturb the conjugal peace of my enemy! May I ask why you refuse me my right?"

"Because Susanna Beaumarchais was not born on your estate."

"Indeed? Well, I am aware of that. The woman swore, in presence of Sartines, that she was the daughter of the chaste marchioness and the pious abbé! Now, I comprehend why, for so many years, I have had the worst in the contest with your son-in-law!"

Diana became pale. "The wretch! did she dare assert that publicly?"

"We must make an end of them," groaned Terray, "or they will be beforehand with us."

"But first I must have my will," said La Blache. "I demand vengeance on both—on him as well as on her!"

"You shall have it!" exclaimed Diana, with bitterness—"even if I perish in the attempt!"

"You will have to wait, however, marchioness," said Maupeau, "until the Parliament and the Châtelet are removed, and we have men in the judges' seats that obey us. Until they are disposed of, every step against Beaumarchais is dangerous, and if we rouse him he will have no mercy. Begin your process with the new Parliament; we shall take care that you gain your suit, and render both harmless; we have the power!"

"Very well," replied La Blache, "but beware how you deprive me of that woman. I would turn the energy of my hatred on you, marchioness, should you protect her! Ha! ha! I do not think she will belie her parentage. Hasten your proceedings, gentlemen; for unless you change the condition of the state, we cannot live merrily in France, and abbés cannot sin with impunity."

The resolutions of the ministerial trio—Maupeau, Terray, and Aiguillon —against the few national rights remaining, were to be executed quickly; for Louis XV. began to show some coolness toward Madame du Barry—an invariable custom of his when any of his creatures were to fall. He was often at Marly, the court of the dauphin, alone or with but few attendants, apparently struggling with some decision, which Maupeau was the more anxious to discover by means of his spies, as he had resolved to become premier, though by the sacrifice of all his former associates. He had his own arrangements, unknown to Aiguillon and Terray, while at the same time he was aided by a determination intimidating in its very audacity.

On the night of the 19th of January, 1771, the police, accompanied by grenadiers, forced themselves into the dwellings of the members of Parliament, giving them the choice either of promising entire obedience to the government, or going into immediate exile. The same alternative was placed in as violent a manner before the councillors of the Chamber of Taxation and the obnoxious intendants of the provinces. More than three-fourths of these officials preferred to be banished, among them Malesherbes and Turgot. Rumors of indignation were heard throughout Paris. A crowd assembled at the Palace of Justice; Maupeau, surrounded by soldiers, entered the hall to survey the few who had sold him their honor, and closed the Parliament. At these tidings, the Châtelet and the courts of the departments also closed their sessions, and justice ceased its administration in France.

Maupeau abolished the magistracy opposing him because he had his new judiciary schemes already prepared; the police were the only executors of right; the will of the officials became law, and bribery the only means of obtaining a favorable decision. After the first public outbreak, terror followed, and the nation became, as it were, a corpse in the hands of the ministers. The new members were chosen solely for their unconditional devotion and blind obedience to the government, and the "Maupeau Parliament," as the people called it, came into existence.

Penthièvre had hoped to see so daring a man as Nassau among his naval officers, but the prince preferred to become colonel of an infantry regiment of the Paris garrison. His amusement consisted in his friendly intercourse with Beaumarchais and Conti, and now and then a visit to Penthièvre. Nassau endeavored to approach Madame de Lamballe, but was hindered by her father-in-law, who always took possession of him to hear something more of Africa; and he also thought he perceived an intentional reserve in Louise, who, besides, was often at Marly. The manner of the princess, particularly her absence of mind, anxiety, and melancholy, justified by no apparent cause, made a deep impression on Beaumarchais, from whom she seemed to have again withdrawn her confidence. Nor could the Countess de Gorzka or Susanna, who was Louise's favorite, explain her gloomy manner.

Toward the latter part of 1771, Beaumarchais was visiting Madame de Lamballe. He was talking of the days at Trianon, and sang the lines he had formerly composed for the Dauphiness Josepha:

> " Im Herzen ruhen stumm und still
> Allmächtig grosse Triebe.
> Wer sie in sich erwecken will,
> Braucht nichts als—tiefste Liebe."

The princess sat at the window, lost in thought. Tears stood in her eyes. "Profoundest love!" she murmured, and a shudder passed through her frame; she looked up, and her startled glance fell on Caron.

"Do you know, your highness, that for a long time past I have noticed something in you I could never have thought possible ? "

"Well, what is it, M. de Beaumarchais ? "

"At Marly you are all cheerfulness; in Paris, all sadness. You also wear a mask."

"And if I do, have you not taught me ? "

"Scarcely. Certainly not with your friends."

"Friends! There are cases, Caron, when one does not even know if he is a friend to himself. Suppose my levity at Marly is feigned, and my melancholy here, my real feeling ?—I pray you do not speak so to me; I do not understand you."

"And you neither understand the glances of Nassau, the despair that drove him into distant dangers, and the longing that brought him back to your feet ? "

"Beaumarchais, he loves Gorzka—not me ! " she exclaimed, in emotion.

"Who has abused you by such a deception ? Who has veiled your eyes so that you do not see—"

"Oh, do not destroy the illusion! He loves *me!* So much the greater is my misery ! As Louise de Savoy, I could cherish such dreams with happiness at Chambery—even as a wretched wife, I could have comforted myself by such a sentiment, if only to have made my life more tolerable; but when I was forced to throw off my mourning, and unwillingly obliged to return to society—when I saw through the web spun about France by the Parces — Beaumarchais, look around, and tell me is this a time for love ? There are but two classes of persons: those who in enjoyment live thoughtlessly and arrogantly at the expense of others, not caring for the future; and those who feel and suffer, and who at last must immolate themselves, uselessly perhaps, but not ignobly."

"But suppose such devotion does not change the course of events?"

"No one would act for another's benefit, if all thought thus."

"No one destroys himself for what he does not love! Who, then, has become so worthy of your regard?"

"And if the sacrifice is so much the more revolting because it is unwillingly but unavoidably to be made, I—For Heaven's sake, I have already said too much!"

Caron rose, and paced the room. A fearful thought passed through his mind. "Princess, does your uncle, the dauphin, or the dauphiness, know of this?"

"Not yet. They will probably not discover it until it is too late. Perhaps they will approve — perhaps hate me, not considering that my heart is breaking."

"Your highness, I pray you, reveal all to me. Let not trouble overtake you when a friend can avert it."

"Poor man!" she said, bitterly, "what is impending over me, neither you nor any other human being can prevent."

"Then I shall soon know it, and, with or without your will, you shall not suffer, should I make use of the meanest of weapons—slander." Beaumarchais seized his hat.

"Caron, do not go! How can you know what I scarcely dare own to myself—how avert what becomes every day more threatening? Do you think you can play with those who can crush you?"

"As I am well acquainted with them, I know my own mode of controlling them."

"I cannot let you go! If you are my friend, tell me your thoughts."

"If you will sincerely answer two questions: Maupeau has approached either you or your father-in-law in a friendly manner? Am I right?"

"Yes!"

"A certain illustrious person appears very often at Marly, and shows great affection for you, and in reference to whom you use all your art to keep him at a distance?"

"I confess I do not know how to escape longer from his attentions."

"Leave that to me, dear lady. You must do one thing, however: under the seal of secrecy you must reveal your position to the dauphiness Marie Antoinette. I assure you, I will put something in motion that will frighten not only M. de Maupeau, but the king."

"And have you the power to save me from a sacrifice that—"

"Yes. Drive immediately to Marly. Tell the dauphiness that I will take the management of the case. The noble personage to whom you refer will appear at her court no more!"

"I will follow your advice, Beaumarchais. You are the only one I trust."

"And poor Nassau?"

"Not another word. Can I think of him at such a moment?"

"But you do, I know." Caron bowed and withdrew. He sent his carriage home, and ordered Gomez to accompany him, took a hired coach near the Palais-Royal, and drove to the Pigeonnier.

Debrelon and Coralie were at this time in great trouble, for Maupeau was beginning to notice them more particularly, and they had temporarily discontinued their orgies, keeping themselves very quiet in view of events at Versailles. They knew not from what quarter the storm would break upon them.

The usual signal sounded at the back gate. Coralie hastened to her piano, and began to sing, while Debrelon opened the door expecting police-officers or gossiping acquaintances.—To his astonishment, Beaumarchais, accompanied by Gomez, stood before him.

"Well, my friend, you look unhappy. Have you had losses?"

"What—what do you wish with us, M. de Beaumarchais? I do not indeed know—"

"Ah, I have arrived unseasonably! Is Coralie at home?"

"Do you not hear her practising?"

"Because she has nothing better to do. As things are now, the opera is all that remains to her!"

"I really do not understand you."

"Very well! Take me to her. I will show you that I am truly your friend."

"Our friend! You are jesting?"

"Do not delay. Gomez may remain here. I assure you, you will thank me for my visit."

Shaking his head, Debrelon led Caron into the boudoir. "It is M. de Beaumarchais who wishes to see you."

"Sir, me? You come at a moment when—"

"When you are already frightened. Well, without any further ceremonies, sit down; we are old friends and neighbors."

"I am really curious to hear what you have to say, who have always been liberal with threats."

"Or with money. You have received considerable from me during many years, though you always betrayed me. You give no more information, yet I discover all I wish to know. Shall I tell you why you are so dejected? The king is very cool toward your dear friend Madame du Barry; there are no more little suppers; he prefers to go to Marly. The countess may do what she pleases, for her power of fascination with him no longer exists. Terray is alarmed, as well as Madame de Ventadour; and Orleans, who well arranged this business, sees his prospects vanish.

Worse still, M. de Maupeau, who has just closed the Parliament, and has the chief authority, is casting his eye on you, ready to send you to St. Salpetrière. Am I not right? Ha, ha! how he will demolish this wasps'-nest! Not that he cares for morality, but he wants all to dance to his own tune, and to become cognizant of their frailties. Many a peer will obey him provided no offensive questions are asked relative to the Pigeonnier. In short, you are ruined, and if you were destitute of money, you would have to resume your old trade of singing in the streets. Suppose I could save you—show you how Madame du Barry could again rule old King Bouquin,* and yourself renew the pleasures at Versailles?"

"M. de Beaumarchais, I know that you are a shrewd man, and can injure us if you wish; but that you have either the power or the will to be useful to us, I beg humbly to doubt."

"Even more, I require nothing in return; I only desire you to succeed."

"Then speak, disinterested man!"

"Well, King Bouquin intends to become virtuous in his old age—he once before attempted it in the society of Madame de Seran; but this time he is in earnest—he is about to marry!"

"Marry?" cried Coralie.

"Yes. Maupeau understands that the government under your friend and Terray will be completely wrecked—that something new must occur, and—"

"M. de Beaumarchais, is this true?" stammered Debrelon.

"As sure as you leave France if the marriage takes place."

"And who is the fortunate lady?"

"I will tell you, if you promise to follow my advice."

"If Bouquin is really in earnest, of course we mean to do all we can to prevent the marriage."

---

* A nickname of Louis XV.

"Then you must go directly to Madame du Barry at Versailles; Terray, Diana de Ventadour, and Orleans, must be roused, and all the courtiers alarmed, before Maupeau becomes aware of your purpose."

"And I will spread consternation among them to your heart's content! Tell me, who is it?"

"He wishes to marry the widowed Princess de Lamballe. Maupeau has already laid the train."

"The old man is always at Marly; it is so. We are brought down to sorrow and shame, if that happens!—To Versailles, a carriage! Debrelon, you must go to Orleans! Every moment is precious."

"Take my hired coach," said Beaumarchais, "and do not forget you did not receive your information from me —you owe me that much discretion!"

"Ah, you demon or angel, I will be silent as the grave!" Coralie was about to embrace him.

"Oh, never mind! You will require all your art where you are going! Adieu!"

On the same day occurred one of those indescribable scenes in the life of Louis XV. when his mistress Du Barry and her friends attacked him like so many Megaras, in order to break his weak will, now by entreaty and allurement, and again by sarcasm and reproach. Every effort was made to dissuade him from a marriage with the Princess de Lamballe, "who had already," so they said, "killed one husband by coldness and neglect." On the following day appeared a notice in the *Mercure Français:* "It is asserted in court circles that the ministers and the Duke de Penthièvre have commenced negotiations for the marriage of his majesty with her highness the Princess de Lamballe!" Paris laughed and exclaimed against it.

Like all feeble-minded men, Louis, who felt ashamed of no evil deed, could not stand ridicule, and he felt humiliated when he believed himself caught in the act of attempting to reform his life. He soon returned to Madame du Barry, in order to forget that he ever had a will of his own. The rage of the terrified courtiers was turned against Maupeau, who found to his sorrow that it was easier to overthrow all the institutions of the country than to displace a favorite mistress. He endeavored to regain the pardon of Madame du Barry and her followers, by concessions of every kind.

The fate that had threatened Louise de Lamballe was now averted in a very comic manner, freeing her from oppressive anxiety. Innumerable anecdotes were related of the mortifying scenes between the king and the woman that governed him, always representing him as a weak and uncertain lover. The merry dauphiness, as well as Conti, whom Louise had informed of the intentions of Louis XV., and who revolted at the idea while they were amused at the result, knew that Beaumarchais had something to do with the matter, but could not discover how he had managed to disturb his majesty's plans. The confusion of the king was the topic of all circles, and the dismissal of an aged lover by a young maiden was termed "*Une corbeille à la Lamballe.*" Among other witticisms, the following appeared in the *Courrier Français:*

" Wer ist's der dem Papa Bouquin
 So wunderschön zur Ader schlug,
Und vom japsn'schen Pavillon
 Dem Engel schalkhaft Botschaftrug?
Wer hat den Berthol'n, der als Arzt
 Uns bie zur Leichenruh' curirt,!
So zum Vernügen aller Welt
 Das Hirn geschröpft, geseift, rasirt?" *

* What famed physician was it who
 So well poor Father Bouquin bled?
And to the " Angel" sent a message true
 That she should Louis never wed?
The same that shaved and cupped Bartholomew?
 Who doctored us as he was doctored too

These lines made quite a sensation, and as they apparently proceeded from some malicious cavalier, who was aware of the facts, Beaumarchais amused himself by answering them anonymously in the *Mercure :*

"Wer dem Bonquin zur Ader schlägt,
　Dem Engel Lind'rungspflaster legt,
　Den Bartel seift und so rasirt
　Dass er einst selbst den Kopf verliert?
　Wer dient wohl seinen Kunden so ?
　Der Hofbarbier heisst—Figaro ! " *

Every Parisian knew this question and answer by heart, and wherever a trick was played on any one it was sure to be called "*à la Figaro.*" "Bouquin" was understood to mean the king ; " the Angel" needed no explanation, and "Bartholomew " was one of Maupeau's names. The police vainly sought both satirists, but Mlle. Coralie Raucourt had been prudent at Versailles, and her interference was unobserved.

It is strange how suggestive sometimes is thought. During his Spanish journey Beaumarchais had received impressions of persons and scenes, which induced him to write a libretto for a comic operà, after he made the acquaintance of Duni, the composer. He had the plot now in his mind ; it was to be a love-affair, in which the principal character was to be an adroit and cunning fellow, a portrait of himself, whom he called Figaro. The poetic question in the public journal suggested a new idea. He changed his piece into a comedy, and gave his hero the trade of a barber. The play was called the *Barber of Seville*, and contained many allusions to the times.

The dauphiness, Madame de Lamballe, and Conti, were highly amused by these effusions, and divined who wrote the answer. Marie Antoinette was curious to make the acquaintance of Beaumarchais, sending him word by the princess to inform her " how Figaro managed to deceive the good Doctor Bartolo," a character in the play.

"Madame, assure her royal highness that I dare not tell her that, as the doctor, like all old men who have been deceived, is malicious and dangerous. But I have written a comedy, in which Figaro's artifices are revealed."

The Princess de Lamballe was requested to present Caron at Marly, and tell him to bring his piece. For the first time, he entered the Pavilion of the Sun under the protection of his patroness. The dauphiness, the Princes de Provence and d'Artois, Conti, and the Duchess de Noailles, first lady of the household, were present. The dauphin, as usual, was absent, busy with his geographical studies, or in his locksmith's workshop, a favorite resort with him, even when a boy at Trianon.

In this circle it was of course not advisable to manifest the gratification of the listeners. Beaumarchais was seriously asked to read his play, and one witty scene after another was recited by the author. Provence, Artois, and Conti were delighted ; the dauphiness was continually pressing her handkerchief to her mouth, in order not to laugh outright. Doctor Bartolo, Figaro, and the distress of Rosina, were too plain, and Count Almaviva so knightly that Marie Antoinette wished that " this lover existed in reality ! " Louise de Lamballe blushed, and Beaumarchais bit his lip.

The portrait Almaviva gave of Bartolo exactly suited Maupeau. Numerous invectives, such as—" I am convinced that a powerful man always shows himself gracious when he refrains from doing us any harm ; " " According to what is at present required

---

* You ask for him who skilfully did quell
　The turmoil in old Bonquin's veins,
Who comforted the " Angel," and as well
　Succeeded with the doctor's brains.
The man who served his suffering patients so
　Is the court barber known as—Figaro !

of a domestic, you will see few gentlemen who would be found worthy of being their own servants;" together with Figaro's description of his own trade, the monologue on slander, and the humorousness of the action,—all drew on Caron after the reading the loud applause of this small but distinguished audience.

"M. de Beaumarchais," said Marie Antoinette, "write more such plays, and rest assured of my protection. I wish this to be represented in the Théâtre Français; I will send orders to that effect to the director of the *Menus Plaisirs*. Do all you can to make it succeed, for I am going to Paris to see it."

"And the police, your royal highness?"

"Why, I heard you had fought them already several times successfully. Besides, if the Dauphiness of France desires to witness a comedy, it must certainly be acted."

CHAPTER XIX.

THE PAGE.

WHEN the dauphiness demanded the performance of the *Barber of Seville*, Beaumarchais spoke of "the police." Though the representation contained nothing against the laws, Marie Antoinette was mistaken if she thought that her will was sufficient. The extraordinary protection which the play had received at Marly aroused the censure of the ministers, and instead of the usual solitary official with his red pencil, four were sent to criticise it. This again stung the pride of the dauphiness and her court; being quite powerless in public affairs, they wished at least to have some influence in trifles, and the comedy had obtained an importance it scarcely merited. Parties were formed for and against it, and the conflict became notorious. Twice the Board of Censure was conquered, twice the play was announced to the inquisitive Parisians, and as often Maupeau had the placards torn down again and forebade the performance. The servants of the government said, "It is meant to shake the foundation of the state;" the friends of Caron replied, "It is the wittiest composition since the days of Molière."

At Conti's desire, Beaumarchais had the play printed at Gauchat's, snapped his fingers at the laws, and sold it for two francs. The edition was exhausted at once, and, as people were determined to find hidden meanings, the rage for its interpretation became so great that it would have been much better for Maupeau if he had permitted it to be acted. He was greatly irritated, and made the king and the Countess du Barry believe that they were attacked, and, as the minister accused Caron of insulting the government, the author was sent once more to the Bastile, in February, 1773.

A similar misfortune never makes so deep an impression on us the second time as the first. We are acquainted with it, and the conviction that we can conquer again ameliorates our grief. When Beaumarchais was this time arrested by Sartines, and heard the accusation, he laughed, and considered the affair quite a jest.

"Honor me by dining in my company, M. de Sartines, as it is dinner-hour. I am having so much to do with the police, that I must repay their trouble by a little politeness. Do not be anxious, dear Susanna, should I be longer separated from you than formerly; my triumph will be the greater."

"Oh, I am not afraid, Caron. We shall see whether their royal highnesses at Marly will be silent, and allow a man to be condemned for that which has the approval of the future queen. The Prince von Nassau and the Duke de Penthièvre will take care that I have no unwelcome visitors here. All those who are inimical to us may find it hard to answer for themselves when a change takes place."

"I hope, gracious lady, you will not count me among those persons," said Sartines, politely. "On the unpleasant occasion to which you refer, I was misled by Count de la Blache, and, though my office obliges me to arrest your husband, I will show him all the favor I can."

Sartines permitted Beaumarchais to make the necessary arrangements, write letters, and supply himself with conveniences for the prison; he also shared the dinner, and enjoyed the conversation, so that a stranger could not have believed that the host was a prisoner in the hands of an officer.

When Beaumarchais embraced Susanna, he whispered to her: "Be cheerful, my love, the Bastile will make a great man of me. Keep yourself quiet, and confide in my good star! Farewell, Susie, or rather *au revoir!*—Madame de Piron, I leave her in your care!" He and Sartines entered the black coach.

Caron really had reason to be of good courage. He had the favor of the dauphin, the interest of the dauphiness, Paris was on his side, and the folly of the accusation was evident. He had found himself in many worse positions, but had always silenced his opponents by abundant resources, the purity of his course, and the boldness of his conduct. His arrest made a great sensation. The dauphin, Marie Antoinette, Louise de Lamballe, and Conti, were highly indignant. Nassau-Siegen and two of his comrades, with the consent of their chief, took up their quarters in the Hôtel Piron, and universal sympathy indemnified Susanna for the separation from her husband, which apparently could not be long protracted.

The lieutenant of police politely conveyed Beaumarchais to the Bastile, and the commandant received him in the same manner, giving him the best chamber toward the outer wall. The petition that his former jailer might attend him was also granted.

When Santerre saw Caron, he was amazed. "What is the matter with you?" said the latter; "do you receive an old friend with such a look of terror?"

"H'm! it is a great friendship which rejoices to meet you here! It bodes no good that I see you again."

"Are you sorry for my renewed imprisonment? Never mind; I have better prospects than before, and you are wrong to grieve when I am unconcerned. I assure you, when I leave, you go with me."

The jailer looked steadily at Beaumarchais. "Your cause may be good, your friends powerful, but we have an old proverb that has never failed. 'He who sees the Bastile once, returns soon; he who sees it for the second time, is rarely liberated; if he passes the gate the third time, he dies here!'"

"How can you believe such nonsense? you look at things from a dark point of view, because you do not believe in your own happiness. In a few weeks you will change your mind."

"Well, laugh at me! It is always good for a prisoner to bring cheerfulness and hope. You will soon need them."

Notwithstanding the confidence of Beaumarchais and Susanna, and all the efforts of Marie Antoinette with the king himself, Santerre was right! Weeks passed, and Caron's case was not decided. Generally so cautious and penetrating, he now only thought of the insufficiency of the accusation against him, not considering that it was merely a pretext to arrest him. All the letters he addressed to the Parliament and the ministers were in vain, and the fact that less attention was shown him in the prison, produced alarm. He knew, however, that his wife was protected, and his fortune safe; once in three days they were permitted to write, and they endeavored to encourage each other, though every week they became less hopeful. The casket, containing the papers of Susanna's birth, was again in the secretary of Beaumarchais, and could as before have been used as a threat; but as Conti did not seem to think it advisable, Caron understood that they must be reserved for real use against his enemies. He became gradually convinced of the sad reality of his condition. Public opinion, at first so favorable to him, became changed by the influence of his opponents; and journals, like the *Gazette de France*, sought to render his life precarious and his honor uncertain. What could he do?

Poor Susanna was still more to be pitied. Awakened from her careless confidence and tranquillity, she became sad and anxious. With a presentiment that in women often supplies the place of understanding, she felt that not the *Barber of Seville*, but the ever-threatening secret of her birth, the malice of La Blache and Orleans, had prompted a persecution that would never be satisfied. She foresaw the time when their patrons would resign them to their fate, and knew enough of public affairs to believe that her husband would be quietly consigned to unending imprisonment. She reproached herself for having read the documents, for, had she been ignorant of their contents, she could not have revealed to La Blache and Sartines a secret that was safe with Conti, but destructive in the hands of the count. Another source of disquiet was the information she derived from Beaumarchais that he had received notice from Vaucresson, the attorney-general of the Parliament, that La Blache had brought his suit before that tribunal, and that it would be decided before the affair of Figaro, as of antecedent date. The permission, however, was given Caron to go out in company with an official of the Bastile, and engage an advocate. He ended his letter with these words: "Do you now see clearly, poor woman? First, our foes attempted to despoil us of our honor, now they are attacking our fortune, and finally they will have our persons, if we do not become too contemptible for their hatred."

Susanna was in great trouble. On the following day she was surprised by a visit from her husband. He had been allowed to go to the city, attended by Santerre, but obliged to return to the prison to dinner, and again in the evening at nine o'clock, so that he had but a short time to spare. She wept bitterly when she saw how pale he was, not thinking that he was equally affected by the evidences of suffering in her own features. On the next day, the 25th of March, he called again toward evening. Unmistakable fear was in his countenance. He evaded the questions of Nassau and Madame de Piron, and withdrew with Susanna, while Santerre waited in the corridor.

"Concealment is of no more use, wife; be prepared for every thing—this time we lose. Brunellerie and Dufour have declared that they cannot undertake my public defence before this Parliament—it would be acknowledging the legality of that body. These lawyers were deprived of their functions when the Châtelet dissolved itself, and therefore their right to appear might be called in question. Six or seven others, whom they named as still being in office, refused to have any thing to do with the matter. They dare not act against the people, who are devoted to M. de Maupeau."

"Then we must quietly allow ourselves to be condemned? Cannot Conti—"

"Conti! Neither he nor any of the other princes or peers have any thing more to do with the Parliament. He has done all he could for us. We are so low in the estimation of the world, that for us to ask the assistance of an illustrious man, is to ruin him. Our only possible safety is in persevering without complaint."

"But what will you do?"

"Request the minister to allow me to plead my own cause before the Parliament. I can depend only on myself. If such persons on principle take as much as they can, I will give them as little as possible." The conversation was interrupted by Prince Otto von Nassau, who asked permission to enter. He held an open letter in his hand.

"I know not," said the prince, "whether this is a malicious chance or not! Just when my presence is your only protection—my friendship the last support in your misery—the Duke de Brissac sends me an order, on command of the minister, to depart with my regiment in two days, and repair to St. Omer, to cover Artois, Flanders, and Calais, against an attack of the English."

"And must you go?" cried Susanna, "my only protector, our last friend?"

"I do not see how I can avoid it, Susie. To demand my dismissal, when I have had the regiment only for so short a time, would be an insult to the army, for which there is no apology, and which I cannot attempt."

"Why your corps, instead of any other, in all the garrison of Paris?" exclaimed Caron, looking at the paper; "there is a purpose in this to remove you."

"I shall not remain here an hour longer," said Susie, in a decided tone, "when the prince has left. I have seen Batyl creeping around the house. Gomez has also noticed him."

"And all this is only a part of the plan to deliver us both into the hands of our enemies!" said Beaumarchais, gloomily.

"Madame Susie must take refuge in the house of your father, my friend," said Nassau. "The retirement of a citizen—"

"Will be less of an obstacle in the way of M. de la Blache to persecute the wife of a prisoner," said Caron, ironically. "The triumph of our opponent will soon be complete. Oh, scoundrels of high rank in France are allied against us, and they are ashamed of no baseness. Ah, my prince, you are foolish to love a beautiful woman! You ought to thank Heaven that you have no wife! Has not my married life been but one series of troubles? Was ever a husband so perplexed and alarmed? I withdrew Susie from the persecutions of La Blache, to starve with her in the Pigeonnier. I was protected from the renewed attacks of that wretch by the court of the princesses, where I had a hundred enemies instead of one. I became rich through my wife, and, tired of court life, I desired to live only for her. I was cast into the Bastile because La Blache wished to rob me of her! Oh, those demons know what they are about. Susanna is my life; if she and those dangerous documents fall into their hands, I am lost!" He paced the room, wringing his hands, while Nassau looked on pityingly, and without having it in his power to advise.

Suddenly both men were startled by an abrupt sarcastic laugh, and looked up. Susanna's appearance had changed, for her timidity and helplessness were gone. "And for this poor little woman, who gave you so much grief, you are losing your mind! Oh, you wise lords of creation—you, who are so greatly our superiors—stand and hang your heads in the hour of danger, and are ready to surrender all your energy and hope! A true woman always knows how to protect herself, and, when a man's calculations fail, she laughs at his great talents!" Susanna walked up and down with fiery eyes and flushed cheeks.

"Have you really discovered a way of escape?" asked the prince in surprise.

"You intend to withstand them alone while I am in prison? Folly! Do not hope to find protection in the Hôtels Conti or Penthièvre, or at Marly; there are no patrons for the dishonored and wretched, and our friends will take care not to compromise themselves with you, after they have vainly striven to save me."

"And suppose I do know of a means of escape? Suppose the shrewdness of a woman greater than all the machinations of a virulent party? Answer me one question. If I am safe from the persecutions of La Blache, Madame de Ventadour, and the ministers—if your heart is no longer burdened by fear for my fate—can you promise me that you will regain the power of your former faculties, free yourself from the devices of your enemies, and pursue them until you have destroyed their name and influence?"

"I can do that, Susanna! But my mind is paralyzed; my heart trembles when I think of your exposure! When you are safe, my own perils are nothing, and unexpected strength would arise in me; whereas now, I feel like a shackled man. And how, dear wife, will you save yourself?"

"By the very method which the adverse party use against me."

"What method?" asked the prince, shaking his head.

"Your serene highness, in two days you must march?"

"Yes."

"Very well, I march with you."

"You, madame!" exclaimed Nassau-Siegen.

"You, Susie?" echoed Beaumarchais.

"Well, I suppose, a colonel of a regiment, who is a prince, will be allowed to have a page as well as Artois, Orleans, and other great men. I will be your page! With the greater part of our fortune, and the documents, you will take me to St. Omer; I can be in no more honorable hands. You will see that I also have a taste for adventure. From St. Omer I will easily reach Calais; at the slightest approach of danger, I can cross over to England, and no one will suspect a poor, sad woman of having been the page of your highness, or Madame de Beaumarchais, the wife of a persecuted poet. Either you escape from your enemies, Caron, and you will know where to find me; or you conquer them, and I return in triumph."

"Well, you are always the same merry Susanna!" said Beaumarchais.

"Truly," remarked Nassau, "a lady's invention is better than all diplomacy! You must be my page, and, if you have only a little boldness, we can delude our enemies."

"Why, prince, should I not have that quality? You do not know of what the wife of a poet is capable in time of need!"

"You dearest wife!" exclaimed Beaumarchais, embracing her laughingly. "Now, let any one say whether it is not worth while for a man to lose his senses from love and grief for such a charming, resolute little woman!— Your highness saved her once before; renew your kindness, and my gratitude shall end only with my life. In your hands, Susie, and in yours, prince, I

"SHE RAN DOWN-STAIRS."

p. 215.

place every thing, and if my relieved mind does not now master all these creatures, I do not deserve the faculties with which Heaven may have endowed me.—Farewell, Susie! No tears at parting! Address your letters to my father; Santerre will deliver them. Do not be troubled about me." He pressed her again in his arms, shook hands with Nassau, and returned to the Bastile with the jailer.

In this hour, when Susanua was suffering all her former pains, the danger of helplessness had roused her to greater action. With a silence and prudence that excited Nassau's admiration, she made her arrangements for flight, so that neither Madame de Piron, Gomez, nor any of the servants, had the slightest suspicion. Two-thirds of the fortune of her husband in papers, cash, and jewelry, together with the documents of her birth, she placed in a haversack, to be carried by one of Siegen's pack-horses, adding only the most necessary articles of apparel. The rest she handed to Brunellerie, taking a receipt for it, and pretended that it was done according to her husband's command.

In order to avail themselves of all means of oppression, the ministers, instead of permitting Beaumarchais to plead for himself, appointed Goesman, a member of Parliament, as his advocate, and had given strict orders that the accused should not be allowed to leave the prison but on business in reference to his lawsuit. Caron had little time left to discover some new expedient, as his case was to come before the Parliament at the beginning of April.

On the 29th of March, at noon, the regiment of Nassau left Paris. The prince took leave of Madame de Piron, and apparently of Susanna, in the morning; and the latter, refusing society, withdrew gloomily to her apart-ments. The book-keeper was sent to Brunellerie in order to explain something in the affairs of Caron, and Gomez went with a farewell note to Morelly, while Susie's maid took another to the elder Beaumarchais. She was now alone, and changed her dress, assuming the garb secretly in her possession by means of Siegen. Half an hour after, a little figure stepped from the back door of the left wing of the Hôtel Piron, wearing a plumed hat on one side, a gray cloak over the left shoulder, and a riding-whip in his gloved right hand, while the blue and yellow bows (Nassau's colors) flourished on the green uniform. The page locked the door, and ran down-stairs ringing his spurs as he passed the servants' room, from which Fanchette, the maid of the chevalière, was just departing.

"Dear me!" The maid stood in astonishment.

"Have you never before seen a man, since you appear to be so astonished?" said the boy. "There, take a kiss as a farewell, my dear!" He put his arms around her, pressing his lips to her cheek.

"What an insolent fellow! A man indeed! You are a mere boy—only a page!"

"Silence, good child! when the regiment of my master the prince returns, I shall have a mustache! I will bring you a dress when we have sacked London. Adieu!" He hastened away.

The page left the hall, and drew his mantle more over his face, as he turned to the Rue Fauconnier. At a little distance stood a person assuming indifference, but keeping a sharp eye on the Hôtel Piron. It was Batyl. When he saw the boy departing from the house, he ran inquisitively across the street, intending to ask a question, while searchingly looking at him.

"Out of my way, fellow, or—!"

The page raised his whip. "Impudent rabble!"

"Ah, excuse me!" stammered the musician, lifting his hat, and slowly retreating toward St. Paul. In the mean while, the youth reached the Fauconnier, where he met two of the prince's grooms, each holding a pack-horse.

"Are you, sir, the new page of his highness?" asked one of them, with a smile.

"Yes, my friend! We have no time to lose; forward to the barracks!" The page walked before them with a firm step.

"What a pretty boy! He almost looks like a girl!" whispered some who met him. He laughed, or seemed angry, as he passed along. His highness had an excellent page.

The sentinel at the barracks presented arms, and the page gave the military salute. "Where is the prince?" he asked.

"In the dining-hall of the officers, sir," said an old corporal. "You might have come sooner to wait on the colonel. You will get a whipping, my little pale face!"

"Very well, cousin gray-beard, you shall have your share of it!" The boy forced his way through the soldiers, toward the apartment on the first floor, whence the tinkling of glasses and loud laughter were heard. When he entered, hat in hand, the officers had already risen from the table; Nassau was surrounded by several chiefs of other regiments, among them the chevalier de Lorges and the Marquis d'Aliaga, of the queen's dragoons, and was drinking a parting-cup with them.

"Why, Nassau, what porcelain doll have you there?" laughed an old colonel, looking at the page. "Surely, you do not intend to take him with you!"

"Am I in my right mind?" cried De Lorges, highly astonished. "Why, that is—"

"It is my rascally page!" interrupted Nassau. "Come here, boy! Where have you been? I shall have to dust your livery as a welcome!"

The youth, seizing the prince's hand, kissed it. "Do so, your highness; it would be no disgrace to be chastised by the bravest man in Europe—better men than I have borne it. What are your commands?"

"That you hold your tongue, and go to my room to pack my saddle-bags. You will find there all I wish to take. Barbillon, show him my chamber." The boy bowed, glanced around, and left, followed by the groom.

"That is the right kind of page!" exclaimed one.

"Where did you get the little fellow?" asked another. "What is his name?"

"Amaranth de Glentrichart," replied Nassau. "He is from Lorraine, but his family have been reduced, so that his mother was forced to accept the assistance of my friend Beaumarchais." He glanced keenly at De Lorges and D'Aliaga. "I think I am acting kindly by tutoring the boy."

"A warrior's life will scarcely suit him," said the old colonel, ironically, "for he looks more like a girl than a page!"

"That will soon be changed," replied Siegen. "He will be weather-beaten and tall enough when we return." The officers took leave, and the last were D'Aliaga and De Lorges.

"How can a man conceal such an interesting adventure from his friends, your highness?" said D'Aliaga, smiling.

"What do you mean? What adventure?"

"Do not be reserved; your page is—"

"Ah, you think he resembles Madame

Susanna de Beaumarchais, and the rogue sometimes affects the manners of his benefactress. But I will soou cure him of his tricks. Adieu, my friends, and be assured I only conceal such secrets of my life as are not my own." He gravely offered his hand and left the room.

"You must have been deceived, De Lorges, or he would have confessed it laughingly."

"And yet I maintain that this page is Susanna de Beaumarchais."

"Then it is a mystery he dare not reveal."

"And he only saved her from La Blache, in order to have her—"

"Silence!" said D'Aliaga; "I forbid you to think evil of the prince, or say one word on the subject, if you would not force me to resent it." ~

"Are you insane, on account of a page?"

When the regiment Nassau left Paris, the Rue St. Honoré was crowded with people, to witness the departure of the troops. At the head rode the prince and his adjutant; after them the band, followed by the standard, to the left of which was the senior lieutenant, to the right the page Amaranth. Then came the main body, with the pack-horses, baggage-wagons, and Nassau's travelling-chaise in the rear.

On the garden terrace of the Hôtel Penthièvre stood Conti, the Princess de Lamballe, Countess de Gorzka, and the venerable grand-admiral. Siegen saluted them, lowering his sword, and casting on them a painful parting glance. Both ladies were very pale. Suddenly Conti recognized Susanna. "It is impossible! My eyes deceive me! And yet, princess, look at that page! Have you ever before seen that face?"

"It is the wife of Beaumarchais!" said Louise, turning away and blushing deeply.

"The wife of Beaumarchais?" repeated the countess, and fainted.

"Abominable!" murmured Conti. "I ought to have kept it to myself. Indeed, I think the Polish lady is in love with Nassau-Siegen."

Beyond the gate St. Honoré the regiment was ordered to halt. "Quartermaster, forward! Amaranth, my boy, you may go with the wagons and horses; ride in my carriage. We encamp at Ecouen to-night. Attend to my comfort, or I send you back to your mother!" Susanna saluted her colonel, hastened to the rear, and entered the equipage; in a few minutes she was on the northern route with the baggage and foragers, arriving safe at St. Omer. On the following night the prince took her to Calais, where she dwelt in a small retired house near the sea-shore.

Susanna's very sudden disappearance created great surprise. Madame de Piron, Brunelleric, and a number of other acquaintances, pitied Caron, for no one knew the true state of affairs except Morelly and the elder Beaumarchais. It was rumored that she had been assassinated, and the police made many investigations, but all in vain. It was forgotten, like many other scandalous reports. On the evening of the 8d of April, Caron received a letter by Santerre; it had arrived at the watchmaker's, and contained but few words:

"Dear Sir: Announce to your son that my page is well cared for. He will soon write to his relatives. Yours,

"NASSAU-SIEGEN."

CHAPTER XX.

FOR FIFTEEN LOUIS D'ORS.

BRION DE GOESMAN, from Colmar, member of Parliament, the man in whose hands was Caron's defence in the process of La Blache against him, resided at the Quai de St. Paul, corner of the Rue des Ormes. Though he never had mind enough to study law, and stammered considerably, he had been enabled to purchase his present position by money, his unconditional devotion to the ministry of Maupeau and Aiguillon, and the flattering amiability of his pretty young wife, who had formerly delighted the citizens of Strasbourg as Mlle. Jamar, the actress. On the 1st of April, Beaumarchais, Santerre, and the lawyer Falconet, went to this gentleman's house, but were informed that he was not at home. They went a second and a third time, always receiving the same answer. Caron could scarcely obtain permission to write a note in the lodge, which the portress promised to deliver after being bribed.

"Confess, M. Falconet," said Beaumarchais, "that it is strange that an interview is denied to him whose cause he is to conduct. You will see that again access will be refused to-morrow. He is particularly interested, beyond doubt, and would prefer the loss of my suit."

On the following morning Caron and his companions appeared, and again two hours later, with the same results. He really did not know what to do next, and went dejectedly to his sisters Margot and Claire, who lived in their own house in the Rue Percée, a property they had inherited from an aunt. While he was telling them of his troubles, one of their lodgers, M. Desrolles, entered and heard an account of the case in question. He remembered the bookseller Le Jay was the friend and publisher of Goesman, and, by losing no time in his application, could perhaps obtain an interview by means of Madame de Goesman. All begged Desrolles to do what he could, so he sent for Le Jay, who came; and, after a private conversation, the extraordin-

ary remark was made that money could purchase an audience. Beaumarchais could have cried aloud for joy, but he controlled himself, and pretended indignation.

"How can I give money to a member of Parliament, in order to obtain an interview, which M. Dufour of the Châtelet never refused me in both my former suits! I would be as much embarrassed to offer as he to accept it. Will it not seem as if I wished to bribe where I had the right to demand? Never!"

His friends all urged Caron not to lose the only chance remaining. "It cannot be called bribery," said Le Jay, "where the conditions of payment are all on the other side. I will make you certain of an audience immediately." He hastened to Madame de Goesman, accompanied by Desrolles. When they had left the house, Caron said, smilingly: "If they take money, my cause is not quite lost!"

Desrolles and Le Jay soon returned, and demanded two hundred louis d'ors for the kindness of the lady in obtaining an interview with her husband. Beaumarchais absolutely refused to pay so enormous a sum for what ought to be granted freely, but he was importuned by all present. "When you have lost one hundred thousand francs, will two hundred louis d'ors more or less make any difference? Even if five hundred were demanded, you ought not to hesitate a moment."

As the money was not at hand, M. Falconet went to Brunellerie to obtain it, and it was to be handed to Le Jay by Margot and Claire, as Beaumarchais had to return to the Bastile and ask permission of De Launay to be absent at night. Le Jay had told Caron, that if he called at the house of M. de Goesman about nine o'clock in the evening, and delivered a note to madame, written by the bookseller, he would be admitted. According to this agreement, Beaumarchais, Falconet, and Santerre, stood at the Quai de St. Paul at the hour appointed.

"The councillor is not at home for you!" cried the portress, in an insolent tone.

"My dear good woman," and Caron pressed a gold-piece into her hand, "only ask the valet of your mistress to come to me; I must deliver this note to him."

"Oh, that is another affair; wait a moment."

The valet de chambre appeared. "What do you wish, sir?"

"I only desire you to take this note immediately to your mistress, while I wait for an answer."

"Oh, sir," replied the servant, in some confusion, "I cannot do that. My master is in the cabinet, at supper with her."

"You are very simple; that just suits me. Therefore, be quick! My best compliments to them both."

Soon the servant returned. "You may go up into the apartment of my master; he will be there presently."

Beaumarchais and his companions followed the valet to the next floor, who showed them into a room and disappeared. After some time, heavy steps were heard. M. Brion de Goesman entered, wiping his thick lips with a napkin. He was short and stout in person, with a broad, red face, and turned-up nose. The servant brought a light, and placed it on a table, and then, catching the napkin which Brion threw at him, he withdrew.

"'Wh-which of you is the ac-accused?"

"I am, councillor, Caron de Beaumarchais."

"Who a-are these ge-gentlemen?"

"This is Solicitor Falconet, a friend whose advice I sought, as I could not have access to you; the other is the jailer Santerre. It is probably not unknown to you that his majesty's government think so highly of my person that they have sent me to the Bastile for safe-keeping."

"I-I ca-care nothing about that! What do you wi-wish to communicate to me? I know every thi-thing concerning your cause."

"I am very glad of that. You have then examined the sentence of both courts of the Châtelet, and are not ignorant of their justice."

"I know! You owe Cou-Count de la Bl-ache one hundred and f-f-ifty thousand f-f-rancs."

"I? I am astonished! Count de la Blache owes me fifteen thousand francs, as was proved by the investigation."

"I know all! The question is about a f-f-forgery in the books. There is a b-b-blot in the place, that is the mistake. I know all!"

"You know nothing, sir, if you will allow me to say so! You have not seen one letter of the deeds, and have restricted yourself to the two principal books, of which mine was declared correct, and that of M. Duverney (which was so long in the hands of the plaintiff) false. Will you permit me to inform you of all the points in the case?"

Goesman smiled contemptuously. "We-well, as you p-please! I know all!"

Beaumarchais drew forth his memorandum-book, and began to describe the course of the suit, emphasizing all those parts where forgery was plainly proved against the count's demands. When he had ended, Goesman rose. "I know all now! I know you we-well enough to give my opinion in your favor. The aff-f-fair is very simple, and I hope to give a just report to the tr-tribunal on Monday next. I bid you f-farewell!" Caron was about to make some further remarks, and Falconet to offer an explanation, but Goesman had already rung the bell. Two servants came; one took the light and preceded the councillor through an opposite door, the other was ready to show the way out to the clients.

When he had reached the street, Falconet exclaimed: "Your nerves must be like a lawyer's, to bear all that! This fellow knows nothing of your business; and such a man, in whom knavery and stupidity are united, is assigned you as an advocate!"

"Ha! ha! If the object is to make me lose my cause, no better defender could be found! I must have another audience, through Desrolles."

"Like this one? And again for two hundred louis d'ors?"

"And suppose I do? Tell every thing to Brunellerie, and drink a glass of water after this excitement. Good-night!" Beaumarchais laughed, and hastened away with Santerre.

On the following morning Caron met Falconet at his sisters'. Desrolles was called, and sent for Le Jay, who was to obtain another interview, by again bribing Madame de Goesman. It was the day preceding that on which the suit was to be decided. The accused handed to Desrolles the watch, set with diamonds and rubies, with which he had never parted even in his utmost need in the Pigeonnier. While the latter was absent, Brunellerie came; he had been to see Goesman, and was astonished at the councillor's ignorance, and indignant at his brutality. Brunellerie had offered ten louis d'ors to the secretary, but the honest man had refused them, saying that he could do nothing, as the case would be disposed of in the cabinet of his master without his assistance. An hour after, Desrolles returned with the tidings that Le Jay had presented the watch to the lady, who was highly delighted with it, promising that her husband should certainly receive M. de Beaumarchais

in the afternoon, if he would be so kind as to send fifteen louis d'ors for the secretary.

"The secretary? How does that agree with your report, Brunellerie?" Desrolles was sent back again to express the surprise of Caron. "Madame de Goesman," said the agent, "insists on the fifteen louis d'ors; she did not care or know what the secretary may have received from others—this sum she required for him."

Beaumarchais threw the money scornfully on the table. "Very well, let this go also! In the afternoon at three o'clock I shall be at the councillor's house." He went, but was refused admittance. This impudence enraged him. "Do you know, M. Desrolles," he exclaimed, when he returned to his sisters', "what I shall do, if I do not have an audience to-day? The name of M. de Goesman and his lady shall be conspicuous at all the street-corners in Paris; I swear that to you, as sure as I am no member of Parliament!"

Desrolles, pale as death, hurried away to Le Jay. The two men ran from one party to the other. Finally Desrolles returned with the report that Caron should call on the morning before the session. If he could then obtain no interview, the lady would send back all she had received.

"Oh, very well!" replied Beaumarchais, gloomily. "I thank you, M. Desrolles!" He paced the room silently and the agent withdrew. "Do you know what I deserve, Brunellerie?" he said, impetuously.

"You?"

"To be whipped like a schoolboy! I have committed the greatest error of my life, so much for blind passion! I wish I had only held my tongue before this Desrolles. The lady's avarice has received a shock. She will restore all to me, and I shall not only lose my suit, but be unable to accuse her and her husband of accepting bribes! I could almost tear myself to pieces!"

Beaumarchais* had played badly. Angry with himself, he returned to the prison, thinking for a long time, without finding an expedient. He discovered among his papers a copy of his communication with Goesman, and he was again tranquil. He sat down and wrote his first famous memorial, beginning: "*Mémoire à consulter pour Pierre-Augustin-Caron de Beaumarchais, écuyer, accusé.*" On the morrow the scandalous parliamentary drama would close, and all know whether as a tragedy or a comedy.

The morning of the 5th of April dawned. A cause was on that day to be decided, the importance of which was not imagined by those implicated. Beaumarchais went to his advocate with a written defence, which Goesman was only required to read to the court, but the councillor was not visible. Caron waited an hour and a half, and even the secretary vainly endeavored to gain the accused an entrance. All he could do was to hand the defence to Goesman. The day passed in sad expectation. Toward evening Desrolles brought the watch and money to the sisters of Beaumarchais. Brunellerie, who was present, assured himself that all was right, except a trifle—the fifteen louis d'ors were wanting which the lady had demanded for the secretary.

"Did she really not send them back?" asked Caron, who just then entered.

"That is a strange question, my dear friend," replied Brunellerie.

"Strange or not," laughed Beaumarchais, "if I am to pay one hundred and fifty thousand francs, I will, with these fifteen louis d'ors, blow up the Maupeau Parliament and my opponents, so that the explosion shall be heard from Dunkirk to Marseilles!"

On returning to the Bastile, he found the decision on the table of his cell. He was to pay one hundred and fifty thousand francs to Count de la Blache, and the costs of the three lawsuits. His enemies had conquered, and began publicly to say that Caron's attempt to cheat the count had been vain, and their success roused them to worse deeds of injustice against him.

Two weeks later it was announced to the prisoner that his second suit, in reference to the *Barber of Seville*, would be determined, and, as if in mockery, Goesman was again nominated his advocate. Seventeen days after the first verdict was pronounced, Madame de Goesman received a letter from Beaumarchais: "You were kind enough to restore my watch and the two rolls of gold; will you not also return to me the missing fifteen louis d'ors, which our mutual friend left with you?" The lady started; she remembered Caron's threats of posting her name, and she was angry against Le Jay, who had been her agent and confederate.

Had Beaumarchais sent the bookseller privately for the money, the affair might have been settled quietly; but the good woman understood enough of pettifoggers' tricks to see that the letter was only a challenge to a conflict in which she would lose her honor. To send him the sum now to the Bastile, and take a receipt for the same, would be proof convincing that she had accepted gifts, and give him the means of accusing her husband of bribery. She desired Le Jay to silence him, but her meaning was that the money should be paid to the sisters of Beaumarchais; as it was, however, to be sent publicly, she was ashamed, and did not send it at all. She showed the note to her husband. He hastened immediately with it to his patron, the Duke de Vrillière and to Sartines.

The duke informed Maupeau of the affair, and the lieutenant of police went with Goesman to Aiguillon, at whose mansion a soirée was in progress. When the minister heard it, he sent for Madame de Ventadour and the Duke d'Orleans, who were among the guests, to come to his cabinet.

"You are a perfect jewel, Goesman!" said Chartres. "This note is a good accusation against Beaumarchais, which may end in the galleys and branding."

"That is true! He can be prosecuted for slandering a member of Parliament!" smiled Orleans.

"Slander and attempt at bribery!—of dishonoring the Parliament and the government in the person of a royal advocate. Is not that next to high-treason?"

"Indeed!" interrupted Diana de Ventadour. "Aiguillon, you must procure the cross of St. Louis for Goesman in return for this letter. La Blache will console himself with the disgrace of the husband since he has lost the wife." Aiguillon nodded, offered his arm to the marchioness, and all returned to the company in very good-humor.

"Do you know, papa," said Chartres, "that I am sorry for this poor wretch Goesman? How Beaumarchais will trample on him!"

"Ha! ha! This Colmar blockhead and his thieving wife we must sacrifice to the lower deities, but Beaumarchais will be completely ruined!"

The third and most dreaded accusation menaced the prisoner. Hitherto his lawsuits had been of private affairs, but, by the new complaint of Goesman, a political and public significance was given to them. If Caron lost, his punishment would be that of a common criminal — the pillory and the galley. If he conquered, the justice of France, the Maupeau Parliament, and the whole corrupt government, would be dis-

graced. Then the process of La Blache would have to be revised, and the mask fall from Caron's foes. With the greatness of the struggle, the strength, courage, and coolness of Beaumarchais increased; now, when he was on the point of losing all, he felt that he should gain all! He finished his first memorial, and sent it by Santerre to Gauchat for publication. It produced immense excitement, being regarded as a theatrical prologue, that announces a startling action, or as the blast of a trumpet summoning to battle! His adversaries were astonished. They saw that he would defend himself in two ways. The pamphlet appeared without naming the printer or publisher, for Gauchat knew what he was about.

In the suit of Goesman against Beaumarchais, the plaintiff had but one witness—his wife. The defendant also proposed that lady as one of his witnesses, the others being his sisters, Le Jay, Desrolles, Falconet, Brunellerie, Santerre, and the secretary of Goesman. "Now the comedy begins!" cried Caron in delight. "Figaro, my boy, bring your shaving-basin, sharpen your razor — this is the time to do credit to your trade!"

The attention of all Paris was absorbed at the beginning of the proceedings. The general-procurator Vaucresson was the public accuser, Durier de Comartin was recorder, and Chazal the parliamentary commissioner who managed the case. The decision had to be made by vote in full parliamentary session. However servile the members were to the behests of the ministers, yet here they found it necessary to engage the best and most righteous jurists to oppose so dexterous a man as Beaumarchais. The examination of witnesses commenced. Le Jay, in great terror, at first insisted that he had received neither the fifteen louis d'ors, nor the watch, nor the two rolls of gold. Madame de Goesman was ill, and excused herself from the preliminary proceedings. Desrolles, fearful of being considered the thief, swore that he had given all to Le Jay, who had handed them to Madame de Goesman. The bookseller was perplexed; finally he said that it was true the watch and the rolls of gold had been received, but as to the fifteen louis d'ors he knew nothing. The secretary of Goesman denied having received any money from madame. She was obliged to appear and confront the other witnesses. For that day Beaumarchais selected the best toilet he had, appearing in the old hall of justice with the graceful smile of a courtier.

"Usher," said the commissioner, "ask Madame de Goesman to step in."

A whisper passed along the judges' bench when the messenger left the hall. All felt that the principal was coming, and that with her appearance was the real beginning of the suit. The door opened, and a lady entered, small and of dark complexion, very pretty, and about thirty-two years of age, wearing a flowered silk robe, which displayed her full shoulders. She wished to dazzle by her beauty as well as by her rank. In one hand she held a fan, and with the other she raised her long dress, so as to show a small foot encased in a high-heeled shoe. Proudly and confidently she threw back her head, cast a glance at the judges, and, without deigning to take any notice of Beaumarchais, bowed, while the precious stones in her rings, bracelets, and necklace, sparkled.

Amid profound silence Chazal began: "Madame, will you be kind enough to tell us your name?"

"I am Joceline Marguerite de Goesman, *née* Jamar, wife of the parliamentary councillor of his majesty, Brion de Goesman."

"Do you know this gentleman?" asked Chazal, indicating Caron.

The lady looked at the accused, and turned very red. "I neither do nor ever will know him."

"I have not the honor to be acquainted with madame, either," said Beaumarchais, bowing, "but while I look at her, I cannot help entertaining a very different wish." The judges smiled, and the lady was embarrassed.

"Have the goodness, madame," continued Chazel, "to have your complaint put in writing, if you have any, against this man Beaumarchais."

"Write," she replied, "that I accuse the gentleman of being my worst enemy, of having a mind capable of any baseness, as all Paris knows, and that he desires to render an honorable woman ridiculous."

"And I, on my side," said Caron, "have nothing with which to reproach this lady—not even the little ill-humor that animates her at this moment. I am only sorry that it is a criminal process in which I pay her my first homage. As to my base mind, I hope to convince her, by the respectfulness of my behavior and the moderation of my answers, that she has been misinformed. —You ought not to be afraid of me, fair lady."

"Afraid of you!" and she cast a scornful glance at him.

"Recorder," said Chazel, "read to madame the examination of the witnesses." The recorder did so. "What have you to reply to this, madame? Have you any explanation to make?"

"None at all, sir," she smiled. "What can I have to say to such absurdity?"

"I must tell you, madame," said Chazal, gravely, "that the evidence, which will be sworn to, is a serious matter, and no absurdity, as you are pleased to call it. Make your objections to whatever you consider false;

I am obliged to remark that you cannot make them later."

"Objections?—oh, yes! Write that I am not acquainted with any one called Le Jay, and that I know nothing of louis d'ors and watches."

"If you are not acquainted with M. le Jay, and know nothing of louis d'ors or a watch, gracious lady," smiled Caron, "it is proved that I cannot be suspected of having intended to bribe or slander your husband the councillor, therefore the letter of the 27th of April was sent you by mistake. I was deceived in this affair by two persons who obtained those articles from me by the use of your pure name.—Then, judges, I accuse Le Jay and Desrolles as guilty of fraud."

"I shall arrest both immediately and confront them with you, madame. The procurator will have to enter a special complaint against them," said Chazal.

"I will take the necessary measures," remarkd Vaucresson.

"No, no!—Yes!"—exclaimed the lady, in great excitement. "I meant something very different! Objections? Well, then, I mean that all the depositions of those persons and of this gentleman are false, and that they were prompted by others to make them!"

"Madame does not feel well," said Beaumarchais, "allow her to sit down!" He politely placed a chair for her. "I see," he continued, addressing her, "that you remember this part of your lesson, only you should have recited it at the proper.place. In the declarations are many points of which you cannot know whether they are true or false. As to being prompted, you have made a mistake. I am aware that I am considered as the head of a clique; this is on account of my former political activity, and you were probably told that I would school others as to their answers—not that I receive such suggestions. But, fair lady, do you really know nothing of that letter from Le Jay; which gained me an interview with M. de Goesman, as has been proved?"

"Yes, sir—wait a moment! Write, as to the so-called audience—the audience!" She endeavored to collect her thoughts, but her mind was confused.

Caron cast a long and significant glance at the judges, in whose features astonishment was visible. The recorder sat with his pen in his hand. Every one stared at the lady.

"Well, madame," Chazal began mildly, "what do you understand by the audience? Make sure of your ideas before you speak. Explain yourself fully, that your objections may be clearly noted."

"I mean," she said, vehemently, "that I do not trouble myself about the affairs of my husband, and attend only to my household! If this gentleman gave a letter to my valet, it must have been done from malice!" This statement was written down.

"Will you be kind enough to explain, madame," said Chazal, "what malice you find in the fact of a note being handed to a servant?"

She stammered and blushed. Suddenly she exclaimed, "If it be true that the gentleman took a letter to our house, to which of my attendants did he hand it?"

"To a young lackey, madame—a man of fair complexion, who said he was your valet de chambre!"

"That is a contradiction, ha! ha! Write that the gentleman gave a note to a fair-complexioned man; but my lackey is not so. What livery did he wear?"

"I really do not know what madame's special livery is."

"Oh, pray write that the gentleman who pretends he spoke to my servant does not even know my livery! I have two, one for the summer and another for the winter."

"Madame, I never intended to dispute that; I even think I remember that the valet in question wore a spring morning vest, for it was on the 3d of April. Pardon me if I do not express myself clearly. As it is natural that your servants, after your marriage, put off your former livery, in order to wear that of the noble house of Goesman, I could not know by their dress whether they belonged to monsieur or madame. I could only judge from the man's expressions on this most delicate point. Whether he was fair or not—whether he wore the Goesman livery or that of the Strasbourg Jamars—" The judges involuntarily laughed.

"Order in court!" thundered the usher.

"It remains, nevertheless, true," continued Beaumarchais, in a louder voice, "that, in presence of two irreproachable witnesses—Messrs. Falconet and Santerre—I handed a note to one of your lackeys on your staircase, written by M. le Jay, whom you do not know, and which the valet would not at first deliver, because, as he said, his master was at supper with madame! This letter he finally carried away, after I had attended to his scruples, and he brought us the reply: 'You may go to the apartment of monsieur; he will be with you soon.' It is remarkable that we went to the room; still more so, that M. de Goesman came to us; and, what is most remarkable of all, gave an audience in answer to a letter you never received, and written by a man you do not know!"

The judges sat motionless; and the silence was such that the lady's breathing could be heard. "All that babble has no meaning!" she cried, very angry, and violently fanning herself. "You and your witnesses did not follow my servant; so you cannot prove that he

15

delivered the note to me. I declare that I never received any note from this lackey or any other, and that I did not endeavor to obtain an audience for the accused! Record all I say!"

"O gracious lady!" exclaimed Caron, quickly. "It is much worse if you did not receive the letter from your servant, as it is proved I gave it to him, and my interview with M. de Goesman agrees with the verbal reply brought by this fair-featured valet. He must have handed the note to your husband, in which you were asked, in accordance with your agreement with Le Jay, to procure an audience for the bearer. We must then conclude that your husband, as inquisitive as he is gallant, fulfils the engagements his wife makes! I really have not the courage, madame, to say any more on that point. Do you decide who opened the note which gained the audience? If you insist that you did not, at least do not accuse me of having compromised M. Brion de Goesman, the parliamentary councillor of his majesty!"

There was a murmur of applause. Madame de Goesman sank back in her chair, covering her face with her fan. "M. Commissary," said Vaucresson, sulkily, "adjourn the court to-day; the lady is ill."

"Then read the proceedings," commanded Chazal. The judges seemed to make light of the depositions, and shook their heads.

"Is it possible, madame," said Beaumarchais, "that any one can place the defence of his honor and the secret of an intrigue in such hands as yours? Pardon me, I am not so much surprised at you as at those who placed you in this dangerous position!" He handed her the pen, that she might sign her name.

Madame de Goesman snatched it from Caron's hand. "And what," she asked, "is deduced from all that is written here ?"

"Oh, that you are a very charming woman, but have no memory. I shall have the honor to prove that to-morrow. It also shows that you are to be pitied in being here at all—you—the wife of a parliamentary councillor—for what ? *For fifteen louis d'ors !* "

<hr>

CHAPTER XXI.

IS THIS FRANCE?

MADAME DE GOESMAN had exposed herself to suspicion on the first day of her examination; but, on the second, the proof of her guilt became incontestable. The calmness and consistency of Beaumarchais, his apparent compliance, and the guilelessness of his questions, so confused the lady, that she was forced to confess she had received and still possessed the fifteen louis d'ors. When she found herself defeated, she became very angry, threatening Caron with violence. She was dismissed, for the judges had heard enough; Goesman had sold an interview with his client, and then purposely made him lose his suit. The proceedings were ended. It was plain that the slander of Beaumarchais against the councillor could not be established. To absolve the accused would be implicating the judges, to sentence him would excite to the utmost the universal indignation already active against the government.

The North American civil war, so long expected, had commenced. The phrases "democratic union," "federative republic," "liberty and equality," assisted by the roll of drums, aroused in the French nation a desire for freedom; the people had been prepared by a sort of mental independence long taught by the philosophers, and there began to glow a passion for national and civil redemption from the tyranny of the privileged classes. The *Éloge de Colbert*, by the financial minister Necker, showed the people how wealthy they had been under Louis the Great, and how impoverished they were now, as the state could scarcely pay its officials, the extravagances of the royal court absorbing its revenues.

Gauchat's press issued the second memorial of Beaumarchais, containing all the scandalous judiciary action, the conduct of Goesman and his wife, and a thorough investigation of the case in question. The public eagerly read the pamphlet, and the name of Goesman, as Caron had determined, became the scorn of every one; public opinion acquitted the accused before the Parliament could come to a decision.

Maupeau adopted another means of silencing Beaumarchais. He had just bought a defamatory poem on the life of the king, by Robin de Bauveset, for a yearly income of two thousand francs. Could not a similar arrangement be made with Beaumarchais ? Maupeau sent word to him, that if he would henceforth be silent, he should be liberated, and the process against him rendered null. Caron, who now had public opinion in his favor, saw his opponents entrapped, and, become aware of the power of his pen, replied that, if set at liberty, the process rendered void, and his suit with La Blache revised, he would be silent as long as his enemies. Beaumarchais left the Bastile a victor, after an imprisonment of six months, having concluded an armistice with his adversaries. He would gladly have quitted Paris, and gone toward the northern coast, where his wife was staying; but how could he? He would have been accused of cowardice; libels would again be rumored about him, if he withdrew before his suit was decided. He felt that the struggle was not yet over, and that to flee would be imprudent, inciting secret vengeance against him, and betraying the refuge of Susanna. He remained quietly in Paris, evading any questions about his wife. His first visit was to his father and sisters, and the second to the Hôtel Conti. The valet de chambre of the prince received him with surprise, and said that his highness was at the residence of M. de Penthièvre. He immediately went there, and had himself announced to the widowed princess, but he was detained long in the anteroom.

"They hesitate to see me! Such is patronage! If a man is unfortunate, he becomes suspected, and the noblest friend finds some excuse for suspending the acquaintance."

At last the servant led the visitor into the garden. " Yonder is his highness, promenading with the princess and the Countess de Gorzka."

Caron descended from the terrace and walked down the middle avenue where their highnesses were. It was plain they would rather not have received him. The princess and the countess averted their eyes, in order to avoid him, and, when Conti whispered a few words, they withdrew. The prince then approached with the coolness and politeness of a man of quality.

"You amaze me by your presence here. Probably you owe your liberty to your memorials, that, as well as others, I certainly admire. As you have sought me *here*, your petition must be urgent. What have you to say ? "

" I really find it difficult to know in what tone I am to answer your highness. You have so spoiled me that I can scarcely take the supplicant's position, into which you force me. No petition brought me here ; I was only ingenuous enough to think you would receive me as usual—as the Caron that exposes himself to danger, but not always for himself. I suppose, however, it requires considerable greatness of mind to have intercourse with a man still in the hands of a criminal court."

"We misunderstand each other," said Conti. "I have not forgotten your services, and on their account I once more received you. But when we found ourselves so sadly mistaken in you, sir—"

"How were you mistaken in me ? "

"In the purest and best respects—in what I esteemed, envied, and praised you before all men ! "

"And what is that ? "

"Your wife, Beaumarchais! I ask you, where is the woman you seemed to love so well ? "

Caron smiled. "Well taken care of, your highness."

" If at mention of her name you do not even start or blush, but smile, you must be the most shameless wretch that the sun ever shone upon."

"What do you know of my wife, that I should blush ? "

"I know where she is."

"I should be sorry for that, your highness ! However, I disquiet myself needlessly ; you do not know it."

"Do you think so ? " said Conti, in a tone of severity. "Then be kind enough to tell me what induced you to give your wife to Nassau-Siegen— the woman with whom you had lived happily so long—the companion of your youth and your adversity ? "

Beaumarchais was greatly astonished. "You speak plainly, my prince! Who told you that infamous falsehood ? "

"I was standing on yonder terrace when the regiment of Nassau defiled past the house. My own eyes, the princess, and the Countess de Gorzka, are witnesses that Susanna left Paris as a page wearing Siegen's colors, and marching under his standard."

"Madame de Lamballe saw her also? Then I owe both of you an explanation! Prince, if my secret were safer by your distrust, I would be silent, and content myself with the knowledge that my honor is untarnished. But, as the princess saw my wife, I must tell you all—not for poor Susanna's sake, but on account of my friend the prince, who loves Louise de Lamballe."

Conti laid his hand on Caron's shoulder, and looked steadily at him. "Nassau loves Louise? Beaumarchais, if I did you wrong, and thought ill of Susanna, may God forgive me! We have become so accustomed to evil, that we sometimes confound the true with the false. But who tells you that my niece loves the prince?"

"Who? I will prove it by a story I will relate to the princess."

"Well, then, come!"

When Louise saw the two gentlemen approaching, she stood hesitating. Indignation was in her countenance.

"Countess de Gorzka," said Conti, "be kind enough to retire for half an hour." Charlotte cast a long, questioning glance on them, and left the garden.

"Dearest uncle," said Louise, coldly, "as you have probably something special to say to me, would it not be better if we were alone?"

"I would only beg you, dear Louise, to listen to a story that M. de Beaumarchais wishes to relate."

"A story? I do not comprehend—"

"Yes, an incomprehensible one, your highness, the meaning of which can be fathomed only by a pure womanly mind which by its own sorrows has learned to sympathize with others' woe, and can separate truth from the mere appearance of it."

"I have no doubt I shall learn to admire the skill of a person who can perhaps influence others better because he is not governed by his own feelings."

"Perhaps," replied Beaumarchais, "those feel most who seem cold. It is sad but prudent to conceal our emotions from those who we believe cannot understand us."

Louise turned pale, and cast an uncertain glance at Conti. "Now, to your story, sir, since his highness desires it."

"I am acquainted with two men, madame—one a prince, brave and magnanimous, but poor and powerless, wandering around the world, and who, among thousands of admirers, has found but one friend. The other was also a child of adventure—a citizen without means, but rich in the love of his wife, who shared his scanty bread and wept with him in his poverty. The latter at last became wealthy, and esteemed at court, and love seemed to embolden him in all his enterprises. These men met at the house of a gentleman of rank, on the day he was marrying his only son to an illustrious lady whom the prince loved, but was too poor to woo! The two became friends for life—the citizen shared his possessions with the prince, that he might be enabled to leave the country, and be no more haunted by buried hopes. The lady was not happy; after a short and sad married life she became a widow. Her lover returned. He found his friend in prison, and his wife oppressed by unfeeling power. He saved her from shame, and gave her back his friend. Oh, he did more! The citizen was again seized by his enemies, hatred bound him in new chains, his poor wife was robbed of her chivalrous protector, for he was sent with his regiment to a distance, that she might become the prey of a libertine, and her husband sent to the galleys! The prisoner saw nothing but dishonor and ruin before him. Then the prince staked his own honor, the newly-awakened hope of his own love, and carried away the wife of his friend in the dress of a page, to preserve her from her persecutors; and he guarded her with the care of a brother! And this friendship, that drew upon the prince the contempt of the lady whom he loved, strengthened the unfortunate captive to overcome his foes and free himself. What could he do for the man who had risked all for him? The citizen went one day to this illustrious lady, and, at her feet, confessed all!" He fell on his knees, and pressed the hand of the princess to his lips.

"O Heaven, what have I done! Sir —ah, pardon me!" Louise trembled and wept happy tears;-she had forgotten the presence of Conti. Blushing, she raised Caron.

"Well, my prince?" asked Beaumarchais, smiling.

Conti approached gently, embraced his niece and kissed her glowing cheek. "Louise, you were unhappy in your first marriage; be assured I will endeavor to make amends." She concealed her face on the breast of her venerable uncle. She was happy for the first time since she left Chambery. Caron whispered:

"O Liebe, zieh mit mir auf duft'gem Rosennachen
Durch Sturm und Sonnenschein. Am fernen Küstensaum
Erglühen schon im Grün die stillen Wonnematten,
Wo Glück und Friede sich mit Ros' und Myrte gatten!"

Beaumarchais conscientiously fulfilled his promise, and remained quiet for several months. Yet he could not obtain a decision in his suit. On the other hand, his patience was sadly tried. Scarcely was the first excitement allayed which his second memorial had produced, when his adversaries endeavored to turn public opinion against him. Numerous pamphlets appeared, and, taking occasion of his silence, the most disgraceful reports were disseminated about him. It was published that he had been married three times; that all his wives died mysteriously, each leaving him a large fortune, and indicating that poison was probably the method used to destroy them. Another rumor was, that he had sold Susanna to a nobleman for a landed estate. He replied in the *Mercure Français* with the indignation of a just and injured man. Pointing directly to the originators of the calumnies, he said: "Those persons who are continually attempting to defile my name and honor, should remember that their friends of the Rues du Petit Bourbon, Garancière, and the Palais-Royal, know better than I about the use of a certain phial, and that it is evidence of my charitable disposition in not recounting facts to the public that would make them shudder more than all the slanders of a concealed scribbler, whose only capital is falsehood, from which stupidity draws the interest."

Caron's temper was not improved by the delay of the Parliament. He felt every social insult the more, because he had no indemnification at home for the malice of the world. Morelly came to see him often enough, but both now felt and thought differently.— Beaumarchais could not bear the liberals by whom Morelly was surrounded, such as Tolendal, Condorcet, and Anacharsis Cloots; and they, on their side, regarded him as a fortune-hunter—an intriguer, puffed up by wealth and court favor; besides, none of them were in a position to assist him against his powerful enemies.

In January, 1774, Beaumarchais heard from Brunellerie and his family of a new baseness of his opponents. A letter was circulating in Paris, purporting to be from a Spaniard, a relative of Don Joseph Clavijo, compromising Caron and his sisters in Spain, in a discreditable manner. The affair of 1764 was distorted so that Marie, the sister of Caron, appeared as the mistress of Clavijo, and Beaumarchais himself as a profligate, and even as a thief. All this was asserted so confidently, that even the kindliest persons shuddered lest some accident should bring them in contact with him. He was deprived of the office of professor to the princesses, though at that time merely nominal. Marie Antoinette openly declared that she would desist from her desire of having the *Barber of Seville* acted, and did not wish to hear any thing more of it. Men of rank, like Richelieu, Luynes, and Penthièvre, requested him to discontinue his visits. His old father was avoided by his fellow-citizens and neighbors, as if he were a leper. Only one man, Conti, believed in the innocence of the poet, but that man could not brave the popular opinion. In vain did Beaumarchais endeavor to obtain possession of the letter so cruelly misrepresenting him and his sisters, and discover the author of it. He was like one persecuted by the Furies, when Marin dared to print the letter, with a rancorous commentary, in the *Gazette de France.*

"A new memorial!" exclaimed Beaumarchais, wildly. He wrote it in one night, with the calumniating sheet before him. It surpassed the two preceding pamphlets in courage, satire, and overwhelming power, indicating the possession of secrets respecting La Blache, Madame de Ventadour, and the Orleans, but secrets which he would not at present reveal. He criticised the Maupeau Parliament and the ministers in an unheard-of manner, made statements that others scarcely dared to think, and refuted the slanders in circulation against him, by publishing the autograph letters of Clavijo, the Spanish minister, and the French ambassador at Madrid, the Duke d'Ossun, and closed his pamphlet thus: "What has become

of the France of Colbert and Sully—the France that Heny IV. and Louis XIV. made the first nation on earth? While America is breaking its chains, and the sound is wafted over the ocean as a *mene tekel,* Frenchmen are dragged to the Bastile by a *lettre de cachet!* While justice is denied, and high-sounding falsehood and illustrious vices increase the misery of the country, calumny, like a bandit, plies its trade on the open highway! Say not, because all has been taken from me, that I am without conscience! Consider me as a criminal, an intriguer, a dishonorable man, if you can; but to what evil-doer was justice ever denied as it has been to me? What institutions of what state ever protracted a cause, in order to let the accused die gradually of the leprosy of public disgrace, except the Maupeau Parliament! I have a right to demand a hearing, to be judged as a Frenchman, who is neither a helot nor the slave of such a privileged aristocrat as would insist on his *jus primæ noctis!* I appeal to you, citizens, to God, to the nation! I demand my right—the right of an independent citizen!"

Twenty thousand copies of this memorial were disseminated throughout France, throwing Voltaire and Rousseau's writings into the shade. The philosopher of Ferney wrote a congratulatory letter to Beaumarchais, and Marie Antoinette expressed her sympathy through the Princess de Lamballe. All those who were adverse to the government were awakened as by a clap of thunder.

What was to be done with this terrible man? The opposing clique had gone too far to remain quiet. They must add injustice to injustice, in order to silence him. He was not again sent to the Bastile, it is true, but secret policemen were posted around the Hôtel Piron to prevent his escape. His pamphlets were publicly burned by the executioner in front of the gray Palace of Justice, at the foot of the Bartholomew steps; he was forbidden to write any more; all publishers, booksellers, printers, antiquaries, and colporteurs of Paris, were admonished not to multiply or publish any of the works of Beaumarchais, unless they desired to be imprisoned. Of course, all this had reference to another process, in which Caron would be accused of high-treason.

It was toward the end of April; more than a year had passed since Susanna fled under Nassau's protection. The old garret at the Pigeonnier was as desolate-looking as ever, with its partition standing in the corner. The same musical sounds were heard from the adjoining room; for Batyl still resided there, though he was doing well, and had saved money; but, as his patrons La Blache and Orleans requested him, he was contented to remain. In order to enliven his solitary life, he had married a chorus-singer of the opera—a fury named Apollina Bonfiant, who knew how to manage him as she wished. A different spirit ruled here now. The space near the door was empty, except that a few boxes and old trunks stood near the walls, and rags, straw, coverlets, and mattresses lying around, indicated that some persons slept at night on the floor. In the background was a large round table, covered with a rather costly cloth, bearing numerous wine-stains. On it was a strange medley of books and papers, champagne and claret bottles, some partly filled, and others empty, plates, silver knives and forks, tin spoons, pieces of coarse pot-ware, heavy silver goblets, with coats-of-arms, glasses of various shapes and sizes, more or less valuable. Those present were seated round the table on stools, chairs, and boxes. It was evening, and candles in empty bottles threw an uncertain light in the large garret. A number of lances, pikes, and halberds, tied together with broad red bands, stood behind the principal personage. The points of these weapons were united, and surmounted by a red woollen cap with ear-lappets. Swords and guns, some of them rare and expensive, were fastened to the beams, and on the whitewashed wall three words were written with charcoal: "*Liberté! Égalité! Fraternité!*"

The society here assembled, at whose extravagant speeches and gestures the venerable Morelly shakes his head, call themselves the "friends of the people," of whom not one but Morelly is of citizen rank. There are three counts and a marquis, who seem to admire the brawling doctrines scrawled over their heads—the apostles of the approaching revolution, of whom but one is destined to die a natural death. Yonder short, stout man with the long reddish hair, large jaw, sharp nose, and broad forehead, is the German Count von Cloots, called Anacharsis, a genius out of order, crazy in philosophy and ancient literature. The one next him is Lally Tolendal, who cannot forget the disgraceful death of his father. That other one is Condorcet, twenty-nine years old, rigid and emotionless, like his favorite science, mathematics. The last is Count Mirabeau, a man of twenty-two, who formerly was obliged to flee from the persecutions of his father, because he had eloped with and married against his parent's will Mlle. de Marignan, and was again seeking a hiding-place, for he had repudiated her as an unfaithful wife. Apollina, that tall, gross woman, with small sparkling eyes, and black hair thrown back in disorder, waits on the company, supplying them with pipes and wine, or sometimes sitting down near Cloots, to listen with apparent interest to the conversation.

"You see how matters are working into our hands; even that fallen fortune-hunter Beaumarchais!" said Anacharsis in a loud voice, "America is throwing off the yoke of Great Britain; the lazy whigs are awaking; avaricious England, deprived of her colonies, will cast her lords and kings overboard! We only require a few years more of the present administration, and France will be in flames, destroying throne and altar. Germany, my native land, will be swept into the current, and a universal republic is the result! Away with dogmas and empty dreams! we must work and prepare the people, that all may have one will and one hand, to annihilate aristocratic privileges and the reign of mammon!"

"But nations, races, and languages, will always exist," said Mirabeau. "Education will always separate the Frenchman from the Sclavonian, the German from the Italian. You cannot advance without civilization and its wars."

"And rebuild the edifice of different classes, officials, and local courts, the evils of the former state!" laughed Cloots. "There ought to be no single nation—no native land. That is what ruined Rome! Man must live free, giving sway to every passion, unhindered by the ties of home, parents, or children, and in contempt of daily labor! I know but one limit, and we must attain it, for the freedom and equality of all. Man is the lord of the world—the only governing deity! Let humanity be our nation, and the earth our fatherland!"

"You are right," replied Condorcet, "and that is the object of our labors. Even Morelly, who first entertained the idea of humanity as it should be, accepts the necessity of its organization and of laws to control it. France or America will open the dance; what follows is hidden in the future. We must first think of our own affairs before we can attend to those of mankind in general."

"And blood must be shed to destroy this tyranny!" cried Lally. "The Bourbons must fall, the aristocracy, and the priests; an iron government must perish by iron! The watchword is to avenge the tears of the oppressed and innocent, and we must faithfully adopt it!"

"Down with the Bourbons!" they all cried.

"Then God grant that I do not live to see it!" said Morelly. "I have tried to build a temple of brotherly love, but you begin with hate!"

"Hatred is a fire that purifies the corruptions of time," laughed Mirabeau.

"In its glow," added Cloots, "liberty will become hardened, and the virtue of Cato, Socrates, and Lycurgus, be regenerated!—Pour out the wine, good woman; on the day of the battle Apollina shall be my Minerva, crowned with laurels."

"A conflict is approaching, and to seek warriors is our first duty!" said Mirabeau. "I am now as a hunted deer, and can do nothing; but you, who are at liberty in Paris, must lay the trains, form associations in all quarters of the city, making them at the same time an asylum for the victims of persecution."

"Oppression increases our hatred," said Tolendal; "it enlarges and energizes our influence; like an avalanche, we shall some day crush all in our path."

"That is my idea!" replied Cloots. "I have spoken to many people that think as we do; such as Danton, Couthon, and Marat. The men will assemble at the right moment, when the call of liberty has no uncertain tone."

Thus this society expressed freely their opinions, for the truth of which they had no other guaranty than their discontent, and the desire that a national catastrophe would come.

As the front door was locked, and hung with a thick mat, to prevent any sound from being heard outside, and the party supposed themselves safe, they did not notice that the side-door leading to Batyl's room was gradually opening.

"Who left that door open?" Apollina exclaimed, suddenly. "Some one stands behind it! Bring a light!"

All sprang up in alarm; Tolendal snatched a sword from the wall, and Cloots drew a pocket-pistol. A tall form in a cloak slowly emerged from behind the door, and a second remained in the doorway.

"What do you wish? How did you gain admittance here?" and Anarcharsis threateningly advanced toward the stranger.

"I came to see M. Morelly."

"I am he," said the old man, approaching calmly.

"Allow the most zealous of your disciples to salute you, the author of the *Basiliade*! I have long desired to make your acquaintance." The newcomer dropped his mantle.

Morelly retreated distrustfully. "You show me an honor to which I have never pretended. Why do you lay that work to my account?"

"But who are you?" asked Condorcet, bringing the light to shine on the features of the stranger.

"Like you, I am a friend of the people!"

"A friend of the people?" exclaimed, Morelly, bitterly. "You, monseigneur? How long has the son of Orleans been friendly to the oppressed?"

"Orleans? His son!" cried the others.

"Yes," said Morelly, coldly, "it is the Prince de Chartres."

Fear as well as surprise made all si-lent. Tolendal grasped his sword closer and moved toward Chartres, who stepped backward, cocking a pistol he held in his hand.

"You see, gentleman, I am prepared. The report of fire-arms would call up those I brought with me as a guard. No one, of course, would visit you without taking precautionary measures. You know faces well, M. Morelly. I am Philip de Chartres. I come seriously to express my admiration for the author of the *Basiliade* and the *Book of Laws*, and to ask him to receive me among his pupils. Banish all suspicion: we are evidently approaching a revolution of the state—only a blind man can deny it. I will be the first of my rank that pays homage to the new order of things,"

"You, monseigneur!" replied Condorcet, sarcastically.

"As openly as certain persons that await the decisive hour, while hiding in their dens, who appear in every seditious commotion, incite the multitude, and then vanish again."

"Prince, we do not understand you!" said Tolendal, "but one thing is certain, you shall not escape to betray us!"

"You excite yourselves unnecessarily, my friends. It may appear extraordinary that a man like myself forgets his rank and blood, in order to devote himself to the liberty of his native land, but the times we live in are extraordinary. I come to you as sympathizing with your opinions, offering you my assistance and protection, and you must acknowledge that I have more to lose than you."

"Sir!" exclaimed Morelly, shocked, "that is unnatural! I know the character of your father well enough not to be certain that the son will be faithful to no cause that does not agree with his dangerous ambition. If in this place we think and act contrary to the laws, we do it at least with a pure heart, with an indignation rendered sacred by the misfortunes of innocence. But what induces you, a prince, to unite with persons of our views? It is the hatred of the Orleans against the Bourbons, envy against those of your own blood! If you really love our wretched France—if you wish to save it from approaching danger—ally with your equals! Attach yourself to your cousin the dauphin, who will one day be king; cast Madame du Barry and the ministers from the vicinity of a desecrated throne, and raise up the right again. Yonder is the field of your labor—undoubtedly not here in our society!"

"Why should he not love liberty?" said Cloots. "Because he is a prince? By no means; did we not cast from us crests, titles, fortune—all the boast of our birth, to serve virtue and freedom? We are noblemen."

"I tell you," said Morelly, placing his hand on his breast, "I will have nothing to do with Orleans; and, if you trust him, you become the slave of his plans. I would warn you against him with my last breath!" The rest were silent, for the distrustful expression of the venerable man's features and his words strengthened their suspicion.

"And so you refuse my friendship because I am a prince? Have you done half as much for the cause of the people as I am ready to do? You say, Morelly, that I act from hatred. Are you acting from love? Oh, you philosophers, who remain doubtful of any existing morality! What urges you to the conflict? Have your passions, misfortunes, and personal advantage no part in it? When liberty has once triumphed what difference does it make as to the means used? If you insist on examining the motive of each combatant, you have but few followers; it is

beyond doubt that passion leads to victory!"

"Leave this place, prince!" exclaimed Morelly, impetuously. "We do not desire your presence!"

"Do you call yourselves politicians and refuse an alliance? Well, take your choice. I can either serve or harm you. I did not come here without having the means of arresting you. Then, you understand, I will have done the king good service. I know you all: Tolendal, Condorcet, Cloots, Mirabeau: I have watched you gliding in and out of this hole—I know with whom you are in association, and you cannot move one step without having my agents after you and your friends. I will warn you of danger, assist you with money, and, when the time comes, supply you with arms. Only by my help can you organize against the reigning tyranny. The Palais-Royal shall be a safe asylum for you. I ask nothing but that you trust me as I do you. Decide!" Morelly seated himself near the table, leaning his head on his hand.

"Very well," said Cloots, gloomily; "we will accept your friendship, since we cannot avoid it. Do you swear to serve liberty, fraternity, and equality, or expose yourself to the danger of losing your life?"

"I swear it!"

"Do you also swear destruction to royalty, aristocracy, and the immoral priesthood?—annihilation to all privileges of the higher classes?"

"I will destroy them, by my life! The republic of free Frenchmen shall undoubtedly rival that of Rome or Sparta!"

"Well, then, give him your hands, he is one of us!"

"I decline to give him mine!" said Morelly.

"Leave the dreamer alone," said Mirabeau; "age makes him timid.—And what would you be called among us,

Chartres ? for now you are no more than any other man."

"Call him Philip Égalité!" exclaimed Cloots. "That will be a sign that in him the first prince on earth has become the equal of the meanest citizen."

"Yes, let my name be Philip Égalité!" responded Chartres. They then shook hands.

"Accept this Phrygian cap!" said Cloots, taking the red cap from the pikes and placing it on the prince's head. "It was an insignum of ancient Rome. Let it adorn you on the day of liberty!"

"It shall, and at my death!" Philip took the cap, kissed and placed it in his bosom. "Until then it shall rest on my heart! Farewell! This man is my friend Sillery; he is also one of us, and will inform you when we meet again." The two visitors immediately withdrew.

All were silent in the garret. They felt as if awakening from a dream. "Do you know," began Morelly, after a long pause, "that we are in his hands? It is certain he has long been on our track, and that Coralie Raucourt has been watching us. That rascal Batyl gave him admission."

"But he will not betray us," said Condorcet; "I have seen through his dark mind. What will he gain by bringing a few unknown men to the scaffold or galley? He intends to make use of us in his ambitious views, and, so long as we are of advantage to him, he will be faithful."

"And then destroy us!" said Morelly.

"Therefore," interrupted Cloots, "he must be entangled in our plans; he must become a traitor to royalty, and be the slave, not the master, of the revolution."

"Does he intend to play the part of Julius Cæsar?" asked Tolendal, gloom-

ily. "By the fates, he may find his Brutus!"

"Henceforth, the Pigeonnier is no longer a hiding-place for us; we can only use it to meet 'Égalité,'" said Anarcharsis. "I must depart immediately.—One word, Apollina, my girl: you must avenge us on Batyl!" He hastened into the adjoining room, followed by the woman. Mirabeau drank several glasses of wine, and then threw himself on the straw, placing his pistol beside him. "I will write to 'Égalité,'—he must force my father to abstain from further persecutions against me!"

Morelly was alone with Condorcet and Tolendal. "There is no escape," murmured the old man—"no salvation! We must go to Beaumarchais to-morrow; he has still some connections, and is rich in expedients; he may advise us. He has never deceived me, and the distressed should not be unfriendly."

"Yes," replied Condorcet, "did you not say that Conti, the dauphin's right hand, is Caron's patron ? At least we shall not be entirely in the hands of 'M. Égalité!'" Lally and Condorcet left.

"Must blood and destruction always be the means of regenerating nations ?" said Morelly to himself. "Must all, whether bond or free, be deceived? Let me sleep, poor old man; perhaps I shall not awake to the terrible morrow!"

On the following day Morelly, Condorcet, and Tolendal, hastened to Beaumarchais, to seek assistance from one who was himself surrounded by enemies. These friends, knowing that Caron was sought after by spies, and that the Rue Fauconnier, St. Paul, and the Quai des Ormes, were patrolled by disguised policemen, took care not to talk of him on the way, and, entering the obscurer wing of the mansion, were announced to Madame de Piron. The lady's age had made her cautious, if not distrustful, and Caron's present position was not agreeable to her, so that it was difficult to gain access; but when she heard Morelly's name, and remembered the happy days she had spent at the little parsonage in Trianon, she received him. He begged her to let him pass to his friend through her apartments.

"M. Abbé, spare an old woman, who wishes to have no more intercourse with the world, from doing any thing that might be considered unlawful. Since Madame Susanna disappeared in such a remarkable, not to say disgraceful manner, I shall be glad when M. de Beaumarchais has left my house, which is always watched by the police. If you must see him, go through yonder glass door, across the terrace and the garden. I have nothing further to do with him."

"I thank you," replied Morelly, in a melancholy tone. "It is nothing new for me to know that the misfortunes of others often harden hearts otherwise kind and good."

The three men reached the apartments of Beaumarchais. He was standing on the terrace, where they had so often met with Turgot, Malesherbes, and the deceased Piron. Caron was looking dreamily at the deserted walks, and the trees just beginning to put forth their early blossoms. He was startled when he saw his visitors, and went anxiously to meet them.

"I pray you, Morelly, how can you venture here? Are you determined to be sent to the Bastile? Do you not know that I am in great danger, and that to-day my sentence is to be pronounced? I was taking leave of these familiar places, where for many years I was so happy!" He entered the sitting-room with them. "What is the object of your visit?"

"Your advice, and perhaps your assistance!" replied Tolendal.

"My assistance? Ha! ha! That is like asking a miserable beggar for money."

"Last night, while we were together with Cloots and Mirabeau, Chartres and Sillery suddenly appeared!"

"Chartres, the son of Orleans!"

"Batyl betrayed us to him. He gave us the choice, either to fall into the hands of the police, or receive him as an associate!"

"Oh, I understand him very well! He thinks the national disease, promoted by himself and his father, has reached its crisis—that we are all ready for rebellion. Orleans and his son wish to be the physicians, you are the instruments in their hands, and their reward will be the throne of the Bourbons!"

"They may err!" replied Condorcet. "The revolution of which they make use will free us, and give the power to avenge liberty on Chartres, should he touch it!"

"Do not think," said Beaumarchais, shaking his head, "to outwit them. I have fought them during my whole life, and now they have conquered me. In all that happens to us I see their hand."

"Do you advise me to go to Conti and have a consultation with him?" asked Morelly.

"So long as Conti is powerless and you have no proof, it is useless. Suppose Chartres should say that he merely visited you to ascertain your intentions and save the state from demagogues? Alas, you are in his hands, and I have no power to save you!"

A noise was heard in the anteroom; Caron started. Gomez entered hastily. "The decision has been made, sir!" he said, "they are coming! The front court-yard and the Rue Fauconnier are guarded by police; Sartines has just arrived, but they seem to be waiting for some one."

"Waiting? For what, for whom? Discover why they delay! When I am led off, you must depart immediately with my baggage."

"Immediately!"

"To my wife, at Calais; in St. Omer you will meet the Prince von Nassau-Siegen."

"You may depend on me, sir!"

"Away! do not let us be surprised by them." Gomez rushed out. "You see the state of affairs!" said Beaumarchais, locking the door. "Come back to the garden saloon, my friends; you can step into the bow-windowed room and witness what is done. You cannot leave the house until the police are gone." Gomez endeavored to open the door from the outside, but, when he found it locked, he rapped violently.

"What is it?"

"The Dukes d'Orleans and de Chartres, with a parliamentary councillor, are just descending from a carriage."

"They are? Then I begin to have some hope! I do not consider myself lost! Farewell, Gomez. Go to your room, and may God reward your fidelity!"

"May He protect you, dear master!" cried the valet, and slowly went down the stairs.

Caron returned to the garden saloon. "The two Orleans!" He smiled. "I believe my former good fortune is restored to me; it is very well that you are here."

"What do you mean?" asked Tolendal, astonished.

"You will soon see. I hope you will show yourselves *men* at the decisive moment. Quick, go into the adjoining apartment, draw the portière—I hear them at the front door."

Morelly, Tolendal, and Condorcet slipped into the room, where they were concealed by the curtain. Beaumar-

chais glanced around, and then laughed ironically, going into the sitting-room, at the door of which the police were knocking.

"Open the door, in the name of the Parliament!" cried the voice of Sartines.

Caron unlocked it. "Ah, gentlemen, are you here at last? I was dozing a little; pardon my inattention!"

The General-procurator Vaucresson, in his red robe and high mortier, entered, accompanied by the two princes. Sartines and his armed guard were stationed at the threshold.

"Are you Caron de Beaumarchais?" began Vaucresson.

"It would be more agreeable to me to be some one else precisely at this moment."

"You were told that your sentence would be finally pronounced to-day, and I, the procurator, have received orders to communicate it to you." He unrolled the document: "'Transacted at a session of the Parliament, being the highest court of justice, Paris, April the 26th, 1774.—Pierre-Augustin-Caron de Beaumarchais, accused and convicted of having slandered and attempted to bribe a member of Parliament; also of having, by his blasphemous writings (notwithstanding the prohibition, and by evading the Board of Censure), calumniated, disgraced, and dishonored the king's majesty, the ministry, the Parliament, and the laws of this land, is sentenced, by the joint decision of this high tribunal, to be publicly branded on the Place Grève in Paris; to be deprived of his nobility, fortune, and civil honor, and to be sent to Rochette to labor in the galleys! In the name of the Triune God, the King, and the Parliament, be it done!'—Thus I deliver you, Caron Beaumarchais, by virtue of my office and this sentence, into the hands of M. de Sartines, lieutenant of his majesty's police, that he may execute the decree of justice against you.'"

Vaucresson was turning away; Sartines placed his hand on the shoulder of Beaumarchais, when the latter roused himself. "M. Procurator, I have still an appeal to the king, and at least six months' time at my disposal, have I not?"

"To the king? Do you dare to appeal to his majesty?" exclaimed Vaucresson. "Very well! You only delay the punishment, for you know you have no mercy to expect. Begin your appeal within six months; but, as we foresaw this, you are ordered to the Bastile until then. The publication of the sentence will, however, not be retarded!" He cast a glance at Sartines and the princes, and withdrew with the ushers.

"I should not have thought that the Duke d'Orleans and his son took so much interest in my fate!" laughed Beaumarchais, sarcastically.

"Because you consider us your worst enemies," replied Orleans, coldly. "But you are mistaken. In this terrible hour we wish to offer you our protection, and save you from disgrace, if you consent to our conditions." He made a motion to Sartines to retire with his men.

"I knew matters could not be so bad as they looked!" murmured Caron to himself. "Monseigneur," turning to Orleans, "since you wish to have an interview with me, let us step into the garden saloon; we may have many things to say that we would rather not let M. de Sartines hear."

Orleans smiled and nodded, then walked into the adjoining apartment with Chartres. Beaumarchais followed, and while the princes took seats on the sofa, he found an opportunity of locking the door unperceived. He glanced at the portière and advanced toward them.

"Now, my most dexterous of dexterous men, my mad Beaumarchais," laughed Orleans, "are you at last in our power? I suppose you remember our meeting at the wedding festival of the Princess de Lamballe? I prophesied that you could not escape us, and you see I was right. I have great respect for your talent for intrigue; you acted against us as no other man ever will act, but you did not know that you were aiding us, and becoming more entangled in the net we had spread around you. I wish simply to say to you that you have your choice between the galleys and freedom, for your appeal will do you no good. I have a ministerial decree of Aiguillon and Maupeau in my pocket, changing your punishment to exile for life. Sartines has secret orders to escort you to any seaport you may select. This will be done if you bind yourself by a written promise to go to England as my agent and act according to my directions. If you refuse, you have the other alternative—the galleys and public branding! You see that you are dependent on my favor. You must be my servant, whose brain I will use as I please, and who, to escape one galley, shall labor in another as the slave of Orleans, who intends to reach some day the throne of the Bourbons!"

"Ha! ha!" cried Chartres, merrily, and both father and son shook with delight at their success.

Beaumarchais bent his head and stepped back. "And do your highnesses compel me to such an intolerable humiliation?"

"Yes, my friend," laughed Chartres. "You have five minutes to write the agreement which sells your intellect to us. You have always been a spy, as you well know!"

Caron was glowing with suppressed anger. He went to his secretary, opened it, and slowly placed pen, ink, and paper in readiness; then he pressed a secret spring, a drawer opened, and two pistols were in a moment in his hand. "Now, M. Philip Égalité," he said, "let us hold a revolutionary session! Advance, friends of the people from the Pigeonnier! Appear!"

The princes leaped to their feet. Orleans rushed to the door, which he found locked. Morelly, Tolendal, and Condorcet advanced from behind the curtain. The dukes seized their swords.

"And are we now equal in the conflict?" said Beaumarchais. "O Lally and Condorcet, you eloquent Spartans, you athletes and fighters about phrases, have you mind enough to see now what these Orleans people are—have you hatred enough to shoot them down for the good of your native land? Take this pistol, Tolendal, son of an innocently-murdered man; draw, Condorcet, and prepare yourself! Shall we be made slaves against our will? The culprit condemned to the galley, dictates to you, Messrs. Orleans—you shall be our vassals! Yonder are paper, pen, and ink. Write what I command you, M. Égalité, or, by all that is sacred, your blood shall flow about my feet. Go, sir, and write precisely as I dictate!"

Tolendal and Condorcet passed around the heavy Orleans and deprived him of his sword. Beaumarchais grasped Chartres, who dropped his weapon. "Do not dare to make an outcry; for if Sartines breaks in the door, you shall both be slain!" Caron drew Chartres toward the secretary. "Sit down and write!" The prince obeyed in silence.

"'I, Prince Philip de Chartres, son of the Duke d'Orleans, of the blood of the Bourbons, acknowledge hereby that yesterday I voluntarily joined the association of the friends of the people, took the name of Philip Égalité, and swore to destroy the Bourbon race, the aristocracy, the priesthood, and the privileged classes; to establish a republic in France on the foundations of liberty, equality, and fraternity, and to do this with all the ability and power of my family!'—Now, sign it! Give me your signet-ring as a pledge!" The prince drew it slowly from his finger. Caron put it in his pocket together with the paper.

"Now, duke, I beg you for the decree of banishment!" Orleans gave it, gnashing his teeth. "You will both go with these gentlemen across the terrace, and leave the house through the apartments of Madame de Piron. I will say but one thing more, monseigneur. So long as you and your son remain quiet, neither harming nor endangering the inhabitants of the garret of the Pigeonnier, and undertake no evil against the reigning royal race, I will make no use of this document." Caron unlocked the garden door. "Farewell, my friends, you shall hear further from me!"

The princes and the "friends of the people" withdrew. Beaumarchais now opened the sitting-room and called Sartines. "M. Lieutenant, you see that I hold in my hand the decree of banishment. I am going to Calais, thence to England. My valet Gomez will accompany me."

"H'm! I see you have made some arrangements with their highnesses. Where are they?"

"They did not wish to leave the mansion in my company, and went through the apartments of Madame de Piron."

"Very well, the carriage is ready; let us go."

Gomez was called, and the baggage of Beaumarchais placed on the coach. Two mounted police-guards escorted him. He departed by the gate St. Honoré, toward the north. At the next station he took extra horses, travelling day and night. At St. Omer he met Nassau, with whom he immediately left for Calais. When he entered the house in which Susanna dwelt, he embraced her with a shout of joy.

"O my dear husband, do I see you again; are you free?"

"Yes, but an exile. We are going to England, my child; but I have brought with me two treasures: for you, prince, the sincere love of Louise de Lamballe; for myself, that which will destroy the malice of the Orleans. Yes, Susie, during my leisure I intend to write the 'Wedding of Figaro,' and how he abolished the abominable privilege of the nobles."

BOOK IV.

CHAPTER XXII.

LOUIS THE LIBERATOR.

WHILE Beaumarchais, a man of such intellect and self-possession, escaped to England with Susanna, the sentence against him was published by the Maupeau Parliament: "branding, loss of fortune, and the galleys!" It was a farce, and at the same time a political stupidity; for the punishment was meliorated to banishment, and in other countries he lost no respect. Strict orders were given to the officers on duty at the boundaries to prevent his return. It was natural that this unexpected and unprecedented sentence should cause universal indignation—a revolt against its injustice, and a sense of insecurity in all circles. The government had stigmatized itself, and the last remains of habitual devotedness were uprooted from the hearts of the people. It seemed as if the blow must soon be struck which would annihilate this unfeeling and immoral of all public authorities, the Parliament.

Orleans and Chartres, outwitted by Caron in the moment of their triumph, unmasked and silenced when they expected to have absolute power over him, returned humiliated to the Palais-Royal, compelled to defer the execution of their intentions to a more convenient season. But iniquity, when united with wealth and influence, is likely to prevail, at least for a time. Anacharsis Cloots had dissipated his fortune, and, being a weak advocate of reasonable and happy liberty, considered all means acceptable that furthered his purposes. As for Mirabeau, he needed, for the most part, protection against his father. These men sought and obtained secret audiences at the Palais-Royal, and formed a league with the Orleans family, becoming their most active agents, under the delusion that the revolutionists would be leaders, when they were really led. From this period dates the secret understanding between the demagogues and certain impoverished nobles, whose standard was the red cap.

Vaucresson had been obliged to announce the appeal of Beaumarchais, but to know that he was in lifelong exile enabled his opponents to breathe freely. The document even of Égalité in Beaumarchais's hand, gradually lost its terrors. The former was the confidential friend of Prince d'Artois, who had great influence at Marly, and while the "friends of the people" established associations under the protection of Chartres, the elder Orleans was on the best terms with the ministers, the newly-strengthened Jesuit party, and Madame du Barry, who ruled the king as unconditionally as ever, while his majesty seemed to have many years yet to live. In a short time the hour would arrive when a change would take place. It was an important hour in history!

The dauphin and his wife were at first greatly beloved by the people. They had always shown themselves humane and accessible, yet no man could have had a less royal deportment than young Louis, according to the ideas of courtiers. Conti, it is true, had some influence on him—he could say all he pleased, but it made no impression. That the dauphin devoted himself to his books, charts, locksmiths, and carpenters, neglecting every thing else, was sufficient to make him contemptible in the eyes of the aristocracy. Marie Antoinette, on the other hand, was cheerful, an enemy to what she believed constraint, and as much devoted to her friend Madame de Lamballe as to the chivalrous and daring Artois. She had scarcely the goodwill of her husband, who did not trouble himself much about her, and their marriage seemed unhappy. The fish-women were accustomed to reproach the dauphiness, when she drove past them, because, though now a wife for three years, she had given no prince to the country. Besides, the miniature court at Marly was so closely watched by that at Versailles, that the dauphin and dauphiness seemed to incur any thing but respect.

On the 1st of May, a mounted huntsman of the Duke de Duras, chief marshal of the king, was announced at an early hour at the Hôtel Conti. He delivered the following note:

"Your royal highness! The king has been suddenly taken ill. The physicians pronounce his disease small-pox, and his life is despaired of! He is supposed to have caught the infection from a person Madame du Barry brought to supper yesterday evening. The countess has just left Versailles in great terror! As you, monseigneur, possess the confidence of the most gracious dauphin, I henceforth await your orders. 'Your most obedient

"DURAS."

A quarter of an hour later, Conti drove to the Hôtel Penthièvre, in order to take his niece to Marly. Young Louis, his consort, and their suite, arrived that afternoon at Versailles. The Princess de Lamballe and Conti were with them, and gave all orders. Vaugyon and the Duchess de Luynes were in attendance. Terray was ordered to distribute two hundred thousand francs to the poor of Paris, that they might pray for the king. "Should this appear too much," said Louis, "then deduct it from the allowance of the dauphiness and myself."

The king was ill ten days. His suffering was terrible, and the atmosphere around him so impure that it acted on him as a poison. His disease could not be kept secret from the people. Orleans and the ministry suddenly halted in their career of vice, and bowed their heads in apparent repentance, waiting for the king's death. The dauphin was more reserved and gloomy than ever. Neither Conti nor Marie Antoinette could engage him in conversation; but when Conti remarked that the future king could not immediately reside at Versailles, he started, as if awaking from a dream.

"At Versailles? No, at Marly!" Vaugyon made his arrangements accordingly.

When the news of the approaching dissolution of the king was known in the provinces, all the partisans of the dauphin's father roused themselves. Maurepas, the witty pupil and colleague of Fleury, exiled by Madame de Pompadour, came secretly to Versailles, informed himself where the new monarch would reside, and hastened to Marley. A number of banished members of Parliament came to Paris, seeking refuge among their friends; the capital was filled with inflammatory material; the people began to talk fearlessly, and laughed at the officials of Sartines, who until then had been their terror.

Louis XV. died on the 10th of May. His whole court, according to custom, had to be present in the audience-chamber. All the halls were crowded with courtiers. But neither the dauphin nor his wife, Conti nor his niece, nor any one of the attendants of the new monarch was to be seen. The travelling-equipages stood ready in the court-yard, awaiting the signal for departure, for the servants had been requested to place a wax-light at one of the windows of the dying king's chamber, and to extinguish it when he ceased to breathe.

Conti stood at the window of the room occupied by the dauphin, who paced the floor, absorbed in anxiety. In the adjacent chamber sat Marie Antoinette and the Princess de Lamballe. They grasped each other's hands and spoke in whispers. At the door of the antechamber stood the Duchess de Noailles, and the Duke de Vaugyon. The Princes de Provence and d'Artois, with their consorts and suites, were in the neighboring rooms.

The wax-light was extinguished! The baggage-wagons and servants began to move. Conti advanced toward Louis; pressing the young monarch's hand to his lips, he said: "He has departed. God bless your majesty!"

"Is he dead?" exclaimed Louis XVI., hastening to Marie Antoinette; he seized her hands and raised her from her seat: "My God," he said, "guide and protect us; we are too young to reign!"

A noise like that of an uproar was heard, as if approaching from the *Œil de Bœuf*. "Heaven! what is that, dearest Lamballe?" asked Marie Antoinette.

"The old courtiers are rushing toward your majesties," replied Conti, in a voice of bitterness.

"I wish to have nothing to say to them! I care to see no one but my aunts, who nursed my grandfather!" cried the dauphin. "Let us pray to Heaven, Antoinette, that we may have to do with persons who, while serving their king, can relieve the wretchedness of our country. It must be done soon! Dear cousin Conti, you have talked much with me, lately, on the state of affairs, and my heart has not been unmoved. You must be my adviser." He was silent, then he smiled in a melancholy manner: "Do you remember three names my father impressed on my mind, and on that of the Prince de Bourbon? It was at Little Trianon, near the grotto of elma."

"My prince!" exclaimed Conti, in astonishment.

"At that time I was scarcely seven years old. One of those men was my first preceptor, a priest, the Abbé Morelly. He must be dead by this time. The other two are Turgot and Malesherbes. My father said: 'Remember these names; you may need them in future!' I have not forgotten them; I have read their works, and observed their actions. Turgot shall be placed over the finances, and Malesherbes be minister of the interior. These places are the most important. Count de Mouy shall have the war department, and I will myself write to M. de Machault."

"My dear and illustrious master!" cried Conti, in joyful emotion, "the spirit of your father is upon you! And what of the late ministers?"

"Send for Sartines."

In the anterooms stood the courtiers and officials, waiting for the moment when the door of the new king's chamber should open, whom they already regarded as their prey. Vaugyon appeared: "Lieutenant of police, M. de Sartines!" The officer entered, and the portière dropped behind him.

"We shall have some interesting business," whispered Orleans to his son; "he sends first for the police!"

Sartines bent his knee before the young monarch. "God bless your majesty!"

"I thank you, Sartines. Let this proclamation be printed immediately, and published throughout France. I have declared in it that the ministers are dismissed, and the Parliament is to be convoked in the old manner. Give these *lettres de cachet* to Messrs. de Maupeau and d'Aiguillon (they have long made an ill use of them); both must not approach within thirty miles of my capital. The Abbé Terray is protected by his clerical robe; but tell him he will be wise if he endeavor to elude my remembrance!" Louis XVI. nodded, and Sartines left the apartment, carrying in his hand the first acts of the new reign.

The Princesses Adelaide, Sophie, and Victoire, were now introduced by a chamberlain. They were greatly depressed. The king embraced them. "My dear aunts, if I did not already love you, your devotion at the bedside of my grandfather would have secured my admiration. I beg you to accompany me to Marly.—My royal consort," and he offered his arm to Marie Antoinette, "I think I am acting according to your desire as well as mine, if I nominate her highness, the widowed Princess de Lamballe, superintendent of your household.—Let us now go, if you please."

The countenances of those present reflected their happiness. When the monarch appeared in the antechamber, the ladies and gentlemen of the old court approached him with profound deference, wishing him joy; he motioned them silently away, for he became again reserved. The visitors made way for him to pass with his suite, and he entered the carriage with the queen; Conti and Louise de Lamballe took seats opposite, and, with the rest of his family, they went at full speed to Marly. After his departure, the courtiers stood for some time looking after the king, who had withdrawn himself from their homage.

"That is a new way to begin a reign!" murmured Chartres.

"M. de Sartines," said Orleans, "will you not give us some explanations?"

Sartines shrugged his shoulders.— "All I know, monseigneur, is, that the ministers are dismissed, and the Parliament convoked after the former and usual style."

"The Parliament to be so convoked?" repeated Orleans.

"We are now dismissed!" exclaimed Maupeau and Terray.

"And I am to deliver these letters to you, M. de Maupeau and M. d'Aiguillon."

"But how are we dismissed?" cried Terray.

"That is my affair!" replied Sartines. "I shall take care that you fulfil the will of his majesty." The "empire of the angels" had fallen!

A few hours later, the Parisians were aware that the obnoxious ministers were discharged, and the Parliament reëstablished, and with it the old judiciary proceedings. The people rejoiced aloud. Crowds gathered at every corner to read the proclamation, and the road to Marly swarmed with happy people, going to see "Louis the Liberator!" They embraced each other in the streets, and a stranger arriving at the French capital in those days might have fancied it just relieved from a besieging enemy. In the following night, a wagon passed from Versailles to St. Denis. Mounted torch-bearers accompanied it, and it went with the utmost speed, as if the driver and escort were anxious to disencumber themselves of their burden. It was the *corbillard*—the royal hearse. Such was the burial of Louis XV. The people sang vulgar songs about him and his favorites, as his dead body rattled over the stones to its final resting-place.

What hopes of a new national life now blossomed! After the unspeakable misery of the country, it was elated by ardent expectations! Thus began the reign of Louis XVI. Conti was commissioned by the young king to inform Beaumarchais that his appeal was accepted, his exile revoked, and that he was to remain only so long in England as to attend to some business which his monarch had confided to him. Marie Antoinette added, smilingly: "Greet him also from me, your highness; I hope we shall now have the *Barber of Seville.*"

"Certainly, since you desire it," replied the king.

The new ruler of France was noble and humane; but he needed encouragement, and long reflection, to rise above himself, as he did in those first hours of his accession. If he took advantage of an unexpected and great opportunity, after his excitement he would again become taciturn and reserved, partly from distrust in himself, and partly from want of knowledge of the world and a freely-developed character. When he arrived at Marly he had an intention of nominating to the premiership M. de Machault, a most capable and faithful man; but the smooth-tongued Maurepas met Louis unceremoniously in the anteroom, and was received in a friendly manner, for his banishment by Madame de Pompadour gave him some respectability in the king's eyes.

The graceful and assured manner of Maurepas, the seriousness with which he seemed conscious of a remedy for every evil in the state, the boldness with which he said, "Ah, your majesty, be not concerned, I can easily teach you to govern!" were so effective, that he became prime minister instead of Machault, to the great misfortune of France. When he heard that Turgot was to be his colleague, he frowned and said, "Your majesty, M. Turgot never goes to mass!"

"He was my father's friend, and that is sufficient. Terray and Maupeau went to church every day." Maurepas bowed; he was in possession of all he cared to know, and had his portfolio in his pocket.

None could be more surprised at their official nomination than Turgot and Malesherbes—the old friends of the Pigeonnier, who met again on the floor at Marly, and shook hands with deep emotion. Their nomination produced great rejoicing throughout the country.

A few days after the death of Louis XV., M. de Vrillière appeared at Ruelle, the estate of Aiguillon, where Madame du Barry had found a refuge. During her days of prosperity this man had been her most devoted servant and eulogist, but now he presented himself with a warrant exiling her to the nunnery of Pont aux Dames. "A good beginning of his reign!", she exclaimed, as she took Zamor, her negro-boy, and four million worth of diamonds, to the cloister.

Beaumarchais was a favorite of fortune. Could any one be more abandoned than he by friends, and humiliated and oppressed by enemies? But scarcely had he escaped destruction, and secured for himself and his wife a place of safety, when he was again raised above his adversaries. Louis XV. could not have died at a better time for him. He could not, however, directly return to France, on accouut of the commission with which he had been intrusted. The revolution in America was progressing favorably, while the old enmity between France and England made a naval war very probable. ' Turgot and Malesherbes begged their friend to give them some account of the state of affairs in Great Britain.

On the 10th of November, Louis XVI. reëstablished the Parliament, amid universal gratitude. The appeal of Beaumarchais was immediately admitted; the process of Maupeau-Goesman against him, as well as the sentence of the former Parliament, was annulled, and his honors restored. At the same time, the queen ordered the *Barber of Seville* to be acted in the Théâtre Français.

Marie Antoinette began to understand her taciturn husband, and love his noble character. Her simple German mind suited his serious temper. There were moments when she could have knelt before him—when her heart yearned for his love; but in vain! He did not seem to comprehend her, and neither her beauty nor her cheerfulness moved him. He was an awkward man in love-affairs, and, distrusting his own feelings, he had little coufidence in those of his wife. He still looked upon her as the "Austrian woman," though he liked to converse with her, and had lately made her a present of Trianon. It was a dark and joyless period in her life to be married four years and remain still an unloved wife, admired by all for her grace and beauty, but neglected by the only one to whom she had brought the treasures of her affection. She needed amusement to drown her heart in forgetful-

ness, and while endeavoring to conceal her feelings, she appeared to have more levity than naturally belonged to her, and to be less regal in her deportment than suited her high rank.

About the time when Beaumarchais closed his affairs in London, the king was at Marly, his favorite residence. This palace, lying in an ancient park, had retained, more than Versailles, the fantastic style preferred by Louis XIV., who considered himself the first of crowned heads, and was proud of his palace at Marly. On the highest part of the mountain terrace he built a large star-shaped pavilion, called the *Pavillon du Soleil*, where he resided. Twelve smaller edifices were crected in a circle, named after the signs of the zodiac, and united by a colonnade. In them dwelt the members of the royal family and their favorites. The ground about these villas flourished with trees and flowers; the royal private garden, into which no one dared enter but their majesties and their satellites, was ornamented with statues and fountains. The wide path, crossing the circle, and adorned with rich pieces of art, was called the king's road.

Here Louis XVI. with his court passed the autumn. He was in the habit of promenading with his courtiers in the evening, when he left his apartments. Besides the royal pair, the company usually consisted of the Princess de Lamballe, Countess de Gorzka, the Duchesses de Chimay and de Tarente Latremouille, the stewardess of the household (Madame de Noailles), who attended to the king's sisters, the Princes de Conti, d'Artois, and de Chartres, the Prince de Poix, Major de Reding and Afry of the Swiss guards, and the Duke de Vaugyon.

"Then these matters will finally be settled," said Louis, continuing his conversation. "From the documents sent by Beaumarchais, we have great reason to be satisfied with him. When do you think he will return, Cousin Conti ?"

"In three weeks at the latest, your majesty, and then he hopes you will permit him to annul the sentence against him in his suit with La Blache."

"Oh, certainly! He will, however, be considerate enough to begin his process in some distant court, at Aix perhaps. That affair created such a public excitement that I do not wish to have it renewed here. A quiet arrangement of this difficulty, and an abolishment of abuses, alone can help us. Beaumarchais is quite too impulsive—we must endeavor to subdue him a little."

"Ah, my husband," smiled Marie Antoinette, "he will find enough to do. I received to-day the announcement from the director of the *Menus Plaisirs*, that he was only waiting for the author, to represent the *Barber of Seville*. Literary success will for some time drive all lawsuits from his mind. And then he is a musician; he and our Lamballe will delight us with their songs, and we shall forget all past troubles."

"Indeed, your majesty," replied Louise de Lamballe. "The poor man and his wife have suffered enough, and only saved themselves from dishonor as by a miracle. Any other person would have given himself up to despair !"

"I can vouch for him, your majesty, that he will obey all your commands," said Conti. "He intends to live only for poetry, and to arrange the affairs relative to his fortune, which has been greatly reduced."

"Oh, he must tell us every thing," said the queen. "His conversation is so impressive and brilliant! He must inform us of all the intrigues which his enemies planned against him, and from

which he escaped so happily. We must hear his whole life."

"And does your majesty intend to call him formally to court ?" asked Artois. "He is a citizen, who, however shrewd and eloquent, has too many mysteries connected with his life to make him suitable to appear in your circle."

"Prince d'Artois, he was the servant and confidant of your noble father," replied Conti, "as well as Messrs. Turgot and De Malesherbes. I know of nothing more becoming than for the son to reunite these men around him. Besides, Beaumarchais has no ambition to obtain courtly rank, and their majesties may take delight in his talent as well as Louis the Great in that of Molière and Corneille."

"You are right, cousin !" said the king. "I shall be as glad as my father to see Beaumarchais."

"He must be very interesting," said Chartres, after a pause. "But he will probably conceal more than he reveals. The best story in connection with him is that in reference to his wife."

"How ?" exclaimed the queen.

Artois looked gayly at the Princess de Lamballe. "Well, while he was in the Bastile, his intimate friend the Prince von Nassau-Siegen amused himself by carrying off the wife of Beaumarchais in the disguise of a page."

"I hope you are not attempting to jest !" The king's countenance darkened. "Who is the Prince von Nassau-Siegen ?"

"A poor adventurer, who sailed with Bougainville," replied Artois; "then brought a tiger's skin from Africa for the Princess de Lamballe, and is now colonel of an infantry regiment at St. Omer. As such he ran off with the wife of his friend Beaumarchais and—"

"Permit me, prince !" interrupted Conti, severely and haughtily. "Judging from the apparent pleasure with which you relate these affairs, you would be glad to undertake them yourself; your friend Chartres would be very useful to you and give you the right direction. With tiger-hunts and voyages round the world, however, neither of you, I imagine, would have much to do.—Your majesty, the Prince de Nassau-Siegen is the bravest soldier in France, and a talented and cultivated man. Ask your officers; your whole army have but one name for him—the Bayard of France! Nassau was poor and in debt; Beaumarchais saved him from his dependent position, and he repaid that act of friendship by protecting Madame Susanna twice from the persecutions of La Blache, and prepared for her a refuge in Calais, while her husband was in the Bastile and threatened with branding and the galleys.—I warn you, Prince d'Artois, not to believe every thing M. de Chartres says, and I remind the latter that certain persons would do well not to call up spirits that might be dangerous to them."

"And did he protect the wife of Beaumarchais against La Blache?" asked the queen.

"I never heard of this Prince Nassau-Siegen—with Bougainville round the world? Cousin Conti, I should like to have him near my person."

"He deserves it, your majesty! He was born to be a defender of his country—a knight of the monarchy!"

"But if he is a prince, dear Conti," asked the queen, "has he no land, no rights?".

"His father possessed the duchy of Nassau. The young Otto, however, was so unfortunate as to have Madame de Chateauroux for his mother, and to be born at Paris four weeks after his father's death. This circumstance was used by the cabinet at Vienna to annex his small principality; and, though recognized as the legitimate heir, all

efforts to regain his possessions have been in vain."

"That is nothing new from such a quarter!" said the king brusquely, and looking at Marie Antoinette.

"My husband, it is the first time that I feel my parents can be unjust. I will write to my imperial mother. Let us indemnify the Prince von Nassau for the loss of his paternal inheritance. France needs heroes, and as you are in doubt as to whom to present the office of commander of the Gardes Nobles, I know of no one more suitable by rank and chivalrous renown. A man who can do so much for an ordinary friend, will do more for his king!"

"Is he not also a sailor, and has he not a daring spirit?" asked Louis, after a short pause.

"I appeal to the reports of Bougainville and the Grand-Admiral de Penthièvre." A longer pause ensued.

"Very well, cousin. Write to him, in my name, that he is commander of the Gardes Nobles, and let him report himself as soon as his successor at the garrison of St. Omer has been nominated. I will speak to Mouy."

"How magnanimous!" suddenly exclaimed a glad voice. All turned to the Countess de Gorzka, who stood tearful and blushing. Conti was perplexed; he looked at Louise de Lamballe, who was pale and trembled.

"Ah!" said the queen, raising her finger in playful rebuke, "how can our little Gorzka so betray herself? The Prince von Nassau-Siegen seems to be victorious everywhere!"

The king smiled. "Well, this matter is settled, cousin; write to him."

"Then we shall have all three at court," laughed Marie Antoinette— "Beaumarchais, Nassau, and Madame Susanna, the much - talked - of page! What do you think of it, dear Lamballe?"

"I share the joy of my uncle, in seeing the array of noble and fearless men around your throne honored by two heroes—one of the sword, the other of the pen."

When the court separated, and Chartres was returning with his cavalier Sillery to the Pavilion of the Scorpion, which he occupied, he said: "Fine news this—it is curdling the blood in my veins! Beaumarchais is coming to court, and M. de Nassau nominated to the command of the Gardes Nobles. I see him already minister or field-marshal! And I dare not move! All has been in vain! We are defeated, Sillery, and we ought to be glad if we are suffered even to remain here. D'Artois is the only one who could be turned to account. And then the love-affairs of the tiger-hunter! The Princess de Lamballe and the Countess de Gorzka both in love with him at once! He really has extraordinary luck; I must try to deprive him of some of it!"

A fortnight later appeared at Trianon—from which Marie Antoinette had banished all etiquette, "in order not to be queen"—Nassau, Beaumarchais, and Susanna. No one was present besides the king and queen, their brothers, sisters, and aunts, Conti, Louise de Lamballe, Turgot, and Malesherbes. The reception took place near the grotto under the elms, as in other days.

When Caron cast himself at the feet of the monarch, and kissed his hand, he said: "In this place, my sovereign, once stood your father, and taught you to love the friends and servants of his cause. The royal son fulfils what the parent could not! I have returned to a happier France, a land that adores its king, and, with Turgot and Malesherbes, I may stand with a beating heart before 'Louis the Liberator,' as we once stood before 'Louis the Desired!'"

The king raised his tearful eyes to heaven, and the queen gently took his hand.

"And have you forgotten the song you composed for the dauphiness, as our dear Lamballe has informed me?" she asked. The song was again sung.

"I feel as I did when the king's father was alive," whispered Malesherbes, "but the times are better!"

Siegen stood lost in adoration of the Princess de Lamballe. All were happy and hopeful, except Marie Antoinette and Louise.

CHAPTER XXIII.

LOVE IN TEARS.

LOUIS XVI. commenced his reign by releasing the larger number of prisoners in the Bastile, so that a small corps of Invalids were a sufficient garrison. On this occasion Beaumarchais petitioned the king, through Conti, to declare the jailer Santerre reinstated in all civil privileges, and at liberty to transact business as any honorable citizen. Like a beast of prey, half tamed by a noble hand, the son of an incendiary entered Paris with his thousand francs, and sought Caron in the Hôtel Piron, where the latter again resided. On his asking the advice of Beaumarchais, several trades were proposed to him, and that of a brewer suited him best. He was accordingly apprenticed to Georguille, the largest brewer in the city. The poet did not foresee that he was letting loose a ravenous beast among mankind, and that Santerre was right when he expected nothing good from himself!

On the order of the queen the *Barber of Seville* was acted in the Théâtre Français. All Paris hastened to witness the much-talked-of comedy, and to have an opportunity of seeing the author, who had so nearly been ruined by the Maupeau Parliament, but who by his dexterity had escaped the galleys and was again at court. His renewed respectability increased the number of his opponents, and they resolved again to humiliate him. How well soever the actors played, the piece was denounced, and many in the audience showed their displeasure by hissing. Such conduct was at length considered unreasonable, and enhanced the interest of the comedy. While the audience were inveighing against it in the parterre, Lecain, one of the principal actors, said to the angry Beaumarchais: "Be calm, my friend, these persons will bring you money! They are insuring immortality to your *Barber!*" And so it was. The representation was given every night, the theatre was always crowded, and Pasiello composed an opera on the same subject.

"Ladies and gentlemen!" exclaimed Caron, when the curtain fell amid many signs of disapprobation. "Those who deride my comedy see reflected in it their own vices; but I have determined to avenge myself as never an author did before!" He was thinking of the *Wedding of Figaro*—the continuation of the *Barber of Seville.*

The great disappointment which the friends of the former reign had experienced by the death of Louis XV. and the unexpected movements of his successor, was accompanied with loss of power and deep humiliation. Turgot said publicly: "No state bankruptcy, whether secret or confessed—no new taxes or loans! There is but one way to save the state: economy and liberty! No half measures!"

Malesherbes, in his celebrated memorial of the 5th of May, demanded the convocation of the Estates-General, as in the reign of Henry IV. He wrote: "Let the whole people give an opinion as in days past; they know what they need!" Such doctrines were death-blows to the old order of things. The clique of Terray and Ventadour had no influence; the elder Orleans, supposing that the time of his uncontrolled authority was near, had become too closely allied with Madame du Barry, for he had intrigued to marry her to the late king, à la Maintenon, but now his courage forsook him. That his house might not be deprived of all prospect of aggrandizement, he resigned further personal activity for the rest of his life, and retired to his landed estates in Orleannais and Brittany, accompanied by his mistress, Madame de Montesson, leaving the conflict in the hands of his son, whom he had so well instructed. Chartres had prudently taken no part in his father's affairs at court, except so far as it was natural for a son to be of the same party; he was not suspected of aspiring to the crown, and seemed rather to court the people, whose leader he wished to be—a position not difficult for him to reach. The Parisians loved the Orleans family as descendants of Henry IV., who had endeavored to retain popular favor; and they never failed to take sides with the citizens in any trouble between them and the kings. The Orleans made the old Palais-Royal, lying in the centre of the most populous districts, a resort for amusements to the inhabitants of the capital. The Paris of the former century could be realized within those precincts at any time; and when such persons as Anacharsis Cloots and his disciples were sent as political missionaries among the residents, it was easy to control the public opinion of that quarter.

Chartres lived very unhappily with Adelaide de Penthièvre. Her rival was Madame de Buffon, the faithless wife of the celebrated naturalist, and director of the Jardin des Plantes. But who took any particular notice of his gallantries? The Princes de Provence and d'Artois lived in the same manner!

It was possible to reform abuses in the government, but the moral degradation of society was incurable.

The tolerance of the young king, his lack of worldly prudence, and the skill for providing entertainment, of which Chartres gave evidence before the queen, as well as the shrewdness with which he managed the frivolous but headstrong d'Artois, gave him position and weight at the new court. Never yet did a royal prince love his first-born brother, who inherits the crown. Provence and d'Artois despised Louis XVI.; they laughed at his timidity and his good-natured weakness, while they spurned his mild political doctrines. They had been educated in deceit, and in disregard of the public well-being. Chartres gave a slavish submission to their opinions, as well as to their efforts to gain influence over the king.

The operations of Turgot and Malesherbes were by degrees misinterpreted to the monarch by the jealous Maurepas, who saw himself unfavorably affected by them. "If these men do every thing, of what use am I?" he exclaimed. He was as seducing a minister as a young ruler could have. His tongue was always charged with jests, bon-mots, and flatteries, and his brain ready for any expedient in emergencies. He saved the king much trouble, regarding the trade of governing as easy, and his arrogance always triumphed over the modesty of his master. Unfortunately, his devices were superficial, and mere tricks from the school of Fleury, while his colleagues regarded their duties as important and serious. Maurepas also worked to estrange the king from Marie Antoinette, that she might have no consideration in her husband's decisions as to the affairs with which he might be concerned. Thus ambition united the premier with the brothers of the king and Chartres for new and unhappy intrigues.

Though the year 1776 was blessed with a fruitful harvest, Chartres joined Bourbon de Condé and several other nobles in raising the price of bread by purchasing large quantities of wheat, thus producing a calamity, afterward called the "Maurepas flour war." A pamphlet of Necker, the banker, against Turgot, was represented to Louis, who, deluded by Maurepas, made a wrong step, supposing he was strengthening the government by means of the peers and aristocracy. He increased the privileges of the nobles at the expense of the lower clergy. The spirit of his father was deserting him.

Trianon was clad in the beauty of autumn; while Nature had made little change from other days in the appearance of field and forest, it was plain that a more frivolous and luxurious society assembled there. At Little Trianon pastoral happiness seemed to have remained, but it was artificial—a world of sorrow lay beneath. Marie Antoinette associated chiefly with her friend Louise de Lamballe, but each kept her own secret.

The more the queen yearned for her husband's love the more she sought the exclusive devotion to herself of Louise—a very slavery of friendship—for every hour of her life was Madame de Lamballe subject to the queen's espionage. When she was not with Marie Antoinette she had Charlotte de Gorzka near her, who had already betrayed her tender sentiment for Nassau. Dissimulation and reserve were the more necessary to the Princess de Lamballe, as she began to feel the encroachments of jealousy. Nassau-Siegen was handsome and chivalrous, his deeds corresponded with his person and character, and it was no wonder that he became a favorite at court. The king liked to converse with him about his travels, the princes and cavaliers were amused by his anecdotes, the ladies were enthusiastic at his gallantry, and (what caused painful anxiety to Louise) Marie Antoinette received him with great favor. When he was absent from the social assemblies, the eyes of the fair queen restlessly sought after him, and her coquetries and attentions betrayed a regard far surpassing that of mere courtly patronage.

Marie Antoinette was unfortunate. Though her virtue could never be impugned, yet, during the first years of her married life, she was sometimes inconsiderate, and lacked dignity. In her love of intrigue, she was betrayed into appearances that gave cause for slander. Conscious of her beauty, and feeling herself neglected by her royal consort, she turned to others, as if to inspire them with a gallantry of which the king seemed incapable. This was but a poor remedy; for D'Artois and Chartres soon discerned her strength as well as her weakness, and played the lover in the pastoral manner of Horace d'Urse. The queen's chief object was to excite the indifferent mind of Louis, and, by making him jealous, to lead him to appreciate the treasure he despised. For this purpose she selected the Prince von Nassau-Siegen, supposing he would be suspected by the king sooner than his brothers and cousins; and, if the poor Countess de Gorzka shed tears, could not the queen richly compensate her?

The king, Provence, and D'Artois, with their suite, were hunting; Marie Antoinette and her ladies and cavaliers were playing blind-man's-buff and other familiar games in the park near her apartments. The Princess de Lamballe received orders to have the repast served at Little Trianon, near the grotto—a place preferred by Louis on account of the reminiscences of his youth—and to make arrangements for the afternoon amusements, for the sky was clear and the birds were singing. Louise and Charlotte departed to attend to the dinner; both were silent and sorrowful. They took care that the servants executed all the orders of the whimsical and excitable queen. The whole court were to assemble at the grotto, and the afternoon was to be passed on the heights of the Arcis. The king had sketched an Alpine hut, which he wished to have built there, and Marie Antoinette had had one erected without his knowledge, intending to surprise him with it on this day. The only persons who knew of this were Nassau, Louise de Lamballe, the court architect, and Vaugyon.

After the princess had seen that the arrangements for dinner were completed, feeling a desire for solitude, she left the Countess de Gorzka in charge, and ascended to the summit of the hill. Charlotte wished also to be alone, and, after having finished her task, she retired to the interior of the grotto, there to lose herself in gloomy meditations, resulting from the rivalry of a queen. In contrast, there was much vivacity on the green in the castle park. The brilliant Marie wore, on her light curled hair, a straw hat, which shaded her arched brows, and the dimples on her cheeks. She ran about among the courtiers; catching one or being caught herself, her play was as natural and graceful as that of a child. The prevailing English style had made quite a revolution in the French fashion of the day. The hoop, powder, brocade robe, and laced coat, had disappeared. The queen wore a white dress of thin barracan, bound at the waist with a broad blue belt; her arms were partly bare, with full short sleeves, and a cashmere shawl completed her simple toilet. The other ladies were dressed in a similar manner. The gentlemen retained, from the former costume, their steel swords, wigs, three-cornered hats, silk stockings, and shoes, but embroideries and very bright colors were banished; brown, black, violet, dark-green, or blue cloth had supplanted the shining satin, velvet, and moire; only Nassau's tall form was clothed in a brilliant uniform: a red coat with gold braid, on which the cross of St. Louis was suspended by a blue ribbon. The tight-fitting small-clothes and top-boots, the sash with the heavy gold tassels, became him; while his helmet, with the horse's tail, and his falchion, were borne by his servant.

Chartres was acting *maître du plaisir*. The game of questions and answers was closed by a remark of the queen that caused great laughter. Chartres, who liked to take a pledge from Marie Antoinette, asked her: "Do you know Homer?"

"Certainly! Homer? He had eyes and played on the hautboy! Do you know more of him?"

The company began the favorite game of blind-man's-buff; it was to be the last, for it was getting late. The lot fell on Siegen and the queen, while the others turned round in a circle. For a long time the prince escaped the hands of the sovereign, but at last they almost ran into each other's arms.

"I am glad I have caught you, dear prince," whispered Marie Antoinette. "Do go and see how things are at our Swiss house; Madame de Lamballe has been away a long time. I will keep the others at play until you return."

"I obey your majesty with pleasure."

However softly this was said, it was noticed by Chartres, who stood near. When the game was broken up, and the bandages taken off, he beckoned to Sillery.

"Watch Nassau, and see what he does. Follow him when he leaves. A rendezvous or something of the kind is on the *tapis*." Sillery hid himself in the bushes.

A new amusement was commenced, in which the queen joined with great eagerness. Nassau pretended that his military duties called him away, and withdrew. When he was alone his countenance indicated seriousness, as he ascended the park road. He had not yet found an opportunity of speaking privately to Louise de Lamballe, who was watched by so many eyes. He had only the word of his friend Beaumarchais as to the love she entertained for him. Knowing all the paths, he struck into a side-opening that led him to his destination without passing Little Trianon. He entered the Swiss cottage, which was decorated with flowers; a gardener and three peasant-girls were busily engaged there.

"Is her highness the Princess de Lamballe here?"

"She has been for half an hour alone in the ruin on the hill, and forbade us to disturb her meditations."

"Probably the princess and the Countess de Gorzka are together. It is warm, and the road steep," said Nassau.

"Oh no," smiled one of the girls, "the countess is at Little Trianon; I saw her just now in the grotto."

"Very well. See that all is prepared according to the orders of her majesty; I will return immediately!" The prince walked slowly toward the ruin, his heart beating violently. "Alone! heaven be praised, she is alone!" He entered by the high, dilapidated arch into the court-yard. The foliage was still luxuriant; the thorn and the thyme flourished among the fragments, and the mullein waved on the broken wall. As the prince passed by the chapel toward the south, he could not but notice how desolate it was in its fallen glory. The altar lay on the ground, some of the columns and the statues of the saints were defaced, and the ivy was spreading its veil over all. In the part not yet fallen into ruins, a Gothic window looked toward St. Cyr, and there sat Louise, with her face turned in that direction, as she leaned against a pillar. Her straw hat was on the floor, her dark hair had fallen over her bosom; she was pale, and her eyes sorrowful, while she clasped her hands as if in prayer. She neither heard nor saw any thing, and in her white robe resembled a Cecilia.

When Nassau beheld the princess he suddenly halted. Ah, who would not imagine the thoughts of a beloved one in such circumstances, and be pardoned in disturbing her solitude? He almost reproached himself for being so near, yet the charm was too attractive. If she suffered, was it not for him? and he felt that it was time for this suspense to end. "Love or misery!" he murmured, approaching slowly. He could hear her sigh, and then speak to herself: "From desert to desert!"

"Louise!"

Madame de Lamballe started with a cry, and was rushing beyond the window, where was a ravine, but his strong arms detained her. "O prince!" she exclaimed, pressing her hands to her eyes, "I did not know what I was doing!" A deep blush suffused her countenance, while she endeavored to disengage herself.

"You were about to cast yourself down from this height, and by my fault!" exclaimed Nassau.

"And how do you know whether it is not well to die thus?"

"It cannot be, princess, if you leave one whose life would then be miserable."

"Your life miserable! No, prince; I think we are both forgetting that we are in the royal service. You come, without doubt—"

"Certainly, the queen's commands

brought me here; but, as fortune has never before favored me so much as to see you alone, will you, dear lady, be gracious enough to grant me a few moments for explanation? Perhaps another opportunity may never return!"

"I cannot reasonably refuse. However, in what you intend to say, consider our position, and—what considerations are binding upon us."

"Are not considerations which force us to silence and dissimulation, grievous enough? Are we also to distrust each other? Must we not have even the consolation of a glance of sympathy rewarding our self-denial and enlivening our hopes? 'From desert to desert,' you were saying, Louise—the words I wrote while long ago thinking of you. Oh, I will not offend the shade of the unfortunate Lamballe, but a dark destiny has hitherto pursued us, condemning you to an unhappy union, and me to a perpetual unrest. Do you think that I, inured to hardships, and delighting in war, have sought a quiet home-service in order to wear this gay dress, and exhibit myself at parades; or, like the effeminate Artois and Chartres, flutter around a queen? Do not class me with them. My heart tells me your own feeling— that the love I have borne you for so many years, and that alone, urges me among thoughtless courtiers, and makes me careless of renown. I am, it is true, a landless prince, having nothing but my honor and my sword, and well knowing how I must fight for your possession; but tell me only that you love me, dearest Louise, and you shall be my wife." He drew her toward him, and he could not refrain from tears.

The princess raised her blushing but joyful face. "Otto, nothing is so grateful to me as your noble emotion. Yes, I love you, and I am proud to confess it. To love each other is a precious

"FROM DESERT TO DESERT."   p. 254.

consciousness, even should we never be married! There is a land where those who, from inevitable circumstances, are separated here, will be united forever!" She leaned her head on his breast.

"But who can separate us if we do not wish it? It requires courage to be the wife of Otto von Nassau, but if you have the fortitude that love inspires, will you not weather the storm with me until the day of our union brings a release from the duties now incumbent on us?"

"I have courage to bear any thing for your sake; I confide more in your love than in myself. But do not let us shut our eyes to the dangers that surround us."

"May I not hope to obtain the sanction of your Uncle Conti, who esteems me?"

"I know he will not refuse you, but you forget that I am not the daughter of a mere citizen, who can marry whom her heart commands. We have to perform the sad duty of living princely, whether we wish or not, or we fall into contempt. I am poor and without a position, as you are, and you will never gain my hand unless you are the chief of a victorious army or fleet, or a sovereign lord. Alas, our happiness does not depend on your arm—not if you had the strength of Perseus—but on the pleasure of the king and queen! I tremble at this selfish favor that so much arouses the envy of others! The queen, Siegen! Ah, you do not see as I do, nor experience the terrible fear that torments me!"

"Speak, Louise, for I have no idea as to what you allude."

"No idea—yes! The unconscious are happy! That remarkable behavior when you are present—that graciousness—laugh at me, call me jealous! Would that I could persuade myself that my feelings deceive me, or that I

calumniate the friendship and condescension of Marie Antoinette, who is so amiable and pure!—But, Otto, I fear the queen loves you!"

"Me? Ha! ha! pardon me, dear Louise, for laughing, but the thought is so new and strange to me that—" He was silent, perplexed at his own recollections. "I cannot believe it, for the sake of woman's dignity—of his majesty! Though she does favor me in an unusual manner, I must be more reserved. Why should her condescension be dangerous to us?"

"Dangerous! that is the word, Otto! It is dangerous to be the object of such attention, for you become the ridicule of slanderers; and yet more dangerous to refuse it, for you would arouse the hatred of a queen! I will not believe that she can so forget herself, but I see no remedy. We have met and loved, only to be eternally separated!"

"No, dearest lady; God will guide us aright. War is almost decided upon against England, and I will conquer happiness with my sword. If we confide in each other, we shall be cautious, and at the proper hour I will kneel before Marie Antoinette, confess our love, and, by my knightly honor, she will not help feeling as it becomes a queen."

"I will pray and hope for it, Otto. I will accuse my jealous weakness for misconstruing the behavior of such a friend.—Let us now return, for why excite suspicion? My uncle shall be our only confidant."

Nassau kissed her hand, and they walked slowly toward the Swiss house, and thence down the mountain. At the cross-road leading to Little Trianon, the princess requested Nassau to go to the palace by another way. This was done for the sake of the Countess de Gorzka. He hastened onward, and Louise advanced toward the Moorish Pavilion.

The princess had long expected the

confession of Nassau's love, but had done nothing to induce it, for Charlotte de Gorzka had betrayed herself to the queen. Besides, Louise feared Chartres and his spies, so that all the circumstances rendered a declaration unadvisable. Now that it had transpired, she was all conscious of the gift of his love, and guarded it silently in her heart. When, however, she noticed the sadness of the countess, and remembered the inconsiderate oath in the Japanese Pavilion, at a time she thought Nassau loved Charlotte and not herself, Louise felt something like remorse. Could she be happy with Siegen without breaking the heart of the Polish maiden? She loved, and had vowed fidelity, but believed in no union with her lover.

The war with England was Nassau's hope; and, while he returned the attentions of Marie Antoinette in a graceful manner, he remained as well beloved as before, but he avoided every thing that could expose him to censure. A glance from Louise, or a stolen kiss, was both a sufficient reward and a token of confidence. Chartres was now certain as to the relation existing between Nassau and Madame de Lamballe; he knew that Penthièvre loved Louise and Siegen, while the old gentleman disliked Chartres since the death of his son Lamballe. Penthièvre could leave his position of grand-admiral to any one he pleased that was connected with his family; and, if Nassau married the princess with the consent of the king, what hindered the venerable duke from conferring that dignity on one who was a sailor as well as a soldier; thus throwing into Nassau's hand the material power of the country. It was necessary, then, by some means to injure the queen and Louise de Lamballe at the same time. Hence arose the slanders that sullied Marie Antoinette's innocency, and made questionable her reputation, so that her movements were subjected to special espionage.

War with England! This was no novel alarm. To assist North America became popular in France, and Maurepas would gladly have promoted the difficulties with Great Britain, if Turgot, Malesherbes, and even the queen, had not resisted him. The ministers thought that their first duty was to reëstablish order, before the cause of others was considered. They urged the abolition of some of the crown revenues, a reduction of taxes, and a convocation of the Estates-General. The latter the king absolutely refused, for he was rendered suspicious by Maurepas; and Malesherbes demanded his dismissal. Turgot, who saw that Louis desired Necker in his place, also resigned, as well as Mouy.

When Malesherbes was taking leave, the monarch said: "You are happy, for you can retire and forget; I must remain."

"Your majesty," he replied, "I have attempted to serve the son as I did the father; destiny seems to wish it otherwise. But, remember, my king, that the Malesherbes are faithful to the Bourbons even to death."

Chartres turned these words into the bon-mot: "*Les males herbes sont fidèles au mort des Bourbons!*"

The farewell of Turgot was more bitter. He said: "If you let your army march to the assistance of North America, sire, your own soldiers will carry republicanism into your palace!"

Turgot was succeeded by Necker, Mouy by the Count de St. Germain, and Malesherbes by the Count de Vergennes. The government was now freed from the philosophic friends of the deceased dauphin, the restless reformers who were always using the word "abuses," which gave occasion to the people for a witticism:

"Der König ist bereits belehrt,
Dass er selbst zu den Missbräuchen gehört!" *

The fair dream of Trianon vanished a second time, never to be renewed.

The *Wedding of Figaro* was finished. The dismissal of his friends Turgot and Malesherbes, the increase of the privileges of the nobles, and, in consequence, the hopelessness of Conti, and the ascendency of the party led by Maurepas and Artois, had aroused the poet's anger, and made the satire more cutting with which his work was infused. An occurrence, that became the court and town talk, added to the pointedness of the allusions.

Count Falcoz de la Blache lived in much disagreement with his wife since her father's death, for his love-adventures were notorious. Moved by an idea of avenging herself on her husband, the Countess Rosa found her page Seraphin de Gaugelat, a young man of nineteen, very interesting, who, as an obedient servant, returned whatever sentiment of regard she entertained toward him. It was no secret, and Beaumarchais used this scandalous history as the groundwork of his new production. Historians are acquainted with the original work, but they do not generally know that the characters of the comedy were persons living at the time. Count Almaviva, the aristocrat, who wishes to seduce Susanna, is Falcoz de la Blache; Rosina, his wife, the Countess Rosa, always neglected and finally tempted to sin; Figaro is Beaumarchais himself, with his merry Susanna—witty persons who at last ruin their enemies. The housekeeper in the judicial scene, called Marceline de Vercatour, almost like Ventadour, is the portrait of Marchioness Diana; the page Cherubin is of course a reproduction of the real Seraphin de Gaugelat; Bartolo and Basilio are Terray and Maupeau; and

the famous stammering judge, Don Guzman-Bridoison, is Brian de Goesman. The interpretation was plain, and every movement of the piece was a representation of the immorality of that age. Such language as involved the dialogue had never before been heard in France; Voltaire's applauded sentences were nothing in comparison. The first who heard the comedy read were Conti, Nassau, Turgot, and Malesherbes, and they were highly delighted with it. "O you assassin," exclaimed Conti, "you kill your victims by ridicule!"

Siegen informed the queen and Artois about it, and they wished to hear it read. A day was appointed on which the king was absent hunting, and several persons were invited to Trianon, a number large enough for an audience, yet so exclusive as to be considered Marie Antoinette's company. Beaumarchais read, assisted by the celebrated actors Lecain, Preville, and the actresses Clairon and Dumeuil, in the small theatre just then completed for the queen. Chartres, Maurepas, and Vergennes, were present. Susanna was in a side-box with the Countess de Gorzka.

The exertions of the count to get possession of Susanna produced great laughter in the first scenes. The dispute between Bartolo and Marceline, and the advice, "Be fair if thou canst, virtuous if thou desirest, but careful of thy reputation, for that thou must sustain!" excited a strange curiosity. "Whom does he mean?" was whispered. The page Cherubin, whose "heart is agitated every time he sees a woman," received much applause, arising from pleasure in the disgrace of one of the aristocratic class. The second act had a still more direct and severe meaning. The company felt such an expression as "To be a courtier is a difficult trade!" when Figaro smil-

---

* The king is already taught that he himself belongs to the "abuses."

17

ingly shrugged his shoulders and replied: "To receive, to take, to ask!—in these three words lies the whole secret!" The queen laughed aloud, thus contributing her share of applause. The comicality of the succeeding action, where the count is so often duped, had great interest, while the decision of the countess that "she would retire to the Ursulines," irritated the more bigoted. The definition of "an aristocrat," as "one who took the trouble to be born," was not relished, but it had to be accepted, because Marie Antoinette, Conti, Nassau, and many others of influence, were glowing with enthusiasm. The monologue on diplomacy and politics next came. "Politics! I know them, and they give no room for boasting. To assert a knowledge of what we do not know, and an ignorance of what we do; to pretend to an understanding of what, in its inconsistency, cannot be understood—to a hearing of what we do not hear; to profess to perform more than we can, and to make others imagine we have important secrets when we have none; to retire with a significant countenance, and appear to be in profound thought, when we have not two ideas in our mind; to publish the same person as both good and bad within a week; to employ spies, pay traitors, intercept letters, and violate their secrecy, and justify all such baseness by some paltry personal interest—if that is not the essence of politics, let me die!"

This could be borne no longer. Maurepas and Vergennes were on the point of withdrawing. "Duchess de Noailles," said Marie Antoinette, in rather an excited tone, "will you ask the ministers whether they feel hurt?" They were forced to remain. The character of Judge Bridoison decided the success of the comedy. When Lecain began to stammer, all exclaimed "Goesman! Goesman!" Rank, etiquette, and personal anger, were forgotten; for there was brought before their eyes the Maupeau Parliament, with Caron's suit. The general hilarity could not be restrained. When the surname of Marceline Vercatour was pronounced, one of the ladies asked quite naturally, "Ventadour?" The secret was revealed, the Marchioness Diana and her much-disputed liaison with Terray could not be misunderstood. The scene therefore of the discovery of the stolen child was listened to in breathless silence. The soliloquy on truth, the count's embarrassment with Fanchette, and the night scene near the pavilion, where the count is unmasked and confounded, concluded a triumph which was the more remarkable as those attacked were themselves the judges.

The queen spoke very flattering words to Beaumarchais, and took from her own arm a costly diamond bracelet, which she gave to Susanna as a keepsake; Caron was surrounded by admirers, when Maurepas approached him.

"Well, since you have gained so much applause here, you will not care about having your comedy publicly acted, will you?"

"On the contrary, it is to be, very soon; her majesty has just promised that."

"Indeed! However, it will not be represented as long as I am minister!"

"Well, I can wait for your dismissal! In the mean while I will publish a collection of couplets that my poetic colleague Maurepas in former times composed for the fishwomen. You alone inspired me, and one good turn deserves another. Besides, whether the comedy is played or not, it must be distributed among the people."

The smiles of others standing by closed the lips of Maurepas, and he left. The Princes de Provence and d'Artois were the most angry with the author. They did not deign to look at Beaumarchais, and the queen's presence alone prevented .them from insulting him. They had become his enemies, while Chartres was highly pleased.

"Is it not curious?" whispered Chartres to Sillery. "Whatever my father and I undertook against Beaumarchais always failed, and yet he is continually doing that which plays into our hands. It would really be foolish not to let him have his way."

On the following day, Maurepas, assisted by Provence and Artois, complained bitterly to the young king of the new comedy, quoted some of the passages, and drew attention to the fact that their publication in any manner would be dangerous to the government. Louis XVI., from a child, paid respect to appearances and regal dignity; and, though so dependent himself, he was anxious to maintain some show of independence. "I command you, M. de Maurepas," he said, "to forbid this insurrectionary work. I am sorry the queen was induced to hear it read."

Maurepas wrote a prohibition to the directors of the Menus Plaisirs, the censors, and publishers, against the performance of the comedy. "Oh, the good man," laughed Beaumarchais, "he means to make my name famous. The *Wedding* will be acted so much the oftener!"

The sensation the piece made among the courtiers was obvious, notwithstanding the opposition of the ministers and princes, the rebuke given the queen for protecting it, and the banishment of Caron from court. Conti said openly to the author: "My birth, I presume, is high enough to justify me in asking to dinner whom I please, my dear sir; and I like to dine with the illustrators of truth."

All who entertained the new philosophic and liberal political opinions among the aristocracy, magistracy, and army, had urged Beaumarchais to read his drama. No royal injunction or ministerial prohibition could affect the private drawing-rooms, and Caron was invited everywhere. It became the fashion to listen to the *Wedding of Figaro*, and its satires passed from mouth to mouth—from the drawing-rooms to the halls of justice, the parliamentary sessions, the coffee-houses, and finally to the boulevards. No one had read the piece, or possessed a copy of it, but every one quoted it.

About this time a noble life terminated its existence — a life spent in the service of the country, and which always labored for its happiness, yet felt that all had been in vain. . The Prince de Conti, the friend of the people, the pride of the Parliament, died, to the great joy of the Orleans, who hated him, as well as to that of the Princes de Provence and d'Artois, who feared him as their mentor, and of Maurepas, who dreaded his influence. Beaumarchais and Susanna lost their oldest patron in him; Nassau-Siegen and Louise de Lamballe their most powerful protector. After he had taken leave of Turgot, Malesherbes, and Caron, he placed the hand of his niece in that of Nassau, saying: "God has refused me my last wish—to see you two united. This is my severest, and, I am thankful, my last disappointment. The unhappy fate of this country is inevitable. Since MM. Turgot and Malesherbes fell, and monarchical France assisted republican America in her revolution, we can hope nothing more from this century. Nassau, be the protector of my Louise! Let your chivalrous heart and ardent love watch over her well-being, and guide her through the storm. May God grant it! —When I am dead, wrap me in the mantle of my order; alas, I bore my cross while living!"

CHAPTER XXIV.

A ROYAL ERROR.

THE new minister of war, Count de St. Germain, was an old soldier who had the greatest respect for the military regulations of Frederick II. He received orders to prepare the army and navy for the anticipated hostile operations. Incited by Chartres, who had his own views, he began to disband the royal domestic guards, because their maintenance was so expensive. First, he deprived the princes of the royal blood of their body-guards; then, he broke up the corps of gendarmes, the dragoon regiment of the queen, the body light horse, and placed the men in the field regiments. He was now projecting also to abolish the Gardes Nobles, only sparing the king's Swiss Guards. Nassau's position was threatened! With it he lost all hope, and would have to return to his adventurous life. He therefore resolved to confess all to the queen; and Madame de Lamballe, though anxious and timid, consented.

Marie Antoinette, on the other hand, the more she felt the king estranged from her by the conduct of Maurepas, and found herself neglected, strove to awaken a spark of conjugal love in the heart of Louis XVI. She showed her partiality for Siegen openly, and indulged in coquetry to arouse the monarch's jealousy. The queen, however, was much depressed by the birth of a son to the Prince d'Artois, who, as Provence had no children, was heir to the throne, and whom the Parisians already called the "Dauphin." The outraged feelings of the neglected wife —of the insulted, childless queen—

drove her to actions the consequences of which she never imagined.

Nassau as well as Louise felt the danger of their respective positions. He was aware of the slander concerning him, though as yet but whispered, and therefore his deportment in the presence of his royal partners was hesitating, for he feared to be misconstrued. It was time to put an end to misapprehension. Several times he accompanied her majesty in her promenades; at first very timidly, and then more urgently, he represented to her the danger threatening him if St. Germain carried out his reduction of the home troops. A fear, natural but perhaps false, had made him silent as to his love for Louise. Marie Antoinette promised to do all she could to save the corps, and several times spoke on the subject with Louis, but he evaded it. The decision, however, was to be made. The queen saw with delight signs of suspicious ill-temper in her husband, and sought to increase it.

Louis was in his private apartments at Trianon. For several days he had been very irritable and restless, avoiding his attendants, and permitting no one in his cabinet but the minister and his brothers. He was idle, neglected his hunting exercise, and had no inclination to engage in his favorite amusements, for he seemed to be disturbed by something which he was attempting to suppress with great effort. Below, in the park, his wife was disporting with her cavaliers and ladies, and with Chartres, Nassau, and Provence; she had secret information of what her husband did, and the more strangely he acted the more careless and frivolous was her behavior.

Louis was walking up and down his apartment, sometimes glancing at the company below, through the window, at which his youngest brother stood.

"I do not believe you, Artois!

And if you swore ten times that Chartres had observed them at a *tête-à-tête*, I cannot believe it of her! Because you are all such faithless husbands, you wish to make me one also. Your dissipated life has taught you to despise women, but I believe in woman's virtue! Her fair and open countenance cannot deceive. A person on whom Nature has bestowed such charms, cannot be false."

"My royal brother, whoever speaks the truth is apt to be ill received. The question now, however, is not the happiness of your life, but the dignity of the crown and the destiny of France. If you are honest you must confess that you have never loved Marie Antoinette, and—"

"But I never hated her, and now I love her! It is impossible to dislike her. I had no eyes when I allowed you to prejudice me against her."

"There are many beautiful women one cannot dislike! Your marriage, as well as mine, was an intrigue of Choiseul, who sold us to Austria. Was there ever a member of the Hapsburg family that was not false? Marie does not love you, and childless queens are the most contemptible creatures under the sun! Why does she detest the Cardinal de Rohan? Because he discovered that she had love-affairs with her chamberlain, while she was a princess at Vienna, and warned Choiseul against this match. But the minister desired you to have no children, because only then could he hope to rule! In the name of your dignity and that of France, I request you to investigate her relations with Nassau-Siegen! Do not fear the consequences. You would not be the first sovereign who divorced a barren consort."

The king did not reply. He put his hand to his fevered brow, where very unhappy thoughts were passing. "The Gardes Nobles must be disbanded to-day! You may tell St. Germain that I will sign the decree. When and where did Chartres see them together?"

"A week ago, about twilight, near the grotto; and, the day before yesterday, on the road to the Swiss Pavilion."

"To the Swiss Pavilion? And she pretended to prepare for me a surprise, while she was providing an asylum for her crimes—a convenient hiding-place for forbidden love! A queen!"

"If I am not mistaken, she is about to take another promenade with Nassau to Little Trianon. I have seen the Princess de Lamballe, the Duchess de Noailles, Chartres, and Provence, retire on a sign from her.—There! she is preparing to go alone with him now! Well, I confess, the faithless wife of a citizen could not act more openly!"

The king approached the window. He saw his consort give orders to her attendants, and, casting a quick glance toward him, turn with a jesting remark, carrying her straw hat on her arm, chatting merrily, and disappearing with Nassau-Siegen. "Artois, accompany me! I will make an end of this!"

"Then act as becomes a king, my brother."

"I will not disregard what is due to outward decorum; I will not permit myself to do that which is not becoming a monarch! Go down at once, and await me at the arcade to the right. See that the path is clear."

Artois hastened away. "Another rendezvous, Chartres?" he whispered.

"So it seems, monseigneur. I am correct this time."

"I heard Nassau, while playing, ask her in a whisper for the favor of an interview!" said Provence.

"Since she is so very imprudent, let her have her deserts," laughed Artois. "Some trouble is near, for our brother is about to follow her; we shall have a charming scene! Take care that you are not in our way; he expects me at the colonnade!"

"I suppose it is not forbidden to be a hidden witness among the bushes?" said Provence, ironically. "If the queen takes a walk, I suppose we can do so also?"

"And it is a mere accident if we happen to meet!" replied Chartres. "Let us go to our place of observation."

Chartres and Provence went to the left, while D'Artois advanced toward the colonnades on the right.

Louise de Lamballe was aware that Siegen intended to come to an explanation with the queen, and felt great fear on account of her majesty's strange levity. She had also noticed a curious expression in the countenances of the ladies and gentlemen, as well as the smiles and whispers of the princes. Though she had not sufficient courage to confess her love to the queen, she cast aside all scruples at this critical moment, in order, if necessary, to warn Marie Antoinette, and by her own presence to divert any suspicion that the queen's thoughtlessness might bring on Siegen. She sent away the Countess de Gorzka, and, losing herself in the middle path, followed the pair in advance of her. The Polish maiden, however, loved Nassau too much, and was too jealous of the queen, to obey the wishes of Louise. She went to her apartment, but, finding Madame de Lamballe absent, hastened through the corridor, and gained the arcade to the right, just as D'Artois entered. She hid behind a statue, while the prince passed on to the peristyle leading to the king's staircase. Scarcely had he crossed the threshold, than she glided toward the right path. When D'Artois reached the inner staircase, the king, whose eyes were red with weeping, met him. His dress was in disorder, and his sword turned the wrong way.

D'Artois hastened to his brother. "Permit me, my king!—People should not notice your agitation by your appearance!" He arranged the king's sword, and the ribbon, from which hung the cross of St. Louis.

"That will do—come!"

The king and D'Artois went down the avenue, and soon saw the Countess de Gorzka in the distance. "The lady of Madame de Lamballe!" said Louis. "Detain her, my brother."

D'Artois' hastened forward. Charlotte, hearing steps behind her, turned and uttered an exclamation of fear.

"Stop, countess, the king commands it!" called D'Artois, while Louis advanced. Notwithstanding the countess's fright, she had some notion of what was transpiring, and endeavored to recover herself.

"Why did you scream, when you saw us, countess?"

"Ah, your majesty, I did not expect you, and was alarmed."

"Indeed, but what are you doing here alone?"

"I?—ah—her highness the Princess de Lamballe is ill, and has gone to her chamber, and—"

"I ask, what are *you* doing here?"

"Oh, the queen has ordered me to follow her."

"You? Whither, if I may ask?"

"To the grotto, I think."

"Are you sure of that?"

"Or to the Swiss cottage. Your majesty, I have really forgotten!"

"Not so bad, to forget the orders of your queen! Very strange! Well, let us go together to look for her majesty; follow us!"

"I obey!" she whispered, and walked behind them.

In the mean while the queen and her escort went their way—Nassau with anxious fear for the result, and the royal lady with a cheerfuluess and excitement that betrayed her anticipation of a scene which she desired. She walked slowly, and, as if she had forgotten Siegen's petition, chatted on a thousand indifferent subjects, about which neither cared much at that moment. Nassau felt badly; he wished to speak, but could not, and would gladly have knelt at her feet, so that his destiny might be decided, but she gave him no opportunity. He would rather have been in the hostile presence of a host of Indian Sepoys, than in that of a woman concerning whom he was uncertain by what feeling or motive she was controlled. At last they arrived at Little Trianon and the grotto.

Marie Antoinette sat down on a stone bench, glancing sportively around.— "Be not angry that I have detained you by all manner of talk. You men have wishes enough, but not much prudence in realizing them. You proposed to speak to me about the danger threatening your position. I know also of your hopes that my imperial mother will be influenced by me to return your confiscated land. But we women, even when queens, are powerless mortals! My illustrious mother is disposed to grant your desires, but my brother Joseph, the co-regent of the empire, is decidedly opposed. 'If Nassau wants his land,' he writes, 'let him enter the imperial service. I give no German land to a Frenchman!' As to the Gardes Nobles, the prospect is not encouraging. St. Germain will have his way. There must be field regiments for this war. I have spoken thrice to the king, but he did not please to accede to my request. There is but one possibility of retaining you here—that is, should Colonel d'Afry accept another post, and you take the command of the Swiss Guards." She conversed with all her grace and amiability, as if she meant to ameliorate bad news by her most friendly confidence.

Nassau pressed his lips to Marie Antoinette's hand. "Illustrious lady," he replied, "your kind condescension surpasses my humble merit; it exposes me to the envy of the court, and my queen to the suspicion of too marked a preference for me. I would, however, never have accepted the high position to which the king called me—my pride would have forbidden me to appeal to your powerful protection, and I would not now cast myself at your feet —if my ambition only were to be satisfied, or I were to obtain a right long denied me. For myself, my sword suffices! I am anxious for more than mere renown and power. I am petitioning for that which embellishes life— the love of a noble and beautiful lady, who is related to you, whose fate as well as mine is in your hands, and without whom I care not to live!"

"What brings you here at the feet of the queen?" asked a rough voice. The king stood before them. Artois, cold and smiling; Charlotte de Gorzka, pale and trembling, were at a little distance.

Nassau sprang to his feet, while Marie Antoinette rose in surprise, blushing deeply. A painful pause ensued.

"My royal husband," said the queen, "the Prince von Nassau-Siegen, knowing that his office is precarious, has just made a confession which I am sorry he did not confide to me sooner. He loves—he loves the Countess de Gorzka!"

"Your majesty!" exclaimed Nassau, amazed.

"But, prince, of what use is hesitation now?" asked the queen.

"D'Artois! Countess de Gorzka!" commanded the king. "Approach!" Both advanced. "Give me your hand, countess!" Charlotte gave it shyly. "I betroth you to Prince von Nassau-Siegen, who has just asked your hand of the queen. The marriage will take place after the war, in which I mean to give the prince an independent naval command."

There was a painful sigh from Louise de Lamballe, who in her hiding-place had heard all and fainted. But the countess, with joyful exclamations, covered the hands of the royal pair with kisses.

"This is all very well, countess," said Louis, gloomily. "D'Artois, make the engagement known in my name.— Your majesty, take my arm." He made a motion with his hand, and departed.

Nassau stood as if an abyss had suddenly opened before him. The fair Polish lady approached now with bent head, awaiting an explanation; but he bowed silently, and passed hastily to the place where Louise had concealed herself, while D'Artois smiled ironically. Siegen found Provence and Chartres endeavoring to restore consciousness to the Princess de Lamballe.

"Here is my place!" he exclaimed, in a broken voice, assisting Louise. "Princess! Let us away!"

"But what does it all mean?" cried Provence, in astonishment. "Let us go to D'Artois!"

"Do you wish to hear the news?" said D'Artois merrily. "The king has just betrothed Nassau to the Countess de Gorzka!"

"Gorzka!" exclaimed Chartres. "Ah, countess, I congratulate you!" Then taking the other two princes by the arm, he drew them hastily away. "For the sake of all the saints, come, your highnesses, or I shall faint with laughter! The queen, caught at a *tête-à-tête*, has given him the wrong bride! And he must have her for the sake of her majesty's honor!"

Louis and his consort took the road leading to the Swiss cottage. She was feverish and excited, while he bowed

his head in grief. When they were alone, he threw her hand violently from his arm.

"You have chosen a pretty juggler's trick, madame, and which seems to please Nassau least of all! If you possess one grain of honor and virtue— if you came to this country to be a pattern to your sex and a blessing to them—then, instead of destroying your happiness by falsehood, immorality, and intrigue, have at least the courage to confess your folly. The Hapsburgs are usually proud! Be queenly enough not to appear better than you are!"

"You are angry with me, Louis; you have always been distant in your manner, and perhaps you even despise me! Then I bless Heaven for your hatred and anger; for they betray feelings better than the neglectful coldness with which until now you treated me; they prove that if I cannot quicken your love, I can arouse your jealousy."

"I do not understand you! Awaken my love? Was that your object?"

"Oh, you have never made the discovery, that your education — your prejudices against the Austrian woman, and your confidants, who gain by our separation, all united to uproot any love you ever had for me, so that you overlooked all my efforts to regain your heart. Do you think it is nothing that our marriage is a laughing-stock; that the Princess d'Artois smiles haughtily upon me, because she is a mother? I came into this country without loving or being really loved, but I came with the honest desire to be your friend, your wife, and the sharer of your troubles. I learned to love your virtues, Louis, and what is my reward? Neglect— nothing but heartless neglect! Am I so deformed and unamiable—so worthy of such conduct—that I can claim from you nothing but good-will, of which you repent as soon as M. de Maurepas desires it? Well, then, send me back to my imperial mother; what matters it if my heart break? Rome has never refused a dispensation to a sovereign ruler!" She stood proudly before him, for the first time a conscious queen.

"Antoinette, but Nassau-Siegen—at your feet!"

"I knew, since his appointment as chief of the Gardes Nobles, that the Countess de Gorzka loved him; that he wished to make a confession of his love for her, and desired me to be his mediator. But I must own, my royal husband, I could not bear the thought of continuing to live unloved; I wished to conquer your heart by strategy. Do you call that unqueenly or frivolous? Then I will be silent, but the woman is of more importance than the queen, and I cannot be the one without feeling myself happy as the other. I yearned to make you jealous, and therefore selected a man whose heart was farthest from me; but who most needed my friendship. Have I again deceived myself by false hopes, Louis? Let me weep, then, since I have in vain excited your suspicion, and degraded myself, and all because I love you so foolishly!"

The king took her hand and kissed it. "Can you assure me of the truth of this?"

"I can! I will never cease to love you—and I would seal my affection with the sacrifice of my life."

"Then pardon me, my true queen! My future life shall be but one effort to make you forget the tears you have wept on account of the indifferent Louis!" He embraced her and asked: "Now tell me truly, Antoinette, who gave you this dangerous courage?"

"A poet's comedy, and one that displeases you—the 'Wedding of Figaro.'"

"It seems to me this Beaumarchais is driving the people crazy."

From that day the king's conduct changed toward his consort. She had purchased, by the misery of her best friend, the happiness of knowing herself beloved. When Siegen, incapable of expressing his sorrow, conducted Louise de Lamballe back to the palace, she pressed his hand gently, and said in a low voice: "As I have promised, I shall ever love you; but you see some fatality attends our steps—we dare not be happy."

On the following day the prince addressed these lines to Countess Gorzka: "It has pleased the monarch, countess, to affiance me to you. I obey because I must, and dare not insult the queen and a noble lady like you. I would therefore spare your feelings, which are sacred to me, even if I do not share them. I shall die as your betrothed, but have the humanity never to expect me to swear that fidelity to you which belongs to the Princess de Lamballe! You have been deceived. Let us both silently endure the evil, and pardon me if I have injured you. It is doubly my duty not to leave you for an instant in doubt of my true sentiments. I hope we shall soon have war with England, when perhaps a bullet may acquit us of our obligations."

Caron and Susanna heard with sorrow of the unfortunate turn the love-affairs of their friends had taken.

"Shall egotism," exclaimed Beaumarchais, in great excitement, "misunderstanding, and the haste of this betrothal, separate two hearts intended for each other, because a king and a queen committed these faults? Shall an error be irrevocable because a monarch was guilty of it; and all our efforts to render you and the princess happy be in vain through the folly of one minute? No, my august friend, do not lose courage. Something important is at the bottom of your misfortune, though apparently caused by accident. That you have now been separated from Louise, dismissed from the body-guards, and your position endangered, seem to me the work of intrigue, and where any thing evil is in question, Chartres cannot be far off. I shall inform myself, and become your advocate, as you were mine in my need; and, if an arbitrary whim deprived you of Madame de Lamballe, either the war or—the revolution, must return her to you! I have still some arrows in my quiver for the hydra."

The war so ardently desired, but so fatal to France, at length began. Burgoyne, the general of the British, was defeated by the Americans at Saratoga. Franklin appeared as delegate from the United States at Paris and Versailles, in order to determine France against an alliance with England. The youthful Lafayette hastened, with others, into the struggle for the transatlantic Union, and Beaumarchais agreed to deliver to the Americans arms to the amount of eight million francs. The battle-cry of the French was: "War against England, and for the Republic of America!" Maurepas was forced to make preparations against Great Britain, and enter into a treaty of friendship and commerce with the United States, through Franklin's personal influence and the demands of the public.

"From desert to desert!" Louise de Lamballe's presentiment was fulfilled. She renounced the happiness of love, devoting herself to Marie Antoinette, whose conjugal peace had been purchased by the princess's misery. She avoided Nassau-Siegen, and delicacy as well as pride prevented her from betraying her grief to her royal friend. Her firm will aided in depressing and disguising her feelings, so that no one imagined that this woman, paler but more beautiful than ever, with so gracious a smile upon her lips, bore a broken heart. She exchanged no word

with Countess de Gorzka, who had been raised to the dignity of a lady of honor by the queen.

Siegen, hitherto a courtier against his nature, from his hope of one day marrying Louise, returned to all that passion for glory which had distinguished his adventurous youth. He shunned the court circles as much as possible, in order to prepare himself, as he said, for the war. He renewed his former soldier life, and to this portion of his history belong the wild feats of horsemanship and the duels which made him famous among the military. The king and the queen might have divined the cause of his altered behavior, as well as of the Princess de Lamballe's gravity, and the Countess de Gorzka's sadness, if they had not been too much occupied with themselves. The happiness of the royal couple made them blind to the wretchedness of others, for an awakened love urged the young king to the other extreme, and made him the slave of his wife. As Nassau-Siegen bore his affliction with courage, they did not understand him, and supposed him to be inspired by warlike ardor and ambition, while he was truly driven by despair; and they considered the countess's melancholy nothing but anxiety for her lover, hastening to the dangers of the battle-field.

Beaumarchais exerted himself, according to the order of the king, to bring his suit for damages before the Parliament at Aix, and now published his last and best pamphlet, in which he laid bare his whole connection with La Blache, from the time when he rescued Susanna from the persecutions of the count at Passy, until the author was condemned to make payment to him by the suit of Goesman. The interest excited by these events as well as by the "Wedding of Figaro," and the curses uttered against La Blache, were beyond description. The count was

"MAY I REALLY SEND FOR HIM?"   p. 267.

sentenced to repay the hundred and fifty thousand francs, besides giving an indemnification for nearly as large a sum out of the inheritance of Duverney, as well as costs and interest. La Blache's fortune, already wasted by dissipation, was ruined, and his disgrace closed the doors of his equals against him. He did not wait long as a victim of his own folly and degradation. On receiving the verdict of the Parliament, he rode to his estate at Passy. In the garden, on the very spot where he first saw Susanna, he shot himself! Thus ended Count Falcoz de la Blache, the mad Almaviva!

The same pamphlet of Beaumarchais brought evil upon other parties also. He exposed the Abbé Terray and Diana de Ventadour to the most dishonorable suspicions by identifying them with Marceline and Bartolo, characters from his comedy. Beaumont, then the Archbishop of Paris, could not rest under the ignominy thus brought upon his profession, especially at a time so inimical to the clergy. He made personal complaints to the king; and Louis XVI., bitterly aggrieved, sent Caron to the Conciergerie. When Beaumarchais was taken away, he requested Susanna to put the queen in possession of the case of documents, by means of the Princess de Lamballe, who, he knew, was favorably disposed.

As soon as Marie Antoinette read these papers, she hastened to the king's cabinet. "My husband, you have imprisoned Beaumarchais. I know you are angry with him on account of the 'Wedding of Figaro.' But read these papers which he has just sent me, and then judge what effect such testimony must have in his hand, if the suit should be pressed against him."

Louis XVI. read the documents, and, rising sullenly, rang the bell. "Send for Archbishop Beaumont; he must come immediately, even if he is in the confessional!" The courier left five minutes after. "Antoinette, I thank you," said the king; "you have preserved me from an act of great injustice. Beaumarchais must at once be set at liberty. It is really a kind of loyalty in him, that he confided these proofs to his sovereign, and not to a court of justice."

"And will you not treat him with more kindness? Shall the ambition of his life—the 'Wedding'—that gave me so much pleasure, never be represented? It is better, sire, to advance such dangerous but honorable men, than by their persecution to increase the number of alienated subjects. Your father loved him, and—Caron feels unhappy that the son should repulse him."

"Well, let him come—I know you like him. Let him hand his comedy to the censorship. But all that is offensive to certain parties must surely be erased."

"May I really send for him, Louis?" asked the queen.

"Certainly. But I must first liberate him and annul all the accusations against him."

"Then do it immediately! One dash of your pen, and—" She held the pen toward him eagerly.

"Antoinette! I am afraid I am falling into many follies for your sake!"

"By which good and talented men are benefited. Is it foolish to do right?" The king kissed her, and then sat down to write to the Châtelet and the Conciergerie. The queen was leaving with the orders, when Beaumont entered.

"Your eminence, I have this moment released M. de Beaumarchais, and destroyed the process against him."

"Your majesty!" exclaimed the archbishop, suddenly stepping back, as if wounded.

"Read these papers; then you will

know what to do as the supreme head of your diocese! Consider the disgrace to the clergy! I give you eight days. Do not force me to appeal to civil justice. I should certainly do so; for such a crime no pardon can be granted, and I do not wish to be considered a—king of Jesuits."

Beaumont turned pale as he read; then, bowing, he said: "I obey your majesty; but, when the guilty persons are removed, shall these proofs still—"

"I will destroy them with my own hand!"

The archbishop did his duty. He called a secret meeting of prelates, and their verdict was: "Imprisonment for life of the Abbé Terray, and incarceration in the penitentiary at Montmartre of the Marchioness Diana de Ventadour!"

Terray had friends among the ecclesiastic judges. One of these informed him of what had taken place. Horrified, the abbé hastily snatched up his treasures and went to the Hôtel Ventadour. "The terrible event has occurred. Beaumarchais sent Susanna's papers to the king. Beaumont was called, and the clerical court have decided our destiny! Eternal penitence! You have caused this, Diana, because, in spite of your hatred of this worthless fellow and his wife, you never dared to make use of the phial, which you were always ready to apply for the advantage of others."

The woman stood as if petrified, and then cast a glance of unutterable contempt on her fellow-criminal. "I never did that, because I possessed one grain less of iniquity than you. You may laugh, but my maternal heart spoke within me. I will, however, make amends for listening to its dictates. I suppose the judges will not be in so great a hurry."

"What are you thinking of? Every minute brings us nearer our wretched fate—the dungeon! We must flee; hasten, for Heaven's sake!"

"I did not know you were such a coward! Believe me, I have always *one* way in reserve to escape my foes. Let them come! I will have the travelling-carriage prepared and make my arrangements. We shall have time, however, to take a slight collation, for we must not tarry on our journey. Are we not going to England?"

"Of course, in that country we may amuse ourselves with these Parisian fools."

"Certainly, I shall be back directly."

The abbé paced the floor uneasily. A waitress appeared with a sealed bottle of wine, glasses, and pastry. "Is the coach nearly ready?"

"It will be at the door in a moment, M. l'Abbé. Will you permit me to fill a glass of wine for you? The marchioness will be here shortly."

"Make haste, then. I hope the lady will not be long making her preparations. I believe, if such a thing were possible, women would make a toilet for the grave." While he was speaking, the marchioness entered in her travelling-costume.

"You are rather severe, abbé. Had you not better take a little wine?" She took her glass and emptied it. Terray did the same.

"Ah, this wine is fiery, passing through the veins like a stream of lava! Give me another glass."

"Do you and Lucien take down the baggage of the abbé, and my strong box, girl.—I carry nothing with me, abbé, but money."

"Very good!" smiled Terray, "money is every thing in this world; an old financial minister ought to know that."

The servant left the apartment. Diana filled her glass again. "A happy voyage, my friend! It is our last journey!"

"What—what do you mean?"

"Well, that henceforth we shall live free from sorrow. But you are fatigued—be seated! Why, what is the matter with you?"—A heavy sound, and Terray was lying lifeless at her feet!

"Are you dead?" she asked, with a smile. "I suppose you are gone to announce my coming?" She sat down slowly in the arm-chair, with her glass in her hand: "Thus I end a life of agony and crime by that method in which I sinned most. I plunge into an unknown eternity with him who made me what I am." She drank. "I deserve and demand no pardon; but while Thou judgest me, Supreme Justice —whose existence I feel and yet cannot believe—do not forget my worst companion, Orleans, and my most daring pupil, Chartres. I thank Thee for one thing, inscrutable Destiny, that, even in my most wicked moments, I was saved from being the murderess of my child. Live happily, Susanna—you are now safe!" The glass fell into fragments on the floor. Raising her hands, she clasped them, as if in prayer. Outside, was a rattling of wheels—a carriage had come, and voices were heard in the hall. A grim smile passed over her lips, and she was dead.

Five monks entered. Nothing of their features was visible, save their eyes, glancing darkly through the holes of their hoods. They stood in amazement.

"They are no more!" said one of them. "*Requiescant in pace, amen!*"

"What is to be done?" whispered another.

"I believe that they are not dead, and should be taken to the carriage," said the principal monk. "They belong to us, and must not die in the profane world. For the honor of the Church, raise them and cover them with the robes of the penitent." The bodies were veiled, and borne quickly away.

As the last sound of the vehicle died in the distance, the servants rushed into the room. "Heaven be praised," exclaimed the lady's maid, "they are both gone, and we are the next heirs! Be sure to throw away these bottles and glasses; the old lady never lacked something to put into them."

Susanna was spared the pain of weeping over the death of her unhappy mother. Terray and Diana had merely disappeared from society. For a short time this caused some whispering, but soon their very existence passed out of mind.

CHAPTER XXV.

CASSANDRA.

THE gravity of Louise de Lamballe, the reserve and melancholy of the Countess de Gorzka, did not at all agree with the cheerfulness and sparkling zest for pleasure which at this time distinguished Marie Antoinette. She did not understand the unhappiness of these two women, often laughed at their seriousness, and teased the countess as a "sad bride only waiting for the orange-wreath which the war would bring." Sometimes she made them understand her dissatisfaction, for she desired to see only laughing faces around her. Thus the friendship formerly existing between the queen and the Princess de Lamballe gradually cooled, and another person stepped into the foreground, whose humor pleased the queen better—Countess Jules de Polignac.

The Polignacs were an old aristocratic family, allied to that of the Orleans since the days of the Fronde, but reduced in circumstances. Urged by the old Duke d'Orleans, the Princess d'Artois had appointed Diana de Polignac, the sister of the count, superintendent of her household, and Chartres managed to present the Countess Jules to the queen as early as 1775. She was not malicious or artful; on the contrary, she was frank, and sportive, and always entertaining, but animated by a desire (very excusable in her position) to raise the credit and fortune of her family by means of the queen. She continued on friendly terms with Prince d'Artois and Chartres, as much from gratitude as policy, and her natural shrewdness failed not to make every effort that could gain her superiority over the other court ladies, particularly the grave and haughty Louise de Lamballe. Her influence became perceptible when her husband, Count Jules, obtained a high position, and Marie Antoinette required her presence more than that of others.

The reduction of the household troops, which so seriously concerned the Prince de Nassau, did not take place, for St. Germain, the minister of war, was dismissed, because he insulted the military nobles in many instances, endeavored to introduce into the army, the Prussian punishment of whipping, and to restrict the expenses of the Hôtel des Invalides. The Guards remained organized, and Nassau was safe; but the prospect of advancing his fortune in the war was not so bright. It is true, the king promised him a naval command; and the French fleet was to concentrate, under Admiral Count d'Orvillier, on the west coast, against Admiral Keppel of the British fleet, a movement which ruined the commerce of the islands of Ouessant and Jersey. Chartres, however, who knew how to influence his father-in-law Penthièvre by numerous artful flatteries, wishing to succeed the aged duke as grand-admiral, claimed the command promised to Nassau.

The king was induced to give the preference to Chartres, through the influence of Madame de Polignac, and the recommendations of the Count d'Artois and Maurepas. This appointment deeply affected the Princess de Lamballe, as well as the Countess de Gorzka, and irritated Nassau-Siegen. It required all the eloquence of Beaumarchais to prevent the prince from resigning his command of the Guards, and accompanying Lafayette to America. This happened at the time when Terray and Diana de Ventadour ended their lives; and the king thereupon gave permission to have the comedy of Beaumarchais passed upon by the Board of Censure.

The queen invited both Caron and Susanna to Marly, for they had become objects of special interest since La Blache's miserable death, and the discovery of Susie's birth. The Princes d'Artois and de Chartres were immediately notified of this gracious invitation, by the Countess de Polignac. D'Artois, the libertine, hated Beaumarchais from the time of the reading of the comedy, and Chartres was aware of the friendship of the author for Nassau, and therefore was the more anxious in reference to the naval command. Both therefore resolved to remain in the vicinity of the king, to frustrate any intrigue against them by their personal presence. Chartres even went farther. He determined to enter the career intended for the Prince de Lamballe, for he had Penthièvre's promise of being made grand-admiral after his first naval campaign. He prepared to start at a moment's notice, for the thought of being deprived of his office, and unmasked by Beaumarchais, the old enemy of his family, filled him with hatred, and strengthened his resolutions. He had heard sufficient about the troubles of his friends Terray and Madame de Ventadour, to fear a similar exposure concerning himself, and made his arrangements with Sillery, concluding with these words: "If I say, on leaving the king's antechamber, 'Do as we agreed,' then do not hesitate a moment. In the other case, I shall say, 'All is well!' But this is not likely to be, for I must make an end of him, and rid myself of this perpetual fear."

The invitation of Marie Antoinette, sent by Louise de Lamballe, made different impressions on Caron and Susanna. The latter was as pleased as a child; for she rejoiced at the honor bestowed on her husband, and that she should see Nassau and the princess again. Beaumarchais was very grave. He considered what he could do for Siegen, resolving to use his appearance at court for his benefit, and repay him as far as possible for what he had done for Susanna in their time of need. Madame de Lamballe begged them to come to Marly about noon, so that they might remain with her until the levee of the queen.

Susie dressed herself in her best style, wearing the bracelet presented her by Marie Antoinette, and the head-dress which Caron had given to Susanna in the "Wedding of Figaro" as a bridal present. The queen was at that time interested in this ornament. Besides, she had on a Spanish dress, representing the full national costume, in compliment to her royal patroness. The old chevalière, Madame de Piron, could not praise enough the little lady's taste, and she really looked more charming than ever. While Gomez, the Spanish valet, was waiting in the dress of a *majo*, with hair-net, ribboned hat, embroidered jacket, and a knife in his sash, Beaumarchais and his wife once more walked through the garden.

"In this toilet," said Susanna, "which you gave my representative in the 'Wedding,' you cannot think, my dearest Figaro, how delightful it is to saunter along these paths, where almost every tree and flower has its own serious or comic history. We almost learn to love our sorrows when we know that they have passed by without materially injuring us, feeling that Heaven has graciously conducted us through all. It was in this place where Conti stood for the last time."

Caron nodded in a melancholy manner. "In that arbor sat Piron, Aumont, Morelly, Malesherbes, and Turgot—some fallen into obscurity, and others dead."

"But we are not dead, and have risen after every fall.—Is not this the door through which Orleans and Chartres glided as serpents, when you were to be sent to the galleys?"

"Leaving their reputation in my power; and, by Heaven, I will use it to assist Nassau in freeing himself from the rascality that seeks his ruin!"

"That is also my wish—I would rejoice to have the prince appreciated according to his worth, and made happy by the hand of Madame de Lamballe."

"We must not attempt too much at once, my child. We should first secure the naval office to Nassau, and thus arouse the princess from her apathy."

"But how will you manage, so that the king will listen to you?"

"I will have recourse to extreme measures. It is a combat—probably the last, and that makes me serious."

"For my part, I find it much more difficult to dispel the misunderstanding of the queen, and the Countess de Gorzka's selfishness. Louis XVI. is just."

"Well, let us go, we must delay no longer. Do what you can to incline all hearts toward us."

"Let me take one more look, that I may be strengthened by my recollections." Passing over the terrace, they entered the carriage and drove to Marly.

The royal couple were residing at the Pavillon du Soleil, which was surrounded by twelve villas, occupied by the highest and most favored members of their suite. To the left, north of the highway, lay the pretty little village of Marly; and, at the right, the forest descended to the valley of Arcis. A fine drive branched off at Roquencourt, leading through the woods to the palace.

As the distance was greater by the way of Neuilly than by Saint-Cloud, Caron and Susanna chose the latter route, especially as they would pass through the valley in view of Versailles and Trianon, with their old and pleasant memories. Riding through the forest shades, Caron thought of the time when, in company with his friends, he went that way, to see the "Desired" for the first time; and how anxiously in yonder parsonage did Susanna await her husband's return from Spain!

"If the evening should be fine, dear Caron, let us return on foot through the park at Vaucresson. The valley of the Mauldré by moonlight is worth looking at."

"To keep you in good-humor, I suppose I must say yes?"

Louise de Lamballe, expecting her visitors, stood at the window of her reception-room in the Pavillon Taureau, situated at the entrance of the road to Roquencourt. She had not seen Beaumarchais and his wife since the reading of the comedy; and she rejoiced when their carriage stopped before the door.

"Welcome, my dear, dear friends," Louise exclaimed as the guests entered. "I have you again, and the last dark cloud of your life is also dispersed. We have plenty of time to chat until the levee, as Countess de Gorzka is on duty to-day.—Dear me, how prettily you have adorned yourself, Madame Susie!"

"In honor of you and to please the queen. I am not Susanna Beaumarchais to-day, but Susie Figaro. Do you not remember that her majesty was curious about this head-dress?"

"That is true! Well, she will be highly delighted. I can tell you, my excellent friend, the royal couple take a great interest in you now."

"Would that it were such as to induce them to listen to me, if I dare speak for a friend!—Has Prince de Chartres already received his command?"

"The order is not yet made out, but the place is as surely his as the king's word can make it."

"The king's word! So had Siegen also, when their majesties considered it necessary to make that unfortunate betrothal. I shall do my utmost to assist him in obtaining his rights."

"That is a hopeless task," said Madame de Lamballe, gloomily. "You will only expose yourself to his majesty's displeasure, and, after all, not conquer influences we are well aware of, and which are stronger than ever. D'Artois is opposed to you, and Madame de Polignac to me; besides, the king will not return before evening from hunting, and your reception will be cordial or cool, according to the luck he has had."

"Then we must gain the queen for our cause, for her will is at present paramount."

"Only not in politics, and then—Let us talk of something else. Oh, I am so wearied of courtier life—this perpetual play of interests—that I was too glad when you were invited. Your presence is as a fresh breeze reviving one in a suffocating atmosphere."

"But do not be angry with us," said Susanna, "if, instead of diverting you, and turning your thoughts to other matters, we speak of yourself, and, as honest physicians, try to heal your heart's wounds."

"Do not be gloomy, noble lady," and Beaumarchais took her hand. "Should it not be our first duty, after you helped us to gain our last deliverance, to prove our gratitude by attempting to unite the only two persons we still love?"

"I have no illusions, Caron. The last foolish hope fled from me on that fatal day near the grotto—I am destined to live alone. Do not let us sadden these few hours by such feelings. I am endeavoring to practise the art of forgetting, and hoped you would aid me. Judge coolly about the position of affairs. Should the prince not receive the appointment, and remain here, Countess de Gorzka will watch me jealously, and I shall avoid him as much from pride as pain. On the other hand, should he be successful and return as a victor, the marriage with the countess will nevertheless take place."

"My dear princess!" exclaimed Susanna, "it will not take place! Do you not know that Nassau sent a note to the countess, explaining the mistake, and confessing that his heart and word were pledged to you? The task is to pave the way to honor for the prince, by a naval command; then, when he has won renown, he will frankly declare himself to the king, and demand your hand."

"Did Nassau-Siegen reveal that to the countess?" exclaimed Louise de Lamballe, "Oh, now I comprehend the gloom that has since darkened the poor lady's countenance! she must hate me, because, having deceived myself, I gave her false hopes, and then robbed her of the man she loves. It is this dilemma, in which my own heart was deluded—this web of most unfortunate accidents, that decides me to say farewell forever to my desires. My heart may suffer, but I shall have done my bounden duty, and possess

18

that peace of conscience which is above all fleeting happiness."

"How selfish you are, princess!" said Caron, harshly; "you forget, in your forced calmness, the woe of the person you love. He will perish in this struggle, if you deprive him of that love without which life is intolerable. Can you still have peace of mind, if in despair he breaks the sword of his king, and, going far away, ends his life in the desert, or on the ocean?"

"And what, you merciless friend, am I to do? Where is the weapon that can conquer all the obstacles that surround us?"

"Love," cried Susanna, "and immortal hope, overcome all things! Where would we be without them? When we were oppressed, without a friend, exposed to a thousand dangers—when men pointed at us, thinking no action too mean with which to tarnish our name—what supported us in such extremities? Love—firm, hopeful love! Wherever that lives in two hearts, they must be happy sooner or later; for, what Heaven has united no monarch's word can separate. Oh, tell us, do you really love Otto von Nassau-Siegen?" Susie looked at the princess, entreating and weeping.

"Yes, Susanna, I love him immeasurably!"

"And will you in future consider it your holiest duty to strengthen his courage, save him from despair, and establish confidence in himself and in your affection, so that he may not be ruined—the noblest man, and the sincerest lover?"

The princess tearfully embraced her enthusiastic friend. "Oh, yes, you speak truly. Who could resist such an advocate as you, or who doubt those hopes of which your life speaks even more eloquently than your lips? And even if you are mistaken, my friends— if your consolations are illusive, and the happiness you promise me a dream

*, —yet to be thus deceived is delightful, for one thing will always remain—the memory of happiness! If I cannot preserve Nassau-Siegen for myself, I can at least preserve him for our native land!"

"I will endeavor to make all this a reality!" exclaimed Beaumarchais. He hastened away to seek the prince, and announce to him the victory Susie had obtained over Louise de Lamballe, to give him new courage, and assure him that every means would be used to assist him in gaining his object. Nassau agreed, to accompany Caron. and his wife, with Louise, a short distance through the park, after the visit to the royal couple.

The Princess de Lamballe announced the arrival of Beaumarchais and Susanna to the queen, at her levee. The example of a firm confidence in others strengthens one's own, and Louise's former cheerfulness returned ; even the Countess de Gorzka seemed gayer, and Marie Antoinette was in the best possible spirits. Nassau demanded leave of absence for the day; foreseeing the action of his friend, he did not wish to be near during certain explanations.

The queen received Caron and Susanna smilingly. "You are really an enchanter, Beaumarchais; as soon as you come, all are merry; I bid you welcome!—Ah! dear Madame Susie! dressed à la Figaro! you are wearing that head-dress; it suits you admirably. Really, ladies, this costume must become fashionable. I wish to have such a one for the next ball. I should really like to try it on now."

"If it please your majesty!"

"Quick, then; and all of you assist me!" Susanna remained seated while many delicate hands were busy in depriving her of her coiffure, to adorn Marie Antoinette.—"Well, how does it become me?" asked the queen, turning to Susie.

"O your majesty, so well that I should be envious if you were not my queen, who ought to be handsomer than any of us."

"Let no one say again that you are not a flatterer, madame! Take it off, and put it in my dressing-room, or I will believe that I am passably good-looking. But, by way of thanking you for this ornament, we shall all wear it the day after the representation of Figaro. You see, therefore, M. de Beaumarchais, that we are interested in having it very soon."

"Your majesty, that is insuring the success of my work beforehand! Who will dare to find any thing objectionable in a comedy, where the costumes are made fashionable by the queen? All will be desirous of seeing the comedy, on account of the head-dress, and the rest will be accepted into the bargain."

"I think your play would make a deeper impression on the public, even if they were not so thoroughly aware of the connection between it and the author's life as I have been, since the day when the Princess de Lamballe handed me the case of documents.— Poor woman!" said the queen, kissing Susie's brow; "and did that wretched relationship become the source of so much sorrow to you?"

"But partly also of our good fortune, your majesty," smiled Caron. "It only confirms the old truth, that malice bears its own punishment, and is powerless against the courage of an honest man."

"Tell us frankly, Beaumarchais, now that you have happily passed through so many difficulties, which of your opponents was the worst? La Blache, Maupeau, or Choiseul?" The ladies present listened with curiosity.

"Your majesty, to answer that question is both difficult and dangerous," replied Caron, seriously. "No man is so sure of victory that his enemies may not renew the battle. I always had two kinds—those who hated me personally, and those who disliked me on account of my activity. They generally united in the same plans against me, at the decisive moment, and so I could not overthrow one without hurting all. It generally happened that my personal enemies were also the abettors of those who endangered the public good and set at naught the good intentions of the late dauphin."

"Do you wish to intimate that they were also those of—our family?"

"Certainly, your majesty."

"Then it is your duty to say which one you had most cause to fear and hate."

"As he belongs to those who are unassailable, and is still living, it would be hazardous to name him without urgent reasons."

"You excite my curiosity. Describe him at least partly."

"Your majesty, I call him a chameleon. If you wish to verify the resemblance, perhaps you may have occasion to-day to notice the change of color."

Marie Antoinette was as much surprised as the others, and was about to reply, when she was interrupted by the noise of hunting-horns. The king and his suite were returning from the chase. The Princess de Lamballe then gave the signal for tea, and the company arranged themselves for the reception of Louis XVI, who soon entered with Vaugyon, D'Afry, and other cavaliers.

"We have been very successful to-day, my dear. You will admire our table to-morrow. A wild boar, an eighteen-antlered stag, besides the small game!—Ah! Beaumarchais, there you are, with your wife! I am very glad you showed yourself a man of honor in this last affair—very glad. I thank you for applying to me; you must always do that. You have outlived so much treachery that it is better in future to make me, instead of the public, your confidant." .

"My gracious monarch, would you really permit this, though at the risk of my being regarded an inopportune petitioner, or an indiscreet counsellor?"

The king raised his head, and looked piercingly at Caron. "I believe you are always troubled about something."

"Unfortunately! At present it concerns an affair important to the country and to justice—in fact, the fulfilment of your royal word."

Louis looked embarrassed. "You have chosen a strange time to speak of it."

"I do not stand every day before my king; and to-morrow it may be too late, if I allow this opportunity to escape."

"Indeed! Well, I hope your request will not occupy much time." He made a motion with his hand, and the ladies retired to the antechamber, the queen only remaining. The Countess de Polignac immediately sent word to D'Artois and Chartres that Beaumarchais was having a private audience.

"Well, what now?" said Louis sullenly, seating himself and taking the cup Marie Antoinette offered him.

"Your majesty, it is nearly twenty years since accident brought me to court. I will not be vain enough to mention the confidence—"

"I know! My father loved you; and that is the reason, in spite of your many eccentricities, we are glad to see you again. Come, what do you wish?"

"My eccentricities were severely punished by the civil authorities, your majesty, and yet time always proved that I was the injured party. Now, however, I myself am not in question; but two others, and a promise which you may remember, sire."

" Name it."

" You promised the Prince von Nassau-Siegen, on a certain occasion, to give him the first naval command in the war, and now I hear that the Prince de Chartres is to have it."

" How long have you concerned yourself with politics and the war service? You write comedies, pamphlets, and memorials; you are an excellent negotiator, and a lucky speculator—are you about to add politics to your accomplishments?"

" Your majesty, I have practised politics for twenty years, and according to the principles of your illustrious father. I make no pretension to statesmanship, but yet I have known men in office more ignorant than myself. The main point is your royal word, given to a man who has few equals in bravery and military science."

" Why do you not say also—'and who is my friend, who has given more proofs of wild daring than of the qualities of a general?' "

" The generalship of the Prince de Chartres, so far as I know, does not extend beyond a rabbit-hunt." The queen smiled, and Louis colored.

" You are speaking of a prince of the royal blood, the king's cousin!"

" He is an Orleans, sire; I wish indeed you had no cousins, for there would then be less misery. I intend neither to accuse nor insult, but, during the lifetime of the late dauphin, the most obscure colonel would have been made general-in-chief before a company of invalid infantry would have been confided to an Orleans."

" Repeat that, if you dare, you wretch!" exclaimed Chartres, who with D'Artois had just entered. The king motioned with much anxiety, and walked up and down in a hurried and embarrassed manner.

" Why this intrusion, princes?" said Marie Antoinette, sharply. "I hope you will not forget your respect for the king or myself."

" Your majesty," said D'Artois, " when a comedy scribbler is listened to in state affairs, I should think it would be permitted to princes of the royal blood to defend their house."

" Silence! *your* honor was not attacked, D'Artois; and I desire no scene here!" exclaimed Louis. A pause ensued.

" You asked me, a little while ago, royal lady, about the chameleon," and Beaumarchais smiled. " His grandfather was a Jesuitical dreamer, and his father an atheist, who knew how to manage matters in such a way that his abettor Choiscul alone was considered guilty. The chameleon is high-born, religious, or infidel, according to circumstances, for he has studied in the society of Madame de Ventadour as well as of Mlle. Raucourt, the friend of Madame du Barry. When the chameleon appears at court he is pure white, and seems loyal; but when at night he glides into a certain street he is spotted with red republicanism. In the Parliament he shines in all colors—at this moment he is black and blue with anger."

This was so true that Chartres trembled, while his eye cast flaming glances. He drew his sword.

" Madman!" said D'Artois, drawing him back, " have you lost your senses?"

" I have but one word to say to this fellow!" said Chartres, approaching his enemy. " If you were not one of those noblemen made by a Pompadour, I would honor you with a challenge. As it is, I ask one question: Where are your proofs as to what you say about me? If you cannot bring them," turning to Louis, " then, my king, send me at once to the fleet! Test my courage and devotion. When I return with honor, I will demand a public recantation from this man, who, in my own person, has insulted a princely house, that, like your own, sire, has descended from Henry IV."

Beaumarchais felt that he was losing ground. "Oh monseigneur, you have wonderful audacity!"

"And did you come here," asked the king, angrily, "with a charge having no shadow of proof?"

"It would be obvious enough, your majesty, if your pure mind would admit it. The prince perverts my words, but later, when facts speak louder—"

"Enough!" interrupted Louis XVI., turning to Chartres. "The command is yours, my cousin, to show you how I regard mere invective. Go immediately to Brest; a courier will follow with your commission.—M. de Beaumarchais, the only thing that protects you is pity that my father's love should have made you so vain. I do not wish to see you again."

"You are right, sire," replied Caron, bitterly. "But if you should, nevertheless, wish to see me again, I shall be provided with proofs at which even you will be amazed, Monseigneur d'Artois.—God preserve your majesty!" Beaumarchais bowed, and, retreating hastily to the antechamber of the ladies, he seized his wife's hand. "It is all over, Princess de Lamballe: the Prince de Chartres is appointed."

"He is!" exclaimed Louise. Madame de Polignac laughed, but Countess de Gorzka concealed her tears.

"Yes, but only for his disgrace, for I know Chartres well.—Come, Susanna, we are forbidden to be here."

"I suppose, however, I am not prohibited from detaining you as my guests to-day," replied Madame de Lamballe, warmly. "Be kind enough to await me in the Pavillon Taurean." Beaumarchais bowed in silence, and left the royal villa. Shortly after, Chartres came from the king's apartments. In the anteroom M. Sillery awaited the prince, who merely said:

"Do as we agreed!" The cavalier bowed, and followed. An hour later, at nightfall, the son of Orleans was on his way to Brest.

Caron met Nassau in the garden path leading from the Pavillon du Soleil to that of Taureau. The former had regained sufficient command of himself to bring Siegen to some degree of calmness, and console him by an interview with the Princess de Lamballe, when they would consider what to do.

It was growing dark, and Gomez was ordered to have the carriage ready, and driven in advance slowly through the forest toward Roquencourt, while Caron and Susanna would follow with Nassau and Louise. Such promenades were at that time not uncommon at Marly, and there was no fear of surprise or interruption. The events of the evening urged the king, who was uncomfortably excited, and exhausted from the day's hunt, to dismiss the cavaliers and ladies early, and, immediately after D'Artois left, he retired with the queen. All was silent earlier than usual, and Louise returned to her pavilion meeting her guests in the colonnade. Her lover greeted her with sad emotion.

"Let us go immediately, princess," said Beaumarchais, "I am certain we shall be watched here."

"I do not think so. Madame de Polignac and Countess de Gorzka are on duty together, Chartres has left Marly, the others have returned to their lodgings. At least take time for a slight repast."

"No, my dearest princess," interrupted Susanna. "Since I know that our object in coming has failed, and we are not wanted, the air of this place oppresses me. The forest path is much more desirable. We can enjoy your hospitality at some more favorable time, and without exposing you."

The party left the garden, following

Caron's carriage, which went slowly before them through the park. The evening was beautiful in the summer moonlight, but their hearts were sad.— "Your highness," said Princess de Lamballe, "no cause was ever better defended than yours by our friend. But you probably know that he has failed. Now, if Chartres is fortunate in the service, his vengeance will pursue us in a thousand forms; but, if he is not, justice will be done you, dark as matters at present look."

"Why should he not succeed?" replied Nassau. "He fights under D'Orvillier, a brave and experienced officer, and he has only to act with common bravery."

"That is just what I doubt—that is the straw to which I cling," said Caron. "I feel, now I am more composed, a little encouragement. As far as I have observed, I have never known real courage dwell in the breast of a selfish man. Chartres knows nothing of his duty as an officer, except on paper. Ah! it requires a pure heart to expose one's self to death for the sake of his country."

"And I, my prince, do not believe that he can or will do this," said Susanna. "His unworthiness will become manifest, and your injured right be vindicated."

"The war is only commencing, and the English are not quickly conquered. M. de Chartres will not find it so easy to advance his military fortune. Believe your old friend Caron, the failure of to-day will become a success. One advantage I have gained—in spite of the king's displeasure, a spark of suspicion against Chartres remains in his mind. It will increase on deliberation, for Louis must feel that no mere slanderer would speak before him as I have spoken. Even Artois, however haughty his manner, was startled. It will be a bad thing for Chartres, if, after such a scene,

he merely does his duty; woe to him, if he performs less than is required of him!"

"The result of all is," smiled Susanna, with her natural cheerfulness, "that we have rather gained than lost. Is our being together, on such a fairy evening as this, nothing? And have we not united two sorrowful hearts in hope and confidence?"

"If I could feel this firmly and joyfully, princess," said Nassau, seizing Louise's hand, "I would devotedly wait for years, and no self-denial would be too great."

"You may," she replied. "I shall consider it my duty as well as honor, to strengthen your courage by confidence. Have we not the example of that faithful couple before us, who triumphed because they clung to each other in every danger?"

"Then Chartres has obtained nothing, except a promise and an uncertain advance," cried Susanna, "but for which he may have to pay dear."

The conversation became more cheerful. They jested about Caron's banishment again from court; and the more Nassau weighed the difficulties in the way of his opponent, the more hopeful he became, and quieted the fears of Louise. When they had gone a considerable part of the way, she remembered that she would have to return with the prince alone through the forest, and took leave of Caron and Susanna.

"Your highnesses," said Susanna, "must let us know when you come to Paris, and if any thing important occurs you must send a messenger."

"Of course, my dear Susie Figaro," smiled the princess, "and I must return your head-dress."

"That you may redeem your hooded mantilla? Oh, have the head-dress as a remembrancer of me; I am now only the Susanna of Beaumarchais. After twenty years' marriage, I cannot seriously intend to wear a bridal wreath; it will suit you better, and you must promise me that I shall be your milliner on a certain happy occasion."

"Oh, I promise you that," said the princess, kissing her.

"How can I ever reward you, Caron?" said Nassau, pressing the hand of Beaumarchais.

"I desire no reward, my dear prince. We are doing all we can for each other. Would I still have my wife, if it were not for you? I can only return good for good." They separated after hearty farewells. Louise de Lamballe, leaning on the prince's arm, returned, while Caron and Susanna continued their route.

"Gomez," cried Beaumarchais, "go after the carriage and let it wait for us!"

"The night is very fair," said Susanna.

"While we were lingering in our farewell, the coach went too far in advance of us. I feel a little fatigued, and the dew is on the grass; you will take cold."

"How careful you are! At home we often sit up later than this in the garden."

"But not in the forest."

"What a pity! It would be well, I think, to live here, far from deceitful faces and mean hearts. How brilliantly the stars shine! I almost wish I could reach them!"

"I suppose you would like to sit on the damp moss, to admire the heavens at your leisure; but it would be rather foolish." All around was silent and solemn; the foliage waved in the night air, and the shadows formed fantastic images in the moonlight.

"Is not some one standing yonder at the bend in the forest?" said Susanna suddenly, with a start.

"Who can it be but Gomez? Surely you are not afraid in a royal enclosure?"

"No, but the solitude of Nature always affects my mind. Now the figure is gone."

"We cannot see very distinctly! Gomez, are you there? Gomez!"

"Yes, señor!"

"I told you it is he; come!" They walked faster, but a rustling was heard in the bushes on their right, and Susanna clung to Caron, who halted. A man leaped into the middle of the road.

"What is the meaning of this; who is there?" A shot answered. Susanna screamed, and the figure disappeared.

"For Heaven's sake, some one is lying in wait for us," whispered Beaumarchais, excitedly; "come, let us hasten!"

Susanna hung heavily on her husband's arm, her head fell on his breast, and her strength gave way. "Caron, God preserve you!"

"Murder! murder! help!" shouted the horrified Beaumarchais, holding his dying wife in his arms.

To use fire-arms at night in a royal forest was a capital offence. Those of the officials that heard the shot, took the first weapon that came to hand, and hastened to the place whence the report came. The first to appear was Gomez. He found his poor master bending over Susanna, and endeavoring to stanch her blood with his handkerchief. The murdered lady was taken into the carriage, and Caron held her in his arms, while they were driven back to Marly.

Nassau and Louise had nearly reached the Pavillon Taureau when the gun was heard. Thinking of Beaumarchais he left the princess, so near her residence, and, hastening back, met the carriage. "What has happened?" he asked.

"Our poor lady has been assassinated!" Nassau felt as if his heart were torn from his bosom.

The body of Susanna lay in the pavilion of Madame de Lamballe, and Caron sat without a word or a tear. His grief was beyond expression. The princess fainted, and her maids carried her away. The ladies and cavaliers of the court were in the utmost excitement. The huntsmen, Swiss soldiers, and noble guards, searched through the forest in every direction. Prince d'Artois appeared. When Caron saw him, his consciousness returned. "Monseigneur, I promised proofs; *here is one!*"

"Unfortunate man, can you entertain the fearful suspicion, that"—Artois did not finish.

"That the shot was intended for me which killed my poor Susanna—yes, prince. The history of my life is concluded. My happiness began with her love and ends with it.—The man who caused thy innocent blood to flow, Susanna, has made me his Nemesis!"

Beaumarchais bore this greatest of sorrows with a composure and silence that surprised Nassau. He lost all that geniality and animation which formerly distinguished him, and rendered harmless his witticisms, by the chivalrous manner in which they were made. It was only while at the harp, or with the Prince von Nassau and Louise de Lamballe, that his heart softened, and he gave way to his feelings. To all others he was sarcastic and even malicious; he was no longer fit for a courtier. But, in the midst of his misfortune, he never lost the feeling of old French loyalty. The unknown murderer escaped, and Artois begged Caron, in the name of the king, to let the matter rest, and he was silent.

Susanna was buried in the church at Marly. by order of the monarch, and Beaumarchais returned to Paris, but not to the Hôtel Piron. He rented a solitary house in the Temple, near the east wall, on the spot that was afterward called the "Boulevard Beaumarchais." Here he was often visited by Malesherbes and the gloomy Turgot; sometimes also by Morelly.

How justified soever Caron, Nassau, and Louise, felt in their suspicion that Chartres was the real criminal in a murder intended for another—however startled Artois himself was at the deed, no one at court could make up his mind to consider the false prince guilty. It was regarded an accident, though sufficiently mysterious by the concurrence of certain events. At that time such crimes in the forests were not rare, and the courtiers soon ceased to pity the bereaved husband, who received the sympathy even of the king and queen with the calmness and indignation of an injured but honest man.

Louise de Lamballe was too much attached to Susanna not to feel enduring sorrow, and was too well convinced of the guilt of Chartres not to warn the queen against him by many intimations. She was often called the never-to-be-believed prophetess by the heedless Antoinette, and the Countess de Polignac proposed for the princess the name of "Cassandra," which was considered quite too applicable to be rejected.

One day, in the beginning of August, Louis and his consort, with their suite, were at dinner, when Nassau-Siegen entered, who was on duty at the palace.

"What is it, prince?"

"I come to announce, your majesty, that the grand-admiral, Duke de Penthièvre, has just arrived at the Pavilon Taureau, and urgently desires an interview with her highness the Princess de Lamballe. He sent word that the affair was of great importance."

"Heavens!" said the queen, "what can the duke want?"

"I hope he brings no evil tidings;

go to him immediately, princess."—
Louise de Lamballe left the apartment.

"Do you know any thing of his errand, Prince Nassau ? "

"No, your majesty. His cavalier seemed much excited."

"I hope couriers are in attendance, Vaugyou, in case we should need them."

"As many as your majesty may desire."

The king was obviously uneasy. Nassau's presence annoyed him. "Very well, 'prince!" Nassau bowed and withdrew.

"Perhaps it is news from Brest ; D'Orvillier was prepared for battle ten days ago," said Artois.

"Then I do not understand why Peuthièvre does not immediately seek an audience; it is his duty."

Madame de Lamballe returned with a letter in her hand. Proud seriousness was expressed in her features. "Sire, my father-in-law the duke has confided to me a report for your majesty. He would personally have performed this duty, but the state of his mind does not permit him to appear in the presence of his king; he has returned to Paris and awaits your commands."

Louis rose impetuously. "Is it bad news from Brest, and does it refer to Chartres ? "

"That is impossible !" cried Artois.

The king took the paper. "We wish to be alone. Remain, Princess de Lamballe." The suite retired while Louis read. He placed his hand upon his forehead, as if greatly agitated.

"My husband," said the queen, "I pray you, do not keep this secret from me."

"How can it be kept secret ? Very soon every child in the street will know that our fleet, which had already surrounded the English at Ouessant, was thrown into disorder by the fault of Chartres, ships and men are lost, and the enemy has triumphed, without receiving a single shot from our dear cousin. D'Orvillier demands a court-martial to decide between himself and the prince, and whether the cause of the disaster was treachery, cowardice, or incapacity."

"And Beaumarchais was right ?" cried Artois.

"Yes, that unfortunate mau is always right. Send a courier after him; I want him and his proofs immediately. Is not the death of his wife sufficient evidence ? Vaugyon, send a cabinet order to Penthièvre. Let him hold a court-martial, and have Chartres and D'Orvillier arrested and tried. I am sorry, Priucess Louise, that the duke makes these disagreeable discoveries as to his son-in-law; he knows my displeasure will not reach him; but inform him that I expect merciless severity. Call the Prince von Nassau." Artois called him. "Prince," said the king, "I gave you my word that you should have the appoiutment which Chartres has disgraced, but unhappily allowed myself to be influenced by family considerations, and preferred him. I am sorry for it ! You are admiral at the next battle, and may God give you grace to wipe away the stain that the honor of our navy has received through this Orleans ! "

"My sovereign, I can only express my thanks by swearing to return as victor—or never ! " The kiug held out his hand, whieh the prince kissed, and Louis went to his cabinet.

All was in commotion ; couriers were dispatched ; consternation was seen on all countenances. Only two persons were happy—Louise de Lamballe and Nassau-Siegen. A few hours later Beaumarchais appeared before the king.

"You were right, M. de Beaumarchais," exclaimed Louis, on seeing him. "Chartres has dishonored his command. Where are your proofs against him?"

"They are numerous enough, if a cousin of the king could be brought before a court of justice without desecrating the head of the state and the dignity of his family; but one item of evidence will suffice. Do you know this crest?" He handed a gold seal with a stone.

"It is the Orleans coat-of-arms."

"It was pledged to confirm the authenticity of this writing, though it is easily recognized." He handed Louis a paper.

The king stared at it as if stupefied. Artois looked over his shoulder, and read in a low voice. "Chartres," exclaimed Louis, "a confederate of republicans! A promise to assist him against my dynasty!"

"To place him on the throne—yes, sire!" replied Beaumarchais, "'Orleans or Bourbon,' is the old party-cry. For twenty years have I fought in this secret, malicious conflict. Your parents fell in it, as you will also, if that family be not rendered harmless. This struggle is the cause of all my persecution, for the Orleans know that I am a dangerous enemy. Because I escaped branding and the galleys in 1774, an assassin was hired to end my life. Your majesty, I can give no stronger pledge of my patriotism—I could offer no more sacred sacrifice, than the life-blood of my wife."

"And I gave this wretched Chartres all the privileges of a friend!" said Artois.

"So did Prince de Lamballe!"

The king seized the hand of Beaumarchais. "How can I reward your fidelity, my friend? Must I own to you that I am too poor?"

"I can point out a way to you, sire. Give all your favor and honor—to me of no use now—to two who love each other, and whom you separated—the only ones for whom I still have any sympathy; the Princess de Lamballe and the Prince von Nassau-Siegen."

"Does Siegen love the princess, and not Countess de Gorzka?"

"Her majesty, the queen, misunderstood his feelings. He was about to demand the hand of Madame de Lamballe, when you surprised him near the grotto."

"I know how to make amends for unfortunate mistakes, my friend, and I will not forget the prince, when he has saved the honor of our fleet."

The position of Nassau at court became happier. Marie Antoinette, informed by Louis of her error, had too pure a heart, and profound a sympathy, not to do justice to Louise de Lamballe, and comprehend her grief. With a delicacy that spared Countess de Gorzka, the queen renewed to the princess all her former affection, and, without much explanation, their hearts were again in harmony. Louise heard from Beaumarchais, that their majesties were aware of Nassau's inclination, and her long-denied happiness was beginning to be realized, for respect was shown her and Caron by the brothers of the king, and Madame de Polignac occupied a more modest position.

The investigations concerning Orleans were made at Brest. The first tidings of the lost battle at Ouessant made public, represented Chartres more unfortunate than guilty. But the examination of the facts proved that Admiral d'Orvillier had done his duty, and given the signal at the right moment for the rear-guard of Chartres to enter battle, but he remained in inactivity, and thus fell into disgrace. Both D'Orvillier and Chartres appeared before the court-martial—the former was acquitted, but the son of Orleans declared "incapable of naval service, on account of negligence." The dignity of grand-admiral was lost.

When this sentence was conveyed to Chartres, in presence of the king, the latter ordered the marshals to withdraw, only retaining his brothers.—"Prince de Chartres," he said, "your rank is your only protection. You committed crimes under its shelter that would have cost others their head. You will leave Paris forever, and remain in garrison at Chanteloup, as major of hussars. As long as you live, neither you, nor your family, must leave that station. Your father also will appear no more in the capital, or at any of our residences!"

"That is to say, the Bourbons have ruined the Orleans!"

"Yes, M. Philip Égalité, since your family have dared to betray the Bourbons to the future republic, and have become conspirators and mutineers, Duke de Vaugyon, and Colonel d'Affry, will take you to your destination." Chartres was staggered, and, casting a glance of fierce hatred on the king, he left.

The hour of the Princess de Lamballe's happiness began. The demons of the royal house, the Orleans, were banished, Prince von Nassau was raised to the post of admiral, and hastened the preparations for the future campaign, that was to entwine the myrtle with the laurel. He equipped a secret expedition to St. Malo, in which D'Artois and Penthièvre were very enthusiastic. The happiness of the royal pair was crowned in December by the birth of a daughter, the stigma of sterility removed from Marie Antoinette, and all malicious reports against her refuted. The rejoicings of the nation were indescribable, and every one was looking forward to a great, hopeful future, except the solitary Beaumarchais and the Countess de Gorzka, who seemed to live in a different world. The christening of the young princess was the beginning of the winter amusements, celebrated by the Parisians, and indeed, by all France. The court began their residence at Versailles, in the beginning of 1779. The brilliant victories in North America, in which French auxiliaries participated, the warlike preparations of Spain, and the secret enmity of Holland, so pressed Great Britain on every side, that the approaching spring seemed favorable to France against England. As the royal family, the navy, the army—in fact, the whole people, entertained the highest expectations of Nassau-Siegen, a happy result was not doubtful, particularly as no sacrifice had been spared to render the fleet of St. Malo formidable. The plan was to take Jersey, by whose possession the English held in check the three largest northern seaports of France—Cherbourg, St. Malo, and Brest, as well as the whole of the western coast. The squadron, consisting of ten ships, was to set sail about the commencement of March. Nassau took leave of the court and his friends.

Penthièvre was informed of the object of Louise's secret love, and delighted to feel that his last days would not be passed in solitude; and, that at least one member of his family would be happy, he not only gave his consent, but resolved, if Nassau returned victorious, to make him grand-admiral, with the consent of the king. The delivery of the instructions gave occasion to spend his last hours among those he loved at the Hôtel Penthièvre. Caron again visited there, and Louise de Lamballe asked leave of absence from Versailles.

"Are you going to Paris, your highness?" inquired Countess de Gorzka of Madame de Lamballe, in a melancholy tone.

"Yes, dearest countess. Why do you ask?"

"I wished to implore your permission to accompany you."

"You?"

"Do not refuse me, princess. I should like to see—him, once more, before he departs; I wish to renounce him, that his heart may be free and cheerful in battle."

"Charlotte, do you wish to overwhelm me with your friendship? The oath I took to advance your happiness, while I was yet Lamballe's wife—"

"I give you back your word! We were both deceived in Nassau's sentiments, and I will no longer be an obstacle. I love him too ardently to bear the idea of a marriage that would be forced upon him, and humiliate me. I will at least preserve your friendship, while, on the other hand, I would lose my self-esteem. Say not another word. I must go with you."

Princess de Lamballe embraced her deeply-moved friend, from whom pride had extorted this resolution, after many tearful nights. No further objection was made. Both ladies drove to Paris, where they met Nassau and Beaumarchais, at the residence of Penthièvre. The former was greatly surprised to see Charlotte de Gorzka.

"Your highness," said the countess, breathing with difficulty, but with an air of determination, "I have only accompanied the princess, to ask you for a few moments' conversation, in order to clear up a misunderstanding which neither you nor I have caused."

"You give," said Penthièvre, "a great proof of magnanimity, dear countess, for which even an old man like myself must respectfully kiss your hand." He pressed it to his lips. "Come, Beaumarchais, let us pay a visit to the Japanese house." Nassau, Louise, and Charlotte, remained alone.

"Prince, do not misunderstand the melancholy with which I part from you. My love for you was a youthful folly. I acknowledge it to have been an illusion, though I feel that such dreams are dear to us. Heaven has provided a remedy for my disappointment—woman's pride, and the desire of sisterly love from her who is worthier of you than I am. I owed this explanation to myself; for I wished you to take with you esteem for me, and peace for yourself. May Providence give you victory, and make you happy!"

"Your disinterestedness," said Nassau, gravely, "deeply affects me, countess. I am to be pitied that fate offered me so much, and withheld so much, that I could not be blessed without wounding some one. To gain a true woman's love, dear Louise," and he seized the hand of the princess, "is something inexpressibly great—to lose it, very sad, countess. You are alone, and friendship only can console the sorrow caused by a mistake. If you could accustom yourself to regard me as a brother, it would lighten my heart. I should then feel that two noble women are praying for me in the day of danger, rejoicing with me when victorious, and weeping for me should I fall! This is a proud thought!" He gently embraced Louise, offering his right hand to Charlotte. "A bride and a sister! I shall live in your memory, and what would divide common hearts will unite yours more closely."

"So let it be," said the countess. "We shall dream of you, as formerly in the Japanese house; and when you return, prince, Heaven will give me strength to witness the happiness of my Louise without envy. Farewell! Return victorious!" She pressed his hand, her eyes were dimmed with tears, and she hastened into the garden.

The prince remained thoughtful, with Louise by his side. "It is curious," he said, "but I am almost inclined to think that love makes a man cowardly. This expected battle will be the first into which I have borne a fearful heart.

Let me disperse all evil anticipation. I do not say farewell, for I do not intend to die."

"Give me a lock of your hair."

"A lock of hair is only taken from the dead, or from one you never expect to see again!"

"A betrothed may ask for it before the battle."

"Perhaps one of yours might render me invulnerable."

"I wish it could! Or that my love would."

"It can! And now away with melancholy faces; no more anxiety! The wife of a soldier should fear nothing but dishonor. Let us go to our friends." They remained together for some time, the gentlemen talking on different subjects. Countess de Gorzka maintained her outward composure so far as to engage in the gayer conversation. The princess, however, was serious. When the carriages came, Nassau, who was going by Nauphle, accompanied the ladies to Versailles, and Caron also went with them. There they separated, Nassau continuing his journey.

"Come for one moment into my apartment, dear friends," said Madame de Lamballe. She drew a small casket from her pocket and opened it. "Gorzka, I have a lock of his hair. Let us share it." She was pale and grave, and the countess fell weeping into the arms of her friend.

"But I beseech you, ladies!" exclaimed Beaumarchais, in great astonishment, "why this seriousness—these tears—when the prince is hastening to the glory of great deeds?"

"Weep, dear Charlotte, weep!" said Louise. "I cannot; but a voice within tells me, 'We shall see him no more!' Madame de Poliguac is right in calling me Cassandra."

"If I were my former self," said Caron, "I should call this folly. Since

Susie's death I too believe in presentiments."

After the prince's departure, Louise and Charlotte were more than ever united in sisterly love. Every leisure moment they employed in talking of the absent one; as formerly, they pondered over their maps, and when Caron brought letters from St. Malo, it was a day of rejoicing.

It was the latter part of May, fragrant with the first verdure of the spring! The Princess de Lamballe stood pale in her room grasping a letter. Countess de Gorzka sat with convulsively-clasped hands, and tears flowing over her cheeks. The letter contained but a few comprehensive lines: "Princess: Heaven has decreed our lot. The attempt on Jersey has failed! Bleeding from six wounds, no ball has spared me the disgrace of living. The wretched man who lost six of his vessels, sacrificed seven thousand men, and yet was conquered, must be forgotten by you. I can never return—a whole life of honor cannot blot out this shame. I release you from your promise. If I succeed in obtaining my dismissal, I shall take service in Spain. 'From desert to desert!' You were right! OTTO VON NASSAU-SIEGEN."

"I knew it," whispered the princess. "I was not destined to be happy, nor he to be victorious! Does it not seem as if Providence itself were in league with Chartres? Charlotte, you are avenged; neither of us will be his bride."

"No," exclaimed the countess, "he will not be dismissed. A man may lose a battle, and yet be a hero. The king will still confide in him, supply him with new resources, and he will conquer."

"Do you think so? Let us hand the letter to their majesties, and hear what they say. Otto von Nassau dared not lose, after the day at Ouessant: they will pardon Chartres, now that Nassau did not succeed."

"And must he again resume the career of a mere adventurer ?"

"Oh no, I know him better ! Heroés arise from despair, and sad hearts bear the mind beyond earthly bounds. You loved him sufficiently to renounce him, and the friend remains to you. I love him so that I would rather see him dead than disgraced; and I promise before God that I would resign my claims to him rather than that he should not enter upon a path of glory. A hero is not born for love—or, if I err, it is the Bourbon blood that makes me thus speak."

The princess had judged correctly. When the official report arrived, the king and D'Artois were beside themselves. They did not consider how well Nassau had fought; they only remembered that he lost more than half of the squadron. Without hesitation he was dismissed.

"I suppose, Madame Cassandra, you will console yourself with the little countess," said the qeeen, ironically. "Even if you could not foresee the misfortune of your favorite, I hope you have enough of the royal blood of France in your veins to forget an adventurer !"

"Your majesty," replied Louise, coldly, "I have resigned him. As a princess of France, however, I am deeply grieved that a defeat is counted a crime, especially as it concerns a man who can atone for it by a dozen victories—that the king in ungenerous anger has deprived himself of the services of one who, notwithstanding this failure, might yet add to the glory of his reign."

"The same excuse might be made for M. de Chartres, princess," said Madame de Polignac.

"I have nothing to answer; for I should suspect you of patriotism."

Nassau went to Spain, entering as captain in the fleet to take Gibraltar from the British. About the same time Count de Gorzka, Charlotte's father, died in Lorraine, where he had lived at the court of the late king Ladislaus Leszynsky, having bequeathed his immense Polish possessions to the Russian crown. He left a fortune of six million francs, and his daughter wished to retire from the French court. She was only withheld by her affection for Louise de Lamballe, which had grown by mutual grief. The position of the princess at court became more painful after Siegen's fall. Madame de Polignac was a tenacious opponent, and had now many advantages over Louise. D'Artois intrigued against the "Wedding of Figaro," and the censors marred the comedy in order to render it unfit for representation. Public matters became worse by Necker's discharge from office, a movement favored by Maurepas and D'Artois. The latter was so extravagant, and involved the court in such expensive amusements, that he had a debt of fourteen million francs. When Necker reproached him with this, he replied, insolently: "Pshaw ! what can you do ?—there are the debts." "Very well, monseigneur, since they give you so much pride, we shall not deprive you of them !" said the minister. He did not pay them, and so lost his office. M. de Sartines, lieutenant of police, was his successor.

Though the house of Orleans appeared to have been rendered harmless, the Sillerys (father and son) were too good political business men in the Palais-Royal not to make amends for the forced absence of Chartres. The altered spirit of the times coöperated with their plans. The freedom which reigned everywhere in conversation, the simplicity of the fashions, giving nearly the same kind of coat to a duke as to a citizen, the republican ideas current concerning the alliance with North America, the continual efforts at reform by the ministers, who were working against each other without reaching the real cause of the public misery, the victory of Washington over Cornwallis, and the deeds of young Lafayette,—all occupied and inflamed the thoughts of the people, and the death of Maurepas left the king melancholy and helpless. Ségur and Calonne, an intimate friend of D'Artois, became ministers on the recommendation of the Countess de Polignac. The people objected and were uneasy, conscious more than ever of the prerogatives of the privileged classes. Having more political knowledge, clubs were formed and a commotion made in the Parliament by men like Mirabeau (who was at last reinstated after numerous scandals and persecutions), Anacharsis Cloots, Danton, Abbé Sièyes, Lamet, Condorcet, Despremenil, and others. Under such circumstances it was considered dangerous to permit the "Wedding of Figaro" to be performed. Marie Antoinette, however, desired it in order to wear the head-dress of the Susanna in the piece, and for Caron it was the last ambition of his life to see it acted.

The comedy was announced, and all classes eagerly visited the Théâtre Français; but, ten minutes before the rising of the curtain, an order arrived from Versailles forbidding the representation! Murmurs of indignation were heard from boxes and from pit! Beaumarchais appeared at the footlights, exclaiming: "If this comedy is forbidden here, I resolve that it shall be played in the cathedral of Notre Dame!" It was the first intimation of the Revolution. About the same time Turgot, the ex-minister, died. Morelly, Malesherbes, and Caron, stood near his bed in his last moments.

"I shall soon know whether the 'Basiliade' is a fable yonder as well as here," Turgot smiled, faintly. "I leave Chaos behind me! Well for him who has neither wife nor children! The North American war and the camp at Compiègne are incurable wounds for France. Rivers of blood will flow from them."

Another event seemed to change again all ill feeling. On the 22d of October the queen became mother of a son, to whom was given the title of Duc de Bourbon. All differences now seemed to be reconciled by this happy birth.

The Princess de Lamballe, who had had the especial charge of Marie Antoinette, took the new-born infant in her arms and knelt by the couch of the queen. "Formerly, your majesty, you drew me to your heart, gave me the sweet name of friend, and honored me so highly that envious slanderers, and even the thoughtless populace, accused me of having a political influence over you and the king, which you know I never had. I pass through life without love, without any of the higher purposes of woman—all is refused me but your favor. Give me something to love. I entreat of you intrust to me this boy; give me the supervision of your royal children. Let me teach them to be virtuous and happy. Let me expend on them the affection of my heart; I am of their family, and I require no other epitaph but the memory I shall leave in the hearts of your children!"

The queen embraced the princess tenderly. "Yes, my only cousin, my dearest friend—you who are never wearied even by my ill-humor, I will share my maternal duties with you; you shall be the governess of my children." It was a reconciliation at an opportune moment, but, alas! of very short duration!

However inimical a prince like D'Artois was against Chartres for having fraternity with the *canaille*, and favoring the republicans—however he despised the duke's cowardice at Ouessant, he was equally disturbed with him at the birth of a dauphin, and the appointment of Madame de Lamballe as governess of the royal children, as well as at the influence the queen had gradually obtained in political matters over her husband. The two princes were alike in dissipation, ambition, hatred against the "Austrian woman," and contempt for the king; they only differed in the means used to manifest their temper; and if D'Artois was haughtier and less considerate, Chartres was less conscientious. D'Artois, therefore, in plotting against the queen, inciting Madame de Polignac (already jealous) against Louise de Lamballe, and disseminating slanderous reports, was involuntarily serving Chartres, and all those who first intended to dishonor the monarchy and then destroy it. The most aristocratic of princes became the instrument of the revolutionary spirit of the times.

The Countess de Polignac did all in her power to render the Princess de Lamballe ridiculous in the eyes of the queen, ascribing to this lady ambitious views in order to supplant her. Marie Antoinette was self-willed and capricious; she was secretly sorry for having bestowed two of the most important offices upon Louise. Small provocations, cool treatment, offensive slights toward Countess de Gorzka, whom the princess loved, produced difficulty and estrangement, sought by the queen and not avoided by Madame de Lamballe. Count de Polignac was raised to the dignity of duke, and appointed steward of the royal household, and Marie Antoinette's affection for his consort was evident to such a degree as almost to make it an insult to Louise. The bitter feelings of the latter were heightened by the deeds of Nassau-Siegen in 1782, turning the eyes of Europe on a man who performed miracles of valor before Gibraltar, who was made a grandee of Spain and a knight of the Golden Fleece, and formally invited by the Czarina Catharine to command her fleet against the Turks.

In the autumn the disagreement between the queen and Madame de Lamballe came to an issue, and about a mere trifle. "Where is the Princess de Lamballe?" asked Marie Antoinette. "I do not see her making any preparations, and yet I expressed a desire to dine in the Temple of Flora."

"Perhaps the princess finds it difficult to attend properly to all her duties," replied Madame de Polignac, ironically, "having a twofold office to perform. So far as I know, she has driven out with the royal children."

"Driven out! and in such weather? That is inexcusable! Go and find her immediately, Gorzka. I command her to appear before me; there must be an end to this." The countess hastened away, while the queen talked herself into greater indignation; feeling that it would require extraordinary provocation to be severe to the princess, Madame de Polignac did not fail to fan the flame. It was not long, however, before Louise appeared.

"I hear your majesty was uneasy at my absence!"

"More than that, I am in the highest degree angry. Where were you?"

"In the Temple of Flora, where you ordered dinner. All is ready for your majesties. As the weather is close and warm, I took with me their royal highnesses, the dauphin and Princess Charlotte."

"And pray, who authorized you to do so? I think it very inconvenient for you to perform the services of intendant and governess at the same time; one of these offices you must resign."

Madame de Lamballe replied calmly: "I felt myself justified in what I did by the trust your majesty reposed in me in reference to your children: but if you think that it is necessary to lessen my duties (which I do not doubt are envied me), I am willing to give up my position of intendant, and wholly devote myself to the royal children."

"The question is not so much about envy as the absurd independence and exaggerated influence with which you flatter yourself. I always intended to recall you from one of your offices, and I shall inquire of my husband whether it is proper to allow you such control over the children of France."

"My influence, your majesty? I never had sufficient to make ministers, à la Polignac!"

"But admirals, princess," said Madame de Polignac, "and such as were defeated!"

"The hero of Gibraltar, madame," replied Louise, proudly, "can bear the sting of an insect; but I feel, your majesty, that I shall oblige you by asking whether it is agreeable to you to dismiss me."

"It is agreeable—you anticipated me."

"I go, your majesty," and Louise's voice trembled; "I will not return unless you should be in trouble, and the Polignacs, Neuillys, and Guemènes, forsake you. May a cloudless future forever separate me from you!" She bent her knee, and kissed the queen's hand; Marie Antoinette became pale, and betrayed her emotion.

"Then accept my resignation at the same time, your majesty!" said Countess de Gorzka.

The queen's sadness turned to anger. "Very well—go, both of you! The court will lose a brace of nuns—that is all!"

Louise de Lamballe and Charlotte de Gorzka bowed haughtily and withdrew. The former handed the keys,

books, and purse of the queen to Vaugyon; then, weeping, kissed the children. On the following day both ladies left Versailles, never to return. It is true, the nuns had gone, and the melancholy tones of Madame de Lamballe's harp were heard no more. The court became gayer, and D'Artois, the Polignacs, and their partisans, invented all manner of amusements to cause Marie Antoinette to forget the loss of a friend whom while dauphiness she had regarded as a sister.

Misfortune seemed to enter at every door after the departure of the princess; it came unsuspected, unannounced in a thousand varying forms, and no one seemed to notice it until it could not be any longer overlooked.

Calonne, Maurepas' successor, paid Artois's debts, and bought Saint-Cloud for the queen at an expense of two million francs. She was grossly insulted by Cardinal de Rohan, (during the visit paid by the Danish king and queen,) who, in order to extort a private audience, forced himself uninvited into the illuminated royal gardens.

The western war ended in the recognition of the American republic by Great Britain, but France suffered from the consequences, for it had consumed the revenue of three years, and increased the debts left by the two preceding monarchs. Of what use to the country was foreign deference, when so much misery existed at home? The troops that had fought under Washington, brought with them a revolutionary spirit, their discipline had relaxed, and they talked of liberty and popular sovereignty as they did in the West. The "Society of the Friends of the People" was often heard of, and Lafayette joined it, bringing his motto: *Our non?* Wherever the glories of the American war were known, the question "Why not we?" was boldly asked.

Countess de Gorzka, assisted by Caron, bought a villa at Sceaux, two miles south of Paris, where she passed the summer with the Princess de Lamballe, and in winter they dwelt with the aged Duke de Penthièvre. Beaumarchais was their favored companion. Their sorrows had united them, particularly since hope had fled, and all selfish feelings with it. Here they dreamed, and the outer life that was rushing by so wildly gave them no concern; they lived in their recollections, as if they had already grown old. Penthièvre felt happy in their midst, especially when Caron received a letter from the Prince von Nassau, now in Russia, and who, at the head of a Russian squadron, had attacked the Capudan-Pacha in the Black Sea, and destroyed the whole naval power of the Turks in that region. His fame became universal, like that of Charles Eugene, who had also been misunderstood and neglected in his native country.

On the 27th of April, 1784, the Parisians again crowded into the Théâtre Français to witness the representation of the celebrated comedy, in spite of the opposition of the king and the ill-will of Artois. Bolder sentiments had been read and spoken in the capital, and the literary world demanded the performance, so that the queen did not desist until Louis reluctantly consented. It had already been acted in the drawing-room of Minister de Breteuil, and considered uninteresting—"not worth the outcry made about it." Prince d'Artois therefore visited his box at the theatre, confidently believing that the representation would fail. But it had great success. What a terrible picture of social disorder was afforded under the guise of graceful wit! Written nine years before, the public enjoyed its irony at this moment, for it was just as applicable to society as in the days of Louis XV. It was not merely en-

thusiasm for the author that inspired the audience; an occasion was given for distinct party feeling. It was the prologue of the revolution, and Beaumarchais its prophet. The comedy was played four hundred times. The poet gave his share of the profits to the foundling hospitals; his ambition was satisfied—he had erected an imperishable monument for himself and Susanna. We cannot perhaps now appreciate all the keenness of this dramatic satire, because we have no privileged classes, parliamentary councillors ready to be bribed, nor any *jus primæ noctis!*

The queen wore the famous head-dress, and 'her ladies imitated her. Dresses, ribbons, colors, phrases, à la Susanna, became fashionable, the page's ballad was sung by the sentimental daughters of the citizens, and Marie Antoinette herself acted the part of Susanna at Trianon, in presence of her courtiers. The epidemic would have been ridiculous, if it had not been too serious—they were playing with the fire before they applied it to their own house. What rendered matters worse was that ominous history about the diamond necklace, ending with the dishonor of the regal as well as womanly dignity of the queen, and advancing, through the follies of the Palais-Royal, the charlatanism of such outcasts as Balsamo-Cagliostro and Lamotte-Valois. From that unfortunate 15th of August all gayety disappeared from the court, and peace of mind from the royal pair. The prophecies of "Cassandra" began to be fulfilled.

Away from the turmoil of Paris, with its false philosophies and rancor, Louise de Lamballe and Charlotte de Gorzka resided at Sceaux, from whose serene heights, as from a Zion, they looked down on the varied scenes announcing the proximity of a great capital. The duke with his white, trembling head, his globes, charts, and folio volumes, before him, sat like a philosopher, while the earth trembled beneath him. Old and weary of life, he retained the name only of his high office. Often Princess Adelaide, the unfortunate wife of Chartres, visited them. Her unworthy husband was endeavoring to ameliorate his banishment by basking in the smiles of Madame de Buffon. Adelaide had long been morally separated from him, 'and, on account of her undeserved misfortune, she again found a place in Louise's heart. The only one who brought them news from Paris, keeping them in communication with the times, was Beaumarchais, the beloved and ever-welcome guest. He had, however, not appeared at Sceaux for two weeks, though the pleasant autumn invited him. All were anxious, and looked often from the balcony toward the north, and every carriage passing on the road was an object of curiosity. The harp rested on Louise's arm, the friend of her sorrowful hours. When she played, it seemed as if spirits whispered to her of other and happier days.

"It is strange that he sends no letter or messenger," said Charlotte. "It is incomprehensible. Besides, he was to give me a report about the purchase of some land near the *Jardin des Plantes.*"

"Do not be alarmed," replied the duke; "your affairs are safe in his hands. He is cautious, and never hurries any thing; that is an inestimable quality in these fast days. He is sure to come as soon as he finds it convenient."

"As if he could not come whenever he pleased, my father," said Louise, smiling. "I am sure he is independent of most circumstances. I rather fear that something disagreeable has happened to him; he might at least have sent Gomez."

"I have no doubt he would have done so, my child," replied Penthièvre, "if any thing had befallen him; he is not the man to hide himself from his friends. Perhaps some new scandal has arisen in the city or the court, and you know he must inquire into every thing." .

"I have often reproached him for it, and yet I always like to hear his gossip. Though that is a little inconsistent, is it not, Charlotte?"

"Not at all, dear Louise. I believe the last feeling that leaves us is curiosity, which seems a sort of sympathy for mankind."

"I see a four-horse carriage approaching; it looks as if it might bring Beaumarchais!" Penthièvre took his old sea-glass and looked down.

"Truly, he is coming!" exclaimed Charlotte.

"It cannot be, my love," said the princess. "It is a state equipage, and Caron does not keep one now."

"But, my child, it is turning to the left into the road leading here, and my eye is strong enough to discover two figures in the coach."

"Two gentlemen?" and Countess de Gorzka blushed.

"Who can they be? But you are suddenly so excited, Charlotte! have you any idea who they are?"

"Oh, I scarcely dare to think it; yet, Otto von Nassau occurs to me!"

"Otto von Nassau?"

"One of them is Caron, and the other an officer in a green uniform. See for yourself."

The princess took the telescope. She turned pale. "It is he!"

"Kind Heaven, is he returning to us?" cried Charlotte, joyfully.

"Returning!" breathed Louise, averting her face.

The carriage drove rapidly to the house, stopping before it. Two men descended, greeting the company on the balcony—Caron and Nassau. The latter wore the Russian uniform, his breast covered with orders. Penthièvre arose, leaning on Louise, to meet them; Charlotte hastened into the drawing-room, for she could not control her emotion.

"Welcome! A thousand times welcome, hero of Gibraltar, conqueror of the Turks, and prince of all women's and brave men's hearts!" exclaimed Penthièvre, stretching his arms toward Nassau. "What fortunate chance brings you to us?"

"I have been sent as ambassador extraordinary from my empress, duke, to manage some business about the Polish affairs, and give peace to that distracted country. I need not say that this was not the only cause, for my heart drew me hither." He took Louise's hand, and kissed it. "I left my heart here, princess. Glory is my bride—but a very cold companion."

"Excuse me," whispered the countess, agitated, "if I withdraw for a moment."

"You are ill, Charlotte!" said the princess, hastening to her fainting friend.

"Permit me, dearest countess," said Penthièvre, "to accompany you. Let us go to my apartments, my child." He arose and left with her.

"Prince," said Madame de Lamballe in a depressed but grave manner, "I am sorry that the great pleasure of seeing you again in the splendor of your fame is accompanied with sorrow that ought to belong to a sad past."

"Louise," said Nassau, deeply moved, "hope has ever lived in my heart, urging me from one victory to another, and filling my soul; it brings me before you to-day the same aspiring, restless man, on whom you alone can bestow the noblest victory by giving me your hand. Do not say it is indelicate, and wounding the heart of your friend

Countess de Gorzka; this cannot outweigh the pangs I have suffered for six years. I have cast the die for my life a thousand times, let me now cast it for your love. Heaven was a witness of our woe as well as our vows, and I ask you, Do you love me still?"

"I need not to be reminded of my promises, prince, to acknowledge frankly that my affection for you is undiminished; that your memory has never departed from me, and will remain to the end of my life. But another—"

"Not so, Louise; listen to me, I entreat you! Let not too great a generosity be the destroyer of our happiness, and without rendering the countess any service. The court has exiled you; nothing attaches you now to the faithless race of the Bourbons. Your father-in-law, Penthièvre, has but a short time to live; his death will leave you alone to combat about his princely fortune with Chartres, whose enmity will reduce your share, and at a time of the most fearful commotions ever known. I appear with seriousness before you, for, after having looked around in Paris for two weeks, with the unprejudiced eye of a stranger, I have noticed the disorder of the government, the defenceless condition of the monarchy, the fury of the people, all inflamed with republican fancies. Nothing now can possibly be done to save the country. Calonne knows that state bankruptcy is very near, and wishes to call the 'notables' to the rescue, where only the sword can decide. Formerly I could have wielded it, but it was broken because I was unfortunate. The equilibrium between the sovereign and the people is destroyed, for they are intoxicated with ideas of American liberty. In France you must look forward to solitude, suffering, and danger; with me you will find a second and fairer fatherland. Catharine has well rewarded me. I am a prince with princely possessions, dwelling among a people simple but faithful, whose virtue is not yet sullied—make that land your home! I pray you, Louise, accompany me and be my wife!" He knelt before her, and covered her hand with kisses.

While Nassau was speaking, the princess was struggling despairingly with the inclinations of her heart. She stood a moment like a statue; then her bosom heaved violently, and she shuddered as if she had some presentiment of her dreadful destiny. "I have patiently heard you, prince, that you may not say my decision is too hasty, or my heart void of feeling. I wish to try myself thoroughly, so that repentance may not remind me of the action of this hour. I never felt so deeply as at this moment the fate of my countrymen and their rulers, and never was it more clearly indicated that this is my place. Receive my reply as immutable —perhaps it is most advantageous to you, merciless as it appears.—Do not interrupt me, prince.

"I saw you first at Chambery, while yet a child. I loved you as a very young maiden loves the embodiment of an ideal—selfishly and thoughtlessly. I became a wife—a daughter of France. Sorrow made a woman of me, and I threw myself into Marie Antoinette's arms. When you returned from Africa, we were all united around the new throne; Turgot, Malesherbes, and Conti were still living, and the whole country was happy. Until the day of my poor Susanna's death, I could love you, immeasurably and innocently, and could call myself yours in spite of Charlotte de Gorzka's withered hopes. Do you know why? Because in you I loved the saviour of my country—the Bayard of the monarchy—because in you I saw the last support to which Conti looked forward, the hero and companion of better times. The unfortunate battle of Jersey broke my heart. I loved you still, but as one dead, with whom all my affection lay buried! Woe to me that you gained a name in foreign lands, and that you proved to the world what you could have done for France! When your honor was regained my love was sacrificed, and you were farther from me than was ever the adventurer of Chambery!

"Are you surprised that the regal blood in my veins is more potent than even my love—that I refuse to leave my native land in misfortune, to accompany a distinguished Russian? In the heart of an exile the lilies of France still blossom! I am a descendant of the Bourbons, and may foolishly expose myself to death, but never can I bow my knee before the sceptre of a czar! To become your wife would be cowardice. I could not remain at your side without feeling degraded, when my country is so miserable—when my queen is growing gray through misfortune, and when, deserted by pretended friends, she may soon seek for the first dear companion of her youth, and find her gone. This short life will soon cease, Otto, and we shall stand before the judgment-seat of God. Shall the king and queen then say: 'And she also abandoned us, our own blood!' No, Nassau-Siegen! I am the Cassandra of my country and people, but I will die with them—that becomes Louise of Savoy!

"And of what use could I be to you, leaving my heart here? The glory reflected by you would only sharpen the pain of my conscience, chiding me with infidelity and ingratitude. Oh, women can also be heroines, Otto; and if I may not be your wife, it is that I may be more worthy to appear in the presence of my God. If you would be truly happy—if you would purchase peace by self-denial, and render me also as happy as I can be in this world: take to your arms my friend Charlotte, who has suffered so much for you. I would only make you wretched. My oath to weave the bridal-wreath for her shall be fulfilled. I cannot see you again except at the altar, by the side of Countess de Gorzka. I may be obdurate and proud, but even in death I must cherish the sentiments of my royal ancestors!" She withdrew, disappearing to her lover as one who had passed into the realm of spirits.

"Lost! lost to me, adorable woman! Self-destroyed by the terrible truth!" The prince's eyes filled with tears, and the hero who laughed in a hundred battles was unmanned by the dignity and resolution of a woman.

Nearly half a year passed. Nassau's mission was accomplished; Louise de Lamballe did not again admit him to her presence, notwithstanding all entreaties. The trial seemed to change his whole nature. One day he and Caron visited the Hôtel Penthièvre, where the duke and the ladies resided in winter. The prince seemed to have grown many years older. He was timidly received by Charlotte.

"Countess, I come to you not as a young, passionate lover, but as a ship-wrecked mariner seeking a peaceful haven. I ask for your hand, and promise to love you as well as it is possible for this wasted heart. I make but one condition: If Louise de Lamballe should ever be in need or danger, you must let me go to save her—even to die for her! Do you agree to that?"

"I do!" whispered the countess.

A few days after, Nassau and Charlotte were married. Louise placed the wreath of orange-blossoms on the bride's head. The newly-wedded pair drove away in the travelling-carriage, leaving the princess, Penthièvre, and Beaumarchais, standing on the terrace.

"It is done, Caron; this was my last pang! I have but one friend remaining of the old times—you!"

"I am your friend, for the remembrance of my Susanna unites us forever."

CHAPTER XXVI.

AN EPILOGUE.

The old, chivalrous, witty France exists no more. Its *esprit*, as well as its follies, was consumed in the flames of civil war; the past is buried in blood and ashes, and the prophecy of the Bourbon Cassandra fulfilled.

On the day when the Bastile was stormed, an act which brutalized Santerre, the leader, as he himself had feared, Louise de Lamballe hastened to the queen. Misfortune had come, the first blood was shed; but, faithful to her promise, she returned. While Orleans-Égalité reigned in the Palais-Royal as chief of the revolution, Artois, Provence, the Polignacs, the Noailles, and the Guemènes, deserted their monarch, trifling away their time on the banks of the Rhine, under the protection of German bayonets. Madame de Lamballe accompanied the royal martyrs on the dreary path that opened with the king's abduction to Paris, and ended in the Temple. Here they were separated, and the princess was thrown into the Abbaye. Her head fell in September, reddening the pavement with her blood, because she would not curse her king and queen, as a "good citizen" was required to do. The lilies became a crown of thorns to her. Her intended protector came too late.

From the same prison Beaumarchais was released by Santerre, and fled to England. He escaped the murderers hired by Orleans, to whom Morelly fell a victim with the *Basiliade* in his hand. Who could be safe when victims were slaughtered by the hecatomb!

Madame de Lamballe opened this dance of death, followed by the king, the queen, and Princess Elizabeth, and closed by Philippe Égalité. He thought he had removed every obstacle to the revolution, but the testimony of Beaumarchais ruined him. Mirabeau had been poisoned by the instrumentality of Chartres, because the former would not place this "soul of mud" upon the throne. The evidence, delivered to Caron by Mirabeau the night before his death, and handed at the decisive moment to Anacharsis Cloots, cost the wretched prince his life.

The mission of Beaumarchais was fulfilled. Faithful to the end, he retained, even in old age, the strength with which he always fought against extremes. When, during that " reign of terror," his opera *Tartare*, written for Salieri, the pupil of Glück, was represented, he introduced the following dangerous lines:

"Meine Freunde, lasst uns ihren Irrthum beklagen,
Sie sind das Opfer einiger Barbaren,
Die mit der Leidenschaft der Menge spielen!
Dies Volk, so treu sonst—wenn es sich empört,
Wird stets geführt von bübischen Gewalten,
Die Herz und Hirn ihm in den Händen halten!" *

---

* My friends! let pity more than vengeance move
Our hearts for those deceived, who sometimes prove
Of barbarous men the bloody sport and prey,
Who with the passions of the people play.
When Frenchmen, once so loyal to kingly right,
Against their rulers rise in angry might,
Great reason is for all the good to fear,
An evil spirit sways its sceptre there.

Caron lived quietly in the small house he had erected, surrounded by a garden, in the quarter of the Temple, near the city wall; on the roof he placed a terrestrial globe, surmounted by a pen, as a weather-vane. In this humble dwelling he dreamed of Susanna and the forest-walk at Marly, of Louise de Lamballe, the dauphin, and the grotto at Trianon, and here he calmly died on the 19th of May, 1799. His last poem is a mirror of his life:

"Im Lenz voll Muth,
Da ging mir's gut;
Der Sommer schwer,
Warf mich hin und her;
Des Herbstes Rast
Eintönig fast.
O, möcht ein Geist noch frisch und grün
Dem trüben Winter mich entziehn!" *

Reader, when you walk through the Boulevard Beaumarchais, pay respect to the place where the intelligence, grace, and fidelity of old France last lingered—where passed away one of the most remarkable men of his time, hiding with him many of its secrets— where the great Mozart recognized an abode of the Muses, and associated with his own imperishable genius the name of a true poet and an honest man.

---

* My joyous youth was as a balmy spring,
That shines within the heart, awakening there
Sweet thoughts that summer's sultry days would
  bring
Their fragrant flowers and ripened harvest fair;
But manhood came o'ercast with stormy care.
Now, driven as one from hope and love exiled,
Weary I wait, while drops the foliage sear,
Along my autumn path, so sadly mild—
Thus let me sink to rest e'er howls the winter wild!

THE END.